MW00978814

Doing it Wrong?

A Novel

by
William N. Rappa Jr.

AuthorHouse™
1663 Liberty Drive, Suite 200
Bloomington, IN 47403
www.authorhouse.com
Phone: 1-800-839-8640

First published by AuthorHouse 2/11/2008

ISBN: 978-1-4343-6236-0 (sc)
ISBN: 978-1-4343-6235-3 (hc)

Library of Congress Control Number: 2008900314

Printed in the United States of America
Bloomington, Indiana

This book is printed on acid-free paper.

To all of my sister and brother educators who have been doing it right all these years. Your legacy lies in the successful lives of the students you have touched.

Preface

My father and best friend, William N. Rappa, Sr., from my earliest memories instilled in me the importance of "the family" to the individual. Following his death in 1999, I learned just how valuable his lessons were to be for the remainder of my life. Although his passing created a wound in the lives of his "family" incapable of healing, his words, deeds, and celebration of life live on in his grandchildren and their children. Without his physical presence in our lives these days are less bright; however, he is as present in our family today as ever. "Until that time, Dad. Until that time", borrowed from the thoughts of William Goldman, "your family" will be one in body again.

The ladies in my life "stepped up to the plate" during my illness by exhibiting a strength, love, and selflessness that only the female of the species possesses. Caring for perhaps the worst patient and "biggest baby" on the planet, unfortunately for them, is not a *Guinness Book of World Records* category.

This book would not have been possible without the love and diligence of my sister, Susan Linda Corcoran, who muddled through my combination of hieroglyphic-like writing and babbling transcription tapes so that her typing-challenged brother's work would see the light of day.

In addition, I offer my undying love and affection to the staff members of Washington Community Magnet School from 1969 through 2005, which had to put-up with me for those 36 memorable years. Not a more dedicated, empathetic, hard-working, loving, group of educators will be found anywhere on this planet in this lifetime.

"This above all, to thine own self be true,

And it must follow, as the night the day,

Thou canst not then be false to any man."

--William Shakespeare from ***Hamlet***

Prologue

At the conclusion of the Massachusetts school year in 2005, a thirty-seven year career in education culminated in a "bitter-sweet" fashion. In the mind of this writer, the "dumbing-down" of education via an impractical, improbable, missed-directed, set of goals mandated by the new educational initiatives had created a "pigeon-holing," easily manipulated, statistically-skewed, and stress generating atmosphere for both students and teachers alike by the Commonwealth of Massachusetts and the Congress of the United States of America. The government had, in effect, created a learning environment that is breeding a generation of neurotic learners as early as grade one who are solely driven to pass arbitrarily designed tests which represent learning via these initiatives. The love, fun, and self-discovery of learning have become the threat, punishment, and self-loathing of today's classrooms.

Forgive this writer if the words offend those who have given much time and effort in such an undertaking, for I do not suggest here a purposeful intent to destroy education...just very poor judgment. The loss of affiliation with students present and former, the divorce of neighborhood parents from their long-appreciated teachers, and the separation from colleagues whose depth of dedication and sacrifice is truly known only by their peers combine to enrage those of us "dinosaurs" of the teaching field who are told that we had been doing it wrong all those years. Be that true, this writer is thankful to have escaped from the scene of his incompetence.

The text before you is a work of fiction. It wrote itself during the first four months of the author's retirement. The work serves in this writer's mind as a love letter of sorts to all who have stood before classrooms filled with eager, restless minds. The reader need not be a member of this ancient brother/sisterhood of educators to relate to the characters. Simply allow oneself a journey to one's past. Perhaps a "favorite" teacher will be remembered as the story of a man who thought he was doing it right his entire life unfolds in these pages.

CHAPTER 1

THE FAMILIAR VISITOR TO THE building appeared uncomfortable; his walk lacked its typical confident stride and bounce as if he were a man on a mission about which he was still not one hundred percent certain. All the opinions, helpful, requested, or offered had been weighed-in and counted. The full spectrum of well-intentioned advice including suggestions such as: "It's a no brainer, friend!" "Man they are paying you to stay home forever!" "How can you leave us like this?" Considering the amount of energy put into this decision it may have become permanently synaptically imprinted on his brain. Hesitating as he looked down the institution-like hallway before him to the doorway of his destination, memories of such a visit of thirty-six years earlier were conjured in his already overtaxed brain. Clutched in his left hand was to him a life-altering document, a single sheet of some secretary's labor but when signed and dated would change his life forever. Many long sleepless nights, an enormous expenditure of physical and mental energies, and several extra doses of lorazapam led to the critical signing last evening. At his destination, he paused once again with a hand on the doorknob. He was sure that were the denizens of this place observing him, he must appear clumsy and plodding in his behavior. The stencil on the destination door made note to all that within the Superintendent of the Lynn Public Schools resided. The glassed top portion of the door reflected back to him the face of a man of average height and pleasant features not very different from the young, ambitious person he knew back in the early seventies. Of course, the hair was strikingly grayer, the pounds had been packed-on and redistributed, and the facial laugh lines had been given a thirty-six year test of endurance. However, the bright brown eyes beneath his unibrow, the ever-present thin-lipped grin that welcomed friend and stranger alike, the always carefully combed hair, though indeed there was less there now than then- held his glance. At fifty-seven years of age, he was about to bring to a conclusion an extended love/hate chapter of his life. The recently signed document in his hand stated that as of the end of the school day on the last day of that very school year, James Thurber Russell would no longer be an employee of the Lynn Public Schools. He was retiring by taking an "early buy-out". He was being put out to pasture, sent out to the stud farm. Wasn't he too young for this? Retirement was for old guys who have lost their fastball! Just ask his students if his skills were still on display. What about his present kids and his former students who visited so often? What about the future students who eagerly waited entry into his class? Yes, there was even a second generation of his kids. Imagine that? His kids had kids whom he now taught or were waiting to be taught by him!

On the other hand, as much as he would miss his kids, he would no longer be forced to endure the daily mental anguish of the circus atmosphere that existed in education for the past several years that so burdened his mind to the point of distraction. Since the Commonwealth of Massachusetts and the federal government concluded in all their combined divine wisdom that teachers and schools have been doing it wrong for the last thirty-something years, new laws were passed. Standardized tests were devised. Teacher competency testing was implemented. Teacher recertification regulations altered yearly as administrators tried to save public education. For teachers, life in education had become a practice of jumping through hoops whenever new and improved definitions of teacher responsibility were created and were deemed to be the next new "answer" to the problem. In his heart and mind these remedial labors of the past several years, though most probably well-intended, were a "fools errand". The alleged causes of all our educational problems were laid at the feet of people on the front lines - teachers. The occupation of teaching made it too damn easy for teachers to receive the blame from the politicians!

Public school teachers were so obvious a target for blame. Their salaries paid by the property tax burdens loaded upon their fellow citizens, the mistaken public belief that summer was a ten week vacation and not unemployment, a gross misconception of having only a six- hour school day and a thirty-hour school week to work... teachers were the perfect foils for the perceived failure of the public education system. But were they truly at the cause of the problem? Politicians took the ball and ran with it, doing what they do best, making promises! Parents were courted by politicians and school administrations alike who convinced them that they represented an integral, vital cog in the renovation of education. In short order, the most obvious and most convenient answer to all problems from both of these groups was "tear it down and rebuild it!" Reteach the teaching staff. Every teacher will be instructed in every new, perfectly packaged, half-million dollar reading, or language arts, or math, or science, or social studies program that promised to rectify the failings of the past. Each new program sold to some well-intentioned school administrator who had not seen, let alone taught in, a classroom in years became part of the professional development agenda. Retrain the dinosaurs...those educators who could or would not accept the newest answer to our educational problems faced ostracism, public embarrassment, and even dismissal.

While our Commonwealth and the federal government viewed the supposed failings of public education as having personnel, curricula, instructional, or philosophic basis, James Thurber Russell had a theory of his own, which he would share with anyone who was willing to listen. According to the accepted "party line", local, state, and federal governments claimed that the new educational initiative guaranteed, a "level playing field" for each and every child. The three hundred fifty-one cities and towns of Massachusetts would treat all of its students equally…each child would be given an equal opportunity for success; each would be held to the same high standards of achievement; each would be subject to the same set of expectations designed by the Commonwealth and our political brethren. Bullshit! And more bullshit! After spending his entire career servicing learners of English as a Second Language, motivating regular education students from severely low socio-economic areas for thirty years, educating the parents of such children at Lynn Evening School and various adult learning centers for nearly as long, JT Russell knew in his heart and mind that not only does a "level playing field" not exist in a society presently constituted as ours, but that it can never exist. Poverty seemed to be the missing or ignored variable in the misguided formula upon which the new educational initiative was predicated. One need not be the second coming of Horace Mann to understand that a child from the City of Lynn who is living in a welfare setting; depending upon food stamps, WIC, and monthly checks for basic needs; existing in a family often times minus a mother, father, or both; being a member of a family unit with some or all of the siblings having different surnames; all contribute to life-altering factors. Such conditions often times create a situation for children that most of us can only have nightmares about. Where exactly was this "level playing field" to those children? That same "field" guaranteed by the government via the new educational initiative was simply another philosophical, theoretical concept as elusive as reaching the speed of light, warp drive on the starship Enterprise, and no new taxes promises!

Compare those children to their wealthier suburban counterparts most of whom being members of a nuclear family, children who have been satiated physically and emotionally from birth, students enrolled in school systems that lacked for nothing via school funding, and families which promoted, valued, and participated in the education of their offspring. The problem was so clear in his eyes. Why was it not as obvious to all? We have a society where "children giving birth to children" is readily accepted. The largest group of live births in this country continues to be represented by the fifteen and sixteen year old population! Societally, there is a desperate lack of parenting skills taught at school and encouragement of education taught at home. Generations of welfare and state dependent families have been allowed to evolve. School systems have failed miserably in the areas of human growth and development due to budgetary limitations for perceived less important subject matter. Generations of self-defeatist, apathetic, unmotivated students have defeated education's attempt to draw them out of their despair. Gang entry and criminal activity have become viable options out of both poverty and isolation. Viewed in its entirety, these factors identified the failure of not the American school system. No, sir! He laid the problems at the doorstep of societal failures, not educational failures. Education and teachers in particular, had become society's "whipping boy" for its own failings in its responsibility to future generations.

How many times had he given the following argument to how many different faces?

"Welcome back Ms. Thomas, it seems like only yesterday that you were sitting in this classroom. Now you are here asking me why your child cannot read at his grade level. Let me ask you, have you ever read to your child either for enjoyment or at bedtime? You need not answer. Do you have appropriate reading materials displayed prominently around your house sending out a signal to your child that you value reading? Do you read in the presence of your child? Do you encourage him to read? Do you know if he has a library card? Have you ever visited the library with him? Ms. Thomas, do you really want to hear why your child is having reading difficulties? This poor kid was defeated before he walked into his first preschool class! He was already behind the average child who enters pre-school able to print his name, having a three thousand word vocabulary, knowledge of colors, letters, numbers and a burning desire to be able to pick-up a book and read alone. Am I placing the blame on you, Ms. Thomas? No, I don't think so. You, he, and many, many others like you and he are victims of our societal system. It is a system that promotes the educational advancement of kids like yours only if the kids themselves are strong enough, independent enough, opportunistic enough to pull themselves up by their virtual bootstraps and beat back the unfortunate environment into which they were born!"

Yes! That was it – his reason to be – the answer to why he entered the teaching field and stayed. Clearly, he was not going to be able to remedy society's ills as one simple educator, but he could reach those kids who had "it". That spirit, attitude, determination, personality, whatever one wanted to call that unknown factor; the "it" was what he sought-out in all of his kids, and he nurtured it to the best of his ability. To him, education revolved around trust. A teacher and a student bonding on an emotional level--love is not too strong a word here – trusting in each other, working together for a common goal. He viewed his classroom as a garden of children when maintained with the proper combination of nutrients, care, concern, affiliation, and love, the result would be a child performing to her/his optimal level of achievement.

Every first day of school, he would give his new group of charges his WTL3 talk. On the front board he would write WTL3. Under that the following phrases were listed:

Willing To Learn
Wanting To Learn
Working To Learn

He would tell each new class of students that the secret of a person's success in school, in life, in everything was right before their eyes.

"If you are willing to learn with me, you will arrive here each day prepared. You will leave any bad attitudes, home problems from that morning, or just the 'ickies' in the coatroom. You will walk into this magical kingdom each day prepared for me to entertain you with the incredible knowledge I choose to share with you. If you want to learn, you will do everything in your power to try to understand each golden pearl of wisdom that I discuss with you. You will put aside your need to socialize with your friends until the appropriate time; you will try your best to keep your mind from wandering. If I am to fill your eager young minds with the wonders that pour forth from my mouth, I need your mind here and in the open position. If you work to learn, you will not complain about the amount or length of your assignments; you will not boo or throw rotten vegetables in my direction; you will to the best of your ability complete your studies during the school day and each evening so that you will not have to tell me some bogus story of what happened to your home work papers! Should you have difficulty with any assignment, and there are no answers for you at home, you will simply inform me in class privately that you 'don't get it'. I will then help you 'get it'. If you combine these three steps with regular attendance (mind and body), our chances of success are great. Now what can you expect of me? I will be here prepared to learn with you each day. I will try everything in my power to help you succeed. I love to laugh and wish to enjoy the people with whom I will be spending six hours each day. Please understand that I do not mean to imply that I believe education is a joke. I take your education very seriously. I take my responsibility to each of you very seriously. I want each of you to take your education more seriously than I do. Sometimes, we will get on each other's nerves. You will at times be jump roping on my very last nerve, and I will probably respond accordingly. This does not mean that I hate you, am mad at you, wish you would vanish into the air, etc. I am human. I have limitations. Some people even say I have faults and make mistakes. Although I disagree, I accept that point of view. One thing that you must remember, and if you never remember another thing I ever say to you, please remember this: I do not expect each of you to be an all A's student. Nor do I expect you to be an all A's and B's student if you never have been. What I do expect of you each day that we are together is that you try to be the best 'you' of which you are capable. If that means you work your butt off and get all C's, great! If you are a B's and C's student and believe in your heart that you have given it your all, great! However, if you are capable of greater things, and you are receiving C's and D's, shame on you because you are wasting a gift given to you by God…"

Over his thirty-six year teaching career, many may not have taken his words to heart, but on the other hand, the success stories emanating from his kids indicated that someone was listening. Their stories became the legacy of his life's work. Teacher and students were forever joined by a bond not easily broken…even though he had been "doing it wrong" for all those years!

CHAPTER 2

THE 1970'S AND EARLY 1980'S version of Lynn, the third largest city in the Commonwealth of Massachusetts, located on what had become known as the North Shore of that historically rich, academically prominent, outrageously taxed, politically hamstrung Commonwealth, looked like many other cities in the country with a population of 80,000ish citizens. "Lynn, Lynn, the city of sin…you never come out the way you went in. You ask for water, and they give you gin. Lynn, Lynn the city of sin!" Sin city was divided if not officially then emotionally into a West Lynn and an East Lynn. West Lynners saw themselves as the blue-collar driving force upon which this great melting pot of a nation was founded. They thought of themselves as tough, no-nonsense people who were the purveyors of family values and the Puritan work ethic. The General Electric Company, with most of their buildings located on the west side of the city, employed a massive number of its residents and actually kept this city from becoming a ghost town.

The East Lynners, on the other hand, saw themselves as what West Lynners wanted to be when they grew up. The supposed West Lynn dream, according to their cross-town neighbors, was to earn enough money to buy East Lynn property. The East siders saw themselves as a suburban, professional, more affluent group from the right side of the tracks. If the facts were to be examined from a purely neutral outsider's point of view, neither side of the tracks was all that right.

The downtown area in the central section of Lynn had been a thriving economic entity with businesses of every category occupying the many large office buildings and storefronts. Prosperity, Massachusetts style, abounded for all citizens who were appropriately "connected." Only a decade ago we had given to the country our favorite son to be its president. In doing so, we had ushered in what was to be viewed as a short-lived, real-life version of the Arthurian legend. Then economic tragedy struck the older cities of the Commonwealth. Some inspired entrepreneurs gave birth to the outrageously popular concept of the Mall. And what a painful birth it was for this city! The citizenry of Lynn like those of the other three hundred fifty cities and towns of the Commonwealth found they could shop more comfortably, conveniently, and less expensively in this new and exciting socio-economic environmental experiment. The many movie theaters of the city could not compete with the multiplexes at the Malls so they became the first casualties. Small business relocated out of town to follow the consumers. Bigger, better, prettier replaced the concept of the neighborhood store. A "Disneyland" for the shopping public had stolen the hearts, minds, and pocketbooks of the citizenry.

The downtown area quickly and quietly became vastly underutilized. The hustle and bustle of times past had given way to the meandering of the homeless in their cardboard box communities. Urban renewal plan after plan attempted to draw the populace back to its roots, but little was ever accomplished in this battle for the consumer dollar. Lynn had to face the truth…her best years were behind her. However, not all of the fine residents of this fair city had forsaken her. Being that one's life, like happiness, is subject to one's circumstances, a community of the city's unfortunate inhabitants took hold downtown in the recesses beneath the train station diagonally across from the first McDonalds's in the country alleged to go "belly-up". At that time, a McDonald's fast food restaurant going out of business was tantamount to the government holding a "bake sale" to raise funds for the defense department.

In this community within a community, an association of brethren brought together by life's cruel jokes took hold. Some of these individuals were victims of circumstances; others were as responsible for their miserable existence, as the moon is responsible for the ebb and flow of the tides. Life for these forgotten souls amounted to a daily battle for survival that involved the attainment of sufficient nourishment and shelter from the elements, which threatened a cruel finality to their "it's barely better than being dead" existence.

One denizen of the underbelly of this fair city, specifically one Newton Spencer Lloyd III, was a charter member of this "living dead" community. In an attempt to be fair to Mr. Lloyd in the eyes of historical accuracy, let it be said that he was an example of a victim and not a conspirator in his own despair. A successful business owner, a loving husband, father, son, and friend, Newton Spencer Lloyd III never knew what hit him. Slightly built, sensitive, always tense, Mr. Lloyd was a critically flawed man. He cared too much for the people and issues in his life and paid for this shortcoming at the expense of his own health and welfare. You see, this man, in the eyes of the world he had known, was just not tough enough. Unfortunately, for him, he was just too weak to survive the death of his only daughter. He was unable to withstand his wife's betrayal of their marriage. He could not function well nor improve his lot in the battle to survive more than a dozen long-term internments at a variety of private and public sanitariums. Ultimately, this weakling suffered the indignity of having his last earthly possessions sold to pay for these long-term health care vacations. The final failing of this invertebrate's miserable life was to have been sent back into an unforgiving and ignorant society without the prerequisite survival skills when the Commonwealth closed his last home, the Danvers State Mental Institution. Yes, in deed, Newton Spencer Lloyd III never knew what hit him!

CHAPTER 3

HER NAME WAS ROSE MARIE, a beautiful flower of a girl, whose life as that of the rose is never long enough. She was born on November 24th 1947 in the year of our Lord and Savior under almost tragic circumstances. Who but the Divine could know this difficult near fatal birth would be one of the lighter times of her short life?

At 2:33AM on the day of her birth, her mother felt a flood of wetness move down her legs as she left her bed to visit the bathroom. She knew immediately that it was "time" and communicated this to her snoring partner. Roused from a fitful sleep, his first in weeks, he barely controlled his natural impulse to

"go to pieces" in any emergency, and he found himself calling his family's home to relate the current events…actually, he did not want to go through this part of the birth process alone! As he spoke on the telephone, his legs refused to cease their constant shaking and shivering. He thought he heard his father say that they would meet him at Lynn Hospital on Boston Street. It never happened.

He carefully and attentively escorted his comparatively relaxed wife onto the front seat of their gray Nash Rambler, which happened to move only forward since it had a defective reverse gear that worked at its leisure, and they had not saved the funds to remedy the situation. Silently cursing his shivering legs, the inventor of the automobile transmission, God's blueprint for the procreation of humankind, and the advent of sexual intercourse, he pulled up to the Emergency Room entrance.

Clearly, it did not take a medical detective to diagnose which of the two new arrivals was most in need of assistance. The attending nurse immediately sat him down and supplied him with water, as he swayed between conscious and unconsciousness. Having him secured at her station under the supervision of a second "angel of mercy", she went about her rather familiar routine of preparing a woman to give birth.

Labor was long and difficult. It was almost as bad for his wife. For ten hours little Rose Marie, Sarah, Jonathan, Charles, or Janice refused to cooperate. The doctor kept saying calming words about long, first birth labor periods that were totally lost on the new father in waiting. In fact, the situation had gotten so bad that the attending nurses on each shift were conspiring to remove him, physically if necessary, from the ward if he could not get himself under some semblance of control. He swore he heard one of them mention his violent demise. As six hours passed, the situation on two fronts, mother's labor and father's irrationality, came to a climax. A pair of nurses, whose size grew exponentially over the years as the story was told and retold, escorted him on a route similar to something seen on a map of the Lewis and Clark expedition. He was told to stay put. He would be escorted back at the appropriate time.

Shortly before 4:00PM, a figure in a white coat approached. In his current state of panic, identification became a challenge. It was his wife's doctor. The doctor's lips moved. He could see that clearly; however, the words were having difficulty reaching his brain. As the physician continued to speak, the processing of the information he provided improved. There was a problem of some sort. The child and the mother were in danger. The situation required that a decision be made as to which would be saved in an emergency such as this… the child or the mother. How could anyone make such a choice? In particular, how could HE ever contemplate making such a choice? The words "time is of the essence, or we risk losing both" struck him like a slap across the face. He heard himself saying, "Save the child." He had no idea from whence the decision or its verbalization originated. When looking back at this life-altering moment of crisis, he was always at a loss to explain his actions and unable to accept the consequences that ensued…and the consequences surely ensued.

The child was born shortly after 8:00PM. That was the good news. He was told that his daughter's condition was stable although the birth process had been a difficult one. She remained in an "at risk" state but her chances of survival were high. The doctor then proceeded to give him the bad news. His wife was clinging to life with little hope of recovery. Although such cases of recovery were documented, they were few and far between. The guilt was immediate and intense. He fell to the floor and lay there in a fetal position. He awoke several hours later in the same position on an Emergency Room bed. He turned and felt for her. Then he called for his wife. The reality of the situation flooded his mind and body.

"I killed her! I killed my wife! God have mercy on both our souls!"

CHAPTER 4

LYNN WOODS RESERVATION, THE SECOND largest public park in the country, was another source for bragging by East and West Lynn residents alike. In addition to being the "shoe" capital of the country, Lynn residents took pride in their "woods" which according to legend was the location at which Thomas Veal, a seventeen-century pirate, buried his treasure booty for safe keeping. It was probably safe to say that not a child in the city neither girl nor boy had at one time or another failed to venture into the forest with visions of exploration and discovery at the famed Dungeon Rock. Aside from the legends and lore associated with this place, the long, shady, winding paths that crisscrossed its boundaries provided a romantic walk for lovers, young and old alike.

Late autumn of 1947 was such a wonderful time for Jim and Charlene Russell. Having just celebrated their first wedding anniversary, they eagerly awaited the arrival of the newest Russell to the planet.

Lynn Woods held a special place in their hearts. She fell in love with the woods upon her maiden visit from California to Lynn to meet his family. It was here that they first exchanged the words "I love you", and knew it was true. It was here that they strolled and shared their most intimate thoughts. It was here that Jim had officially proposed marriage to Charlene. It was here that she accepted his proposal without reservation. Moreover, it was here that little James, Susan, or Maria was very close to being born!

At eight and three quarter months pregnant, Charlene insisted on a visit to their "woods". Jim knew it was a bad idea but the memory of his mother's insistence that a pregnant woman should be denied nothing was so ingrained in him that he had no choice but to agree. They agreed upon an automobile tour only. No walking would take place. At the first sign of any baby activity, they would immediately go to the hospital. He felt somewhat secure with these limitations. He felt in control. How was he to know that a tire would not cooperate?

"I told you wait in the car. I'll have this fixed in no time."

"I want to help."

"You'll be the most help to me inside."

"I'll check the spare tire. Where is it?"

"Where is it?" he echoed sarcastically. "My love, did you see it inside the car? Why don't you look in the trunk?" This suggestion was followed by a murmured exclamation in Italian questioning her intelligence.

"Jim, it's flat..."

"Shit"

"Jim..."

"WHAT?"

"My water just broke."

How was he to know that fate would pick that very moment to start "screwing around" with him? How did he know that he would react with the panic he swore to be incapable of harboring? In his state of over-exaggerated emergency and blind cursing at any and all who had him in this situation, how was he to know that Charlene had torn a length of her while skirt and used it to signal a distant motorcyclist? How was he to know that only a driver and one overly pregnant woman could ride the cycle at one time? How was he to know that he would miss the birth of his first son by twenty minutes following an exhausting ten-mile run to the hospital? How was he to know that the worst day of his life would turn out to be the best day of his life?

"Are you OK?"

"I hope I look better than you, Jim. We have a son." Then to the infant in her arms, "Don't worry, honey. It's only your daddy, and he cleans up real well."

CHAPTER 5

"PLEASE STOP TAPPING ON THE window. That is very disturbing to the infants! Can you not read the signs? This is a hospital-zone where one is expected to exercise quiet and act reserved in deference to our patients and other guests. Individuals die on these floors every day! Please, exercise self-control when in this area. Not everyone here has cause for delight!

"We apologize, Miss, this is our first grandchild. We're new at this," responded the largest member of this despicable Gang of Four, Mike McDonough, maternal grandfather of the newborn. Embarrassed beyond words, the maternal grandparents, Aunt Betty and Uncle Richard Russell apologized repeatedly for their unintentional breach of hospital rules and etiquette regarding James Thurber Russell. However, this happy group would not allow anything or anyone to interfere with their moment of absolute joy. As she turned to walk away, Richard gave her the Italian "salute". Following a brief meeting of the minds, they agreed to curb their enthusiasm at the risk of losing continued access to the baby. A brief time later, the same nurse from hell returned to the viewing area. This time she acted as if she had just had a major attitude surgically removed.

"Which one is yours?"

"The most beautiful one, nurse. Russell, baby boy, is on the front of his basket," said a smiling Anne McDonough without the least hesitation.

"Now, you sound like a grandmother, Angie," volunteered Mike looking up at his bride of twenty-seven years.

A third opinion, expressed by Betty Russell, boasted about the bundle of perfection that her sister-in-law and brother had brought into this strange and often times hostile new land of theirs.

"I think he looks just like me," added Mike McDonough.

"The only thing you two have in common is you both shit yourselves," responded the smiling Richard Russell.

"Remember where you are, you two," admonished the new grandmother, Anne McDonough.

The nurse could not help but be moved by the sight and sound of the ecstatic foursome. Their joy was infectious, and their warmth toward each other seemed genuine. She wanted to be part of their happiness. This nurse had seen too much despair this day. Compelled now to explain her earlier behavior after viewing the happiness before her, she truly regretted the tone of her earlier admonishment. Sidling over toward Anne and Betty, Nurse Clancy began to share with them the story of the baby in the basket next to their grandson. The front of the basket read "Lloyd, baby girl". As she spoke, tears filled the eyes of all three of the women. Mike and Richard strained to hear the words that brought their joyous welcoming party to an abrupt halt.

"So we don't know right now if the little girl will have her mother or not. The doctors have done all they can do. The woman's desire to live and God's plan for her will determine the ending of this story."

Almost on cue, both women made the sign of the cross, hugged each other, and took turns embracing their newly found best friend.

Turning to Mike, Richard whispered, "Women…Am I right?"

Mike nodded in agreement, "They sure ain't like us".

"Thank your God for that, my friend…thank him good and all the time," mumbled Richard.

CHAPTER 6

"YOUR WIFE IS BATTLING, MR. Lloyd, and that is a positive sign, in deed. We should know more within the next twenty-four to forty-eight hours. She has received the best care that any hospital could offer. We are simply not advanced sufficiently at this stage in our knowledge of the human body to combat all contingencies that may occur during the miracle of birth. You must stay strong for your wife and that little girl awaiting you in our nursery. Have you understood all I have told you? Good. If we remove the restraints from your arms and legs, will you exercise the self-control expected of a man with your education and intelligence? Good. Nurse, let's get these things off of Mr. Lloyd."

This had been the introductory experience of Newton Spencer Lloyd III with external physical restraint. It would not be the last. The nurses in the Emergency Room were neither able to control nor pacify the grief-stricken new father who deliriously confessed repeatedly to the murder of his wife. Following several incidents that caused injury to hospital staff, physical restraint was the only option along with a few healthy does of a tranquilizing drug that help bring the distraught man to his knees.

"I must see her, he whimpered. I need to tell her. Please take me to her. Please..."

"There are many critically ill patients on this floor, Mr. Lloyd; I cannot risk having your out of control actions jeopardizing their wellbeing!" The pathetic sight before him caused a crack in the doctor's self-protective, emotionally devoid, façade.

"If you promise me your best behavior, I will allow you to visit your wife. Any inappropriate actions on your part will conclude this visit. Am I understood?"

"Yes, thank you. Please take me to her."

The doctor and two nurses walked the weeping new father to a ward not far from his emergency room incarceration. The room was large enough for six beds, each surrounded by a curtain that barely offered the privacy it promised to provide. A female in a various degree of the birth process occupied each of the beds. Emily Franklin Lloyd occupied the last bed on the far right side of the room. She lay without movement, save for the shallow breathing, which was the only indication that she was still among the living. A monitor connected to her by a series of electrodes evaluated her vital signs constantly. Newton Spencer Lloyd ambled over to his wife followed quickly and closely by his medical guardians. He looked upon her pale, still face and fell to his knees.

Theirs had not necessarily been a happy union. Most of their family and friends believed that the eccentric, fun-loving, beautiful blond Emily, having chosen the intense, introverted, very average Newton Lloyd as a life's partner was at least strange if not downright bizarre. Some skeptics even alluded to the fortune that awaited Mr. Lloyd upon the passing of his parents. To others, the match was simply one of fates cruel jokes played upon human beings as they plodded along blindly through life. Still others, being more optimistically bent, felt that predestination at work resulted in this odd coupling. Regardless of the reason for the union, it existed; it lasted; it continued…until now.

On his knees, he was holding her hand begging her forgiveness; Newton heard a high-pitched alarm sound! The medical staff quickly and professionally went into an emergency response indicating a dire need for action. Lloyd was pushed away from the bedside hastily and the staff acted to save the life of Emily Lloyd.

Emily felt herself rising to the ceiling. She was able to look down upon herself in her bed as the staff worked upon her still body. She watched her husband crawl to a wall and cling there for support. She could see and hear everything so clearly. She felt wide-awake and full of energy so unlike the form being worked upon below her.

"If he only knew I was fine, she thought to herself. What were those rants coming from him?"

"I'm sorry I killed you. I'm sorry I chose our daughter's life over yours. I don't' know how or why it happened! Please don't leave me! Please forgive me! You mean everything to me. Don't leave…"

Suddenly, Emily felt herself moving upward at an incredible speed. She was unencumbered by any physical constraints such as ceilings or roofs. As suddenly as it occurred, it halted. She found herself looking toward a long gloriously lighted cylinder of some sort. The last earthly words lingered in her consciousness with her doctor saying somewhat somberly, somewhat matter of factly, "She's gone. Nurse, please note the time."

The glowing light was so comforting, so warm, and welcoming. She felt herself drawn very willing forward. Upon entering the light, she immediately was greeted, though not with words, by her grandparents and her mother who had been awaiting her arrival. Wordlessly they encouraged her to journey into the cylinder, to follow the path to the light. This encouragement was not needed. She felt as she never felt before. Her sense of well being and belonging increased as she drifted through the light. In the distance, she sensed a presence…an all-protective, all loving being. The closer she came to her destination, the more she sensed that this presence did not radiate the qualities of her earthly male counterparts. She sensed compassion, maternalism, and an unconditional love that surrounded her and filled her with a feeling of attraction and affiliation unknown to her before. Surrendering herself totally to this new experience, Emily longed to reach the end of the cylinder. At that point, her progress stopped. Wordlessly, the light communicated to her that this event was a mistake – her time had not yet arrived to be welcomed here. Emily resisted. She did not wish to leave. A sense of belonging had already overtaken her. Unfortunately, for her, she had no say in the decision-making process. At a speed equaling her ascension, she descended re-joining herself on the hospital bed.

"Nurse, I said she's gone. Please note the time!"

"Doctor, unless you wish to bury a live patient, I believe you should revise your pronouncement!"

CHAPTER 7

"HELLO, YOU HAVE REACHED 978-555-5000. I am not at my desk now. If you leave a message at the beep, I will get back to you as soon as I can. If you need immediate attention, dial "0" for the operator. Thank you."

"Call me at home when you get a chance please." JT hung-up the phone and opened the refrigerator. After taking out a bottle of Poland Spring water, which he used to wash down his blood-pressure pill, he thought about how automatic his actions were upon arriving home. Will he still call his wife, as was his daily habit, when he became a retired gentleman? Things will be different. Will I be different? Will my life be different? I guess we are going to find out. He was about to walk down to his mother's apartment as the phone rang. He called out, "Ma, I'm home." To which she simply responded, "How are you, James?" He focused on the ringing phone and JT picked it up before the second ring. It was his wife returning his call. At fifty-something years of age, his wife was still a beautiful woman. After too many years of marriage to James Thurber Russell, she had maintained her looks and her sanity – no small accomplishment. Theirs had been a classic love story… both of them deeply in love with him. She had been his perfect complement. Her even temperament and optimistic view of everything, her calm approach to emergencies, her lack of complaining and ability to live with pain made her the perfect partner for JT who possessed none of those qualities. She was his ying to her yang, his ping to her pong; she filled-in all the things missing in his nature. She was everything he was not nor could be.

"Jamey? His wife was one of the last who still called her husband Jamey. Most everyone else called him JT, James Russell, or worse.

"Hi. I did it. As of June 30th, I will become a retired old fart".

"The only difference I hear is the retired part."

"Wow! For a woman who had her sense of humor surgically removed at birth, that was pretty quick!"

He had called her Jupiter Probe for years. The reason was while reading 2001:A Space Odyssey, he was captivated by the concept that messages sent to Jupiter from earth would take six months to be received. That was about the same amount of time it would take her to understand all his hilarious comments he would say to her. She would eventually laugh at his humor though long after hearing it…sort of a processing thing. Thus the Jupiter Probe moniker was born.

"Well, you will be more impossible than usual to live with now. I cannot stand the idea of you watching me go off to work each day to earn the bread for the family. You'd better get some kind of job fast!"

He could not remember exactly when he fell in love with her, but the why was so much easier to remember. Her beautiful eyes and long dark brown hair, her nose-wrinkling laugh, her incredible gullibility… at Fenway Park for a Red Sox game he told her about the seventh inning tradition that everyone stood and stretched at the same time. After explaining the tradition and watching as she participated in the seventh inning stretch, having her full attention, he told her about the eighth inning cattle grazing, when cows were to appear from behind the center field doors to mow the outfield grass. Of course, she was skeptical, but "hot damn" she watched for those cows! She was a perfect foil for his sense of humor. She was smarter than he and possessed common sense that he was lacking, but "hot damn" could he ever tell her a story!

"Will you be home at the regular time?"

"I have to pick up your cleaning and stop at Shaw's. Do you need anything?"

"How about a celebration steak tonight?"

"OK. I'll get steak, potatoes, and mushrooms."

"You know the way to this carnivore's heart."

"Bye."

"Bye."

As he hung-up, he started to feel very nostalgic. That was about the last thing he wanted to happen. Too late. The gods had decided that his reward or punishment for that day, whichever way he chose to perceive the anointed task, was a couple of hours of down time to walk down memory lane. He sat back in his recliner and dosed off to an earlier, simpler, freer, wilder time.

CHAPTER 8

IT WAS GOING TO HAPPEN again. All that guilt and disappointment, he hated himself. He knew it would happen, and he wanted it to happen, subconsciously of course, but damn it, that feeling after it was over…

Tara Anne Carleton kicked off her shoes and slipped down on the front seat of her blue 1962 Chevy. She slid her foot towards Jamey and began to tickle his very sensitive sides with her big toe; that action tended to break whatever relationship ice that might have set in and seemed to set the mood for the evening. It was not that James Thurber Russell was shy. It certainly was not that he was turned-off by Tara. His masculinity clearly was never a question. It was just that damn feeling he hated. Again, he tried to fight his instincts as he had tried for the past three years. It just was not natural to suppress a sex drive like little JT's.

"Jamey? Jamey?"

"What?"

"What's wrong?"

"Nothin."

"Jamey there's something wrong, now tell me, or I'll get dressed and…"

"There's nothing wrong!"

"I've known you for almost four years, and if there is one thing I do know about you, it's when you're trying to hide being upset. Now, what's wrong?"

"For the love of Christ, Tara, will you get off my back? There is nothing bothering me. Nothing. Oh Jesus! Don't cry, Tara, please, com'on will ya. Christ, I'm sorry that I yelled, but, Jesus, I'm just sorry. Stop, please."

"Jamey, do you still love me?"

"Why is it that when a guy blows off a little steam, which by the way was in no small part brought about by your constant nagging and directly attributable to an aggravating niche in your personality, why does that automatically bring to the surface all of your petty insecurities and hang-ups?"

"Showing off your education again, Jamey?"

She always kidded him about his schooling mainly because she envied him. It was not jealousy that she felt; she genuinely envied the determination of a person who was labeled in high school with an average I.Q., a higher educational disaster, for working his way towards a future which would have escaped a less ambitious person. Although her I.Q. was higher and her college entrance exams were higher in both the verbal and quantitative sections, she still found that college was wasted on her, probably because she spent all of her time in the snack bar or the student lounge playing cards. Because of that and her love for him, she could not help but envy the guy who was working with "less heavy equipment" than she had and was succeeding nicely, thank you.

Jamey looked up from the floor of the 62 Chevy and a smile cracked the somber look on his face. He stretched out his hand to touch her face. She half smiled then closed her eyes.

"I'm really sorry."

"Do you want to talk about it now?"

"There's nothing to talk about, really."

"OK, but, I think we should have a talk soon. You know we don't talk much anymore. We used to talk a lot, but now we just take everything for granted. I think it's time for an 'inner most thought' talk."

That was Tara's description of her favorite type of conversation. They would spend the entire evening telling each other their fondest hopes, make plans for the future, and discuss any hidden fears. She always felt more secure and sure of Jamey following such a discussion. Innermost thoughts never ceased to make her closer to Jamey than ever before even closer than while they were doing it.

"Sure thing, honey, first thing next week, no, let me see. OK, first of next week; I'll just jot that date on my calendar. No, I'll have my girl call your girl to set up a date."

"You know, Jamey, sometimes you...."

"Yeah, I know."

CHAPTER 9

IT WAS THE BEGINNING OF the last semester break of Jamey Russell's college career. He did not sleep much that night, so he awoke quite late that morning. He cleared the remains of sleep from his eyes and rolled over towards the only window in his newly wallpapered bedroom just in time to see his sister Bina jump quite ungracefully, into a snow drift. Bettina Charlene Russell became Bina at birth because her new big brother could not pronounce Bettina. Bina, four years his junior, had the same beauty possessed by Charlene Russell. Her blond hair and blue eyes, her petite developing figure, and her out-going personality had already made her a target for the males of West Lynn. He smiled to himself with brotherly pride. He was proud of Bina, although he'd die before he'd say that – he was proud of his entire family as they were of him. The family structure was everything to the Russells; all for one, one for all and anything for the children was the rule of thumb at Rancho Russell. The closeness of the Russell family unit arose not by accident. It was a tradition passed on, through both sets of Jamey's grandparents to his father and mother. Guisseppe (James) Lorenzo Russell, the breadwinner of the clan, was a man of average height who, quite obviously, was carrying a few too many pounds for it. If ever there were a truly nice guy existing in a world so prone to lethargy, alienation and selfishness, that man was Jim Russell. People often said that JT looked just like his mother, an opinion that was probably true. Jim Russell would be the first to say amen to that. It was evident that he was not a handsome man, nor was he an unattractive man; he was one of those millions of people thrown under the heading of average, normal, or plain. Yet, the man was far from plain. He was a sincere, honest, truly empathetic man. His deep-set eyes perched at the bridge of an Everest type nose seemed capable of viewing one's soul. He forever had a smile ready and used it quite leisurely. Jim Russell had seen much in his forty-five years. He lived through times both good and bad. Unfortunately for him he had been down looking up most of those forty-five years. Jim was the second oldest of two brothers and two sisters, the son of an immigrant Italian carpenter and his wife who upon arrival in America soon learned the meaning of bigotry. Thus, the name Ruselini became Russell but not out of submission, but rather for the sake of their children. All of the children of Teresa and Dominic Ruselini were born in America. First came Richard followed on alternating years by James, Mary, and Betty. Although Richard was the oldest, he lacked the leadership qualities necessary in the oldest sibling of a family. Therefore, to Jim fell the role of guardian, protector of the young, and keeper of his brothers and sisters. He accepted the role eagerly and practiced it seriously all his life. As the years passed, money became very scarce. Life being as difficult as it was at the time, the pressure was on the oldest children in the family to add to the family's finances. Life had placed Jim Russell in such a situation. Although he did manage to graduate from high school and he knew in his heart that had he been given the opportunity he would have been successful in college, he accepted a $40.00 a week job at a Lynn shoe factory the day after graduation. The factory was only a five minute round trip walk from Jim's home so he returned for lunch each day in time to hear all of the latest disasters and family catastrophes reported by his loving mother in Walter Winchell fashion, except for the heavy accent, of course. During that time Richard, who was a frail almost delicate young man, received a full scholarship to Boston College. Jim was often heard saying that he thanked God for Richard's good fortune. At the age of five, Richard was stricken with a form of paralysis, which left him lame and quite susceptible to disease. Fate had to compensate the young man whom it had seriously wronged. Richard's misfortune was only the beginning of a number of tragedies, which would befall the Ruselinis in America. When Jim was nineteen years old, he lost his mother, a woman whose only mission in life was to make a new life for her children in a world, which was both strange and hostile to her. It happened in a matter of seconds. One morning she walked down the stairs leading from their six-room apartment to return a cup of borrowed sugar to Mrs. Bloom on the first floor. A sharp piercing pain sheared through her head causing her to fall forward. The diagnosis was a brain hemorrhage which took her life instantly. Exactly one year to the day later, Dominic Ruselini succumbed to his loneliness. Life went on, and the living survived the pains of death. The Russells remained a closely-knit family unit and shared each other's joys and sorrows. Richard graduated from Boston College and went to work with an accounting firm in Boston; Mary took a job with a clothing manufacturer; Betty continued to be smothered with attention and got increasingly more spoiled; and Uncle Sam called Jim to war.

CHAPTER 10

IT WAS A COLD DAY in March when James Lorenzo Russell boarded an Army bus and waved good-bye to his family. He looked at Richard and winked, "You're the leader now pal, keep'em healthy." He looked down at young Betty who was sobbing uncontrollably. He blew a kiss in her direction which she pretended to catch and hold tightly in her fist. The bus began to roll as a single tear found its way to the corner of his mouth. He was gone. He received the governmental grand tour over the following ten months: Fort Bragg, New York to Camp Campbell, Oklahoma to Fort Burns, California. His mail trailed him at various times due to his travels, but he always kept in touch with home. He hated the Army. He hated the fact that his family was three thousand miles away, and he hated the loneliness he felt.

On a weekend pass, his last before shipping to places unknown, he met Charley. Charlene McDonough, the only daughter of a first generation Irish immigrant, was a truly beautiful girl. Long brown hair, light blue eyes, a magnificent smile, which exposed the most beautiful, and perfectly even teeth imaginable; all this and she had dimples too. Jim flipped for all five foot two, one hundred and seven pounds of her beautiful figure. Charley McDonough was doing her part to support our fighting men; when she was not taking freshmen courses at Summer Valley Junior College, she was handing out donuts, coffee, and a little home conversation to lonely service men at her local Red Cross station. Everything that Jim felt when he first saw Charley was reciprocated to some degree because she broke a long-standing rule and allowed him to walk her home that evening. They talked, walked, and laughed. Jim laughed, really laughed, for the first time in months. In that one evening, over a period of two or three hours, Jim learned that she had no special boyfriend, eagerly looked forward to the day she would marry, wanted at least two children, was a virgin and would remain that way until her wedding night, and had never allowed a first date kiss, probably because there had not been all that many first dates in her sheltered life.

"I know we've just met, and I know we're still practically strangers, but well Charley, would you write me? It doesn't have to be anything too long, you know, a line or two or five. I know it's a lot to…"

"Of course."

"You will."

"If you hadn't asked, I would have asked you."

"Really."

She nodded and dropped her eyes to the pavement to hide a much-reddened face. He lifted her face with his fingertips and gave Charley McDonough a very special kiss. They spent the next two days together. The hours went by quickly as do all good things. Before they knew it, the time had come to say good-bye. They stood together outside her house hand in hand.

"You'll write?"

"Of course."

"You know I… well, I've never met a girl… I mean to say that you are…Oh shit! I'm in love with you, Charley."

"In love with me?"

"Yeah, I love you, Charley."

"Jim…"

"No. Don't say anything; just tell me you care, and that there is a chance for me."

"I do care, but…."

"But there's a chance."

"Yes."

He kissed her for the third and final time in three days, turned and walked down the concrete path. He pushed open the gate with his knee, turned and said, "Get your trousseau ready, doll. I'm coming back to marry you." He did. On May 12th, 1946, James Lorenzo Russell took Charlene McDonough for his lawfully wedded wife. They moved to Massachusetts where Jim's family welcomed them into a small three-room apartment.

Things were quite different at home for Jim. Mary had married; Betty was engaged to a Marine; and Richard had found a girl. They were grown. It seemed to happen over night, but three long years had passed. The family dissolved in body, but never in spirit. With a long life to look forward to together, Mr. and Mrs. James Lorenzo Russell set up housekeeping in Lynn, Massachusetts.

CHAPTER 11

"JAM-EY! JAM-EY! JAM-EY!"

"What the hell do you want?"

"Are you ever getting up?" yelled Bina.

"Bina, what time is it?"

"About eleven, I guess."

"Oh Christ! I'm late. Old man Lloyd will shit himself."

Mr. Lloyd was the owner of a small drugstore, which happened to be the sole source of income for JT Russell. JT had worked for Mr. Lloyd since the summer before he entered college. During that time, he had received raises totaling fifty cents. His wages skyrocketed from $1.50 per hour to $2.00 per hour.

"Four years of back breaking, insult taking, intellectually stunting soda jerking and a miserable fifty cents in raises. Jesus, that's twelve and a half cents a year. I know I'm worth more that that. I think I'll tell Mr. 'psycho' Lloyd that I'm gonna stop breaking mine, and he can take his goddamn job and stuff if up his big goddamn..."

"Jam-ey! Jam-ey!

"What?"

"Ma says Mr. Lloyd called to see if you were sick."

At that moment, Charlene Russell entered the room.

"James Thurber Russell, aren't you supposed to be at work? I am ashamed of you. If you no longer like the job, the wages, or the boss, and you wish to give up your position, the truly fair thing to do is tell him face to face. Give him a fair amount of notice."

Charlene Russell always called her son James, never Jim, Jimmy, JT, nor Jamey, always James, and when angry she would pronounce his entire name in round high-pitched tones. She was still a beautiful woman. Everyone said so. She carried her years well, and her figure had weathered two children quite well. After twenty-two years of marriage and two difficult births, she was the same size as the day she married.

"OK, I'll talk with Mr. Lloyd to submit my formal resignation."

"By the way, James, do you have plans for tonight?" asked his mother.

"Yeah."

"May I ask what they are?"

"Sure."

"What are they?"

"I'm going out with Tara."

"Oh."

That "oh"! That goddamn "oh"! There was not a word on the face of the earth that had more negative meaning to JT. He heard it almost every time that Tara's name came up in discussions with his mother. He knew it was not Tara, not personally that bothered his mother; she would react to any girl with whom he had become serious in the same manner. She simply feared losing her only begotten son.

Lloyd's Pharmacy was a fairly modern establishment located at the ground level of the Walsh Building in the downtown area of Lynn. It had a ten-seat soda fountain, a relic of times past, as well as a number of well-stocked shelves offering the same goods probably seen on similar drugstore shelves from Boston to Los Angeles. Mr. Lloyd was in the backroom filling out a prescription when JT arrived.

"Mr. Lloyd."

"Well now, Mr. Russell is in the building."

He always called JT Mr. Russell, and it never failed to burn his ass.

"I'd like to speak to you."

"You're late, Mr. Russell. Maybe I should take this from your pay."

"Look, Mr. Lloyd, I'm finished; I quit. If you wish, I'll stay on until you find someone else.

"What? You're leaving?"

"Yes, sir."

JT was puzzled. The old man looked both surprised and hurt. Holy Jesus, he was hurt.

"I'm very sorry, Jamey."

For the first time in over four years, he addressed him in a familiar manner.

"I'm sorry more than I can tell you. You were like," he hesitated, "well no matter, Rose Marie and I will miss you, Mr. Russell. But perhaps now I will hire someone who doesn't eat all of my profit."

"Well, I'm almost finished with college, and after graduation I'll probably get drafted or something, you know, so I decided to take a pre-graduation vacation."

"Youth is a very precious possession; the only trouble is too soon it depreciates. Enjoy it, Mr. Russell, because one day you will wake and find in the mirror an old man."

"Well, if you don't need me, I'll be going".

"Wait, please, one minute."

Newton Spencer Lloyd III walked to the back of the room and opened the rusty old safe, which had seen many better days. He removed a long white envelope with the wording Mr. Russell on the front. With the envelope extended in his left hand, the druggist reached for the boy's right hand.

"This is for you. I was saving it for June and your graduation, but it seems now is a more appropriate time."

Jamey took the envelope and read the outside writing. His glance moved towards Lloyd silently asking for permission to look inside. Mr. Lloyd nodded and Jamey proceeded to find a stack of ten-dollar bills.

"Holy Jesus! What is this?"

"Your back salary."

"But...."

"I put some in the envelope every month you worked for me. In there you'll find maybe fifty pictures of Alexander Hamilton."

"Five hundred dollars? Five hundred dollars?"

"OK at arithmetic you're good, at soda jerking you could improve."

"I don't know what to say."

"I know. Don't say anything. That's all your money; you earned it. I just kept it safe for you."

Usually, James Thurber Russell had a difficult time expressing his true feelings, yet sometimes tears of joy say it all. They embraced. How could he have been so wrong about a man with whom he'd spent so much time?

"Come back sometimes to visit me. Rose Marie and I will miss you terribly."

"I will sir. I want to...."

"Please, you have said everything that needs to be said. Now let a poor working man get back to his trade."

JT had in his hands that proverbial string from which the world dangled, and he was not about to let it go.

CHAPTER 12

TARA CARLETON COVERED HER TYPEWRITER and leaned back trying to gather her thoughts after what had been a very difficult eight hours. In fact, every day at J. Hollingsworth Furniture was a difficult one. Competition in the furniture business being what it was in Lynn at the time tended to make the man, John Hollingsworth, a task-master driven by a need to succeed, a sincere respect for his bank account, and a wife whose clothing bills accumulated geometrically. Having married very well, Mr. Hollingsworth parlayed Mrs. Hollingsworth's inheritance into six stores from Lynn to Springfield, an annual income calculated to be in the high six-figure neighborhood, and a peptic ulcer, which made him the second most miserable person on the planet. Tara remembered her first meeting with the man – a disaster! How was she to have known that the short, balding, lisping man who mistakenly happened into the woman's rest room was J. Hollingsworth and not the neighborhood pervert? How was she to have known that without his glasses, John Hollingsworth could not read a sign the size of a billboard? How was she to have known that striking J. Hollingsworth on the skill with her purse would get her a job in the largest furniture store in the city?

She had certainly come a long way since that day. Upon leaving college after the first semester of her sophomore year, she applied for a secretarial opening at Hollingsworth and won the job over fifteen other applicants. After six months on the job, she was the best secretary in the office. Within a year she had been promoted to her present position of inventory control, customer service and credit department supervisor.

Tara watched the second hand of the clock located over the exit sign and grinned with anticipation. She would be seeing Jamey in just over an hour. Just as soon as she could get home, change, and motor over to his house, the best part of her day would begin. Regardless of her fatigue, she was never too tired to see Jamey; she loved him. She loved to be with him were it only to window shop at a mall or watch TV together at this house. At exactly five o'clock, she lifted her five foot four, one hundred twenty-pound, very feminine frame from the chair and walked briskly from the Hollingsworth building. She smiled at Douglas, the parking lot attendant, as she half ran half-skipped to her car. Once inside, she knew everything tiring and bothersome was behind her for at least another day.

As if she had awakened for the second time that day, Tara looked forward to the evening. Within a matter of ten minutes, she was pulling into the circular drive that led to her front door. As was usual, on a Monday, neither her mother nor father was at home. Monday was club night for the Carletons at Nahant's only and very selective country club. Being long time members of this club carried with it the responsibility of attending all club functions as well as the maintenance of a regular schedule that underscored their standing in the community's closely-knit social structure. Therefore, as was usual on Mondays, Tara came home to an empty house. She unlocked the front door and ran non-stop to the telephone. A call to Jamey was of top priority each night with the exception of those nights on which he worked.

"Hello, Mrs. Russell?"

"Yes."

"Mrs. Russell, this is Tara. May I speak with Jamey?"

"Certainly, how are you Tara?"

"Fine, thank you, and yourself?"

"Very well, thank you. Here's James."

"Hi. How was work today?"

"Ok, what did you do?"

"Oh, nothing too much. I quit my job, found out I was an asshole, and became a rich man. Other than that I took it easy."

"What are talking about? You are talking stranger than usual."

"Mr. Lloyd gave me, hold on now, he gave me five hundred dollars, fifty ten-dollar bills!"

"Why did, and I believe I am quoting you directly here, 'that cheap old mother who squeezes nickels so hard that the buffaloes scream', give you five-hundred dollars?"

"I'll tell you when I see you."

"Hey, where are you taking me tonight, sport?" she teased.

"How about a pizza and a sundae?"

"For an appetizer of course?"

"No, my dear, that is main course and dessert."

"Well, since this is Monday and one, I have no money, and two, I've had no better offers, I accept your less than prolific proposal. My car or yours?" she smiled already knowing the answer.

"Yours."

"Of course, sport. I'll be over by six, ok?"

She dropped the receiver and ran up the stairs to her room. After washing her face and reworking her make-up in record setting time, she made a final stop at her desk for the renewal application for Cosmopolitan, which she had forgotten that morning. It was then that she noticed the calendar on the desktop. The twenty-fifth circled in red grabbed her attention. She was almost a week late. Her "friend", as she called her monthly cycle, was due six days ago.

"I hope Jamey isn't counting this month. He is neurotic when this kind of thing happens. I wonder if all guys are like that. If he is counting, I am in for a hell of an evening. Oh well, maybe this month will be different. I just hope he's not counting."

Normally she could reach the Russells' home in fifteen minutes, ten if she broke the law. Having broken several laws on the way, Tara pulled in front of Jamey's house at exactly six o'clock. Jamey who was standing on the porch walked around to the driver's side of the car and watched as Tara slid over.

"You're late."

"Are you crazy? I set the land speed record getting over here."

"I don't mean that."

"Oh shit."

To understand the logic that lay the foundation to James Thurber Russell's paranoid-like behavior at such times of the month, one had to walk a mile in his moccasins, so to speak. At best, such a task was very difficult to accomplish. For a mere mortal, the task was impossible. JT's feeling about their sex life had as many layers as a piece of fine French pastry. If he did really know what love was, he knew he really loved Tara. In every part of him that made decisions, she was his perfect match. Part of the problem lay here. JT had spent so much of his adolescence allowing the little head to do the thinking for the big head. His sex drive was always on automatic and always stuck in high gear. To keep his hands off Tara required God-like strength unpossessed by JT. He loved everything about touching, squeezing, holding, hugging, and kissing the girl. They thought they were being responsible by practicing coitus interruptus regularly. Condoms were a poor second choice because he loved the feel of her. Now at that point the weird part begins. JT was so aware of the difficulty any girl would have being accepted by his mother, he became very defensive whenever the subject of Tara arose at home. That intense sensitivity had been at the root of several mother/son screamfests in the past. Therefore, he set as his goal to eliminate hostilities and encourage pleasantries between his two women. In other words, he labored to get his mother to accept Tara unconditionally. The logic of his plan was well intentioned. The practicality of forcing people to like and accept each other via the manipulations of a third party was faulty at best, yet he was not to be deterred. JT had that plan so imbedded in his mind that it was as if he had been brain branded! If his mother was at least accepting of Tara, and some unexpected event occurred, the storm might be more easily weathered.

"Hey, Ma, you know that girl, Tara, about whom you have no bad feelings? She is pregnant! I am the father! We have to get married!"

Whenever he thought about this scenario, and that was just about once a month, he would make himself physically sick and emotionally unbearable to other carbon-based life forms. How in the name of God would he ever succeed in having Tara accepted into the Russell Family were they to show up at the front door pregnant? That was at the crux of his sullenness every month. On the other hand, he could not communicate that monthly scenario to Tara simply because as smart as she was the answer would be obvious; Tara would stop doing it with him! That would not be acceptable to either JT's big head or little head. JT's "little head" had no intention of surrendering its desire for the pleasures of her flesh. He was willing to put himself and Tara through Dante's Inferno each month rather then exercise the self-control required of abstinence.

CHAPTER 13

IT WAS QUIET AS THEY drove; it always was at this time of the month unless of course everything was normal, which was not often. Tara sat at JT's side though not as close as was her habit. She really hated him at times like these. She could not understand or accept his petty fears, irrational behavior, and unsympathetic disposition. After all, what was she to do? Was she to blame? Month after month for the past three years, since they had been doing it, he had subjected her to what she considered the cruelest of all treatments – silence. Between lovers, silence holds an ambiguity disdained through the centuries. Consider the silence which passes before eyelids close and lips meet, when eyes search deeply and longingly into eyes, when two hearts beat steadily in the night each knowing that one is there to answer the other. In comparison, consider the silence, which is borne of disappointment, disillusionment, anger, and hurt. This hurtful silence builds walls as the parties persist in their need to maintain real or imagined positions of debate. Silence had come to mean more to them than not speaking. It said many things in many ways.

JT remembered, as they drove past the beach, the day he met Tara. The last thing he needed was another girl. At the time he was seeing a very obliging lady of sixteen who had "the biggest bosoms" since Janice 'Watermelons' Kelly, a young lady who had been officially measured at 48D by every male in Lynn except Monsignor Blackman and Jack Thurman the city drunk. What else was there on earth: an obliging female, enough tit to choke an alligator, and a car in which to perform the dirty deed. All served to make life a dream for him. Yet, shortly before dusk on June 28th, 1965, fate entered JT's life. On that day at the Revere seashore, he simply stumbled across Tara's path, both literally and physically. He and Joanna Fortucci sat killing time at the beach until darkness would allow them to return to his car to get down to some serious loving. JT did not see Tara until it happened. In an effort to run free from Joanna's grasp, JT fell over, on, and for Tara. Following an apology, a laugh, and an introduction, he and Joanna returned to the car. He went through the motions that evening. Their love that had burned so brightly so quickly died as rapidly as it had grown. Tara was the focus of his thoughts from the moment he fell over her.

He returned to the beach alone each of the next four days searching for Tara and putting Joanna off with a variety of excuses. JT's persistence paid-off on the fourth day of his quest, and soon thereafter, he and Tara were together quite regularly that summer. With September approaching, the uncertainties of a new relationship began to raise its ugly head. Both Tara and JT were to enter college in the fall. Tara would attend Fairlawn, one of the big money out-of-town schools, while JT was going to attend Blake College, a medium-sized relatively inexpensive, local school. By the time school was about to start, Tara and JT were in the vernacular of the time "into each other" very deeply. Both felt they had found what William Goldman once called "the handle" – all that there is to make life worthwhile. They planned their lives together. They sealed their love with all the physical intimacies two people in love share – with the exception of the big one. The night before Tara left for Fairlawn, JT gave her his class ring. He remembered that night so well. They parked at Lynn Beach and watched the waves rush to shore. There was little to say. She was leaving him, going two hundred fifty miles away. It might just as well have been another planet! There she would be meeting all kinds of smooth-ass college clowns who would try to "slap the make on her as soon as look at her". What was there to say? He held her and kissed her. Mostly he just looked at her and smiled. He just could not help but smile whenever he looked at her; he could not understand why. At midnight without saying a word, he took the class ring from his finger and slipped it on hers. Without saying a word, she told him that she would be his for as long as he wanted her.

CHAPTER 14

THAT FIRST YEAR IN COLLEGE was what JT called "an ass-breaker". He missed Tara but found less time to miss her than he had anticipated. He saw her on some weekends and at Christmas break; it was at Christmas that he had the first real heartbreak of his life. During Christmas vacation, Jamey looked forward to the break from book boredom, as well as being with Tara, six hours a day. They visited that night. They stayed at both their houses for a short time, and then they went to the Delvanes' home, JT's second family. Anthony James Delvane and James Thurber Russell had been friends since their days together in Miss Landry's third grade class. They went through both grade school and high school together. Now they were entering college together. The two were virtually inseparable. No one ever asked where Tony is or where's JT? They simply asked, "Where are Tony and JT?" Where one appeared, the other was soon to follow. Tara and JT visited with the Delvanes until it was time to leave for Mid-Night Mass. That was, in fact, the last time he went to Church; it seems a college education has that kind of an effect on some people. After Mass, Jamey drove Tara home, where they exchanged gifts in his car. He gave Tara a skirt and matching sweater that he very proudly announced he chose all by himself; she, of course, said she loved them. He reciprocated by "loving" the maroon sweater she gave him. Something was not right. He felt it all evening, and could see through her façade. She was so quiet all night long, yet he hated to bring up possible unpleasantries at such a happy time. But, James T. Russell could not leave well enough alone. She was troubled and confused as he soon discovered. He could remember the dialogue verbatim:

"What's wrong, Tara?

"What?"

"There's something bothering you. What is it?"

"Jamey, I love you; you know that, but I have to find out for myself if you are the one; the man I'll spend the rest of my life with."

"Go on."

"Well...I want some freedom. I want for you and me to date others, as well as each other. Do you understand?"

"Yeah, I think I do...After three goddamn months in goddamn college, you get the goddamn hot pants for some goddamn football gorilla. Well, listen sister, you take your goddamn freedom; you have your goddamn cake, but I'll be goddamned if you'll goddamn eat it too. Merry Goddamn Christmas."

"Jamey, are you going to shut me out all night long?" He snapped back out of his thoughts.

"What? Jesus ,Tara, you know how I am."

"But that doesn't stop the hurt, Jamey! You hurt me every time you do this. Can't you understand? My periods are irregular. You are incorrigible. Many girls are irregular. God, Jamey, what else can I say?"

"Listen, I can't turn my feelings off and on. They are what they are. When I'm down, I'm down; that's all there is. I'm sorry."

"Great, then I want to go home!"

"All right, but would you like to eat something first?"

"No!"

It was almost dark when they reached his house; the moon was full and only a handful of stars were visible overhead. The ride had been a long one, not distant, yet very long. He caught Tara wiping away tears several times during the drive. On one hand, he could count the times when she had raised her voice or "told him off" in their three and a half years together; therefore, these times remained vivid in his memory. One other such time was the night she discovered how sexually active he had been during their three-month separation. He had not tried to keep it quiet, nor on the other hand did he advertise his escapades. The month following their reunion, Pammy Livingston quite vindictively filled Tara in on some of JT's busy mornings, noons and nights following their break-up. Tara knew Pammy was telling the truth when she volunteered information too intimate to create. Pammy described a beauty mark that she had located on JT; she even graphically and descriptively explained where it was located and how she had discovered it. JT Russell would be the first to refute the significance of the mark, but Mother Nature knows more about beauty in that area than a mere mortal. JT's beauty mark was located on the right hemisphere of his penis. Tara had not fooled herself into thinking that he sat at home in front of her picture swearing celibacy during this time apart, but neither did she think he would have gone forth single-handedly and try to populate the world! She was furious! The next time they were together, she did not leave out a derogatory term, nor did she fail to link those terms with appropriate adjectives. A dock worker would have had difficulty keeping up with her that night. In the end, she wanted to believe him, an obvious conclusion, since she did not question Jamey's explanation that Pammy had gotten him drunk and had taken unwanted liberties with his body. Bringing him back to the present, the car bumped the curb as he pulled into the driveway. JT slowly looked over at this silent passenger. Neither spoke. He began but stopped. She did not speak. He left the car closing the door behind him. JT walked quickly towards his back door. As he turned upon opening the screen door, he watched Tara slide over behind the wheel and in one sweeping motion pull from the yard onto the street.

He went to his room and flopped down on his bed. Sleep for him never came when it was needed most; that night was no exception. His ceiling turned into a huge screen on which memories flashed by at a frightening pace. Not surprisingly, Tara was the featured player. The night they got back together was always something pleasant for him to dwell on; it helped replace his black mood. That was some day.

CHAPTER 15

MARCH 23RD, 1966, SEEMED JUST like any other Friday when Jamey awoke: Psych of Adolescence at 10AM, Educational Philosophy at 11AM, and Experimental Psych at 1PM. He would breeze through both late morning classes, have a bite to eat and then struggle through Experimental Psych with Dr. Feldon Fox, an hour of sheer nausea. It always amazed JT how so much bullshit filled a five foot two inch Ph.D. Fox was chock full of brand new education complete with brilliant new theories of his own in some cases; yet, no one could identify with him as an instructor. He was like the loud mouth bore that used to sit at the front of every class. He was the one who would engage the instructor in debate and possess the answer to every question. If the teacher happened to sit down suddenly this poor bastard would probably get his nose broken or at least have it buried in the teacher's ass. Rolling over towards the clock, JT saw that he had twenty-five minutes to get to Psych of Adolescence. After debating and rationalizing, he decided to give Tony a call and forget classes altogether. What he needed was a nice little break from the routine, away from home, away from those possessive females, away from everything. Tony was on his way out of the door when JT called.

"What' da ya say, buddy, New Hampshire for three days and two nights? We'll make it back for classes Monday morning, I promise."

Tony was not the kind of guy that JT had to badger. He was "in" immediately! After talking to his mother about his newly devised plans and setting up his finances for the outing, he hopped into "Black", his 1962 Corvair, filled her up with gasoline, and picked up Tony shortly before noon. Oh boy, it was going to be some day. He found that to be so true.

They decided to drive up to Laconia, New Hampshire, a two-hour trek to a little ski lodge where, according to a friend, the ladies were lovely and agreeable. Hundley's Ski Heaven was the name of the lodge, and a more inappropriate name never existed. Heaven consisted of cold water and no heat, ripped sheets and bad food, not enough snow to ski, and Tara Ann Carleton.

Unbeknownst to JT, Tara and several of her friends had also taken a long weekend having arrived late Thursday evening. Tony and JT arrived close to three o'clock that Friday. After checking in, they started to "check it out".

The snow was so thin in many spots that the ground showed through, but that did not stop the guys from grabbing a toboggan. The slope was "jammed" with seven or eight people including JT and Tony.

"I can't believe we paid slope fees to go sledding," complained Tony.

"When in snowless Rome, do as the sledding Romans do, my friend" consoled JT.

"Together or alone?"

"What?"

"I said do you want to go down together or alone?"

"I'll hold your hand Delvane".

JT hopped on the toboggan after Tony boarded and wrapped his ankles and arms around the inexperienced driver.

"Ready?"

"For what?"

"Hasta Leugo-o-o-o-o-"

They had looked for an area with the most snow disregarding the angle of that particular slope. They chose a black diamond slope usually reserved for the most experienced skiers. In hindsight, the slope seemed later to have a 90-degree angle. They were flying down the slope scared shitless. Suddenly, in front of them, lay a disabled toboggan. Panicking, the inexperienced driver, veered sharply to the right throwing JT off the sled in the direction of the toboggan. Several bounces and a short roll later, JT found himself on the snow covered ground one leg and one hand draped over Tara Carleton!

Thankfully, he did not lose consciousness, but he was lightheaded. It took several moments before he realized that he was not alone. He tried to shake the cobwebs from his throbbing head; as he did so, he turned toward the body he partially covered. Turning away, he did a perfect double take. She lay there eyes open with a very red face surrounded by very fluffy white fur hood. She smiled, as did he.

"Excuse me ma'am, haven't we met like this before?"

"Yes, it seems to me we've bumped into each other but who knows where or when?"

They just looked. That old silence spoke again, as it had in the past. She drew his face close. When she kissed him, he knew that she was not hurt. When he kissed her back, well no injured man could kiss like that! They lay there, he on top of her, for what seemed to be minutes, but in reality was only seconds.

"Russ, Jesus Christ, are you all right? Who is she…? For Christ's sake, Tara, what the hell are…?

Jesus Christ what's going …?"

"Relax Tony."

"Ellen, how's Ellen?"

"Who's Ellen? "

"She's my girlfriend who was driving the toboggan."

"Look behind the toboggan, Tony. We're alright. Isn't that right Tara?"

"You bet, Jamey."

The four casualties staggered down the slope with little more than a few bruises and a couple of scrapes. After a refreshing breather on the ski lift, all shock and nervousness disappeared. The lift was a two-seat model that allowed Tara and JT to talk on the ride back to the lodge.

"You look well. Fairlawn must agree with you."

"Actually, I haven't been well at all. That is why I am here. Jamey, I have never had three more miserable months in my life. I've missed seeing you…I've…I've missed you so much.that…

"Tara, please don't cry."

"I know a girl who transferred from Blake to Fairlawn and she was bragging about a guy she'd dated at Blake. When I found out it was you, I got so jealous. I don't mean envious. I mean hate type jealous. She had my property type jealous!"

"But, you…."

"I know; I wanted to be free. Nevertheless, Jamey, I have changed my mind over the past three months. Do you think that we could date occasionally when I am home? I would not take up every weekend. I know how busy you must be, but I'd love to go out with you again, if you'd like to go out with me."

"You know, Tara, all my life I've seen everything very simply, black or white. If something was agreeable to me, and I liked it, I'd accept it cut and dry; on the other hand, if something wasn't as I liked it, I'd reject it in the same way. There has been no room for negotiation in my life, no room for the shades of gray. I was so hurt last Christmas, more hurt than I have ever been or probably will ever be again. You were the first girl I ever loved… You are the only girl I have ever loved. I had seen scenes in movies like that night a thousand times; I had read accounts of such things before in novels, but when it happened to me…"

"Jamey are you saying that you could forgive me? Would you possibly want to try again? I mean you and me together?"

"I think that you deserve me; Lord have mercy on you."

"He already has Jamey; he already has."

CHAPTER 16

WHEN HE FINALLY AWOKE THE following morning, he was very anxious. Fighting with Tara was something he hated to do. Additionally, the tension he lived with at that time of each month usually led to blinding headaches. He wanted desperately to call her to set things straight; however, personal telephone calls were against the policy of J. Hollingsworth Furniture Company unless, of course, the call was of an emergency nature. Well, he decided that the present situation was indeed an emergency to him. If he did not speak to her soon, his goddamn skull would blow apart! He dialed the Hollingsworth telephone number as fast as he was able.

"Hello," he stated in his most profound voice, "I must speak with Miss Tara Anne Carleton. This is her physician, Dr. Quack. I must discuss her blood test results with her immediately!"

"One moment please, I will connect you," recited the voice at the opposite end of the line.

"You bet your ass you will, Missy! The doctor is in the house," laughed JT.

"Hello, this is Tara Anne Carleton speaking."

"Good morning, hon. Please forgive me," he begged.

"Jamey! Do you want to get me fired and pregnant?" questioned the object of his attention.

"Miss, this is Dr. Quack calling to discuss your recent blood test. You will be pleased to know that you have some in that great body of yours!" he teased.

"You are insane, and I must be as equally insane! I have to go; I'll call you tonight."

"Wait, Tara, I want you to marry me – tonight! Please say yes," he pleaded.

"I don't have time for a demented boyfriend or husband, Jamey! Oh! By the way, I have it. I awoke with it this morning. I guess you can stuff that proposal now," she continued. And while I am on this mini-rant, I'm not exactly sure what possesses you at this time of the month, but I can't help but think you could handle it differently. Right now, friend, you are doing it wrong! Good-bye!"

"Bye honey."

JT hung-up the telephone, threw his fist into the air, and patted his crotch.

"We made it through another month, Little JT. We'll be back in business in a few days, little buddy." whispered JT to his penis.

As history has shown us repeatedly, some people just never, ever learn.

CHAPTER 17

THE NEXT FEW MONTHS FLEW by. They attended his Senior Prom, Senior Week, and the senior concert with the Velvet Hockey Puck, and finally graduation. As Tony put it, Graduation Day is the decorating of the four year casualties. Three hundred five graduating seniors took turns accepting diplomas with the left hand and shaking the Chancellor's hand with the right; the three hundred sixth one, James Thurber Russell, not only accepted with his right confounding the Chancellor's attempt at shaking his hand, but he also walked off the stage at a juncture where there were no stairs – painful. After picking himself off the floor, he returned to his seat to the sounds of a standing ovation. He thought to himself "always leave 'em laughing."

Until that climatic moment, Mrs. Russell, Bina, and Tara had sat crying while Jim Russell's chest almost burst from his shirt. After the incident, all four were ready to sneak out the back door.

"Well, Mr. New College graduate, that was quite a stage right exit you managed," called Newton Spencer Lloyd who along with his daughter Rose Marie joined the Russell Family and Tara on their way out of the auditorium. JT hugged both Lloyd and Rose Marie.

"Hey, Rosie, you look wonderful," he smiled.

"Thank you, Jamey. Do you really mean that?" she asked blushing.

"Have I ever lied to you?"

"Yes, Jamey, you have, often!"

"Today?" he volleyed.

She laughed long and hard. The two had shared a bond that went beyond being born on the same day, same year, at the same hospital, at about the same time. Actually, they first officially met in Miss Reynolds first grade class on their first day at school. It was then that James Thurber Russell won the heart of the young woman. He became her knight in shining armor, elementary school style. On that day, one of their fellow classmates questioned Rose Marie about her constant stuttering – an embarrassing situation even for a five year old. Jamey made it known to the questioner and everyone else around him that James T. Russell will answer all stupid questions for Rose Marie! From that moment on, a relationship blossomed that grew and matured through grade school, junior high school, high school, and college.

"Mr. Lloyd, we're having a little party for the twinkled-toed graduate. Will you and Rose Marie please come?" asked Charlene Russell.

"We'd be honored to join you, Mrs. Russell," responded Newton Lloyd.

The last guests departed just before midnight. JT flopped on the sofa with envelopes in his hand. He seemed to have found new life in opening his gifts. In a little over five minutes, JT had opened and tabulated the contents of fifty-five envelopes that now lay at his feet. Three hundred twenty-five dollars was his total. His father teased that it was a good profit for only one-day's work. As he and his father continued their conversation, his mother entered the room carrying a small box wrapped in yellow paper with a green ribbon and bow. Tara followed with a bigger box wrapped in white paper with a red bow. At the end of the line was Bina who carried a box bigger than his mother's but smaller than Tara's box wrapped in gold paper with white ribbon and a white bow.

"Now it's time for our gifts," his mother said.

"Open mine first, Jamey."

"Thank you, Tara."

He wrestled with the ribbon and ripped at the paper. Finally, he won a clear-cut decision. It was a cassette tape player for his car. Exactly the one he had picked out but never bought.

"You're kidding, Tara, this is too much. Really, this costs too much money."

"How many times do you graduate from college?"

"Only once if we're lucky," cracked his father based upon his son's earlier header off the stage.

He leaned over and kissed her. He kissed her for the first time in front of his parents. He must have been happy.

"Open mine next, Jamey."

"Bina, I hope you didn't go crazy too."

Again, he battled the packaging, and again he won decisively.

"Tapes!"

Bina had given him six cassette tapes, all of which were JT's favorites.

"If I understand the workings of the player I just received, these will be very handy." mugged the center of attention.

"Jamey, aren't you just the wittiest college graduate ever?" teased Bina.

He hugged his younger sister and buzzed her cheek.

"Well, I guess we're last, Mother. Why don't you give sonny our present?"

"From your father and mother, James."

"Thanks Mom. Thanks Dad."

The package fit in the palm of his hand. The excitement had left him a bit groggy so he hesitated a moment. He finally unwrapped the small container, shaking it gingerly trying to identify the contents. Inside he found a sheet of cotton. As he picked it up between his thumb and index finger, it revealed a green key. His eyes bugged. He looked at Tara, who was crying and smiling. He looked at the key; he could not speak. He looked to his mother and father whom were smiling very proudly and finally toward Bina who had joined Tara crying.

"Holy shit! A car? A goddamn car?"

Jim Russell shook his head affirmatively. JT jumped up, grabbed both his parents, and cried.

"No, I don't believe it. A car? How could you? I don't ...."

All five of them came together in the center of the room laughing and crying simultaneously.

"Let's stop this foolishness, right now!" ordered his mother.

"Would you like to see your new car, James? It's in the garage."

"One thing, James, we hope you agree with us that "Black" should be given to Bina."

"Abso-fucking-lutely!"

"James!"

JT ran out of the house to the garage. He grabbed the handle and stopped. He took a breath. Up went the door and his eyelids. Sitting there headlights facing him was an olive green Toyota Mark II complete with automatic transmission, bucket seats, and black interior. He had been saving for this car! Again, he grabbed both his parents; this time he was already crying, as were they.

The Russell's and Tara spent the next three hours riding all over Lynn. At 3:30 AM, JT drove his car into the garage and closed it up for the night. He spread his arms and gathered the four people he loved most in the world, and they walked into the house.

CHAPTER 18

"TONY! TONY! IT'S TEN O'CLOCK…" The human alarm clock was Jessica Delvane, an attractive, second-generation, Italian mama, whose claim to fame was giving birth to Anthony James Delvane.

"OK, Ma, I'm up."

"What time did JT have to go this morning?"

"Six o'clock. You know the goddamn Army."

"Tony, your language gets more offensive each day."

"Well, Jesus, Ma, we're only out of school five days and whamo the goddamn army hits him! What a graduation gift. I wonder when they'll catch me."

"Don't be so pessimistic; you know that Jamey should be found unfit for the army. Remember he had that rheumatic fever when he was fourteen."

"I hope so, Ma."

"And you and your knees, you have nothing to worry about according to Dr. Motherson. The doctor told me that they reject boys with knee cartilage surgery on one knee; you've had two."

"Yeah…well, let's wait to see."

Ten miles away at the Boston Army Base, JT Russell was completing his psychological test. Only an hour before, Sergeant Brown, a huge man whose name also described his race, stood feet spread, legs straight, chest out, stomach in, and chin out awaiting the next batch of future gladiators.

"You men are here by request of the United States Army. You are guests of the United States Army. You will not fuck around because the United States Army will not stand for it! If you do fuck around, you will be subject to immediate induction! Do you understand? My Assistant, Corporal Breath, will administer the Army Intelligence Test to you. Corporal Breath, they are all yours."

A pale, slope shouldered, mousy looking, young fellow dressed neatly in army fatigues complete with two stripes on each arm, three ribbons of various colors on his chest, and an impressive medal located beneath the ribbons walked forward almost apologetically.

"I am Corporal Breath. You will now take the intelligence test. You will write your level of completed education in the appropriate square. If you do not attain a grade, which is comparable to your level of education, I will give you a complete battery of tests. That consists of seven one hour tests."

That was all JT needed to add yet more humor to the surreal experience in which he found himself. He did not even remember falling down the rabbit hole into fucking Wonderland! The reality of the situation finally struck JT. He had not dropped into Wonderland. He was in Hell! Should he have to take seven one-hour exams, he would be there forever. Up to that point, JT had laughingly been lost in the bizarreness of the situation including the bus trip from Lynn to Boston, which required several stops along the way to herd on more perspective Vietnam casualties. The situation, as grave as it appeared to JT on the surface, became one of absurdity when two young men boarded the bus at Chelsea. The taller and thinner young man of the two was wearing the loveliest shade of bright red lipstick and a simply divine pink shirt and slacks outfit. His companion, a muscular, broad shouldered, young man of perhaps twenty-one, wore only a pair of crocheted slacks, no shit! He wore no shirt, no socks, and no underwear.

There he was in his birthday suit modeling a pair of crocheted slacks, which covered little to none of his masculine "package". If college had taught JT anything at all, it had taught him to be broad-minded, tolerant, and inquisitive. JT found himself locked in a situation wherein all three of those desirable qualities could be shelved for future reference. He felt as if he were a spectator at a village idiot convention. Everything was unreal – the abusive attitude of regular army personnel toward the draftees, the unique collection of draftees with which to socialize, the highly impersonal mechanical method by which the draftees were processed, the sheer idiocy of having sergeants with the intelligence level of bottle tops completely controlling the present and possibly future actions of their intellectual superiors. The tremendous anxiety level that he began to feel at noontime of the day before yesterday was now in overdrive. Everything served to make that scenario something from a "what's wrong with this picture" puzzle. JT's personal list of mishaps and indignities became legion. The medical technician could not draw blood from one arm, so he decided to seek a "gusher" on the other arm. Unfortunately, the young army technician lacked both technique and expertise in his mandated profession. The result was a pair of arms, which would have caused a drug addict embarrassment. The trip to the diabetes-testing center lasted an abnormally long period due to a lack of cooperation between JT and his urinary system. Once he was successful in opening his urinary sphincter, his cup overfloweth over his hand. He experienced total degradation when an army doctor ordered he and six other draftees to bend over and "crack a smile". It was JT's introduction to anal examinations. The army doctor was not at all pleased with him regardless of the dazzling smile, which JT presented at this command. Having a strange hand on your organs of sexuality prodding, pressing, and weighing on the command of "turn your head and cough" proved to be just another in a series of embarrassments. The final surprise of this day of days occurred when an army doctor informed JT that rheumatic fever victims were not automatically exempt from the draft unless they had had a case of the disease within the past five years. JT had not. The army trumped his trump card. His family doctor all but guaranteed JT's family that his medical history would make him a reject in Armyland; however, it seemed that this army doctor had read a different script. The only element separating JT from a new khaki wardrobe was a case of severely elevated blood pressure. The doctor insisted that he retest JT at the end of the day. According to the army physician, elevated blood pressure was a common occurrence in draftees, although in JT's case a reading of 155 over 120 for a twenty-one year old man was quite high. The army doctor was going to keep JT there overnight in order to test him in the morning in the event the young man purposely ingested a blood pressure elevation enhancer. He theorized that after an extended period, JT's blood pressure, free from any artificial stimulant, would return to normalcy. Were JT ever in his life closer to a complete mental collapse, he could not recollect the occasion. Very tactfully, he discussed with his newly found adversary a chapter of his medical history, which he had previously failed to relate --unstable blood pressure-- a condition with which he lived for years. Apparently, he was successful, for the army doctor allowed JT to relax for forty-five minutes before re-testing his blood pressure. The incredible consistency of his readings, 154 over 120 on the second examination, convinced the doctor that holding him overnight would serve no useful purpose. However, he did require JT to have blood pressure readings on three consecutive days mornings and evenings at a physician of JT's choice. The draft board would evaluate the results of these readings. The decision of the draft board would then determine JT's classification.

CHAPTER 19

"1A? HOW THE FUCK DID that happen? You are a complete physical fuck–up!"

"Don't know, Tony, but it came today."

"What're you going to do?"

"I guess I'll enlist. I was thinking the Marines. If you have to go, why not go first class?"

"Russ, the average life-span for a Marine second lieutenant in Vietnam is a minute and thirty-six seconds!"

"Well then, perhaps you should come with me to cover my ass."

He did. They joined as part of an enlistment program known as the Buddy Program. Join with your buddy, and the two of you will go everywhere together. At the physical, Tony's knees did not eliminate him from the service just as JT's unstable blood pressure and rheumatic heart had failed to keep him stateside. Perhaps the country was in such dire need of sacrifices that the physical exams were more lenient than in the past. After all, if you are going to get your ass blown-off in a minute thirty-six, what the fuck difference does your blood pressure make? Following the customary send-off parties and the series of mandatory good-bye visits with family and friends, Tony and JT headed for Parris Island and the Marine's version of basic training. They discovered that "being gone" was a lot less painful than the preparations for leaving. Among JT's many weaknesses, perhaps right at the top of the list was crying females. He just did not know how to deal with that particular feminine response to anything from joy to heartbreak and all the emotions between the two. The past three months had been horrible for him in that regard. Neither Tara nor his mother had a dry eye when he was anywhere near their vicinity. Bina was somewhat better but still not good. The last good-byes were the absolute worst. He was almost happy to get on the train so that he could grieve privately, or as privately as one could with sixty-five other people experiencing the same separation anxieties.

Both he and Tony thought basic training would kill them. At times, they hoped that it would.... fortunately or unfortunately, depending upon your point of view, they both made it through as lean, mean, fighting machines. They chose not to go home before the expected assignment to the "big dance" in Nam. He and Tony just did not want to go through all that stuff again. The downside of the situation was their inability to show-off their new muscular bodies to their friends back home. Hey, they were the first guys on their block to be able to kill a man using only two fingers! The upside was that they did not have to leave all over again. Following diligent thought and discussion, they solved both issues. JT and Tony photographed each other making Mr. Universe-type poses for their friends back home. They sent photos of themselves in their marine dress uniforms to their families. They shared Kodak moments for hours until just the right poses were packaged for delivery home.

The news traveled quickly throughout the camp about the impending thirteen-month tour of Vietnam. Hearing the news was more of a relief than a shock. The waiting was murder. "Let's get this shit over with so we can go on with the rest of our lives" seemed to be an attitude held by many of their fellows in the corps.

Vietnam was a nice place to visit, but the new marines were not crazy about living there. If you liked fucking bugs and leeches, temperatures that made your sweat sweat, all the rice in the friggin world, and little yellow guys trying to blow your fucking head off each day, you would love this place. Tony and JT did not. Eight months into their thirteen-month tour found them to be old hands at this war stuff. After seeing your first man die a hideous death, and then be able to get over the nightmares that kept it so real that one woke in cold sweats for weeks, one had this Vietnam thing knocked! JT and Tony solemnly pledged to each other to cover each other's asses, stay clean and sober while there, and get each other home in one piece. The atmosphere there in war central would have seemed comical if the bad guys had not have been using real bullets. The inmates or enlisted men were running the institution or the army. The amount of therapeutic marijuana used by our troops made a Cheech and Chong movie seem tame. Those people who did not want to be in Vietnam in the first place developed an attitude toward life and death that scared the shit out of JT and Tony. Some of those strung-out guys on your side became as dangerous to you as the bad guys on the other side! Therefore, the childhood friends lived by a simple code, "Take care of you".

The closest thing to a "firefight" that either of them had experienced was senior year in high school when Tony in his father's station wagon cut-off some ape from Lynn English High School on the way to Roland's Ice Cream Parlor on the Lynnway. That firefight involved finger signals, harsh words, and some terrifying gestures. Your basic Vietnam firefight involved constant, nasty fighting up to and including the hand-to-hand type. On a reconnaissance mission during their ninth month in the jungle, their squad was cut-off from the main unit. After having been shot at, over, and around for hours, the eight man squad dug in close to midnight. They were dog-tired from a day and night of following "Charlie" through the local landscape. They appeared to be out-numbered and very possibly surrounded. As the Lone Ranger said to Tonto when surrounded by Indians, "I think we're in trouble, Tonto." Tonto then replied, "What do you mean we, white man?" Tony and JT were the Lone Ranger to the other six guys' Tonto. As perilous as the situation appeared, the sergeant and his remaining squad, sans JT and Tony, settled in for an evening of smoke and relaxation. After several "feeling-out" attacks, "Charlie" got serious. A constant barrage of enemy fire and friendly response rang out in the darkness of the night. JT thought it so weird that one could actually see the path of projectiles leaving from rifles fired into the black of night; it was almost hypnotic.

"Sergeant, we're pretty low on ammo."

"Hold tight, Russell, they can't keep this up all night."

They friggin-well did. Shortly before dawn, the scene became amazingly quiet. They theorized that the other side was as short on ammunition, patience, and good judgment as the good guys. Word passed from trembling man to man to prepare for hand-to-hand combat.

JT nodded to Tony, "Take care of you."

He responded, "Take care of you."

The first attack struck suddenly and from all sides. The shock at actually seeing "Charlie" close-up was numbing to the senses. These guys wanted the good guys dead, and they did not care if they made themselves dead getting that done. That was the reality of the situation – as irrational as it sounded – if the good guys did not terminate the bad guys, then they were going to be terminated themselves. A wave of screaming enemy soldiers engaged what was left of the squad. JT and Tony stood back to back as each squared off against knife welding opponents. All that torturous training at P.I. became a great advantage. The autonomic nervous system seemed to take over their bodies enabling them to make Bruce Lee type moves of which they were consciously incapable in the sane world. A quick look around and JT saw that the two separated in the midst of combat. JT found himself facing a foe that seemed to hesitate in taking the fight to him, so JT initiated the action. Hand to hand, blade clashing against blade, helmets leaving heads to find their way to the bloodied ground. JT saw his opening and thrust his knife into the throat of his nemesis. With his last gurgling breaths, the mortally wounded enemy maneuvered his knife toward JT's right shoulder and plunged it in to the hilt. Pain shot through his body like an electrical charge. JT rolled off his victim onto the helmet that had left his opponent's head at the onset of his attack. On the ground next to the helmet he found a photo of a man, woman, and child along with a letter that had fallen from the band holding the items within. Upon hearing the sound of a copter overhead and the rattling of machine guns from above, he felt safe for some strange reason. He grasped his victim's documents and allowed himself to relax before consciousness left him. He awoke some hours later with the photo and letter held tightly in his left hand.

The corpsman who treated him greeted him back to consciousness with, "You lucky son of a bitch! You have yourself a million-dollar wound here. This will get your ass home in a hurry."

JT responded by saying, "Tony", but once again he lost his battle with unconsciousness.

Three days later, he awoke in a hospital bed. He found his right shoulder and arm in a cast. Immediately he needed to know two things: Where's Tony? And, for some reason, where are my papers? Strangely enough, the Vietnamese nurse knew exactly of what he was speaking. As the attending nurse, she pried the photo and letter from his hand prior to his going into surgery. She had left them in the bed stand to his left. Unfortunately, she had no information about any of the other members of his squad. However, she promised that someone from his platoon should appear shortly. All his questions would be answered in due time. He asked the nurse to get "his papers" from the bed stand. In doing so, she made mention that the letter appeared to be unfinished. She handed JT the documents and offered to translate the letter for him when he was up to it. He thanked her and closed his eyes.

As he awoke, his eyes slowly focused on a form beside his bed. He recognized his company chaplain standing somberly at the side of his bed. JT was inconsolable when told that he was the only surviving member of his squad. He had lost his other half, his alter ego, his best and lifelong friend. JT just could not "wrap his mind around" the idea that there was no more Tony. The caregivers needed to medicate him for the following two days. While in this state of forced unconsciousness, he relived some great moments from home.

He, Tony, and Tara were together as always sharing their lives as only intimates are capable. When the dreams left him, the reality of his situation struck him immediately though this time he more readily comprehended and accepted the fact that Tony was dead. JT did not keep his promise to bring Tony back in one piece. How could he ever forgive himself or this fucking war? A familiar face looked down upon him asking if there was anything she could do for him. The Vietnamese nurse, whose name he later learned was Ngyyen Thi Hong Kim, smiled at him and he returned her kindness.

"I saved something for you, Corporal Russell," she whispered.

"Yeah, the photo and letter…" JT responded.

"Yes, I have those also. But I thought you would like the souvenir that the doctors removed from your right shoulder."

Upon his bed, she placed a photo, a letter, and a knife all of which had been in her safekeeping locked in the nightstand at his bedside. He lifted the knife to his eye level and viewed it from every angle. Burned into the handle were a name, Phong Ho Cheung, and several markings, which the nurse described to him as Buddhist holy symbols.

"What does the letter say? Do you have time now, nurse?"

"Well, my first impression is that this was written by an educated person. The form and substance are excellent. The letter is to his wife, Tram, who he has not seen in several months. He asks about his son, Twan, and their living conditions back in the North. This part is quite interesting, Corporal. Basically, he reiterates their plan which she should enact if she does not hear from him after six months. Can you believe this? She has family in the states. Of all places! She is to journey to the South and extract herself and their son from Vietnam using any means possible. She is then to contact her family in the eastern part of the United States for aid. He will meet them there, his fate willing. The letter is unfinished."

"And the back of the photo, nurse?"

"The date must indicate when the photo was taken. Behind each person in the photo, there is a name and number. I believe these are the identities and ages of the subjects. The man is twenty-four years old. His name is Phong. The woman is twenty-three years old. Her name is Tram. The child is five years old, his name is Twan."

"If I didn't already have enough self-pity to wallow in, I am now responsible for murdering another human being brutally, taking the husband and bread-winner from a young woman and her family, and causing a five year old to be fatherless. Jesus, by any chance did I kill his dog or rape his mother?"

"Corporal Russell!"

"I apologize nurse, forgive me. I've," he hesitated, and then with a louder sudden tone, "been under a bit of a fucking strain lately."

With these words, she left the items on the bed and removed herself from the hospital room. JT felt even worse when she left. She had been nothing but caring, kind, and considerate. He just kept on shoveling that self-pity up his ass.

CHAPTER 20

WHOEVER FIRST SAID, "WHAT GOES around comes around" must have been talking about Newton Spencer Lloyd's life. The time had arrived for Newton Spencer Lloyd III to face the consequences of his decision-making.

"You miserable, motherfucking, poor excuse for a man! Well, Newt, you pathetic worm-prick, you'll wish I HAD died before I'm finished with you!"

Not even a "but dear" would emerge from his paralyzed vocal cords. He was dumb struck. The doctor's pronouncement of his wife's death had seemingly just reached the confirmation center located deep within his brain when one of the attending nurses corrected the doctor's call, as suddenly all of Emily's vital signs registered within normal levels. Not more than a minute later, his dead, now quite alive wife sat upright in her hospital bed, looking surprisingly evil and spewing forth a volley of angry damning accusations directed at the further shell-shocked Newton Spencer Lloyd III!

"She will never be mine, Newton! That little girl belongs to you and you alone! I will have nothing to do with her. You wanted her; you'll have her; you disloyal piece of shit!"

Communications central in Lloyd's head hurriedly worked up to speed. He was hearing his wife's words, comprehending their meaning, embracing their emotional bent, but the scene was so indescribable and incomprehensible...she had emerged from her calm, quiet, deathlike sleep like an evil "Jack in the Box". The performance lasted several minutes before Mrs. Lloyd was subdued and set to rest via the accurate placement of a nurse's hypodermic needle into the screaming woman's right hip. Almost immediately, her rage subsided, and she shortly returned to her pre-death level of calm. Now that he had a moment to gather his thoughts, he ran some of her rants through his memory. His eyes focused upon the smallish woman on the bed whom he once knew so well.

"How did she know we had a little girl? How did she know I chose the child's life over hers? How could she hold an innocent newborn responsible for the desperate actions of her inadequate father?"

It was now 2:30 in the afternoon, some twelve hours since the onset of the final stage of the birth process. Mr. Lloyd had experienced a lifetime's worth of pain, suffering, embarrassment, and confusion during this time. Unfortunately, for this poor wretched creature, that day was only the beginning of his worst nightmare. Fortunately, his emotional expenditures on the events of the day finally affected the man still huddled on the floor of the hospital ward when consciousness gave way to the blackness of sleep.

CHAPTER 21

Not many would argue that one of the most outstanding benefits to living on the North Shore of Boston, Massachusetts, was the fabulous Atlantic Ocean. The seashore which traversed Winthrop, Revere, Nahant, Lynn, Marblehead, Swampscott, all the way up to Gloucester was a tourist magnet during the late spring and summer months, but to residents of the area, all four seasons offered their delightful version of this wonder of the natural world. Watching the waves as they crashed against Red Rock during early fall would draw Lynners to their public beach as if the summer concert series was still taking place. Every now and again when the populace of this fair city would be "treated" to a hurricane, hardy souls would brave the ruthless winds and pelting rain to view huge breaking waves leaving their walled-in confinement to submerge Lynn Shore Drive with their constant, rolling attacks against the sea wall. With the horizon offering its audience the illusion of a sky and sea meeting, sunset over the ocean presents a dazzling display of color and delight. The driftwood and debris piques one's imagination and curiosity about the origin of the miscellaneous items along the shore. The remnants of sand dollars, crabs, jellyfish, clamshells, and other assorted residents of the sea and shore lay lifeless upon the sand fulfilling the cycle of their existence. The dog walkers, runners, power walkers, bicyclists, and skateboarders take turns sharing the paved walk around the nicely landscaped sea wall.

All of this and much more cast a spell upon those fortunate enough to live in this area and appreciate it enough to enjoy the experience.

Not surprisingly, with the exception of being among his family and friends, JT had an urge to visit his favorite locale --the seashore. Up to this point in his twenty-two years of existence, he had not found a more relaxing, calming place to be. Memories of Tara; the wild, careless, fun days and nights; the conquests of the ladies in his life; and Tony, his unibrowed partner in crime, his shadow, his guide, his confessor, all of these served to make this place special--no sacred--due to recent events. JT and Tony were of about the same height and weight. They shared the dubious distinction of having a single eyebrow. Tony was perhaps a bit on the quieter side, but equally capable of causing "shit-hitting the fan" moments. The two were inseparable, kindred spirits since grade school. In fact, JT swears that Tony was Rose Marie Lloyd's harasser on the first day of first grade. Though he denied it to the end, he had more than made amends over the years if he, in deed, had made such a transgression. The youths did not become fast friends immediately. In the third year of their educational lives, they crossed paths once again being in the same classroom – Miss Sheehan's third grade. Through the years, Tony was fond of answering the questions about the beginning, duration, and durability of their friendship by saying, "I pulled a friggin thorn from his paw, and he hasn't let me alone since!" They shared their lives, loves, families, first jobs, driver's education school, proms, junior and senior high school graduations, college life and graduation, basic training and Nam, but that was where it all ended. Life without Tony would take a major effort. JT faced an imposed transition, but one with which he would inevitably have to deal.

CHAPTER 22

HE WAS HOME – NOT for a visit – for good. The corpsman that treated him was correct. He hit the lottery with his wound. Stepping from the plane was a bittersweet experience for JT. Sure, he was home for good. Yes, he would mend completely. The last report he received indicated that Tony's body and those of the other squad members were missing. His entire squad with the exception of himself ceased to exist. The Defense Department declared them MIA, missing in action. During the past two months, grief had made living amazingly difficult for JT. Nightly, Phong Ho Cheung visited him in his dreams. They fought their fight night after night with the results virtually the same. During most of his nightmares, there was always a time when he spoke with his opponent. Sometimes, before the onset of the combat, Phong would introduce his son Twan and wife Tram to JT. Cold sweats and startled awakenings became normal nighttime occurrences. Oh yes, Tony was there usually. However, Tony always lived to laugh about the outcome with JT. Nighttime became a dreaded adversary. Daytime became a constant challenge to his senses to maintain his sanity. The physically and emotionally crippled marine, as part of his pre-discharge physical, was ordered to see the camp psychiatrist, Major Axel T. Rosen, a short, balding, mustached man with a ready smile and the most gentle manner JT had yet to experience. Dr. Rosen and JT met three days a week for about a month. JT never complained about the imposition. The doctor diagnosed JT as clinically depressed with possible stress related symptoms. He prescribed a menu of an antidepressant medication and muscle relaxing tranquilizers. JT simply followed directions, took the pills, played the game, and did not give a shit.

He neither expected nor desired a large-scale homecoming. At Logan Airport in Boston, about a fifteen-minute drive from Lynn, JT saw his parents, Tara, Bina, and the Delvanes as he walked through the plane's departure tunnel into the airport. All ran toward him with tears. When Jessica and Mario Delvane hugged and kissed JT, he totally lost his composure and became inconsolable. The welcoming party "closed ranks" and surrounded the object of their attention and affection. The group sidled over to a relatively empty visitors waiting area and somehow were successful in getting JT to sit. Jim Russell did not know whom to help first. Charlene, Tara, and Bina were crying hysterically. Mario and Jessica Delvane held onto JT with a vise-like grip. The center of attention whose bloodless face indicated an immediate need for fresh air and liquid seemed on the verge of collapse. JT's Dad, who had suppressed his own emotional needs to bring a kind of order to the proceedings, pulled the group together. He led Tara, Bina, and Charlene to adjoining chairs. Next, he walked Mario and Jessica Delvane away from JT to the other side of the waiting area. Quickly he returned to his sobbing, wavering son and held him in a very unmanly like chest-to-chest embrace. A fellow passenger had notified airport security, which in turn notified the airport paramedics. Within moments, JT was fitted with an oxygen mask and began to regain color in his cheeks. Jim noted to himself that his women-folk had returned to a less debilitating state. Bina helped Tara and Charlene walk over to JT and Jim. The medics were talking to the Delvanes. The situation had begun to take on stability. Jim nodded to Mario Delvane who gestured to him that he and his wife were leaving. JT was able to sip water once the paramedics removed the oxygen mask. Bina, Tara, and Charlene positioned themselves about JT taking turns hugging and kissing the recovering patient. Jim Russell walked away from the scene and fell apart against a bank of pay telephones.

"That was almost as good as your college graduation exit, kid!"

The voice was that of Newton Spencer Lloyd III. In the company of his daughter, Rose Marie, he had been a distant observer of the goings-on.

"Is there a second show tonight?"

"Dad, please."

"Rosie, I was just fucking with them."

Recently, McGinn Hospital released Newton following a stay that lasted several months. Several months ago, Mr. Lloyd opened his Union Street drug store early one morning while being in the nude. As he warmly greeted several of his early arriving regular customers in this unusual attire, the police arrived. An overnight evaluation at Lynn Hospital's mental health center indicated a need for additional testing. Therefore, Newton found himself transported to McGinn Hospital, a private sanitarium, just south of Boston. Once again, this latest episode of mental health incapacitation just added to his growing list of incarcerations. Rose Marie had experienced so many of these moments over the past decade that she had built a protective wall around herself to keep from taking a similar route herself.

"This wasn't a good idea, Dad. Let's go. We'll see JT later."

"Hey kid, I heard you killed a gook!"

"Dad! Let's go, now! We are sorry. We'll visit later when Dad is feeling better."

"I'm fine, missy. No one around here can take a fucking joke."

"The car is this way, Dad."

Following a pregnant pause, a voice spoke from the background.

"Well, do you guys know how to throw a welcoming home party or what?" a now smiling JT Russell observed.

CHAPTER 23

"WET NURSE? EMILY, MY DEAR, what is a wet nurse, and why do we need one?"

"You need one for your daughter, Newton, unless you have breast milk for her."

He had been hoping that the incredulous happenings of the previous evening were just figments of his hyperactive imagination and not the heartbreaking reality he was experiencing once again.

"Before you leave this hospital with that child you had better make arrangements for a twenty-four hour/seven days a week, three hundred and sixty-five days a year nurse."

"But Emily, surely now that you've had time to think…"

"Newton! Nothing has changed. You wanted the child more than me. Now raise her without me. By the way, I won't be divorcing your miserable ass, but you'll wish I had, you little prick."

Thus, life began for Rose Marie Lloyd, a child who was at the center of a real-life melodrama revolving around an inept man, his "hell hath no greater fury " wife, one set of grandparents in very poor health, and the other set of grandparents "stoking the fires" of their mortally offended daughter. Talk about one's lack of a support system. Little Rose Marie's nurse, who was paid to love her, and her father, who most of the time was unable to love her, formed the only loving family this child was to know for the next twenty-one years. Miss Take did all that was required of her and more. At twenty-six years of age, Miss Alexis

Take was serving her first prolonged engagement as a full-time nanny. The very attractive, blue-eyed, blond had striking features – movie star quality – an incredibly fit five foot three inch figure upon which a slender one hundred five pounds were spread, an amazing smile and disposition, and a deeply held secret as to why such a woman was willing to forego a real life of her own to be a supporting player

in the dysfunctional soap opera in which she soon found herself involved. A friend of a friend had directed her to Newton Spencer Lloyd upon hearing that the desperate man needed help immediately. Alexis caught Mr. Lloyd at his home between visits to the hospital and applied for the wet nurse position in person. Lloyd saw her as an answer sent from God. He hired her on the spot without benefit of anything that resembled an interview nor with a single recommendation. Basically, she fulfilled all of his requirements. Alexis Take was alive, eager, and filled with the milk of human kindness both literally and physically.

The "happy" family left Lynn Hospital to begin their lives with the now seven-day old Rose Marie. Alexis had spent the previous several days suckling her new charge in the hospital under the supervision of the maternity ward nurses. Although she had little experience with this aspect of her job, she took to it quickly and formed a bond with the otherwise, essentially, motherless child. Routine was established immediately at home with Alexis having one hundred percent responsibility for Rose Marie and her needs. Newton continued to grow his drug store chain, which now stood at three with the help of an infusion of capital from his ill parents, and Emily became more rancorous and unforgiving by the day. She unilaterally decided that she should work so she took the Union Street pharmacy for her own. This decision, in no way objected to by Mr. Lloyd, was to become the new passion in her life. She sublimated all her earthly wants and needs into a career. Newton, at the same time, managed the pharmacy in Nahant and was in the process of opening a Lynnfield store when he fell from his tightrope walk with reality. Rose Marie was close to a year old. Emily had abided her existence although she had no emotional and little physical contact with the child. Rose Marie simply existed to Emily. A story was concocted by Mrs. Lloyd for the benefit of the growing child. Alexis was informed that Rose Marie, when the proper time arrived, was to be told that her birth mother had died when she was born, and Emily married Newton shortly thereafter. In this way, Emily felt more justified in having the child address her by her first name as opposed to mother. So it was to be. To Rose Marie, Emily would be her stepmother and was to be addressed as Emily. Somehow, in her warped view of her life's situation, Mrs. Lloyd found peace in that fashion. Not so, Mr. Lloyd....he had accepted separate bedrooms, total absence of intimacy, no communication, and independent lifestyles. The more he thought about this newest perverted angle to their miserable existence, the more it weighed on his already last nerve! How could she carry that anger for so long? He accepted his wife's hatefulness toward him. Why couldn't she give the child a break? Repeatedly in his mind, day upon day, he ruminated over his life's situation until finally one Sunday while Alexis and Rose Marie were at the park; he decided to address the situation with his non-communicative wife.

"Emily, this has gone on far too long. Things must change for the good of all involved. I think you should see someone for help. In fact, I demand you see someone. I cannot continue like this. If we are to continue together in this fraud of a marriage relationship, you or you and I must seek outside help."

"Fuck you," matter of factly rolled from her lips.

"Is that all you have to say? Have you no concern for the possible psychological damage to which you are subjecting our little girl? Are you so unforgiving and self-centered that you cannot see past your own good for the good of others?"

"I said 'fuck you'. And she's not our child; she is your child."

What happened next most would say Newton Spender Lloyd III was incapable of initiating, but it did happen. He lunged at the physical body that had come to epitomize everything he despised in the world. He struck her gaping mouth with a right-handed closed fist. The look of shock that registered on her face gave him such satisfaction. The worm had turned, and he struck her repeatedly left fist following right.

Emily dropped lifelessly to the living room carpet. Blood from her facial wounds sprayed the oriental carpet at the spot where she fell. Newton jumped upon her and wrapped his unmanly hands around her throat. He felt nothing. He knew it was right. He wanted her out of his daughter's life forever. Returning to partial consciousness, Emily instinctively fought back by placing an extremely well placed knee into Newton's crotch. She broke free as the aggressor rolled around the floor in agony. She grabbed the lamp from the end table, which stood to the left side of the long tan sofa, and she struck the disabled attacker upon his head. Newton's lights went out. The next thing he remembered was the ministrations of a firefighter while the police waited with handcuffs at their ready. His arraignment at Lynn

District Court was brief, and the result preordained. The Magistrate sentenced Newton to thirty days at Bridgewater State Hospital for evaluation and observation. Newton Spencer Lloyd III would not be hearing that Magistrate's nightmare like decree for the last time.

CHAPTER 24

Alexis held Rose Marie's hand firmly as she walked into Breed Elementary School. The only mother Rose Marie had known in her brief six years of life had kept the conversation positive, upbeat, and enjoyable on their walk to the child's first day of school. The insightful Miss Take harbored apprehension over this day. Her many restless, sleepless nights that led up to the moment had taken an emotional toll upon her. She found herself crying inexplicably and often at the most insignificant occurrences. A patient, passive woman by nature, as of late the nanny found herself fighting the instinct to grab Emily Lloyd by the hair and slap her back to her senses! Alexis had seen all of Rose Marie's warning signs over the past several years: the stuttering that worsened with each new day, the withdrawal from all others but her nanny, the refusal to enter into play with other children, and the distancing of herself from her father. Rose Marie Lloyd was a child in trouble. Unfortunately, only Alexis was there to care about it.

The first grade classroom was filling slowly with those who would be her classmates for the next one hundred eighty school days. All were warmly welcomed by Miss Reynolds, a tall, well postured, nurturing woman of sixty years. Rose Marie hid behind Alexis as Miss Reynolds introduced herself. A gleam in the veteran teacher's eyes warmed the nanny immediately. Rose Marie was encouraged to introduce herself to her first teacher. The frightened little girl wanted to accommodate the request. She desperately tried to say the words, but her mouth would have none of it. After an awkward moment or two, Alexis smiled at the teacher and led Rose Marie to a front row seat where the two were able to relax and whisper encouragement to each other.

At the same time, Charlene Russell with James T. Russell in toe entered the same classroom. He immediately walked up to the teacher, introduced himself complete with a handshake, and explained her options in addressing him.

"You can call me James, or Jamey, or JT. Whatever you like, but I kinda like JT."

"Well, young man, why don't we start with James and see where we go from there?"

"OK. Mom, I'm going to walk over there," he said pointing to Rose Marie and Alexis.

"James," reminded his mother, "behave yourself."

As Charlene Russell and her child's new teacher exchanged introductions, JT walked directly to the fragile, blond haired, blue-eyed girl sitting with the pretty woman in the front row.

"Hi, I'm James Thurber Russell, but you can call me Jamey or JT. I kind of like JT best but…"

"Hello, Jamey," replied Alexis Take holding out her hand. "How do you do? I am Alexis and this is Rose Marie."

"Doesn't she speak?"

"Yes, she does, but she is a little shy right now."

"How come? We're all just kids."

"Good point, Jamey. Rose Marie, would you like to say hello to this young man?"

James Thurber Russell thrust forth his hand and took Rose Marie's hand in his.

"I am pleased to meet you, Rose Marie. Want to be friends?"

The embarrassed girl nodded her head affirmatively and smiled at the precocious little boy. She then stuttered out "hello" and "my name is Rose Marie" which took a while to communicate.

James Russell looked to Miss Take and asked if she always spoke like that. Upon hearing her answer, he said, "Don't worry she'll get it fixed here. School fixes things. I'll take care of her for you."

He held the girl's hand and led her to the back of the room to a chart that listed numbers from one to ten in words and numerals as well as the primary colors. He began to read the numbers and point them out to her, and she smiled. When he started reading the colors, she joined him without a trace of stuttering. Alexis joined them smiling at the little man who had just entered her child's life. She had an immediate affection for the boy. She reasoned that her attraction to the little man was due in part to his magnetic personality and partly because he was protecting her baby. When it was time for the parents to leave the classroom, Charlene found James who very quickly introduced Rose Marie and Alexis to his mother. Mrs. Russell kissed him on the forehead and told him she would be back to pick him up for lunch. He was barely listening to her, but he said OK and waved good-bye. As Alexis turned to say good-bye to Rose Marie, a moment she had dreaded, to her surprise Rose Marie kissed her cheek, waved good-bye, and walked away hand in hand with her new acquaintance.

"I'll pick you up for lunch, Rose Marie. I'll be right here. Wow! She is not even listening. Isn't that something?"

Alexis and Charlene Russell walked out together sharing some not too personal information that people exchange at first meetings. However, at this meeting, Alexis Take could do nothing but "gush" about Charlene's little man, James Thurber Russell.

"I'm not going back! They make fun of me! I tried real hard, Lexy, but the words just wouldn't come out." The distraught little girl whimpered and sobbed while holding on to the schoolyard fence for dear life.

"What about Jamey? Didn't you have fun with him? Isn't he your new best friend?"

"The teacher sat him across the room from me. I sit next to a boy who makes fun of the way I speak. He repeats everything I say. I'll never speak in that room again."

"I'll tell you what, honey. If you will trust me and walk back into the classroom with me, I will fix this problem. What do you say?"

"Can you Lexy? Can you make it better?"

Alexis smiled, nodded her head, crossed her fingers, and said a silent prayer.

The discussion with Miss Reynolds proved to be fruitful. Having given the kindly teacher more information than she thought herself capable of sharing, Alexis requested that Rose Marie sit next to James Russell. Now, many teachers would have had their noses out of joint over the intrusion in classroom management issues; however, the wise, old, veteran of thirty-nine years in the trenches saw an opportunity to assist a child in distress who needed more stress in her life as much as the kindly teacher needed another gray hair on her silver head. Marjorie Reynolds made it happen. To the forever gratefulness of Rose Marie Lloyd, Alexis Take, and yes, James Thurber Russell, Rose Marie was moved to a seat adjacent to James where he kept his promise to "take care of her". At afternoon recess, James Russell had some unfinished business that needed attention. He began by reintroducing Rose Marie to every member of the class, as his best friend. He told them that they did not have to like either of them, but they could not like just one of them. He made it known that school was a place that helps everybody so they were there to help each other. The tiny peacemaker then confronted Rose Marie's morning menace. Little Mr. Russell simply told the misguided youth that should he or any of his comrades wish to poke fun at anyone in the future, JT Russell should be his one and only target. One would have thought that this little kid was a primary school peace negotiator. Rose Marie Lloyd thought he was like the knight in shining armor that Lexy had read about to her, the one that had risked his own life to save the damsel in distress. From that day on, James Thurber Russell and the fragile Rose Marie Lloyd were friends for life.

Her school life became the only constant, aside from the knowledge that Lexy was there for her, in Rose Marie's life. From day to day she had no idea if her father was going to be with her or not. She recognized that Emily seemed polite enough to her; however, she was always so distant that Rose Marie sensed a feeling of anger directed toward her from her stepmother. Newton, on the other hand, attempted to perform his fatherly duties, but sadly for Rose Marie, the rigidity of his personality since his return from his latest mental health internment made him appear cold, indifferent, and preoccupied. Following the evaluation at Bridgewater State Mental Hospital, Newton was sent to McGinn Sanitarium for treatment of his emotional meltdown, which almost resulted in the death of his wife. Emily Lloyd needed no further motivation to fuel her utter disdain for her lawfully wedded husband. In point of fact, she was able to end their marriage at her will. Strangely, Mrs. Lloyd chose to bring her husband back into the home after each of his past three stays at various private sanitariums. The question in the minds of all familiar with their case was simply why she endeavored to continue in the relationship. Perhaps the fact that his mother and father insisted upon clinging to life, thereby delaying Newton's acquisition of their combined wealth, was a factor in her decision making process. Could it possibly be that she was not yet finished torturing a man whom she once allegedly loved? Whatever the reason, the following were facts of their lives: Emily Lloyd's wrath had no limits or boundaries. Rose Marie Lloyd's childhood was a disaster from day one. Newton Lloyd was slipping deeper and deeper into a mental health state from which few people are able to exact themselves and live to talk about it.

Jamey, as she was fond of calling him, and Rose Marie spent the next six years sharing the same classrooms perhaps because of divine intervention at work. JT was the ever-present protector of his best friend, and through the years, this role became the source of much teasing from his male friends over his "girl friend", Rose Marie. JT took everything in stride, and he never once flinched in his devotion to his Rosie. Over the years, he was quite dedicated and persistent in assisting her with her stuttering treatments after school each day. By the sixth grade, Rose Marie had her problem under control with the exception of those times when extreme emotional situations overwhelmed her defenses. Jamey was her whole world. She absolutely loved him. At the age of twelve, she knew that Jamey would be her husband some day, and they would live happily ever after. The advent of the Anthony Delvane and James Russell friendship in Miss Landry's third grade class was the only event to that point in time, which ever threatened Rose Marie's relationship with her Jamey. The two boys "clicked" being in the same classroom. They had known of each other for a couple of years, but they became inseparable in Miss Landry's class. Let it suffice to say that Rose Marie was perplexed over this new alliance. She chose not to share Jamey with anyone for any reason. She languished at recess when he played with Tony. She cried after school when JT visited at Tony's house. She suddenly had a total relapse of her stuttering. The little girl sensed that she was about to lose someone else that she loved. One evening as she and Lexy were lying on the grass in the backyard surveying the heavens, Rose Marie raised her concerns about her relationship with Jamey. Alexis sat her upright and stared straight into her eyes.

"Rosie, you can't make someone love you, and you can't keep someone loving you simply by the force of your will. All you are able to do is to be the person that you are. You can offer to another the qualities you possess, your friendship, loyalty, and support. Remember, honey, no one can be owned or should be controlled by another. Love is something given not taken. Do you understand?"

"I think so. I just don't want things to change."

"Rose Marie, change along with death and taxes, as you will learn, are aspects of life that we mortals cannot avoid."

They embraced and continued looking skyward. Rose Marie ran Lexy's lines through her mind over and over until they made more and more sense to her.

"I guess I can use your ideas when it comes to everybody in my life, huh Lexy?"

"Yes, you can, hon. Yes, you can."

JT and Rose Marie survived the entry of Tony Delvane into there midst. The twosome became a threesome. Perceptively, little Mr. Russell recognized the threat to Rose Marie and made additional efforts to include her in his new friendship. They became as close a threesome as they were a twosome. One thing had not changed in time; Jamey still owned Rose Marie's heart. However, at the doorway to junior high school, all three of the friends were battling that disease known as adolescence. The physical, chemical, emotional, and intellectual battles taking place in their bodies were sure to influence their words and actions, and they did.

CHAPTER 25

SHE AWOKE WITH "THE ITCH", as she had begun calling it. God, she was so tired of having to scratch it by herself. How long had it been now since someone had scratched it for her? Had it really been over thirteen years? How had she held out so long? She thought to herself, "I'm fucking fortunate that my hand hasn't fallen off my fucking arm." Emily moved her right hand down into the triangle of darkish hair that lay at the entrance of that place which brings men to their knees. Upon reaching her clitoral destination, she began to please herself by making slow circular movements over the protruding nubbin. As quickly as she had begun, she jerked her hand away cursing to herself.

"Fuck this! I'm going to get laid!"

She leaped from bed and began her morning routine to prepare herself for the workday. She was now in charge of the Nahant pharmacy after concluding a prolonged and quite successful stint at the Union Street pharmacy in Lynn. Desiring a change of pace and seeking to deal with a "higher class" of customers, Emily had informed Newton of her plans to move on-up and, as usual, he fell right into line with her wishes. Two years had passed since his mother died, and ten months later, his father gave in to his battle with cancer. Newton progressively found life in the real world more and more difficult to negotiate. The Lloyds now owned and operated a fourth pharmacy located in Peabody at the North Shore Shopping Center thanks to a more than substantial gift from his deceased father's will. Being an only child of well-to-do parents had finally paid-off "big time" for Newton. Too bad the poor bastard could not enjoy it.

After applying her make-up and drinking her coffee, Emily hopped into her shiny new Thunderbird convertible with nary a good-bye to anyone to begin her drive to work. She kept her window partially opened as she wove her way down Lynn Shore Drive toward the rotary. The day was a beautiful example of autumn in Massachusetts complete with the long-awaited turning of the leaves. The trees were turning from their summer hues of green to lush yellows, oranges, and reds... so beautiful, so wonderful to be alive if you were Emily Lloyd. She made her way around the circular rotary and entered the causeway leading to Nahant. On her left she glanced at the beach, a place of such passionate memories for her. Parked in front of the tall bushes about mid-way across the causeway, she had many "hot" evenings with a bevy of Lynn's high school jocks. She was a prize, but only the truly worthy needed to apply. With her looks and personality, and her penchant for life on the wilder side, Emily enjoyed every pleasure of the flesh imaginable throughout her high school years.

"Stop it, bitch. You're bringing the friggin itch back," she chastised herself. She glanced to her right where Revere Beach lay in the distance. Yes, she was no stranger to that place either. However, the memories of that beach were more associated with Newton Spencer Lloyd III, the awkward, college senior whom Emily Lloyd, high school senior, dated for a lark. Perhaps his pathetic hound dog expression and utterly impeccable manners found a place deep inside her where the woman in her resided. He was by far the most asexual male she had yet to meet. Perhaps, after all her "fucking around", she liked that aspect of their relationship. The guy never even "tried" anything with her. After their fourth date, no one would have thought there would be a fourth or even a second one, he asked her for a kiss on the cheek. She responded by sticking her tongue so far into his mouth that she swears to have hit his epiglottis. Even in the dark, she could see the bright red coloring of his embarrassment. Shocking him, in particular, and people, in general, was a major "smile" for Emily. Running into the surf in her birthday suit, flashing her boobs at passing truckers, grinding her dance partners to the slow songs, that was Emily Franklin in the raw. She wondered, "How the fuck did I ever end-up with that useless piece of shit that I married? Just lucky I guess, huh Emily, just lucky."

As usual, she wheeled a little too fast into the small-unpaved parking lot of Lloyd's Nahant Pharmacy causing a cloud of dust to rise and circle the Thunderbird. Emily fixed her make-up while waiting for the dust to settle, popped-out of the T-Bird, and walked happily into the white, mid-sized, wooden building that had been her sanctuary for the past several months. The pharmacy was perhaps the size of a single-family five-room ranch house. She employed a druggist and two part-time stock boys who job-shared that position. Emily, to her credit, was no stranger to hard work both opening and closing the store every day except Sunday when the store remained closed. On this day, Reggie Fields was due to work after his classes at Lynn Classical High School. Douglas Fowler, her druggist, sat reading the Lynn Item in his car as she "landed" in the parking lot. Following her to the front door, Doug, a tall, thin, attractive man of twenty-seven, sing-songed his usual "good morning boss" and entered directly after her. Today, she gave Doug a little bit warmer greeting then usual, and he recognized that immediately. Emily and Doug drifted off to their separate destinations, he to the pharmacy area at the rear of the store and she to the checkout area at the front of the store. The interior of the store was comprised of six double-sided aisles, a stock room behind the pharmacy, and a converted utility room that served as her office. A desk, table, and two chairs pretty much filled that area to maximum capacity. Adhering to a custom of times past, in part perhaps due to tradition, but more realistically due to a lack of personnel, the store closed for forty-five minutes each day at the twelve o'clock lunch hour. Emily enjoyed that store branch so much more than the downtown Lynn branch. The clientele in Nahant was more to her liking than the diversity of cultures with which she dealt in "the city of sin". The atmosphere was so different in her new assignment. She usually felt that the day and early evening hours seemed to fly by. That day was one of those "where did the time go" days. Reggie Fields had swept-up just before 6 PM and left on the hour while Doug Fowler was in the backroom preparing a final prescription for early the following morning. Emily wandered into the backroom to check on Doug's status. The pharmacist was standing with his back to her, apparently deep in thought, concentrating upon his task. Emily slipped into the room unannounced, edged up to the unaware druggist, and from behind placed her petite right hand on his private parts. Startled to death, Doug left his feet and swung around to face his very intimate intruder. During these seconds of rapid response, Emily's hand never left its placement. As he recognized the familiar face of the violator of his private region, Emily looked directly into his eyes and smiled as she continued to toy with his unit.

"Holy shit, Emily! You scared the life out of me. What's all this about? Why the sudden interest in me? You know I'm very married, Emily."

"I'm married too, Dougie. I'm not asking you for your fucking hand." She continued her ministrations by separating his testicles within his boxer shorts and rolling each around with her fingertips.

"Emily, I can't do this. I couldn't, wouldn't do it to Christine. Please stop."

Doug moved his hand gently to push hers aside, but Emily brought her left hand into play blunting his protestation.

"What if I told you that your job depended upon your, let's say, your cooperation?"

"Emily, are you telling me that if I don't do as you wish, you will discharge me?"

"I didn't say that, Dougie. I simply asked a goddamn question. What if?"

The dazed pharmacist found his voice and tried to reply in as forceful a tone as he was able to muster.

"I would say thank you for the opportunity you have given me here. I have enjoyed working for you."

Emily released her hold on his now ready organ.

"Well, you shock me my friend. You are a man with strong moral values, especially impressive since your nuts were in the hands of a very eager woman."

"I'll see you tomorrow, Doug."

"Do you mean here at work, Emily? Do I still have my job?"

"But of course, Dougie. I was just screwing with you. Let's lock up and get out of here."

The emotionally drained yet still erect druggist followed the boss out of the room.

"Oh, Doug, you'd be best to lose that boner before you go home."

Chapter 26

Breed Elementary School and Breed Junior High School were adjoining buildings; therefore, the transition from grade school to junior high was less traumatic for the students who were continuing their education within that building. It appeared to JT that coming from one of the "feeder" schools such as Burrill, Tracy, or Callahan was a far more difficult and scary thing for a kid to do than simply move to a new section of the same old familiar building. The entering seventh grade students would spend the next three years of their lives at Breed Junior High on Hood Street before moving on to either Lynn Classical High School or Lynn Trade School. Junior high school in Lynn vastly differed in this way from other cities. The traditional eight years of grade school format followed by the four years of high school did not exist in Lynn. Nor did the six years of grade school, two years of junior high, followed by four years of high school format exist in the city. In Lynn, you went to grade school for six years, junior high for three years, and high school for three years. As young as he was, JT could not understand the logic in this plan. He would think about the kids from St. Patrick's, St. Michael's, and even St. Mary's, all Catholic feeder schools that contained eight grades. The poor shits at those schools would have to go to a new school for one-year, their ninth grade year, and then go to another new school the following year for high school. Lynn was doing it wrong. He knew it. Why didn't they? Since it was so difficult being a kid to begin with, why was not a whole damn city unable to remove such obstacles to their educational lives as opposed to erecting them?

The next three years turned-out to be intense, trying times for Rose Marie and JT in particular. In Rose Marie's mind, JT was the love of her life, her reason to be, her destiny. JT loved Rose Marie in return; however, he was not in love with her the way adolescent boys feel about "hot" girls. Rose Marie, in his mind, was like another sister, a best friend, a lifelong companion. What was developing here turned out to be a sure-fire cure for friendship. The seventh, eighth, and ninth grade years witnessed the drifting apart of Rose Marie and JT. She wanted, and at times demanded, much more from him than one friend ever should of another. JT's flirtations and crushes over the next three years eventuated into earth-shattering life events for Rose Marie. The pressure on JT to be to Rose Marie what he was not, weighed on him mightily toward the end of grade nine. She was always upset with him. He watched her cry many times. What was he doing wrong? Seeing his friend in such distress was extremely painful for him. Seeking counsel from Tony was generally tantamount to asking a blind man for directions, but the Rose Marie thing had JT so confused and upset, he was desperate enough to listen to his old pal.

"Russ, what is your problem? You are absolutely the most perceptive person I've ever known, but when it comes to Rose Marie Lloyd, your judgment develops amnesia."

"How so, Tony?" he responded defensively.

"Russ, the girl has been in love with you since birth. Man, I cannot believe you. You're there for her all the time at any time from first grade to today, and you cannot see what's happening?"

"But, Rose Marie and I are not like that."

"Wrong, big guy, you may not be like that, but she is definitely in L-O-V-E."

"Yeah?"

"Yes sir, and I can't believe it took a self-absorbed, insensitive, slob like me to point out the obvious to Mr. Wizard."

"What do I do? I can't remain the cause of her pain. I love her too much for that."

"I see two options if you're interested in listening."

"I have so far, oh great one."

"The first choice, and as I see it, the less desirable of the two that I shall propose, is to reciprocate her feelings. Give her what she wants – you. You can try to love her back as she loves you. In other words, you can fake it. You can string her along until she gets tired of you and ditches your ass."

"Yeah, like that's liable to happen."

"I know. I'm not a big fan of my number one option myself. Number two option requires attempting a maneuver at which men are incredibly poor practitioners. Tell her the absolute truth. Pull no punches. Give her the facts and just the facts so help you God."

"Jesus, I would be the last person to believe that I'd be going to you for advice about women. I agree, number two is the only way to go. I just can't stand to see her hurt."

"Russ, either way she is going to get hurt. Get over it. Deal with it now because it will be way worse later."

He purposely stayed away from her that weekend at the cost of two whole days in bed battling a suspiciously sudden arriving "bug" which totally incapacitated him and left him incommunicado. JT used the time to work out exactly what he wanted to communicate to Rose Marie and how he was going to go about accomplishing the task. Such was a labor of waste. He was no closer to a plan on Monday morning than he was on Friday evening. Of course, JT could not avoid Rose Marie for the rest of his life, right? When he saw her that morning for the first time in several days, he knew he was acting strange. He was never uncomfortable with her, not until today. They agreed to go to the library together after supper. JT would walk to her house, and they would walk to the library together.

"So far, so good," he thought to himself. "I didn't pass out."

CHAPTER 27

NOVEMBER 24, 1942, ON THE road to Las Vegas Nevada, Jeffrey Fine, a twenty-two year old draft-dodger from Torrence, California, and his twenty one-year-old girlfriend, Rita Bowles, pulled-out of a roadside diner back onto the highway. Fine knew that he had thrown his life into the "shitter" the moment he ignored his draft board's notification to report. So what did this hero turned genius decide to do? He convinced his beautiful but incredibly naïve girlfriend to join him in escaping across the border to Mexico. Unfortunately, for this minor criminal and geography-limited ner-do-well, he went the wrong way. Currently, he had found himself just outside of Las Vegas with enough cash to purchase a pack of gum. Mr. Fine then used his incredible sex appeal and attractiveness to persuade Rita to seek a job exhibiting her God-given attributes at some local gentleman's club on the strip to support them. With constant and not so gentle prodding, she consented. Following two days of living in his car, eating free food samples offered at the casinos and cleaning-up in gas station bathrooms, Rita impressed the owner of Mario's Men's Club, Mario "The Barber" Mesana, to hire her two fabulous breasts and incredible ass. Rita worked her ass-off literally and figuratively to keep her man in clothes, in food, and in drugs. Reciprocally, Jeff did not work anything off and did absolutely nothing to enhance their lives except to keep his meal ticket sexually satisfied. Three long years later, Rita was still removing her clothing for compensation, and Jeff was attempting to set the indoor record for consecutive days on a drug-induced high. One memorable evening, Rita returned home from a hard night of pole dancing and stripping to find the love of her life playing "show me yours, and I'll show you mine" with the bimbo from two doors down the hall. Caught in the act, Jeff really did not have a defense, nor did he feel a need for one. Rita's reward for her loyalty and hard work was the right to watch the asshole to whom she shackled herself demean her, their relationship, and everything she valued. Jeff, obviously offended by Rita's inopportune appearance, reacted as most scum sucking, bottom dwelling, pieces of shit would react. He slapped her around the room for a couple of minutes, watched her as she crumbled to the bathroom floor, and then went back to screwing the bimbo. The "termination of relationship" handwriting was on the wall. Now she had to figure out a way to exit that unholy union alive.

Rita continued to dance and live with Jeff; however, she became steadfast in her refusal of sexual relations with him. At first, he responded by beating the piss out of her. This behavior would never do. He was destroying his one and only meal ticket. Who in hell wanted to pay to see a bruised and battered stripper regardless of how great her tits were? So, taking the path of least resistance, Jeff and Rita cohabited in a sexless union with good old Jeff getting his rocks off with any female foolish enough to fall for his many lines and endless supply of drugs. In June of 1945, the exit from her hell-on-earth relationship appeared in the form of Bruno "Bocce Balls" Bernardi. Long enamored by the beautiful, big bosomed, blond Rita, Bruno, a "made" man in the Gambini crime family, but a real pussycat in life outside the mob, asked her to dine with him after one of her performances. Bruno was a hulk of a man. Extra huge immediately would come to mind. He was also gentle and kind in his way with Rita. Always a gentleman, never disrespectful, if he were not a cold-blooded, maniacal killer, everyone would have probably loved him.

"So, Bruno, why do they call you 'Bocce Balls'?"

"Do you know our game, honey, the Italian game of bocce?"

"Yeah, isn't it kinda like bowling?"

"Yes, the balls are rock hard and as big as oranges."

"OK, so what's the connection?"

He pulled down his zipper and exposed "the bocce balls".

"Oh my," she exclaimed in admiration.

Their relationship went from "parked to high gear" in little to no time at all. She informed Bruno about her present relationship and its liabilities to her health and welfare. Bruno told her he had the answer in his shoulder holster. She begged him not to kill that miserable plague of her existence. Instead, she convinced Bruno to discuss Mr. Jeffrey Fine's fugitive from the law status with a Las Vegas jurist who was known to be sympathetic to the mob, for a monthly fee. In short order, Mr. Fine was not so fine. He found himself in stripes at the federal penitentiary at Levenworth, sharing a cell with a massive, angry, bisexual by the name of Salvatore "The Salami" DiPasto. As time passed, being Bruno's girlfriend definitely had a downside to all the romantic, monetary, materialistic upsides. His huge penis and incredible testicles were killing her. This guy could fuck a manhole and get stuck. She could not enjoy normal relations with her man. The bloom was soon off the rose. The good news was that she had accumulated a substantial bankroll should she wish to relocate speedily. The bad news was that Bruno, with his mob connections, would most probably find her wherever she went. Rita understood that if she wanted to maintain her normal-sized vagina, she must move quickly. Making no move to escape would result shortly in a "choochie" inside of which she would be able to hide a watermelon. How many excuses for not having sex with a murderer can one girl contrive? To add to her predicament, Rita learned that she was pregnant. She needed to do some serious, fast thinking. Her condition threatened to expose the secret she kept from "Bocce Balls". If only she could make Bruno fall out of love with her. The exit plan she created was priceless. Manhood and pride were the common denominators valued and solemnly guarded by all mobsters. Wise guys protected these qualities religiously at any cost. If the world knew that a "made-man" was a sissy-boy, a homo, or simply an unmanly kind of man, his career path would surely end. Yet, the worst of all the embarrassing situations that could befall a wise guy involved his relationship with his woman. Having his woman impregnated by a member of a different, darker skinned race was the unforgivable sin to the wise guy. It was upon this concept that Rita Bowles designed her exit strategy.

"So, Bruno, you have three choices: kill me and this unborn negro child in my womb and burn in hell for eternity; keep me around until my delivery time to prove I'm lying and take your chances with what pops out from my loins; kiss me good-bye saying what we had was sweet but over."

"I loved you, bitch. How could you do this to me? Didn't I treat you good?"

"Yes, love, you treated me very well, and I still love you, Bruno. We just don't fit, you know what I mean?"

"Get the fuck outta here! I don't wanna know you, see you, or hear about you ever, capice?"

"What? No kiss good-bye?"

Good-bye to Las Vegas. Hello to anywhere else! With no real family to whom to turn, the three month pregnant, financially independent Rita boarded a cross-country airplane for Boston, Massachusetts. She had fallen in love with the 1946 World Series losing Boston Red Sox baseball team and although her initial plan was to go to the home of the World Series winner, she just did not see herself in the Midwest milking cows and waving a St. Louis Cardinals pennant. So Boston it was. A smaller version of big city New York, Boston was just the right size for her. Her sole complaint involved her distaste for New England weather. New Years Day, 1947, found her alone, pregnant, and content in a clean, warm, three room furnished apartment less than a five-minute cab ride from Massachusetts General Hospital. The girl was always thinking ahead. She already had her bag packed and at the ready for her trip to the delivery room five months hence. Those five months flew by. Before she knew it, she was being assisted from a cab by its owner, Bernie Diamond, and into a wheelchair. From there she was checked into the maternity ward where she waited for little

Bruno or Bruna to arrive on the planet. It never happened. At least not the way it was supposed to happen. Her little Bruno was stillborn, a victim of strangulating umbilical cord. On July 4, 1947, Rita laid her son Bruno B.B. Bernardi, Jr. to rest in an unmarked grave, in a little known cemetery, in a little known area, somewhere in Boston. The woman proved to be extremely resilient. After a period of depression and mourning, she started planning for her future. The first order of business was to lose herself. What she needed was a new start, a rebirth so to speak. The now twenty-six year old Rita Bowles changed her residence, her lifestyle, and her name. Lynn, Massachusetts, became the new home for the brand new, Alexis Take.

CHAPTER 28

"SO WHAT YOU'RE TELLING ME is that after all these years you are willing to walk away from our friendship because I don't feel the same way as you do?" asked JT with a tear in his voice.

"Do you have any idea what it means to a girl to have the guy she adores tell her she is like a sister to him, Jamey?"

"You just answered a question with a question, Rose Marie."

"Jamey, if you can't love me, I can't be near you. I hurt to the very core of my being." Her stuttering began. He knew they were in serious straits at that point.

"Should I have pretended, Rose Marie? Would that have been better for you?"

She looked from his face to the cement stairs of the library. Her tears made spots on the cement.

"Only one thing would be better for me, Jamey, and I just lost it."

She ran down the stairs into the darkness.

"Rose Marie! Wait! Please, Rose Marie!"

She was gone. At the time, he really did not understand how far-gone she was.

"Look," admonished Tony the following day, "you did what had to be done. People can't go on kidding themselves about what is or is not real."

"I called her. She wouldn't take my calls. I waited outside her house to walk her to school this morning, and she did not come out.

I feel so fucked. Was I doing it wrong with Rose Marie all these years, Delvane?"

He shrugged, and they walked in silence.

High school now beckoned. New and more complex situations waited. Out went some old relationships, in rolled some new. Life at Lynn Classical High School was difficult for most sophomores. A small but active group of junior and senior class members made life miserable for selected victims. Fortunately for JT and Tony, the bad guys tended to leave them alone. The boys felt that keeping a low profile for that first year was the prudent thing to do. Although she had not spoken to him in months, JT managed to stay attuned to Rose Marie's comings and goings. He was intensely displeased that she began "running" with a group in which the old Rose Marie would never have fit. He knew she had started smoking cigarettes. There were reports of her attendance at some questionable parties where drugs were readily available. He even kept track of her dating. She had pretty much chosen the bottom of the barrel dwellers as her romantic interests. Of all her downhill activities, the dating thing most concerned him. JT had this feeling deep in his heart and mind that she was punishing him by abusing herself. As strange as it sounded to him as he tossed it around in his constantly active mind, the possible reality of the situation grew and disturbed him greatly. It was at the end of their sophomore year that Rose Marie's shit hit the fan! Not only was she found at Lynn Beach naked in the back seat of a car with some Neanderthal moron she had been dating, but they were also in possession of marijuana. The arresting officers gave her just enough time to make herself presentable before loading the two lovebirds into the rear of the cruiser for a trip downtown. Upon answering the telephone at the Lloyd residence, Miss Take informed the arresting officer of Mr. Lloyd's incapacitation and Mrs. Lloyd's choice not to get involved. The veteran nanny queried as to whether she could be of service since the young lady had been in her charge for years. Alexis posted bond for Rose Marie and transported her home. As they walked into the house, they were confronted by a furious, Emily Lloyd.

"A drug dependent slut! Is that what you have raised for us, Miss Take? I have a reputation on the North Shore. The success of our stores depends upon our good name. What the fuck did you think you were doing, young woman? No, do not say a goddamn word! No matter what you say will not make-up for this blot on my reputation. Wouldn't you know it? That spineless father of yours is not where he is needed once again because he is making yet another visit to his mental home away from home. What a fucking circus of a family! Well, Rose Marie, here is the bottom line for you. You will enroll at St. Clarissa's Catholic School for Girls as of tomorrow. You will be boarding there. Miss Take, when a nanny has no one to attend, that person becomes expendable. Pack-up. Your services will no longer be necessary."

The shocked look on Alexis's face, the hysterical crying of Rose Marie, and the smugness on the face of Emily Lloyd all served to emphasize the joy of victory and the agony of defeat emotions of the moment.

"My father won't let you do this, bitch! You're not my real mother. You have no say in my life! You certainly haven't for the past sixteen years!"

"Well, hold on to your panties, little girl. Here's a news bulletin for you..."

It all came out. Venom flowed from Emily's lips as she informed the girl of the truth about her parentage. Alexis screamed at Emily in protest to stop before she went too far, but her words fell upon deaf ears.

"You knew, Lexy?"

"Of course she knew. It was her fucking idea," sneered Mrs. Lloyd.

"Listen to me Rose Marie!" cried Alexis.

"No!" she screamed. "I've heard enough. Get away from me, both of you! I hate you! I hate you both!"

"Run away you little bitch. You truly are your father's daughter. Run fast and far away from life like your piece of shit daddy!" screamed a totally out of control Emily Lloyd who ranted and raved all the way to her bedroom.

The two women faced-off in the dining room the following morning. Neither appeared to have slept well. Rose Marie, who ran to her room and locked the door last evening, had yet to rise that morning.

"What fucking contract are you talking about, Miss Take?" queried a mystified Emily Lloyd.

"Now that I have your attention, Mrs. Lloyd, and you seem to have returned from the world of the delirious, I feel obliged to correct an errant assumption of yours regarding the terms of my employment. You see, you miserable excuse for a woman, I have a twenty-one year contract, signed, sealed, and in the possession of the Lloyd family attorneys. Mr. Lloyd and I made that commitment to each other over sixteen years ago. He knew he was in dire need of someone to protect his little girl so he put his money where his mouth was. Oh yes, Mrs. Lloyd, there is a provision for you to buy out my remaining contract years at double my salary per year. Removal from my position would require proof of negligence, neglect of duty, moral turpitude, a felony conviction, and so on. So, get this straight, you miserable bastard, I would love nothing more than never to see you or deal with your warped, demented view of motherhood for the remainder of this lifetime. But, I love that girl upstairs, and I will kill you before I will allow you to hurt her anymore."

"Really…is there anything in your contract that spells out your duties as Rose Marie's nanny?" smiled the evil queen.

"I'm not sure, but I presume so," responded Alexis Take.

"Well, you had better pray that those duties have been specified in writing, my dear Miss Take, because if they are not, you will be given every shit job that has to be done either here or at the stores. I'll have you wiping my ass on a daily basis," smiled Emily Lloyd seemingly trumping the Take trump card.

"Since you are still in my employ, and I shall closely review that contract with our lawyers, wake the little bitch and get her enrolled in her new school. Also, make sure she is properly withdrawn from Classical High School. Lastly, see our lawyer about her embarrassing run-in with the law last evening. Just get it done," commanded Emily as she turned and walked away.

"Is there anything else, madam? Perhaps you would like your ass washed," yelled Alexis.

"There will be plenty of time for that, dear," smiled the lady of the house looking back over her shoulder.

CHAPTER 29

JT DID NOT SEE ROSE Marie very often during their junior and senior years of high school. He often lamented the direction that this lifelong, truly important relationship in his life had taken, but if nothing else, JT was a realist. Crying over the spilt milk of the past, in his mind, was a sure way to spill some more. After not hearing from her or seeing her by his graduation day, he had assumed the relationship dead. He set about burying it and allowing it to rest in peace. Yet one never knows in life when or where fate will throw Rover a reward bone. JT was home alone on that late June day uncharacteristically sleeping late. He awoke at the announcement of the front door chimes that someone did not want him to continue his sleep. He pulled on his jeans and threw on a jersey before answering the call that disturbed his rest. Pulling open the door and seeing his visitor made his mouth drop open. There stood the lovely Rose Marie Lloyd.

"Rosie, what a terrific surprise! Hey, you look great."

"Hello, Jamey, may I talk with you?"

"Of course. Please come in."

As she entered the hallway leading to the living room on the left and the upstairs to the right, she threw her arms around the shocked young man. Just five minutes ago, he had experienced a somewhat unceremonial departure from the world of dreams. Was this part real? Was this really happening?

"I miss you", she wept. "I'm so sorry about...."

"You don't have to say another word, hon."

"Yes, I do. I was so wrong to hurt the one person in my life who deserved it least. Can you please forgive me?"

Crying now also, JT took her pale, delicate face in his fingertips, pecked her lips, and held on to her as if to keep her from escaping again. Catching-up was great therapy for the recently reunited couple. The old familiarity was right there. They spoke and laughed without missing a beat. The easiness of their more than a decade of friendship was obvious to both of them. It was as if nothing bad had transpired between them. Although they knew this not to be the case, in their good judgment they both silently decided that the past should be left right there. Rose Marie informed him that she had been dating a very nice boy from Bishop Fenwick High School for the past six months. He had recently graduated, but her experimentation with the darkside of life for all that time had cost her the opportunity to graduate on time. She would have to return to St. Clarissa's to repeat her senior year. She thought that a mild punishment for the asinine way she behaved for so long. She related to him that shortly after experiencing the regimentation at her new school, things deteriorated for her. The more that people tried to help her, the more she repelled them. Were it not for two great new girlfriends, Angela and Andrea Arrington, twins from Nahant, her supportive and caring boyfriend, Patrick Cross, a rich kid from Marblehead, and her senior class advisor, Sister Joan-Michael, she feared that she would still be wallowing in her life of self-pity, hostility, and self-destructiveness. These four individuals put-up with all her crap and reintroduced her to her misplaced understanding of unconditional love, a concept so alien to her due to her perverted upbringing. JT heard the sordid truth about Emily Lloyd and her perverse view of non-parenting. She described her troubled father's constant battles to stay out of hospitals. The amusing revenge of Alexis Take was the final subject of her conversation. Following the night of Rose Marie's first arrest and the hideous ramifications that followed, Alexis had taken a new more powerful role in the house. Alexis learned from the Lloyd family lawyers that she held "mommy-dearest" Emily by the "short hairs" in any dealings with the saintly Lexy. As the proud possessor of an ironclad contract with four years remaining and an outline of duties specifically limited to those that directly affected the good, health, and welfare of Rose Marie Lloyd, Alexis was now Emily's "worst nightmare" in the struggle for Lloyd family supremacy. It reminded Rose Marie of Emily, the little devil, on one of her shoulders and Alexis, the little angel, on the other. Alexis found herself in a position of strength, legally speaking, in her dealings with Emily. Therefore, Alexis would not stand for any of Emily's shit storms, ever! When it was JT's turn to open up, Rose Marie learned that he had been playing the field when it came to the ladies with no one special in his life. However, he told her about the night before at Revere Beach and the girl he stumbled over in the sand. He told her how he could not get the girl out of his mind.

"Are you all right with me talking like this, Rosie?"

"Jamey, I will love, no, adore you, for the rest of my life, but I am over that romantic fantasy in which I had us starring. All I want is my best friend in the world back if he is willing."

"He never went away, kid. He was just waiting for your return."

They embraced yet again. This time they clung to each other and covered themselves in a flood of tears.

"Well, look at us, Jamey. Quite a pair, huh?"

"Always have been, always will be, Rosie."

Before leaving his house, she remembered the request her father had made of her the night before when she told him that she was going to visit with Jamey.

"What are your plans for the summer?"

"Tony and I are still looking for jobs. We're looking for something that will continue when summer ends to give us money for college."

"You're hired."

"What?"

"My dad would love to have you and Tony work for him. If you like the job, and he likes your work, you can schedule your part-time hours around your college schedule."

"Both of us? Get out of town!"

"Of course, you'll work at different branches. I advise you to pick the Lynn store. Emily is not there. Tony can have the pleasure of working for the 'dragon lady' in Nahant."

"That's it? We're hired?"

"Yup. When can you start?"

"Today if you want."

"Let's say Monday. How about that?"

"Wonderful. Oh, Rose Marie, these are paying jobs, right?"

"Only if you're nice to the boss's daughter!"

CHAPTER 30

UPON HER MAPLE CHEST OF drawers immediately in view as one walked into her bedroom, she found a note-sized, pleasant smelling envelope resting against the framed photo of her and Rose Marie. Written on the front in a lovely hand, she saw her name. She knew immediately it was from neither Mr. Lloyd nor Rose Marie. Alexis slit the top of the envelope with the monogrammed silver letter opener given to her as part of a desk set by Mr. Lloyd last Christmas. The note inside dated that very day was from the lady of the house, Emily Franklin Lloyd. To Alexis's surprise the greeting was actually cordial. She commenced reading the body of the note not quite grasping its significance.

Dear Miss Take:
I realize that our relationship at best has been a rocky one. I take full responsibility for this circumstance. I would be pleased if you would accept my invitation to dine with me this evening. I believe the time has come for me to repent for my offenses against you. Chef will be serving dinner at 7:00 PM. I truly hope you will attend.
Sincerely,
Emily

"What the hell is this all about? Repent for her offenses against me? What about her incredible abuse of her daughter? I should take this invitation and stick it up her…yes, but then I will not know what is behind this 'reaching-out' of sorts. Shit, I'll do it, even if I have to hold down my food to see just what she's up to."

Rose Marie, as usual, was out with Patrick that night; Mr. Lloyd was inventorying the Lynn store so only the two ladies would be dining that evening. Alexis decided to take the high road, putting aside her harsh feelings for her dinner companion, since it was only for that one evening.

"Miss Take, thank you for coming. I know this is not an easy task for you."

"Thank you for the invitation, Mrs. Lloyd. Needless to say, I was surprised by the invitation."

"It was long over-due, Alexis, may I call you Alexis?"

"Certainly, Mrs. Lloyd."

"Please, call me Emily."

"If you wish, Emily."

"Alexis, aside from your dealings with me as a parent, you and I have had little opportunity, and I take the complete blame for this, to get to know each other."

"Well, Emily, the truth be known, I had no desire to know you on any level so I take my fair share of the blame for our lack of socialization."

"You are a very straight-forward speaking woman, Alexis. I like that."

"I try to be open and honest in my dealings with people. I've found that philosophy works for me."

"Of course, Alexis. I perceive myself to be an astute businesswoman. I pride myself on knowing my products, my clients' needs, and talent. I have an offer to make you that I hope you'll not reject 'out of hand' simply from whence it came."

"Emily, I pride myself on being a good listener regardless from whence the information comes."

"Good. We have four stores now. I am sure you are well aware of this fact. We currently have stores in Lynn, Nahant, Lynnfield, and Peabody. I desire to expand our territory. Unfortunately, Mr. Lloyd's health makes him a liability to me on a number of levels. I do not know if the man will be running his store or wearing shackles from day to day. I need to surround myself with good, intelligent, honest, hard-working people in order to succeed in my quest."

"And your point is…"

"I want you to learn the family business. I would like you to come aboard and eventually manage your own store or stores."

"You must excuse me for being at a loss, Emily. After all, we have been less than forthright with each other, and our relationship would have to improve in order to be considered bad."

"You are so correct. I thought of all the potential questions, concerns, and fears that you might direct at me. So why don't you just ask away."

"Emily, is this a way for your to circumvent my current contract so you can get rid of me?"

"The precise question I expected first. I shall put into writing, notarized by our attorneys, whatever safe-guards you mandate, fair enough?"

"That is very interesting. Why would you be offering this opportunity to someone who doesn't like you in the slightest?"

"Another excellent question, Alexis. We need not like each other to be successful associates in business. That fact appears to be a universal truth. However, I would welcome the opportunity to expand and develop our relationship. I have been truly impressed over the years at your absolute dedication to Rose Marie and her unquestioning love for you. Perhaps learning about each other on different levels will alter our perceptions of the past. The obvious, I have found, my dear Alexis, is not always the accurate."

"Pardon me, Emily. This conversation is dizzying. I am at a loss. My mind is spinning in utter confusion."

"Why don't we dine now? We will continue this discussion later."

With a nod of agreement from Alexis, Emily called for their meals. Dinner conversation was much lighter than that of the earlier evening. The women shared life stories, as much as either wanted the other to know. Emily talked about her work, and Alexis tried to answer questions about her career choice and marital status. Alexis's ears perked-up when Emily broached the subject of her marriage. Perhaps the several glasses of wine with dinner loosened her lips and her previously closely guarded privacy.

"Newton's health has become such a liability to the business. His trips to private sanitariums are costing us a fortune. I spoke with our lawyers, and they are in the process of putting the business solely in my name to protect us from foreclosures or bankruptcy. Newton will remain the boss in name only. His medical needs will be accommodated. I just cannot risk everything for which I have worked. I have also asked them to begin divorce proceedings. I won't continue in this farce of a marriage any longer."

"Well, that certainly added to the information overload of the evening, Emily. I'm beginning to see you as a very complex yet interesting woman."

"Good. I want your acquaintanceship, and if I may be fortunate enough, your friendship. We are about the same age aren't we, Alexis? I'll be forty-three in a few months."

"Yeah, forty-three and counting."

"Let me ask you, Alexis, how does a beautiful woman such as yourself live a life of celibacy? Don't you ever get horny?"

"Hold on Emily. Who said anything about celibacy? Besides, isn't that a very personal question?"

"So, you have men friends with whom you have relations?"

"I didn't say that Emily. Men are not a priority with me. When I have the urge, I just take care of myself."

"What a waste of beautiful womanhood! I did that for so long until I finally took charge of the situation."

"What about Newton?" queried Alexis.

"I haven't fucked that piece of shit since we conceived Rose Marie."

The wine was now making Emily more talkative than she had been in forever. She talked of her "boys" in muddled references. The fact that she did not have to scratch her own itch came through loud and clear to Alexis. The more she spoke, the more curious Alexis became. Unfortunately for the now eager to know Alexis, Emily was approaching maximum capacity on her personal alcohol gauge. The end of their evening was rapidly approaching because of her companion's incapacitation. Nonetheless, it had been one hell of an interesting session.

"You had what with whom?" asked Rose Marie in a panicked voice. Why did you do that? You feel the same way as I do about that bitch. She is dead to me, end of story. I cannot help but feel betrayed Lexy. What were you thinking?"

Never once did Alexis consider how her socializing with Emily would affect Rose Marie. Thinking on her feet, she rationalized her decision to her young charge by repeating to Rose Marie the old saying that the devil that you know is better than the devil you do not know. She theorized that by establishing a relationship with Emily, they would be able to anticipate her moves, protect themselves from the unexpected, and evaluate her strengths and weaknesses. Alexis knew she started to sound like a James Bond clone, but her gut instinct told her that Rose Marie was in dire need of a convincing argument to alleviate the doubts she now harbored about Lexy's loyalty and credibility.

"I don't like it at all, but I trust your judgment, Lexy. Please don't expect me to join in this undercover operation of yours. I will not even acknowledge that woman's existence. I shall never break bread with her nor speak to her in a voice civil or otherwise."

Alexis had not expected to see Rose Marie that night. Rose Marie's recent habit had been to come home late, go right to her room, and sleep until late morning. On the night in question, Rose Marie had arrived home earlier than usual and knocked on Alexis's door shortly after the "dinner party" ended. Following their brief but potentially destructive meeting, Alexis kissed Rose Marie goodnight, watched her sadly exit the room, and prayed that the repercussions from this night would not be cause for her everlasting regret. That evening sleep was elusive. Alexis's mind wandered to and from her responsibility and emotional bond to Rose Marie. The offer from Emily frequented her deepest thoughts. The reality of her nonexistent sex life, Emily's mysterious sex life, and at some point, though she labored long and hard to remove the mental pictures, of hers and Emily's sex life together cluttered her mind. The question of her future haunted her that night. What happens to good old Alexis when Rose Marie turns twenty-one? Her contract will be completed. She will be cut loose. She will be on the downside of forty. Alexis Take viewed starting over again as such a frightful undertaking.

"To thine own self be true," rattled around in her head. "Have I actually been doing it wrong all these years? Have I painted myself into the proverbial corner? What to do? Where to go? Time was not an ally. What about Rose Marie? I'm needed…but for not much longer, Alexis. To thine own self be true, Rita…"

"Well, what are your thoughts, honey? Should I take her offer? Without you on board, there is no deal. Rose Marie, I did a lot of thinking last night. Without you in my life, where do I go? What do I do?"

For the first time in her lifetime with Alexis, that was the only time Rose Marie could remember Alexis speaking about her own needs. The thought conjured-up the picture of a woman with an evaporating present situation-- her contract-- and an opportunity-less future, which was on the immediate horizon. Was she being selfish? Alexis had given her everything a mother could give her – more in fact. It was time to give back, Rose Marie reasoned.

"Look, the only thing that matters to me is that you always remember how much I love you, Lexy. I'm old enough now to fight my own battles. You helped make me this strong. I'll never be able to repay you in this life. Whatever you decide upon, I'll know great care and concern were involved in the process. It's time to think about yourself for a change. I support whatever decision you make."

They embraced, wept, then looked at each other and smiled. Rose Marie was not sure her affirmation was the right thing for her to do; however, in her heart, she knew it was best for Alexis. Alexis was not sure that sharing all the information arising from the Emily dinner was the right thing to do with Rose Marie; however, she knew in her heart, she had to do it for herself.

The following morning upon returning from her morning bathroom routine, Alexis found another envelope. Exactly as the previous in handwriting and smell, she opened the note quickly, impatient to unlock its contents.

> *Dear Alexis,*
> *I loved our dinner. I pray you have similar feelings. The offer outlined that evening was not a casually considered proposal. Months of planning then gathering the courage to address you were well worth my trouble. I think, dear Alexis, that you and I may be more alike than either of us could have even imagined. I await your positive response.*
> *Your friend (I hope),*
> *Emily*

Alexis held the note to her chest, smiling. She knew the ball was in her court. It was time to enter the game.

CHAPTER 31

"Hurry-up, sweetie! Don't keep mama waiting." The hulking footballer followed his fantasy into the small office. Closed for the evening with the doors locked, all the lights, save one, were out. She closed the door behind him and immediately began to explore his mouth with hers. The eagerness of youth always disturbed her at times like these. She felt obliged to teach him how to properly handle a woman. Often times she felt like an animal trainer offering rewards for the correct response. Yes, that was it. It was reward and punishment, Pavlov's dog, Skinner's pigeons, Emily's young men. The first time, some four years earlier, eventuated out of her abject sexual desire. The day following her rejection from that foolish, now former druggist, Douglas, found her "itch" unbearable. She had vowed never to scratch it herself again, but the best laid plans of mice and men... Around the noon hour, back then, just as she and Douglas were closing for lunch, a nervous young man probably seventeen or eighteen years of age walked to the door. Sending Doug to lunch, Emily waited on the young man herself. She could see immediately that the choice she made for the young man would not have been his first choice. His errand was to secure condoms. Most certainly, dealing with a fellow male would be entirely more desirable than confronting the opposition. The young man was about to turn and leave when Emily reached for his arm. Unconsciously, she moved her hand up and down his hairless forearm.

"We were just about to close for lunch, but we always have time for our good customers," she smiled.

She had seen him in the store recently. She remembered him because he looked so ill at ease as he approached the pharmacy counter to speak with Doug. Because Doug was up to his elbows in prescription preparations, Emily asked if she could be of service. Visibly shaking, the young man bought twelve packages of Juicy Fruit gum, thanked her, and walked, almost jogged from the store.

"Are you out of gum already?" she teased.

"Yes m'am, no m'am. I mean I don't need gum, m'am," stammered the very uncomfortable youth.

"And what is it you need today?" purred Emily Lloyd.

"I need condoms, m'am."

There he said it. It was as if someone pricked a balloon inside of him. The nervous energy whooshed out of his body. The difference in his composure was immediately noticeable.

"Certainly, sir. Come this way, please."

The boss lady slowly and sexily walked to the back counter where she displayed a selection of the various manufacturers' brands located in a drawer behind the counter.

"Don't you think it would be much easier for everyone if the Commonwealth would allow us to display these things and allow self-service sales?" teased the saleswoman.

"You know it. I can't tell you how long I've put off buying these things. I plan it out each time, but something always goes wrong. I've gone into stores from Nahant to Gloucester without any luck. I've tried going in just as the store opens or just as the store closes…"

"Or just as its closing for lunch?" cooed Emily.

"Yes, m'am. I always chicken out."

"Until today," she said trying to build his confidence. "What's your name? I'm Emily Lloyd. I own the pharmacy."

"I know, Miss Lloyd. I've seen you here a lot. I'm Brady Nelson."

She put forth her hand, and he shook it.

"Well, Brady, now that we're old friends, next time shouldn't be such torture for you," she smiled licking her upper lip. "Let's get you taken care of, Brady."

And she did. Emily Lloyd on that day and year invented the concept of "test-driving" the condoms that she sold to high school boys. Part of her service involved lessons on the proper application of the condom both manually and orally. Once the condom fit properly, she offered a "try before you buy" money back guaranteed concept. She smiled to herself as she thought that she had yet to have anyone ask for his money back. How many had there been in the past four years? Probably twenty or thirty a year not counting repeats. Emily had become a sex surrogate to a whole generation of Lynn Classical, Lynn English, Lynn Trade School and St. Mary's of Lynn high school boys. Not to speak of the boys from neighboring towns who had heard about "the condom lady" from a friend. How well had this practice served its purpose? She had not scratched an itch in four years.

"Honey, that was fine. Next time be sure to warm up your partner first to make sure she's ready for that meat club of yours. If I forget, remind me that we should work on your oral skills too. Give mama a kiss goodbye."

As she dressed, the tingling in her still wet vagina reminded her why this part of her life was worth all the potential trouble her secret life held in store for her. For the second time that evening she locked up the store, this time with her on the outside, and she then hopped into her T-Bird and started home. She would be arriving home much later than usual, so she grabbed a burger and fries at Christy's at the end of the causeway just around the rotary. As she ate, she relived that night's events.

"Be careful, dear. You can't afford to get all wet again," she admonished herself.

The T-Bird pulled into the drive, and she bounced out. She walked upstairs to her room and upon opening her door noticed an envelope propped against the cosmetics on her make-up table. The envelope looked familiar. It was one of hers. Her name was printed across the front and the smell of Alexis Take emanated from its form. She quickly tore it open and read the contents.

> *Dear Emily,*
> *Please forgive my borrowing your stationery, but I have none as beautiful as this. I, too, thoroughly enjoyed our dinner together, and nobody is more surprised about this than I am. Concerning your generous offer, if you are still interested in my participation, and you are still willing to place in writing the safeguards to my present contract, you can see I am still not firmly convinced that our joint venture will succeed; I wholeheartedly accept your terms. I look forward to learning from you and working with you to make the Lloyd Pharmacies even more successful in the future. I am at your disposal to meet, dine, visit your lawyer, etc.*
> *Your friend,*
> *Alexis*

She was quite used to winning; however, she figured the odds to be strongly against her in this endeavor. That made her victory so much more satisfying. She lifted the letter to her lips and brushed it across them taking in the fragrance of Alexis Take.

CHAPTER 32

ROSE MARIE COMPLETED HER HIGH school requirements at St. Clarissa's that May and received acceptance to Blake College for the following September. JT, Tony, and Rose Marie continued their special relationship as if nothing had ever happened. The boys did Mr. Lloyd proud by performing above and beyond the call of duty. The life of college men probably could not have been more difficult for JT and Tony, but they persevered and graduated right on time. Rose Marie became a model student and good citizen attaining Dean's List grades for her first three years. Emily and Alexis were dynamic together. Alexis was a sponge having absorbed all the knowledge she could from Emily. Within a year of their teaming together, Alexis assumed sole management of the Lynnfield store. At the same period, Newton Lloyd was in and out of mental health facilities, mostly in. The difference to him this time was the quality of residence. Since the finalization of the divorce, it was state hospitals only for poor Newton. No more high priced sanitariums were budgeted for the former boss and founder of Lloyd Pharmacies. Shortly after the boys graduated in May, Newton experienced another episode, which left him overly medicated, under evaluated, and infrequently examined at Danvers State Mental Hospital just off Route 1 in Danvers, Massachusetts. Newton and Rose Marie had just recently attended JT's graduation party. A day or two later, Newton was doing his "nude thing" again, but this time he walked into Lynn City Hall to pay his tax bill. Needless to say, he never reached the

Tax Collector's Office, but he did take up residence in a familiar cell at the Lynn Police Station where he remained until yet another magistrate sent him away for yet another evaluation.

Soon after JT received his 1A classification from the draft board, he set about informing the people outside his family and Tara, who were important to him. Rose Marie was at the top of his short list. He decided to tell her in person so he called ahead to find if she were going to be home. They were to meet at her house around mid-afternoon. She reacted as he expected. He had already experienced similar hysterics from his mother, sister, and Tara. When he left her house, she had settled herself down, and after having him promise to write her faithfully, she kissed him and allowed him to leave.

The truly interesting relationship developing at this time was that of Emily Lloyd and Alexis Take. Since their partnering three years ago, the women had become inseparably close friends. With a single year remaining on her contract with the Lloyds, Alexis allowed Emily to tear it up and throw it away. In return, Emily adjusted her friend's salary to compensate her for her brilliant contributions to the growing successes of the Lloyd Pharmacies. Further, she insisted that Alexis remain at her home for as long as she wished. Emily suggested that since her home had been Alexis's home for twenty years, she should continue to reside there. The lion had truly lain down with the lamb. What could possibly happen next?

Rose Marie graduated from Blake with honors in elementary education. She immediately accepted a position at the Freed Elementary School located in the Highlands section of Lynn. Tara kept herself occupied with her Hollingsworth position, Bina transferred from Boston University to Merrimack College, Charlene and Jim Russell, Jessica and Mario Delvane worried day and night about JT and Tony, and Alexis Take and Emily Lloyd fell in love!

CHAPTER 33

THE CITIZENS OF LYNN AWOKE one morning with news that two of their number who had been fighting in Vietnam were in the headlines. The story explained that Corporal James T. Russell, USMC, and Corporal Anthony J. Delvane, USMC both of Lynn, Massachusetts were involved in a ferocious hand-to-hand combat firefight in the DaNang region of South Vietnam. Corporal Russell sustained severe non-life threatening wounds, and Corporal Delvane was missing in action. Having been notified earlier in the day by the Defense Department, the Russells had already been fortunate enough to speak with the physician at the hospital to which JT was transported. They held out hope that a follow-up call later that day would lead to hearing their son's voice. Although this did not happen, both Jim and Charlene were thankful that there was still a JT to talk with. The Russells immediately visited the Delvanes who had received less encouraging news about their son. The commiserating parents sat close together amongst several other supporters. Charlene held Jessica close to her sharing the grief that so many mothers had experienced recently over a war that was officially not a war, fought in a country whose people did not want the U.S. there, for some convoluted reasoning the truth of which was known only to our military and political leaders. Was that to be the true destiny of woman? To bring life into the world to be destroyed for every cause deemed necessary by their male counterparts? Homo sapiens had fought since some cave dweller had wandered onto some other cave dweller's territory. Humans had been killing each other as long as man had walked the earth. What was the common denominator in all the previous conflicts of our world? Man! Wars had been started by man, fought by man, planned by man, for the gratification and glory of man. To woman, man had been doing it wrong all through the ages. If woman ruled, not a mother's son would be sacrificed at the altar of war.

"I know he's alive, Charlie. I know in my heart. I would know if he were dead," wept Jessica Delvane into her friend's shoulder. "Since he was born, I always knew when he was hurt, always. I would feel it even before it happened. We're connected like that, you know?"

Charlene squeezed the agonizing woman's shoulder, "He'll find his way home to you, honey. He'll come home."

The following several months brought no relief to the Delvanes. Not knowing was so much worse than knowing for certain. The Delvanes finally understood the meaning of that "closure" term that had come to be so casually discussed when all types of personal tragedies were at issue.

Finally, JT phoned home. He was coming home. His war was over, at least the one-waged 8000 miles away. His wounds were healing, the physical ones anyway. Arrangements were made to meet him at Logan Airport. His arrival would come strangely enough only two days before the memorial mass celebrating the life of Anthony James Delvane.

The mass for Tony was both solemnly sad and incredibly uplifting at the same time. It was served by three priests from Sacred Virgin Church who had known Tony as he was growing up. The pews were completely filled. Hundreds of other celebrants stood outside of the doors and formed a ring around the old West Lynn parish church. Everybody of import in the city was there even the mayor and his wife. JT received a great deal of attention as he, Tara, Bina, and his mother and father left their car to walk across the street to the awaiting Delvane family. Unlike the emotionally explosive scene from the other evening, they greeted each other warmly and with a sense of calm and resolution. They were doing that for Tony. Their individually held feelings had to be "placed on hold" until their duty was fulfilled. Following the service, the church goers exited in a serious, orderly manner sharing only fleeting glances and nods of recognition until they found themselves outside of the building that was held in such a loving and devoted fashion by so many. Rose Marie approached the Russells as they walked toward their vehicle. There were hugs shared by all and the final remnants of the tears that were to be shed that day were cried.

"Jamey, I want to apologize for my father's behavior the other night. Well, you know his problems as well as anyone. He just seems to be making no progress since he was released from Danvers State when the Commonwealth closed the place down. The divorce apparently caused him a set back though God knows why. He hasn't really been married to that woman for twenty years. I hope you can forgive his interference at your homecoming."

"Come on, Rosie, you never have to make excuses to me especially about your Dad. I owe him a lot. Perhaps I can start paying him back now that I'm home again. What do you say? Do you want to autograph my cast?"

"But of course, sir. Is there any room left?"

"If there isn't, just wait a second and I'll break something else."

She hugged him and whispered into his ear, "I adore you, James Thurber Russell, past, present, and future."

He kissed her and whispered back into her ear, "You have always had the best taste in men."

She cracked up though the two of them were the only ones aware of the humor in the situation.

Rose Marie offered her good-byes and turned to catch JT mouthing, "I love you, Rosie." She smiled her beautiful smile, turned, and walked away. He never saw her again, alive.

CHAPTER 34

"LEX, ARE YOU COMING TO bed or do I have to come after you," teased Emily Lloyd.

"My dear, Ms. Lloyd, all good things are worth waiting for," responded the now disrobed Alexis Take.

"You know for an old broad you are one gorgeous piece of ass."

"Stop, you'll turn my head with your sweet talk, Miss Emily, m'am."

She dropped down beside her first lover in over twenty years and immediately began fondling the previously impatient Emily Lloyd.

"I look at you, Emily, and I still can't believe what's become of us. How did this happen? I never dreamed I could feel this way about another woman especially that 'bitch on wheels' you were in my mind."

"Why try to define it, examine it, explain it, when we can simply enjoy it, Lex."

Emily slowly kissed Alexis as Alexis removed Emily's final piece of clothing – her panties. Safely ensconced in the master bedroom once again, no one ever intruded on their lovemaking even during an afternoon encounter such as today. Alexis felt additionally secure because the only person she even cared about hurting was Rose Marie, and Rose Marie would never dream of visiting Emily's portion of their joint dwelling, especially not the dragon lady's den of inequity.

As Rose Marie rolled her Volvo into the driveway, she was seething. All the way home she wondered why Lexy did not make an appearance at the memorial for Tony. Rose Marie had worked herself up to such a state that she even started to question why Emily, Tony's boss for four years, did not have the decency to attend the service. Not that she gave a shit about Emily any more or less then she had for the past twenty-one years. She simply had felt that with her father's disability and social ineptitude some executive from the business should have attended the memorial. She walked into the great room and called for her father and Alexis; neither of whom answered. Chef could be heard in the kitchen preparing for the evening meal. Quite contrary to her nature, Rose Marie walked to the liquor cabinet and poured herself about four ounces of vodka. It went down without hesitation. So easily did it disappear that she poured herself yet another four ounces. Not being used to such inbibement, the effect on the young woman was immediate and intense. The anger she harbored upon returning home was now a maniacal desire for someone's blood. Cursing the bitch that gave birth to her and utterly disappointed in her "real" mother, Rose Marie strode towards Emily's bedroom to have it out with her! Without reservation and steeled by the liquor controlling her delicate mind and body, the hostile feeling young woman pulled open the door to Emily Lloyd's bedroom and allowed it to slam against the wall. The embracing women reacted to the intrusion in terror! Rose Marie's brain tried to process what she was seeing as she entered the room. Mere seconds passed before a frightful scream of "No!" passed from her lips but emanated from her very soul. Both naked women attempted to cover themselves to little or no avail. Alexis ran toward Rose Marie to offer an explanation and comfort. Rose Marie grabbed her by her blond locks and ripped her to the floor.

"I hate you Lexy. You were my world. I have nothing left. I hate you, and you're fucking girlfriend!" Off she ran through the opened door, out of the house, into her Volvo. The two traumatized women upstairs heard only the squeal of her tires as she left the drive.

CHAPTER 35

Perhaps the most colorful location for stories about the local lore of Lynn legends was High Rock and the tower built there on December 16, 1906, that sits at its summit. In modern day Lynn, High Rock Tower houses a mini-observatory opened to the public at precisely scheduled hours. The surrounding area is a city park that had become as of late more frequently visited most probably due in great part to the concerted effort to make the area safer and more accessible to the citizenry by local government. High Rock Tower had begun to experience a rebirth in interest of sorts. Standing eighty-five feet high atop the highest point in the City of Lynn, the dome of the stone structure, and it's church-shaped windows offered visitors a panoramic view of the Commonwealth's capital of Boston, as well as many of Lynn's sister communities. High Rock, a Pawtucket Indian meeting place and headquarters of their great chief, Nanapashemet, in pre-English settlement days held the reputation of being a spiritual, mystical, some say sacred site in this old city. The clairvoyant, Moll Pitcher, who lived for fifty years at the base of High Rock on Essex Street, was the vilified subject of a John Greenleaf Whittier poem in which he makes mention of her evil in the mystic's dealing with the sailors whose fortunes she told for a price. John Murray Spear, a former Universalist Church minister, turned spiritualist, became the leader of a cultist group, which in and around 1854-claimed guidance from the spirit world in an attempt to create a new and improved God out of metal and wood. High

Rock, being the closest Lynn location to heaven, served as their base of operations. The spirit helpers guided the group's labor by designing the contraption and outlining its composition. According to legend, only Spear was in communication with the spirits; therefore, he became the conduit between the two worlds. Legend has it that the mechanical deity was in fact created. However, the contraption failed to Iive up to its highly promoted promise after failing to be infused with energy from the extraterrestrial world during a public exhibition. The new deity, according to local lore, made nary a twitch of a movement. The less than godlike showing of the machine became the source of further ridicule and derision for both Spear and his followers. Regardless of the truth or falsity of the legends, such tales served and will continue to serve as fodder for discussion for future Lynn residents for years to come.

It was here at this legend-rich location that a Lynn police cruiser approached an abandoned late model Volvo that had struck a cluster of three large maple trees causing considerable damage to the front of the vehicle. The patrolman found that the automobile was registered to Newton Spencer Lloyd III who both men recognized as a very successful owner of local pharmacies. The lateness of the hour and the condition of the Volvo made the officers decision to search the area a foregone conclusion since the driver of the damaged car could be nearby and in need of medical assistance. With flashlights in hand, the patrolmen separated to commence their search. Within a matter of moments a call for assistance from one officer, a rookie police officer, to his more experienced partner had the veteran running. Upon reaching the younger officer, he found the rookie on his knees vomiting. As he attended to the officer in distress, his flashlight illuminated the twisted and broken, blood-soaked form of a young woman. His immediate radio call for assistance resulted in a parade of fire trucks, emergency vehicles, and squad cars to High Rock. Now recovered, the rookie related to his partner how he had stumbled and fallen over the female's body. As he got to his feet to investigate the cause of his fall, he found his hands and pants were coated with a thick, sticky liquid. He was stricken with nausea born of terror by the gruesome scene before him. In a heap of broken humanity, the body lay motionless at the foot of the ominous tower of High Rock. The victim, transported to Lynn Hospital's Boston Street branch, was pronounced dead on arrival. Examiners theorized that the victim either had jumped or been thrown from the top of the tower.

The ownership of the vehicle presented the police with a starting point for their investigation. The only other significant piece of evidence was clutched in the victim's rigored right hand. A blood-spattered note was pried from the dead woman's hand. It was composed of three lines:

I am sorry, and I love you Dad and Jamey.
I forgive you, Lexy.
Thanks for everything, MOTHER.

A team of detectives was assigned to the case. Sergeant Tom Walker and Lieutenant Shane Gillis, both veterans of the L P D, gathered the physical evidence, reassessed the scene as daylight broke, and pretty much confirmed their earlier theory of death from a fall either accidental or intentional. The heavy smoking Walker, the older of the two by ten years, thought he had seen it all until that night. He had never seen a body so contorted, a head wound so profound, and more blood than he thought a human being capable of containing. The much younger, college educated, Gillis, who had been tabbed as kind of a "whiz kid" at the station due to his rapid rise through the ranks simply had returned to his vehicle after the initial examination of the scene and called home to ask his wife if their fourteen year old daughter, Jackie, was alright.

The drive to the Lloyd residence was a somber one for the detectives with each lost in his own thoughts. The hour was now seven in the morning. Gillis hoped the residents to be early risers. As they pulled into the driveway not a creature was stirring, perhaps a mouse, as they exited their vehicle and made their way to the front door. Several rings of the door chimes brought a disheveled, frail looking man, still in his underwear, to the front door.

"Lynn Police, sir, I'm Detective Gillis and this is Detective Walker. Are you Newton S. Lloyd III owner of a white 1969 Volvo sedan?"

"Why, yes. That's my daughter's car."

"And her name is what, sir?"

"Rose Marie Lloyd. What is this about?"

"Your car was abandoned on High Rock following a collision with a cluster of trees…"

"Is she alright? Rose Marie, is she hurt?"

"May we come in, sir?"

The peals of anguish bursting forth from the hysterical father followed by a volley of ranting denials brought Alexis Take down the stairs toward the men.

"Newton, who are these men? What on earth is going on?"

The hysterical man had suddenly ceased all activity. His eyes were fixed as he stared directly at Alexis. She had a fleeting vision of him as a stone statue.

"M'am, you are?"

"I'm Alexis Take. I take care of the Lloyd's daughter, Rose Marie, and have for the past twenty-one years."

"We are police officers, Ms. Take. We have reason to believe that the Lloyd's daughter, Rose Marie, died late last night."

At the feet of the catatonic father, Alexis Take fainted dead away.

"Holy shit, Shane, I don't know who to help first."

"Let's take care of the lady. This guy doesn't seem to be going anywhere soon."

A call to the fire department brought a paramedic squad to the Lloyd's dwelling within three minutes. They attended to Alexis who was now conscious and hysterical. Her screams of anguish brought Emily Lloyd to the top of the stairs.

"What on earth, Lexy? What is it?" yelled Emily Lloyd.

"They think Rose Marie is dead, Emily! Oh Emily, what if she's dead?" sobbed Alexis.

Without a change of expression, Emily Lloyd turned and walked back to her bedroom.

"What the fuck was that about Shane? Was that the kid's mother? Close knit fucking family circle we got here, partner."

"Speaking of family circle, Tom, where's the statue?"

"For the love of …he's gone, Shane!"

Unbeknownst to the officers, Mr. Lloyd had refocused, shed his cloak of silent surveillance, and left the building. He was nowhere to be found. With some difficulty and after some time, officers were able to obtain the name of Rose Marie's dentist from the now quite heavily medicated Alexis Take. Within a short period of time, the police would know positively if it were Rose Marie Lloyd who had met an untimely demise last evening.

Based upon the dental records and what was left of her skull, the identity was confirmed. The handwriting on the note was compared to a sample of the young woman's writing and again – confirmation.

"Shane, everything points to a jumper."

"I agree, Tom, but I would like to have a talk with the mother and nanny before we sign off on that."

"You're the boss, Lieutenant, sir."

Bad news travels just as fast if not faster than good. Charlie Russell's friend, Sylvia, from the Bookbinders Book Club, worked the morning shift as secretary to the LPD Chief of Police. Her call to the Russell residence was short and all but sweet. JT's mom now was in possession of devastating information to her son. What would she do? She knew she was not very good at these things. Breaking bad news to people, telling little white lies, complimenting outfits that she found hideous, all these tasks were concepts alien to her personally. She decided to contact Jim at the warehouse; he would know how to handle it. As she dialed the phone, she talked herself through the script to use on Jim. Dialing incorrectly for the third time, her conversation with herself got heated.

"Ma, what are you doing? I heard you talking to someone from upstairs, but you're alone."

Charlie was startled to see her son, so much so that she simply blurted out the shattering news as she grabbed JT and fell to pieces in his arms.

"Rose Marie's gone, James! She died last night in an accident."

JT released the weeping woman from his arms and sat on a kitchen stool. With his head held firmly in his hands he began the grieving process for his poor, misguided, star-crossed lost love. He had not been home a week and he will have attended a memorial service for his best friend and a funeral service for an irreplaceable character in the story of his life. Strange, he thought to himself since he was beginning to feel somewhat more upbeat about life. The nightmares of his war engagement with Phong Ho Cheung lessened considerably of late. He even had to concentrate to remember the names Twan and Tram, Phong's family, who also often visited him in his nightmare world. And now this....

The detectives revisited the Lloyd home later in the day. Their intention this time was to secure background information that might help explain why a beautiful, intelligent, young woman with her whole life ahead of her chose to leave this plane of existence in the form of a splat on High Rock cement. Several employees from the various Lloyd pharmacies located themselves around the large house hoping to be able to offer their support to the grieving family. Unfortunately, there was no grieving family to comfort. A single, heavily medicated, devastated nanny sat amongst them for a while. Not knowing how to keep her sanity from separating from her being, Alexis returned to her bedroom where she gratefully slipped into sleep. Upon awakening, her first impulse was to seek out Emily. She thought out loud about where the fucking bitch was. Did she really react to the news in the way Alexis believed she had observed? Perhaps Alexis had entered into a deal with the devil and Rose Marie's death was her punishment. Perhaps her selfishness clouded her judgment and allowed her to make the biggest mistake in her mistake-filled life.

She slowly walked up the stairs and at the top turned towards Emily's bedroom. Without so much as a knock, Alexis opened the door and entered. Emily was sitting at her make-up table touching-up the face that she had put on several hours before. Her casual brightly colored outfit offended both Alexis's senses and sensibilities.

"Emily," Alexis said softly, "your daughter, your flesh and blood is dead. We'll never see her loveliness again, and it's our fault!"

"Firstly," Emily stated matter of factly, "we may have shared the same flesh and blood, but she was never my daughter. Secondly, I bid good riddance to her."

Alexis could not believe the callous words torturing her ears. As recently as last evening, she thought she loved the woman before her who had now once again taken on the appearance of an unfeeling monster.

"Furthermore, Lex, that sorry-ass Newton has disappeared. I figure we killed two birds with one death."

She refused to hear anymore of the venomous, offensive, horrible things leaving those lips that she loved to kiss. She rushed toward her former lover whose back was now to her and gracefully left her feet in a dive that resulted in Alexis tackling the shocked Emily. Alexis fell to the floor with Emily and found herself on top of the screaming woman. Emily absorbed blow after blow from the fists of the empowered attacker. Blood appeared on Emily's nose and lips. She screamed for Alexis to halt her attack. Alexis would have none of that! The bleeding woman's freshly combed hair was the next target. With a strength she had no idea she possessed, Alexis grabbed Emily's locks and repeatedly bounced her head on the floor. Blood now escaped from a gaping opening on Emily's forehead. Yet still, the attack continued. She tore away Emily's clothing that was so offensive to her. Body shots took the place of the head banging. And then it stopped. The woman beneath her ceased her crying and screaming. She looked directly into Alexis's eyes, which froze the attacker's actions.

"You're fired!"

Emily then lost consciousness. Alexis rolled from her victim and surveyed the damage to her own body. The nanny stumbled to the bathroom, applied some disinfectant to a scratch or two, and quickly sponged herself clean of Emily's blood. Filling Emily's douche bag with cold water from the tap, Alexis doused the unconscious woman back to consciousness.

"How appropriate, Emily, a douche bag for a douche bag."

When Gillis and Walker asked to speak with the nanny and the dead girl's mother, the chef gave them excuses as to why that would not be possible at the time. Gillis would have none of that and insisted that the two ladies speak with him here and now or speak with him at the station in the time it would take them to drive there. His message was relayed to Emily Lloyd who had made a vain attempt to make herself look presentable. Next, the chef, who served as messenger, visited Alexis in her room; she woke the tired, aching woman and insisted she join the detectives in the great room. Within ten minutes of the Lieutenant's ultimatum, a battered and bruised Emily Lloyd, the possessor of two blackened eyes, hobbled down the stairs with great difficulty and successfully reached her destination thanks to the sturdiness of the stairs' hand railing. From the other side of the house, a slightly stooped-over Alexis Take made her way toward the officers.

"Holy shit," Walker whispered to Gillis. Do you fucking believe this? They look like Ali-Frazier after the Garden fight.

"Seems to me there was a clear winner, Tom," whispered Gillis in return. "The one on the stairs should be seen by a medic. Right after we question them we'll offer to take them to the ER."

Walker half smiled and whispered back, "Think we'll be safe alone with them, Lieutenant?"

"Sure Tom, we got the guns, man."

The story, although not a pretty one and if made public would most certainly cause a mortal wound to Lloyd Pharmacies and their immoral owner, came gushing from Alexis. The events of the previous night containing all the graphic details had the detectives "eyeballing" each other. Alexis held that they were responsible for Rose Marie's decision to end her life. Emily simply sat and listened, nodding in agreement or shaking her head, very gently, when in disagreement. Her lips now twice their normal size were a perfect compliment to her two bulging, black and blue eyes and the lovely reddish pink long horizontal cut on her forehead.

"Well ladies, we thank you for you cooperation. After hearing your story, I believe we can put the investigation to rest," said Gillis. "You've committed no crime that I'm aware of at least according to the laws of the Commonwealth of Massachusetts. How you two deal with the consequences of your actions is up to you and your consciences. I'm not even going to ask about your appearance, Mrs. Lloyd and Miss Take; however, I will offer you transportation to the hospital should you wish to go."

Emily nodded her head in acceptance, but Alexis graciously declined the offer. Walker and Gillis assisted the loser to the squad car and helped her inside, as the winner asked all visitors to leave the premises immediately. Following the mass exit, Alexis returned to her room and cried herself to sleep.

CHAPTER 36

THE SERVICE FOR ROSE MARIE Lloyd was a private one. Her only family member in attendance was Alexis Take. Miss Take was surrounded by the Russell family and Tara Carleton, the Delvane family, the Arrington twins, Rose Marie's former boyfriend, Patrick Cross, and sister Joan-Michael, her counselor at St. Clarissa's. A short, religious service was held at Samuel's Funeral Home on Ocean Street in front of the closed casket. A longish drive to St. Joseph's Cemetery for the internment followed. The few in attendance more than made up for the lack of mourners with a non-stop flowing of tears, sobs, and moans of agony. JT fell to his knees at the gravesite unable any longer to keep his composure. Jim and Tara immediately tended to him and sat him in a waiting folding chair. JT did not know if he were going to faint. For moments he balanced at that delicate border between consciousness and unconsciousness. Of all things, his guilty conscience finally returned him to consciousness. Could he have, should he have handled their relationship differently? Had he done so, perhaps they would not be at this place today. The few in attendance there assisted each other in completing their duty of laying poor Rose Marie Lloyd to her final rest. The mourners trudged back to their vehicles after sharing farewell hugs and headed off in separate directions back to their world of the living.

That night JT found sleep next to impossible. If he had been more intuitive, he would not have even attempted to sleep for when sleep did finally occur, so did the nightmare return. JT and Phong were facing each other with knives drawn. Prior to the encounter, JT looked to see Rose Marie talking with Twan and Tram. She waved to him and mouthed, "I'm sorry, Jamey; I love you." She then returned to her conversation with Cheung's son and wife. Phong smiled at JT and nodded that he was ready. The battle between them was different this night; Tony was there again cheering JT on, but something strange happened in the dream…JT was killed for the first time ever! He watched as Tony and Rose Marie rushed to his side before his eyes closed for the final time. Then the nightmare was over. His eyes snapped open as he shot upright in his bed.

"I fucking need help! I'm going nuts!"

He did, and he was. Fortunately, he refused to allow his stubbornness to interfere with his good judgment. He started seeing a psychiatrist in nearby Swampscott who modified his medication, worked closely with JT on his guilt and fears, and within the course of six months had JT at a new level of daily functioning. He felt reborn. As long as he remained on his medications, he was a new and improved JT. Therefore, being the bright guy that he was, JT faithfully medicated himself precisely as directed. The possessor of an improved lease on life, JT, forged with encouragement from Tara and his father, began to explore career opportunities. His Uncle Richard had offered to introduce him to a Lynn School Committeeman friend of his when JT had first arrived home. A call to his Uncle Richard led to a visit to the gentleman's home. The time was not wasted. Because JT did not possess a teaching certificate, he had two options: He could return to school, take the courses he lacked, and intern for several months in a classroom under the supervision of a cooperating teacher, thereby securing his certification. The second option required having the good fortune to obtain a waiver from the Commonwealth in order to accept a teaching position at which he would remain for six consecutive months, undergo a series of three to six evaluations by the principal of that school, then apply for permanent teacher certification status. It was a good news/bad news type thing for JT to hear. He definitely was opposed to returning to school for he knew at that point in time he lacked the focus and drive to be a student again. The second option piqued his curiosity. He would be earning a living at the same time he was earning his teaching credentials. Thanking the committee member profusely, he and his uncle left the meeting with an appointment in hand to meet with the Deputy Superintendent of Elementary Education of Lynn Public Schools, Dr. Horace Clifton, on the following day.

JT ambled around the administration building looking for the correct office, tried to maintain his nervous tension, and prayed not to sweat through his suit. Locating the correct office, JT greeted the secretary with his usual good humor that appeared totally lost on the woman. She neglected to look up at him for what seemed like minutes, and when she did look up her stone faced countenance did little for JT's confidence. Of course, he knew nothing of the secretary or her attitude problems. It was not up to him to judge her in the way she went about her business. He had no idea that this worn, older, fairly attractive woman had been so beaten down by her job and her interaction with Dr. Clifton on a daily basis. Finally, she directed him to have a seat, reminded the deputy superintendent of their appointment, and returned to her typing. Ten minutes later and perhaps one minute from JT's total perspiration saturation, he was invited into the office.

He thought to himself, "What's the big deal here? I've killed men before!"

Dr. Clifton was a tough interviewer. JT immediately identified his game as intimidation. He tried to put his visitors on the defensive probably due to a deep-seated sense of insecurity, social ineptness, or an inferiority complex. JT impressed the hell out of himself with that thumbnail sketch of his adversary and the speed in which it took shape in his overly burdened brain.

"He doesn't know he's dealing with a psychiatric patient who was a psychology major. Bring it on, Horace, I can be just as crazy as you," surmised JT.

JT did not back-up once during their verbal sparring match. He looked the man in the eye, which seemed to make the educator uneasy;

he gave clear, cogent answers to the interrogator's questions; he even made the man crack a smile or two. As weird as it seemed to JT, he and his perspective boss clicked.

"Well, Mr. Russell," began the now much friendlier Clifton, "if by the close of school tomorrow, you are able to present evidence from the Department of Teacher Certification that you, in fact, have the qualifications to be certified a teacher by the Commonwealth, I will offer you a position in the school system that will allow you earn that certification."

JT could not contain himself. He hugged the obviously embarrassed educator. He then shook his hand and exited quickly on his way to Boston.

"Sir, I'll see you tomorrow. Believe me, Dr. Clifton, I will be here. I want this to happen more than anything."

He did, and it did.

CHAPTER 37

ALTHOUGH THEY STILL RESIDED IN the same house, at least for the moment, Alexis had not seen Emily since the fight of the century. The firing apparently had been sincere since Alexis's Lynnfield store position now belonged to another. She suspected that the next assault would be an eviction notice so she went about getting her finances in order and her possessions prepared for transport. As Alexis entered her bedroom, she was shocked to see several vases of red roses positioned about the room. The all too familiar stationery of Emily Lloyd was also present to her utter surprise.

"What could that bitch possibly say to me? If I had had a gun that night, I would have blown her fucking head apart!"

Still, the curiosity of a woman would not permit her to destroy the note and be done with her forever. Opening the communication rekindled some old feelings from a kinder, gentler time, or a time that she convinced herself was such. The hand and the smell were Emily's without question.

Dear Alexis,
I am writing to you to apologize for my callous behavior when last we met. I regret that my actions brought to a conclusion such a rich, beautiful relationship as ours. I am very much still in love with

you, Lex, and I want us back together. Perhaps, we will be able to turn back the hands of time to shortly before that terrible night and rediscover the lovely moments we, two, have shared. Please give my words serious consideration. I have never been more sincere about anything in my entire life. Lex, I need, want, love, and lust for you. I pray you find it in your heart to forgive me and reenter my now miserable existence. Please contact me soon. I cannot go on like this.

Love,

Your Emily

The pieces of paper, like snowflakes, floated to the floor after having been ripped into micro-pieces by Alexis and tossed toward the ceiling.

"Sure, you horny fuck, I'll forgive you," she murmured to herself. "I'll forgive you when I'm squatting on your fucking grave pissing on you."

Composure, her composure, was the key to her revenge. In her mind, she owed Rose Marie more than she could repay, but dealing with that miserable fucking excuse for a human female required that Alexis be well prepared and devoid of the boiling caldron of emotion that burned deeply within her.

"In due time, Emily, you will receive everything that you deserve," she thought out loud.

In Las Vegas, a much older and wiser, now head of the family, Bruno Bernardi received a call from an Alexis Take. Not knowing who that was, he refused to accept her call. The same thing happened five more times over the next two days until he finally received a call from Rita Bowles!

"Who the fuck is this?" inquired the aggravated crime boss.

"You don't remember old friends, Bruno?" teased the voice at the end of the phone line.

"How do I know it's really you, Rita?" he asked gruffly.

"Well, how about these clues, Bruno: Negro baby, left ball a little larger than right, shaved my private parts with your knife..."

"Rita, you bitch, I told you...."

"Yeah, I know Bruno, but we're both older and wiser now. We're a lot closer to the grave than before. I want to set things right with you."

"Fuck you, whore!"

"You used to love to didn't you, Bocce Balls? Do I hear a trace of hostility in your voice, love?"

"What the fuck do you want from me, '*mulignane*' lover?" he sneered.

"I told you, old friend, I want to set our record straight," she lied.

"Why now after twenty years, do I hear from you?" he asked starting to soften his tone.

"You did tell me that you never wanted to see my face again, lover."

"Yeah, that's right", he whispered regretfully. "I hated you for what you did."

"Well, Bruno, I have a confession to make. There never was a Negro baby, love," she started to cry. "It was our baby, and he died on his birthday, Bruno."

"No, '*moolie*' knocked you up?"

"No, my sweet Bruno, it was a ploy. I didn't know how to get away from you alive. You were physically killing me. You were too much man for me, Bocce Balls."

"You're sure it was our kid? And a boy? He died?"

"Yes, I am more than sure. I have experienced the pain of our baby's loss every waking moment since the time of his death, Bruno. Now you know, and I ask your forgiveness."

"Where are you, Rita?"

"Massachusetts."

"Will you see me?" he asked tentatively.

"First, do I have your forgiveness, Bruno?"

"I never stopped loving you, Rita, even at the worst of times. If you are being honest with me now and swear on the soul of our son, I will not only forgive you, but I'll come to see you."

"I'd like that very much. But there is an ulterior motive to my calling you after all these years, Bruno. I want someone dead.

CHAPTER 38

A CLASSROOM TEACHER OF ENGLISH as a Second Language for children ten years of age and over was JT's reward from Dr. Clifton for his rabid perseverance and staunch determination. The location of his new position was at the T. Lewis Carroll Community School on Blossom Street, the site of what turned-out to be his home away from home for the next thirty-something years. The large rectangular-shaped two-story building appeared in excellent condition considering its 1914 unveiling. The cream-colored brick exterior and its white-painted cement trim looked particularly striking to JT at first sight. The building was located in what was termed "the brickyard" section of Lynn. This area had been a culturally rich section of the city where families of every nationality came to settle. This "melting pot" of a neighborhood developed into a proud, hard-working, loyal group of citizens to mother Lynn, and although the identity of this section of the city had faded over the years, those who grew up in the "brickyard" wore their hearts on their sleeves when it came to discussing their roots. The entire building was surrounded by schoolyard space and was enclosed by fencing. Inside there were ten classrooms on each floor, an auditorium with a balcony, a full gym, a cafeteria, a main office, an ominous looking boiler room, a custodians' office and a teachers' lounge on each floor. The interior woodworking reflected the craftsmanship of a time long passed. JT pretty much fell in love with the place at first sight.

Room 4 housed the oldest group of non-English speaking learners. The ESL program was comprised of three classes: Level 1, Mrs. Chadworth's class, contained kindergarten/first grade-aged students. Level 2, Mrs. Waldron's class, contained second through fourth grade-aged students, and the newest addition, Mr. Russell's Level 3 class, contained fifth/sixth grade students and up. The job description was clear enough. Prepare the non-English speaking and limited-English speaking students to enter a regular self-contained classroom with the skills required of them to function successfully. As with everything else in his twenty-two years of life, JT threw himself head first into his new challenge and found he loved it. Not only was his new job interesting and challenging, but also the city actually gave him money to do it. His first full-week's paycheck bought presents for Jim, Charlie, Bina, and Tara. His first $106.00 weekly check in his possession, a job that he could not wait to go to each day, a supportive, loving family, and a girlfriend who loved him more than anything in her world, JT Russell had actually found happiness. The combination of his quick wit, good looks, and intelligence allowed him to be accepted readily by the veteran staff at the school. He was by far the "baby" in an impressive group of educators at TLC. Women, by far, outnumbered the men on the community school faculty probably five to one, but that was more good news for JT because for some reason, totally lost on him, women loved him. He, in turn, loved women. He loved everything about women, not only the obvious physical things. Their thought processes, so different from their male counterparts, enchanted him. He was envious of the way they were able to express themselves emotionally and openly. He adored the way they pretended not to be "randy little tarts" when, in fact, JT believed that a group of women friends would always "out-raunch" a group of men friends every time. However, the females would do it in such a well-mannered fashion. Finally, their femininity was perhaps that which he loved most. Having a mother and sister who epitomized the feminine side of women, it was no wonder he sought-out such a trait in potential mates. In Tara Anne Carleton, JT had struck the mother lode of femininity!

CHAPTER 39

ALEXIS HUNG-UP THE PHONE, TOOK a deep breath, and relaxed in her chair. If calling Bruno had not been the most difficult task she had ever performed, it was in the top two or three of her lifetime. She thought it went well, in fact, so much better than she had anticipated. A smile came to her lips, the first since Rose Marie's passing. Then musing to herself, "*Well, Rita/Alexis, the murderer who passionately hated you for the past twenty years now knows exactly where to find you – good thing or bad thing? The incredibly delusional/psychotic woman with whom you shared your body and love wants you back – good thing or bad thing? You are unemployed, though not impoverished, but you have no security or roots remaining in your life – good thing or bad thing? You just entered into a 'devil's deal' with the mob to have a fellow human being, regardless of the quality of that person, killed – good thing or bad thing? You certainly have been a very busy little girl of late Miss Take/Bowles.*"

The thrust of the conversation with Bruno resulted in a plan that had him coming to Lynn two days hence to visit with his former love. The impression she received over the phone brightened her outlook on their future relationship; however, any life with "Bocce Balls" would present her with the same physical problems that caused her to leave the first time. She thought to herself, "Am I doing it wrong? Have I opened-up that proverbial can of worms never being able to put the lid on it again? Look, anyone can second-guess. You put up your money, dealt the cards, now play the hand to its conclusion. 'Que sera, sera' as the old song says, right?"

Alexis received directions to leave a photograph of Emily Lloyd in a large manila envelope addressed to Mr. Smith at the Hotel Everson in downtown Lynn. In addition, outlines of her comings and goings, work schedule, and after-work habits were to be included. Alexis did all of that immediately. She was now to re-establish communications with the lovesick Emily Lloyd and help put her at ease in her day to day living. A reply to Emily's last note seemed to be the first order of business.

> *Emily,*
> *A note was the last thing I expected from you. On seeing the familiar stationery, I pretty much determined that I was getting an eviction notice. Yes, much has transpired in a very short period. Yes, we were in possession of a relationship that became the center of my life. Yes, we can probably blame our emotional meltdowns for the unforgivable way we treated each other. And yes, now that the dust is settling, the time for healing may be at hand. Yes, let us meet and discuss the past, present, and future. You set the time and the place, and I'll be responsible for the agenda.*
> *Sincerely,*
> *Alexis*

Alexis placed the return note in its customary spot on Emily's make-up table, turned, and walked quickly from the scene of their near-mortal combat. Now her role was to sit and wait – wait for Emily's response; wait for Bruno's arrival; wait for Emily's well-earned death.

A tall, thin, well-dressed man approached the check-in desk at the Hotel Everson.

"Mr. Smith checking-in. You have a room for me right, bud?"

The young clerk behind the desk looked up and was impressed with the Italian-silk suited man standing before him.

"Smith? Mr. A. Smith? Yes, sir, you're in Room 201. I'll have a porter take your bags upstairs."

"No need. I'll carry them myself."

"Whatever you wish, Mr. Smith," said the clerk handing the new customer his key and a large manila envelope. "The envelope was waiting in your box."

"Thank you, bud. Take this for your trouble," the stranger said handing the young man a fifty-dollar bill.

The kid fell all over himself after witnessing the size of the gratuity in his right palm.

"If I can be of further…"

The stranger had already gone on his way.

Alexis telephoned the hotel and found that Mr. Smith had indeed checked-in; however, her attempts to reach his room were fruitless. She left a message for him with the front desk.

> *Mr. Smith,*
> *Should you wish to see me this evening, I will be unavailable until quite late following a dinner engagement at our home with my former boss. Should you wish to contact me for anything, you have my telephone number and extension.*
> *Rita*

Mr. Smith had spent the early afternoon perusing the contents of the manila envelope now in his possession. Hunger called, and he dressed to find a local eatery. At the front desk, the same clerk saw the generous stranger leaving the hotel. He called to him that he had a message. The now smiling clerk handed the note to Mr. Smith in anticipation of an additional gratuity. After reading the brief message, he stuck it in his pocket and was about to turn as he saw the clerk's hand reaching out.

"Hey, bud, we're not getting greedy here, are we? Fifty bucks a message is pretty steep, you know? Besides, being greedy can cause a guy only one thing – trouble, capice?"

The trembling clerk nodded and left the desk area for a much-needed infusion of oxygen. As the stranger walked the downtown area looking for a decent restaurant, he formulated his plan for the evening. He had everything he needed, and he had filled the rental car with gas before he checked into the hotel.

"It will be a good night," he said to himself, "if I can find a fucking restaurant that won't poison me."

Later that night, Alexis and Emily sat facing each other from opposite ends of the very long dining room table.

"You're so far away, Lex. Should I take that as a bad sign?"

"Do you mean physically or emotionally, Emily? Because right now, I am where I believe I should be. Let us not evaluate each other's every word, movement, and gesture, Em. Let's just try to enjoy each other's company and let nature take its course."

Lifting her wineglass, Emily proposed a toast, "To old times in hope that they'll return".

They drank to each other and were replacing their glasses when Alexis noticed a movement behind Emily. A tall thin man holding a handgun with some kind of long device on its barrel made his way quickly and quietly into the dining room.

"Sorry to interrupt ladies, but I have business with Mrs. Emily Lloyd which is you, correct dear?"

"What the hell is going on?" thought Rita. "Who is this?"

Without hesitation, the intruder stepped to the side of Emily Lloyd, held his gun inches from her lovely head and pulled the trigger! The sound was muted leading Alexis to identify the device on the front of his gun as a silencer.

Alexis threw herself to the floor in fear and protest!

"This is not how it was supposed to be! Who the fuck are you? Does Bruno know you're here?"

The almost headless body of Emily Lloyd twitched and shook as it finally came to rest in a pool of her venomous blood.

"Greetings, Rita, from Bocce Balls. He sends his regrets, but he will not be here tonight. He did want me to read this message to you."

> *My Dear Rita,*
> *I am so sorry. I wish things could have been different, but I cannot ever forgive the death of a male child of mine. If you had stayed with me, we would be enjoying the fruit of your loins together to this day. You fucked-up in the worst possible way, love.*
> *Good-bye, I love you.*
> *Bruno*

Mr. Smith then shot one silent bullet into the forehead of Alexis Take or Rita Bowles. In either case, both of them died at the same time. He placed the handgun minus the silencer in Emily's right hand and pressed his gloved fingers over hers to leave her markings on the weapon. He then made sure that both women had ceased to exist, searched the area for any witnesses, and took a piece of rolled beef from the table and ate it as he exited the way he entered. Chef discovered the bodies upon reporting for work the next morning. The Lynn Daily Item's headline declared that a murder/suicide at the Lloyd mansion had left the co-owner of a string of many successful area pharmacies and her family's nanny dead.

At the airport hours earlier, Mr. Smith made a very brief call from a pay phone to Las Vegas.

"Boss, it's done."

On the other end of the line, Bruno Bernardi laid the phone in its cradle, placed his hands over his eyes, and cried like the baby he had never seen.

CHAPTER 40

Time passed quickly for JT in his new position. Following the receipt of his teaching certification after the six-month evaluative period, he enrolled in the graduate school program at Salem State College. He began work on his master's degree in education. JT was invigorated. The job was going well. He had become very goal oriented, and he finally asked Tara to share the rest of her life with him. Theirs was a wedding void of tradition. They were married during an evening mass at St. Michael's Church in Nahant, on November 5, 1972, but they opted to forego a reception in favor of quick get-a-way to the Ritz Carleton Hotel in Boston to begin their married life together. Just over a year later, on December 8, 1973, Katherine Anne Russell was born to Tara and James Russell. Katie was a perfect little baby in every way, and Tara was born to be a mother. Fatherhood for JT was more of a challenge then motherhood was for his wife. By his own account, for the first three months of Katie's life he averaged about three hours of sleep per night. He was forever checking on her, watching for signs of her breathing, praying that she would make it through each night. The new father required several medication adjustments by his psychiatrist before he felt relaxed enough around the baby to sleep through the night.

The overriding impression JT received from his job was one of gratitude. Every child in his classroom shared one common hurdle, which was the ability to function comfortably in an alien environment.

He began to view his job as seen through the eyes of his students. How many of these uprooted babies had any choice in the decision making process to change lifestyles as drastically as they had been asked to do? If he were they, what would he need from his teacher to adapt to his new world? What would be some of the potential problems he would face as a student dealing with say a Russian teacher, who spoke no English? By placing himself in the proverbial "shoes" of his students, JT's teaching style evolved. Empathy with equal portions of patience, humor, understanding, and high expectations became his trademark. He labored mightily to establish an atmosphere in his classroom that offered both a sense of security and a productive learning environment to each child. He strived to establish personal relationships with his kids and found many non-verbal ways to do so. The man was not difficult to read. His students took to him as if he was made of ice cream and chocolate. He became their one constant in a sometimes hostile, often times confusing new world. For this, he received their "thanks" offered in so many different ways. What was to be the physical, mental, and emotional cost to JT in totally immersing himself in the lives of his students? He never thought about it for a moment. That was just part of being James Thurber Russell.

September of 1974, was the beginning of the third year of his tenure in an ESL classroom. He felt his first two years went well, but he knew he was learning "on the fly" with his students. For the first time in his brief career, he felt that he was ready to spread his wings in this field, which offered no set curriculum for Lynn's teachers. He was ready to implement some of his own ideas, practices, and theories. This third class was an interesting mixture of cultures: six Greeks, four Hispanics, one Italian, one African, two Asians, and a Russian – a true United Nations of the elementary type. Knowing that the fifteen children, who comprised this class, came to him at fifteen different levels of comprehension and verbalization, the first few days were usually "to the bone" exhausting. Looking back, he blamed this fatigue on his failure to notice one very special student in his class. JT's preparation for each new class involved the review of any and all information available on each new student. Because paperwork was often stockpiled on some secretary's desk, stuck in the parents' folder at the Bureau of Immigration and Naturalization, or simply still in the student's home country, more was known of some children than others. All the available information for each child had to be entered on a City of Lynn Public School Cumulative Record Folder. While completing those folders that year, the name Twan Cheung slipped right by JT. Other than his name, age, and legal guardian, JT had no historical data on the child. Sometime about mid-September, he received documents from an American school in the Philippines attended for a short period by the same Twan Cheung who sat in the first seat third row of his present classroom. Having a duty-free period that day, JT emptied his bulging mailbox and sifted through his mail separating "the wheat from the chaff" so to speak. The official looking document in his hands added greatly to his knowledge of young Master Twan Cheung. Born in Vietnam some ten years ago, Twan Cheung, the son of Phong Ho Cheung and Tram Thi Cheung Lam, both deceased, arrived in this country one month ago from the Philippines under the guardianship of his maternal grandmother, Lai Thi Lam Ho. According to that document, the child was born in the South and departed Vietnam with his mother from Saigon at the age of seven. The document failed to shed any light on the child's travels from that point to his arrival last year in the Philippines. Initially, JT could not see the forest for the trees. He had done a very good job burying his Vietnam experience and those nightmares. Nothing about that new information registered for a few moments. Then in a moment of enlightenment, though this one flavored with horror, the puzzle pieces of Phong, Twan, and Tram fell into place!

"Holy shit! No, this cannot be happening. What are the odds? No fucking way it could be the same kid."

It was.

CHAPTER 41

THE SUN HAD BEGUN ITS daily journey across the September sky. Its streaming light slipped through the sleeping man's eyelids delivering him from a restful yet uncomfortable sleep. Sharing a bench at the train station for the past week, scurrying for food day and night, entering fleeting relationships intended only to keep all involved alive, was now life for Newton Spencer Lloyd III. Rose Marie's death, which he had yet to accept, had pushed the former well-to-do executive over the edge. Sanity was now an alien concept for the man; however, one might argue that when one considered Lloyd's life in its entirety, perhaps he was presently a happier man. Rubbing the remnants of sleep from his eyes, he dropped his protection from the chill of the September evenings. The stained, wrinkled, paper comforter slid from his shoulders to the floor of the train station. He quickly bent to retrieve the day old front page of the Lynn Item, his only protection from the elements, and folded it neatly in sections. As he was about to hide it behind the bank of lockers to have access to it that evening, he saw on the folded papers what looked to be a familiar face. Then he seemed recognize a second face next to the first. Laboring to recollect to whom the faces in print might belong, Newton's memory failed him totally. Therefore, he moved on to the next order of his business. Unable to comprehend the headline that announced the murder/suicide of one Emily Lloyd and one Alexis Take, the unaware and uncaring Newton Spencer Lloyd III hid his protection from the elements behind the lockers, smiled to himself at his ingenuity in doing so, and wandered off to face the challenges of the rest of his life.

CHAPTER 42

PERHAPS THE MOST INTRIGUING CITIZEN of the fair City of Lynn, Massachusetts, to her inhabitants was the former CIA operative who had been held captive in a Chinese prison for nineteen years and was recently released by the Chinese in a politically motivated gesture of friendship prior to President Nixon's historic visit to mainland China. According to those in the know, two American CIA agents on a surveillance/rescue mission over China at the height of the Korean War had crashed. The pilots of the aircraft died in the crash, but the two operatives survived, became prisoners of the Chinese, and stood trial on spying charges. The United States government absolutely denied the spying charge. The captured Americans were found guilty. One received life imprisonment because the Chinese thought him to be the leader having graduated from prestigious Harvard University. The other and older of the two received only twenty years for he had graduated from lowly Blake College. It appeared that the Chinese were higher educational snobs.

Leo T. Leonard of Lynn, Massachusetts, and Blake College, and Bruce C. Fishbain of New Britain, Connecticut, and Harvard University, spent the next nineteen and twenty-one years respectively as prisoners of the Chinese government. After experiencing years of solitary confinement, constant threats of torture, and feedings that barely sustained them, Leonard was released in 1971 at the age of forty-four. Two years later, Fishbain was handed his freedom at the age of forty-three. It had taken all those years for the US Government to do something it could have done on day one, which was to admit to the Chinese something that everyone in the civilized world had known all along – the men were spies and not civilian Army employees. The two returned heroes today hold legendary status with the Central Intelligence Agency for time held captive and living to tell about it.

"Hey, Russell, you were in Vietnam weren't you?" the pompous, self-important, incompetent, special education teacher, Arnold Landers, yelled before a filled teachers' lounge.

"Yup," answered JT curtly not wanting to engage the bore in conversation.

"Listen here, Russell."

JT rolled his eyes to the ceiling knowing he had been cornered. He tried to relax the tension from his body for he knew the bore now had the floor.

"According to this morning's Herald, a millionaire whose son was MIA in Vietnam hired a bunch of military mercenaries to investigate reports that U.S. soldiers were being held in makeshift prison camps in the jungle near the border with Laos. Sure enough, they found the reports to be accurate. Following a bloody battle, fifteen captives were rescued from the jungle prison including, get this, the millionaire's son and a kid from Massachusetts!"

JT shot to attention. To that point, he had allowed the self-absorbed asshole's words to enter left ear, exit right. The mention of a Massachusetts soldier being rescued pumped adrenaline throughout his previously bored to tears body.

"Does it give a name, Arnie, I mean for the guy from Massachusetts?" he spat out, unaware of the emotional fashion in which he responded.

"Let me see. Yeah, down at the bottom the page it says Corporal Anthony J. Delvane of Lynn, Massachusetts was…"

JT heard no more. He slumped to the floor as he lost consciousness. His fellow teachers gathered around him as one went to call for assistance. The principal of TLC, a wise and gentle man, who JT was proud to call a friend after being in his building for only a short period of time, knelt at JT's side applying cold packs to his forehead. The fledging educator fought his way back to consciousness and immediately began to cry uncontrollably. He must have been a sight to his colleagues. Had they known at that moment what he was experiencing, there would not have been a dry eye in the house. Pulling himself together, JT was able to talk, just as the paramedics entered the lunchroom.

"I'm fine, really," insisted JT.

"Hey, Teach, we'll tell you when you're fine, all right?" mused the lead paramedic.

Of course he was fine. He was more than fine. He was wonderful. He would be getting his other half back. Tony had returned from the dead. He had to see the Delvanes. Principal Walter Holloway, a tall, handsome, dark-haired man of forty ordered JT to take the remainder of the day off after the paramedics cleared him medically. His green Toyota steered a course straight for the Delvanes' home not very distant from his school. Cars were parked all over the place. It looked like a bad used car lot. Apparently, the word had circulated quickly – Tony was alive!

JT ran into the Delvanes' house as usual without knocking, took the red-eyed Jessica Delvane in his arms, and held her as if letting her go would cost him his life.

"Jamey! He's alive! I knew it! I told your Mom! He's coming back to us, Jamey!"

Mario Delvane walked over to the two and added his strong arms to their embrace.

"He's coming home, kid. He's coming home. Things will be just like before, right Jamey?"

"You bet, better than ever, Mario," whispered JT.

He was so wrong.

At a military hospital in the Philippines lay the newly released prisoner of war, Corporal Anthony J. Delvane, in a restless, dream-filled sleep. The nurse had no choice but to awaken him because his rigid course of medication required him to ingest the chemicals at precise times.

"Corporal Delvane, awake please, it's time for your medication," cooed the highly attractive army nurse. "Now be a big boy and swallow everything," she flirted to a non-interested Tony. "You know, Corporal, I haven't seen you smile since you arrived here. Perhaps this news will do the trick. The doctors say that you'll probably be home for Christmas, Corporal."

There was no response from the stone-faced figure on the bed.

"Won't that be great? Christmas at home with your family."

That time he felt obliged to reply.

"Yeah, lady, happy fucking holidays! I am going to ask Santa-fucking-Claus for a new right leg and a new left eye. Merry fucking Christmas to me!"

The shocked nurse dropped her eyes to the floor, picked up her refuse, and left without turning back.

"Christmas, fuck that, why didn't they just let me die in the fucking jungle?" lamented the distraught soldier.

Tony could clearly remember how he ended-up in the jungle prison. The firefight on the night that JT died was not as clear to him at all. He remembered standing back to back with his friend, and then they were separated, each involved in his own battle for survival. Tony remembered how he quickly dispensed of his opponent, and then turned to look for JT before he engaged a second attacker. Tony was less fortunate with this opponent having received a bayonet wound above his right knee. He could still feel the blade enter his thigh sending shock waves through his already hyper-tense body. Pulling the blade from Tony's leg, his opponent then used the butt end of his rifle to hit Tony in the head twice across his left eye. He folded up and dropped to the jungle floor as if he were dead. The next thing he could remember was a return visit by the enemy seeking-out prisoners. Only he and the millionaire's kid, whom he unmercifully verbally abused all through basic training and there in Nam, were loaded on stretchers and removed from the scene of the carnage. The Vietnamese threw the others into a quickly created mass grave. The journey was torturous. He prayed constantly to be put out of his misery. His wounds were now festering and life threatening. Upon arriving at their destination, their Viet Cong conquerors tossed them into what seemed to be a bamboo constructed corral. Several inhabitants of the prison attended to the two new arrivals. One of whom, an army proctologist, examined the men. Although not in his sphere of expertise, he was doctor enough to recognize the gangrene that had settled into the newcomer's thigh. However, a butcher could have diagnosed the problem with the same man's eye that lay upon his left cheek.

Gaining the attention of a guard, the M.D. forcefully mentioned Geneva Convention, medical care, medicine, surgeon, all the terms that might strike a familiar note with his captors. Something worked. Moments later, the guard returned with a knife, saw, needle, thread, several towels, and a container of Vietnamese moonshine. The M.D. received his operating instruments as the guard shoved a tray under the door of the bamboo cage.

"Well, gentlemen, we have a decision to make. If this man does not lose this leg as soon as possible, he is certainly going to lose his life. If I operate in this ungodly manner, he is most probably going to lose his life. What say you? I'd ask him, but he seems to be unconscious."

"You're a fucking doctor, man. Do something for him! He's one of us. He didn't fucking ask to come to this shithole country!" yelled one of a group of prisoners surrounding the patient.

"You are correct to a point, Greenberg; however my specialty is operating on assholes, much like yourself."

Several others restrained the angry Greenberg from rushing the medic and held on to him until his anger subsided.

"I apologize, Greenberg, that was very insensitive of me. Please forgive me. On second thought, I should be apologizing to assholes everywhere, shouldn't I?"

Up again rose Greenberg as if to defend his honor. Once again he was restrained.

"Thanks, Greenberg, now I'm in the mood. Let's get this guy fixed up," smiled the medical man.

Major Snow, the proctologist turned jungle saw-bones, explained the part each of those present would play in the operating theatre. The key to the success of the operation was to keep the patient from bleeding to death. Snow had several men locate coconut-sized rocks, which they placed in an open fire. The rocks, he hoped, would serve to cauterize the wound once the leg had been removed. The problem was in the logistics of transporting the hot rocks from the fire to the patient. Appleby, a quiet, ex-waiter from New York suggested using the tray on which the operating instruments were delivered along with a few sets of their chopstick eating utensils for maneuverability.

"All right, Appleby, you're in charge of rocks and sticks. Pick two guys to assist you," ordered the doctor.

"The other major problem is the patient waking up," frowned the surgeon. "This guy will enjoy the operation much more if he is unconscious. Greenberg, you want to hit someone. If this poor bastard moves an eyelash – by the way you are a righty, correct – if he even appears to be coming to, I want you to hit him on the left side at the point of his chin as hard as you wanted to hit me. Look, Greenberg, do not be shocked if that hanging eye tears off. We will worry about that later. Are you up to it? Sure you are. Just think of me. The rest of you guys who have the stomach for it will be holding the patient down, just in case…"

Using the knife now sanitized with jungle-made moonshine, the surgeon cut the unconscious young man to the bone. He then began to saw as quickly as humanly possible through the bone.

"Get those fucking rocks ready, Appleby!"

As he had feared, the patient began to feel the excruciating pain. Six men were holding him down when Greenberg stepped to the plate. He pulled his fist back six inches and rocketed his right fist at exactly the designated place. The patient moaned and lost consciousness. His eyeball hit Moseby, the first holder on the patient's right-hand side directly in the mouth! Following a few moments of nausea all around, the doctor had the leg removed. Appleby and his assistants sacrificed their own body parts to roll the burning rocks toward the openly gushing lower thigh. More jungle juice over the rocks cooled them a bit, and the patchwork surgical procedure was working as advertised.

"It's working, right doc?" questioned the now composed Greenberg. "The blood is slowing down big time!"

"One more rock, guys. We've still got to slow this baby all the way down!" called out Major Snow.

The flowing was controlled. The last of the jungle juice was used to clean the area around the hanging connections to the lost eyeball. The doctor cut away the nerves and ligaments that remained.

"Cook me up a small rock, will you, Appleby? I want to use it on the eye socket bleeding," yelled the incredibly fatigued surgeon.

The fact that he made it through the operation alive was a miracle. To see him actually improving steadily could be compared only to the raising of Lazarus from the dead. From then until the night of their escape from their captors, the new guy had no other name except Lazarus.

CHAPTER 43

"MR. RUSSELL, MAY I PLEASE have a drink of bathroom?" requested Twan in what he thought was appropriate English.

"Whoa there, little man. I do not think you would like that. Twan, in English we say, may I get a drink of water. We say, may I go to the bathroom, but we do not say, may I have a drink of bathroom, buddy," smiled the amused teacher.

He received a huge toothy smile in return and sent the little boy out of the room. The majority of students in the room, all of whom were at a more advanced level than Twan, shared a good-hearted laugh at the cool little kid's expense.

"Good try, right kids?" asked the smiling educator. Do you remember when you would say things like that? Sure you do. Back in September and October, Angeliki would come to school each morning, walk into the classroom and say, Good-bye, Mr. Russell. Sergio kept asking me for a piece of water. Juana would smile at me and say, Excuse you, Mr. Russell, for me. Kids, we are all in this together so let's enjoy ourselves. Besides, the one thing I know for sure is that you will be speaking better English than I speak by the end of this school year."

After school that day, Twan was the last to clear his desk, pack-up, and head out the door. On that day, he was obviously delaying his departure. He walked to the blackboard where JT was busy copying the class work for the next morning. JT turned around suddenly, saw that mop of hair, that big toothy grin, and jumped back in surprise.

Twan stepped forward and wrapped his arms around JT.

"Mr. Russell, you are best friend for Twan."

JT smiled back at his admiring little student, placed his hands on his shoulders, gave them a squeeze, turned him about, and playfully kicked him in the pants as he left the room.

"Twan," JT called out, "you're my best friend too."

The choked-up teacher completed his duties, packed his briefcase, and headed out the door shaking his head.

CHAPTER 44

"WHY DIDN'T YOU JUST LET me fucking die? Who made you God, Major? Oh! I am sorry, sir. I should be thanking you, shouldn't I? Well, thank you for allowing this fucking freak to continue to live!"

"Lazarus, it is not uncommon for patients to experience severe depression following a loss of a limb or other body part. You have lived through two traumas under the most extreme of circumstances; I know what you are going through, "commiserated Major Snow.

"Do you, sir? I see two eyes and two legs on your body. How the fuck can you possibly know how I feel? If you really give a shit about me, you will help me end this miserable life instead of allowing me to exist as some sideshow freak. Kill me, damn you! Kill me! Kill me, please!" screamed the young man until he exhausted himself and fell into a deep sleep.

That jungle prison became their home for almost five years, and each of those years enhanced the anger and self-disgust of the man known as Lazarus. He failed more than a dozen times to end his life. The pathetic soul redirected the hate he felt for himself to the other prisoners in general and his captors in particular. Let it suffice to say that Lazarus did not have enough votes to win an election for prison compound president. His act had gotten very old, very quickly. Everyone in that prison had perfectly rational reasons to hate their circumstances, but to a man, they felt that the new guy was drowning himself in self-pity and brought down everyone else around him. Life was tough enough. That soldier was making it unbearable. When prisoner morale appeared to be at its lowest, the rescuers arrived! At dusk without the least warning, shots began to ring out all round the compound. The prisoners scattered in all directions seeking cover. They watched in glee as several of their captors yelped as they began their trip to join their honorable ancestors.

"Holy shit! Whoever is shooting is on our side!" yelled a smiling Major Snow to Appleby.

The thoroughly surprised prison guards were initially target practice for the unknown attackers. Gunfire seemed to be coming at them from all sides. The attack, having interrupted the evening meal, was well underway by the time the diners were ready to respond. Explosions occurring concurrently from the north, south, east, and west brought down barbed wired covered bamboo fences, blew huge holes in the guards' compound, and toppled the lookout tower, which the enemy obviously had not been using lately. Following the salvo of ground shaking explosions, an assault of gas canisters commenced. On the heels of the debilitating gas attack, the attackers revealed themselves. Perhaps twenty men in camouflage dress each wearing a gas mask and carrying a second one rushed the prison from three sides. Every Asian was a target. Machine gun fire lit up the now dark sky. The screams of agony as death came to pay a visit intertwined with the victorious bellows of the attackers. The final battle lasted a few minutes; the bad guys knew it was over so they stuck their hands up over their heads and stooped down into a submissive pose. The attackers would have none of that. The carnage on the way to release the prisoners was eye opening. Body upon body of former captors lay dead or in the final stages of life. The commander of the outpost along with his personal protection staff of three stood in the center of the former prison camp laboring for air once chased out of hiding from their now fallen jungle hellhole. The attacking angels of mercy searched out the prisoners and upon finding them, fitted each with a protective gas mask. The battle was over. The guns were silent. By count, fifteen ex-prisoners survived. They thanked their saviors with hugs and tears of joy. Their rescuers, in return, allowed them the honor of placing the prison commander and his staff of three – the only bad guys remaining--on trial for their crimes against the living and dead members of their pathetic brotherhood. Tried and sentenced in moments, the duty of carrying out the sentence went to the former prisoners. Of the fifteen survivors, nine accepted weapons from their liberators. The man known as Lazarus walked toward the company commander slowly maneuvering his makeshift crutch that served him well for all those many years. He stopped before the restrained officer who was in the control of the rescuers. He guided the bayonet toward the crying man's face. With a twist of his wrist, he plucked the left and then the right eye from his head. Screaming in utter agony, the officer begged for death. Lazarus granted his pleas by digging his blade into the man's stomach and ripping upwards gutting the commander. The former prisoner's anger did not stop there; he stabbed the now near death body repeatedly until the rags he had worn for all his imprisoned years were soaked with the man's life fluids. The remaining three prisoners who soiled themselves watching that demonstration of man's inhumanity to man were not going to wait to be butchered. All three broke free of their captors and were machined-gunned down after several steps. One nightmare ended for the newly freed captives. A second was to begin involving their readjustment to home and family.

CHAPTER 45

THERE WOULD BE NO WELCOMING home celebration for Anthony J. Delvane, at least not immediately at any rate. Following his transfer from the hospital in the Philippines, he was to be located at the Veteran's Administration Hospital in Charlestown, Massachusetts. There he would be fitted for and taught to use a prosthetic leg. In addition, the fitting for the prosthetic eye would be taken care of there as well. Upon relocating at the hospital not far from his home city, he refused to see anyone, including his mother and father, until he was in one piece again. Therefore, Jessica and Mario Delvane were limited to telephone conversations with their son for the immediate future. The nurse in the Philippines was correct. He was going to be home for Christmas, but he was not going to be at home for Christmas. Depending upon his mood, he would accept short calls from only his mother and father. Tony would discuss his progress in the hospital, but he did not wish to hear or discuss family, local, national, or world events. Jessica became more distraught by the week. That person she spoke with ever so briefly was not her son, at least not the one she sent off to war. In comforting her, Mario explained about posttraumatic stress syndrome, the psychological torture he may have endured, and the time he may require to adjust to his new appearance before he was ready to return to his home. Following long and frequent conversations, both of them agreed that they should seek counseling if either or both were to survive this period.

Christmas and New Years Day of 1975 passed without the reemergence of Tony "Lazarus" Delvane. Martin Luther King's birthday, Ground Hog Day, and Valentines Day also passed without a sign of the marine hero. With Easter approaching on the calendar, a mellower Tony Delvane set a goal for himself.

"On Easter Sunday, Lazarus will rise again from his grave," he vowed to himself.

He shared this timeline with no one. His was a self-imposed deadline. He vowed to walk without a hint of a limp and learn to keep his shiny new eyeball from rolling around in his head. He diligently worked the therapeutical routines assigned to him, and then he "pushed" his physical therapist to allow him to do more. For the first time in years, there were times when Tony felt no anger, no hostility, almost a calmness that had been missing from his life for so long. The conversations with his parents lasted longer and were more cordial. Their counselor had suggested that such might be the case. The Delvanes held out hope for the first time since Tony's return. Honoring his wishes, no one other than his parents communicated with Tony, and he initiated all conversations. During one such conversation with his parents two weeks before Easter, Tony learned the truth about one of the terrible falsehoods with which he had been living.

"Beside you, Ma and Dad, the only other person I wish I could talk to is Russ. I miss him so much. Was he buried at home?"

Jessica looked in shock at Mario who was on a second line.

"Tony, what do you mean?"

"Did the fucking Marines send my best friend's dead body home to be buried, Ma, or is he lying out there in some fucking shithole dug by a bunch of gook bastards?"

"Tony, Jamey is home, alive!" blurted out Jessica.

"What are you saying, Ma? I saw him lying on the ground with a knife in him!" the now utterly confused soldier replied.

"He's alive, son, and he can't wait to see you," added Mario Delvane.

Tony dropped the phone, broke into a massive grin, and screamed, "Russ, you bastard, you made it! You made it! Thank God, buddy."

Picking up the phone again, he asked his parents if they were playing with him. He would not stand for such a thing. He wanted to see JT. He needed to see JT. He asked his parents to arrange it for him.

"I want to see the three of you, right away, all right?" yelled the completely overcome with joy patient.

The next day was not soon enough for Tony. His physical therapist worked him out on the Stairmaster, helped him put on his dress blues, and popped in his new eye. Then he waited. From early

morning to late afternoon he had eagerly anticipated their arrival. Shortly after four o'clock, Corporal Anthony J. "Lazarus" Delvane was informed he had visitors. He rose from his chair, adjusted his uniform, and asked his nurse how he looked.

"Good enough to eat, handsome," she flirted.

"Let's talk about that later, Lorraine," he teased back.

Jessica and Mario went in first obeying the hospital's not more than two visitors at one time policy. When they witnessed the decorated marine before them in full dress, both halted in their tracks and cried into each other's shoulder. The marine then moved toward them without a hint of a limp, grabbed them in his arms, and squeezed. They shared kisses followed by more kisses. They could not get close enough to each other. While outside of Tony's room, a nurse approached JT. Her identification badge identified her as Lorraine Swift.

"You must be JT," suggested the nurse.

"And how would you know that, miss?" quizzed JT.

"Well, Tony forever talks about his other half being as good looking as he is and you certainly fill that bill," cooed the attractive care giver.

"Why are you out here alone?"

"They are your rules, m'am. I'm just following orders," saluted JT.

"Screw that, buddy. Get your ass in there where it's needed!" encouraged the nurse.

He thanked her with a hug and gently pushed open the door. Five extremely wet, red eyes looked at him as he entered. Tony told him not to move, released his hold on his parents, and walked directly to his best friend. He grabbed JT around the neck.

"I thought you were dead, Russ. I thought we were over!" lamented Tony in a wave of tears.

"You thought I was dead? Shit, we already had a burial mass for you, buddy," mocked JT as the tears flowed over both of them. The four embraced, kissed, and cried until they were hugged, kissed, and cried out. They spoke of that day as being a new beginning for all of them. They saw no sign of the hostile, self-pitying, angry man who had been on the other end of all the phone calls. The visit was much longer than hospital regulations normally allow, not that this foursome cared.

As the visit concluded, Tony held his parents hands and looked directly at his friend, "Where's Easter dinner going to be? You are going to pick me up, Russ. Please invite Tara, Rose Marie, and your family, Russ. It is finally time to celebrate. The two Lazaruses have returned from the dead."

CHAPTER 46

FOLLOWING THE DEPARTURE OF HIS last student, JT turned from his paperwork to answer a knock at his door. Two women of Asian decent walked into the room toward his desk. JT stood to welcome the two visitors. One was a short, grandmotherly-looking, older woman, very nicely dressed, hair newly coiffed, and a smile from here to there that revealed two gold front teeth. The second visitor was a much younger woman who walked respectfully behind the older woman. Strikingly attractive with long, black, silky hair, the younger of the two women was tall, curvy, and seemed to float as she walked. JT welcomed them with his ever-present smile and asked how he could be of service. Having already focused his attention on the younger woman, JT was all ears as she spoke.

"You are Mr. Russell, yes? I am Mai Lin Sun Lam, and this is my mother Lai Thi Lam Ho", the younger of the two woman began with barely a trace of an accent. "My mother is the grandmother of Twan Ho Cheung, your student. I am Twan's aunt."

JT practically tripped over his tongue expressing his pleasure at meeting the women. Since his "little head" was processing most of the dialogue from his visitors once again, the big head did not register the importance of the visitors' identities.

"My mother felt that she must come to meet the man that her grandson speaks about all the time at home," continued the focus of

JT's attention. "Mr. Russell, you are idolized by Twan. He even wishes to become a teacher, like you, when he grows."

The older woman smiled and echoed, "Twan teacher", and shook her head affirmatively.

JT finally dragged his attention from the lovely vision before him who was doing the speaking for the pair toward the older woman whose smile lit up her face. JT smiled again, nodded his head, and reached to take the grandmother's hand in both of his. The older woman practically swooned at the gesture that brought a smile to her companion's beautiful countenance.

"It is a pleasure to meet Twan's grandmother and aunt. He is a wonderful little boy. He is so smart and eager to learn that his progress has been excellent."

JT stopped to give the translator time to communicate his words to her mother. He was hoping that he did not appear to be staring, but Ms. Mai Lin Sun Lam had the complete attention of "Little JT". As the translator paused, JT resumed his comments.

"I love the little guy. He is so funny and such a fun person with whom to spend time. Twan is so eager to please, hard working, extremely well-behaved; ladies, this young man is the All-American Asian boy."

He paused again, as the grandmother learned the meaning of the teacher's words. The older woman smiled mightily with pride and then giggled at the description. She stepped forward and placed her arms around the surprised JT. He was sure that he was blushing, but not too embarrassed to hope for a similar response from auntie. It did not happen to his everlasting disappointment.

"Please, Mr. Russell, if there is anything we can do to make Twan's transition easier, or if there is anything we can do for you...."

JT did not hear the end of that line because "Little JT" already had his own ending in mind. Once again, the grandmother hugged the flustered teacher followed by the aunt who extended her hand to JT.

The gracious educator took her hand between his two hands and applied a gentle squeeze as his eyes and the eyes of the source of "Little

JT's lust" met and locked. The women turned to leave as JT saw a mop of dark hair peeking around the doorway. As the women exited the room, he heard Twan yell, "See you tomorrow, Mr. Russell."

"Right you are, Twan. Right you are," smiled JT.

As "Little JT" returned to his pre-visitor state, the reality of the recently concluded visit finally registered with the now rationally functioning JT.

"Holy shit! That was Tram's mother and sister, the mother-in-law and sister-in-law of Phong Ho Cheung. They treated me like a member of the family and unbeknownst to them, I murdered Twan's father. I am most probably responsible for Twan's becoming an orphan. Why did I ever pick-up that damn picture and letter? Can I deal with this shit now that they are at my doorstep? Fucking war! Fucking Vietnam! Fucking "Little JT", behave yourself!"

CHAPTER 47

"YOU ARE MARRIED? YOU HAVE a daughter too? Russ, I have been gone a long time."

Tony Delvane and JT Russell sat side by side in the green Toyota as they had so often in the past. JT picked-up the war hero at the hospital, and they headed directly to the Delvane home for Easter dinner. Tony had an all day pass, but he was required to be back at the hospital before 10 PM. Jessica and Mario's counselor offered that the comfortability factor for Tony on his first non-hospital attempt at socializing would increase in his most familiar setting. Therefore, he suggested the locale for the feast. The guest list included the Russells, JT and his family who Tony had just learned about, and the Delvanes. All had ample reason to celebrate this Easter together. Wanting to be unencumbered by all the preparations of cooking, serving, and cleaning up after the meal, Jessica and Mario arranged for a catered dinner by a Revere service that offered Italian food for which Tony would die. Pietro's Restaurant would send its experienced team of caterers to keep the guests up to their ears in veal parmagiana, chicken cacciatore, veal piccatta, eggplant parmagiana, ziti, spaghetti, ravioli, lasagna, meatballs, and sausages. The feast would then conclude with the most decadent selection of Italian pastry the world has yet to see.

Having broken the exciting, good news to Tony about his and Tara's marriage and the birth of Katie Anne, JT felt it was incumbent upon him to break the sad news about Tiffany to Tony. Who else would be better to deliver the news than he to his other half?

"Well, Tony, you heard the good news. Now I have some bad."

"What is it, Russ? Are you okay?"

"Rosie Lloyd is no longer with us."

"Did she leave Lynn?"

"She died, Tony."

The passenger sat silent for a moment, head in hands.

"How did it happen?"

"She killed herself."

"How? When? Where? Oh no, Russ, was it over you? I gave you all that advice on how to handle that relationship, so I'm…"

"No! No, Tony. It was not over me, and you have nothing to do with it. Rose Marie suffered greatly in this sick world, friend. She was too good, too pure. When she could stand the pain no longer, she brought it to an end in her own fashion."

"My God, Russ, "lamented Tony.

"I promise there will be no more good or bad news today. Today is the celebration of the rebirth of the two Lazaruses, you and me, on the day the Lord himself rose from the dead," grinned JT.

The green Toyota pulled into the drive and the "rejoined halves" marched into their old, familiar, stomping grounds. After all the hugging and kissing greetings, the first thing Tony wanted to do was hold Katie Anne. Tony lifted the almost two year old, kissed her on each cheek, and then on her forehead. Not knowing who this strange person was and why he was holding her and crying, Katie Anne responded to the strange person by not crying. She returned his kisses with one of her own.

"You know, man, when we baptized her, I refused to have a godfather present. I insisted on that until the parish agreed that one Anthony James Delvane became her godfather posthumously. Bina and I stood alone in front of the priest as my beautiful little angel, Katherine Anne Russell, received the sacrament of Baptism. I knew you were with me that day. I knew you were there for Katie."

Tony passed Katie Anne to Tara and grabbed his alter ego. They clung together, and as they separated, Tony whispered, "I love you, Russ. Thanks for being you."

JT responded with, "You always had great taste in friends, Delvane. Just how friendly did you get with the boys in that prison camp?"

Tony playfully pushed JT away. "Hey Tony," called JT, "me too, buddy. Me too."

The dinner was wonderful. JT could not remember a more enjoyable time with a closer-knit group of people. Tony, Tara, Bina, and JT entertained their parents with amusing coming-of-age anecdotes, censored appropriately where necessary, of course. They ate themselves into a stupor as they forced the last mouthfuls of pastry down their throats. Then it happened. While serving coffee to the guests, one of the servers, who happened to be of Asian decent, lost his balance when bumped by Mario Delvane in his haste to reach the bathroom in time. The pot of hot coffee emptied on Tony! Fortunately, for him, his prosthesis received the brunt of the spill while he sustained minor burns to his cheek and hands. Tony's eye met those of the profusely apologetic servant. Moving awkwardly to gain his feet, the previously smiling, happy dinner guest assumed the countenance of one appearing to be pure evil. He grabbed the servant by his collar and began to shake him roughly.

"You goddamn gooks! You are no good for fucking shit! I should send you to meet your fucking ancestors, Charlie, just like you sent so many of us to meet our maker."

He slapped the man and sent him to the ground. The stunned group was incapable of action for several moments. JT leaped to his feet and restrained Tony as Charlene and Jim attended to the now crying servant.

"Get your fucking hands off me, man! Do not touch me, ever! I will kill you, man! I'll kill you."

Jessica ran to comfort her son who was now howling obscenities and screaming for assistance from Appleby, Snow, and Greenberg. At the first inclination of trouble, the lead caterer had phoned the police who appeared almost immediately. Witnessing the proceedings, they pushed JT aside and both officers proceeded to immobilize the ranting Tony Delvane. One officer had a headlock on the hysterical man and had to look twice as he watched an eye pop from the man's head! The second officer had the marine secured around his waist until he lost his footing, slid down the man's thrashing body, and lay on the floor with an artificial leg in his arms.

"You can't do this to me! I am a war hero! I am a big deal. I left parts of me in that little shit's shithole of a country. Get off of me."

A shot of a tranquilizer administered by a paramedic brought the situation to a halt. JT explained that his friend had been under hospital care for months. In fact, he was due back there within the next hour. The police unilaterally decided to supply transportation to the hospital for the now sedated Anthony Delvane.

"We'll sort things out in the morning at the hospital," said one of the officers. "Right now, this guy needs to be back there, fast."

The Russells, the Delvanes, and JT followed the police car while Tara packed up Katie Anne and headed for their Bernard Street apartment.

As JT drove in the parade following the police cruiser, he wondered to himself, "What the hell is next?"

CHAPTER 48

"Mr. Russell, my aunt thinks you so handsome," teased Twan Cheung.

"Well, I think she's handsome too, "joked the smiling teacher.

"I say you look like movie star," smiled Twan.

"Really?" mugged JT.

"Yes, sir, Porky the Pig! Ha ha! Ha ha! Ha ha!" The little guy laughed himself into hysterics.

"I'll get you for that, buddy," laughed the amused teacher as Twan returned to his desk.

"I knew she dug me," lied JT to himself in his style of self-effacing humor.

He could use a good laugh right about now. The events of Sunday had left him on edge and discouraged again about Tony's prognosis. He understood the hell one may experience in readjusting to the real world after returning from war. He went through it, and at times, he felt he was still going through it. Considering the extraordinary circumstances of Tony's hideous experiences, who knew the depth and severity of damage, temporary or permanent, done to his psyche? He certainly believed that the man he drove to Easter dinner was not the same man who accosted the server at that dinner. A Jekyll/Hyde allusion rolled through his mind. The one certainty in his heart and mind was he needed to have a healthy Tony back in his life. Now that he had him back, he would do whatever he could to keep him there.

The police did follow-up the complaint the day following Easter as promised. Fortunately, for Tony, the poor traumatized server with whom he tangled refused to press charges probably out of fear of losing his job. Tony's physician and the hospital psychiatrist requested statements from those who were most closely involved in the incident. JT, Charlie, and Jim Russell provided their perspectives during the early part of the week following Easter when they visited with Tony. The young man they observed was clearly not the same happy, good humored, young man with whom they dined on Sunday, nor was he the violent, foul-mouthed, petulant bully who required physical restraint and sedation. The Tony they viewed was unable to relax. He circled his hospital room nervously and reacted to every loud noise. He was incapable of carrying on a conversation that day so the Russell family's visit was brief.

At mid week, Jessica and Mario Delvane were contacted by the hospital as to their availability to meet with Tony's mental health team. After telling the caller that they were at the disposal of the hospital staff, an early morning meeting was set for the following day. Jessica made a late evening call to JT questioning as to whether he could take the day off from school to attend the session with them. He immediately telephoned his principal, Walter Holloway, who understood the situation and encouraged him to attend the session. Walter, himself, would cover JT's class until his return. After thanking his boss, JT telephoned Jessica and arranged for a 7:30 pick-up the following morning.

"Mr. and Mrs. Delvane, Mr. Russell, I can not say that I am shocked by the incident at your home recently," offered Dr. Sheldon Brown, doctor of psychiatry. "Several weeks prior to the scenario that you witnessed we had an episode here at the hospital that required medication to restrain Anthony. A new nurse on his ward attempted to attend to Anthony when he reacted angrily forbidding her to touch him, warning her to stay clear of him, using profanity and racist remarks toward her. The nurse left the ward in terrible distress, and as I said, Anthony had to be sedated. There was a common factor involved in the two episodes. The nurse was, as was your server, of Asian decent. We believe that the horrible experiences Anthony endured during the past five years have done considerable damage to him psychologically. The depth of that damage is unknown at this time. As a staff, we feel it is in the best interest of our patient for him to remain in this hospital's psychiatric ward. He will receive a thorough evaluation. Upon reaching a diagnosis, we shall put in place a treatment program aimed at remediation of his problematic behavior. Following sufficient progress, we will be able to reinstate home visits. Of course, we understand that this is disconcerting to you. You want him home. I want him home, but now, we, as a staff, believe your son is presently a danger to himself, as well as to those individuals who ignite the tremendous anger he possesses."

"Will he be allowed visitations, doctor?" queried JT.

"Following our evaluative period, we will initiate a regular visitation schedule for Anthony," he responded.

"Doctor, how long do you think he will be confined to the hospital?" questioned Mario Delvane.

"I wish I could answer that, Mr. Delvane. We will know more following our evaluation. Are there any other questions?" asked the psychiatrist.

"Doctor, will he get well?" sobbed Jessica Delvane.

"We will do everything in our power, Mrs. Delvane, please believe that. Your boy has given a great deal to his country. We owe him the best that we have to offer," replied the doctor with undoubtable sincerity.

Anthony James Delvane began yet another period of incarceration. The difference between his past and present situations was he was now in the hands of people who cared about him. Yet still, the question of the moment was whether Lazarus had it in him to rise once again.

CHAPTER 49

"Mr. Russell? This is Mai Lin Lam, Twan's aunt. I am so sorry to telephone you at home, but I was not sure what to do. Twan has not returned home from school. My mother is very worried."

JT looked at his wristwatch. "Ms. Lam, its 7:30, and he hasn't been home at all? Call the police right now! I'll go over to the school and search toward your house."

"Thank you so much, Mr. Russell."

"Tara, one of my kids did not get home from school. I'm going to look around."

"Jamey, be careful."

He pulled out of his driveway and immediately applied his brakes. Across the street leaning against the large oak tree directly across from his front door sat a small figure possessing a familiar mop of dark hair asleep against the tree. He leaped from his car, crossed the street, and gently shook the sleeping child. Awakening with a start, Twan was soon flashing that toothy smile so familiar to JT.

"Hi, Mr. Russell," beamed the ten year old.

"Twan, do you have any idea what's going on at your home? Your grandmother and aunt are terribly worried about you. We have the police looking for you."

"For real, Mr. Russell?"

It was impossible for JT to be upset with this kid. His disarming smile, his bubbly personality, and his obvious hero worship left JT putty in the boy's hands.

"What are you doing here, Twan?"

"First, are you mad with me, Mr. Russell?"

"No, Twan, I'm not mad. Everyone is just very worried about you."

By this time, Tara had joined them across the street. She had been watching JT's departure from the living room window with Katie Anne in her arms.

"Is this Twan, Jamey?" asked Tara.

"Who's Jamey?" asked Twan.

Katie pointed to her daddy.

"What's he doing here, Jamey?" questioned Tara.

"I haven't gotten to that point yet, hon."

'You're Jamey? I thought you Mr. Russell," the little visitor wondered aloud.

"It's a long story, kid. Let's go inside," suggested the now relieved teacher.

Two calls were made immediately from the Russell residence. First, JT notified Twan's aunt and grandmother that Twan was safely in his care. After some needed nourishment, he would return his young charge safely to his home. The next call to the Lynn Police Department called off the manhunt for the at large ten-year-old. Twan was like visiting royalty to Tara and Katie. While Tara prepared a meal for the little adventurer, Katie took Twan into her bedroom and introduced him to all her dolls. The two children got along famously. Katie followed Twan around like a shadow.

"Twan, your hamburger is ready. Would you like chips and a pickle?" inquired Tara.

"Yes, I thank you, Miss Russell," smiled Twan. "Are you Mr. Russell's wife?"

"Yes, honey, I'm the lucky girl," teased Tara.

"You are beautiful lady, Miss Russell, and you good cook too," complimented the happy diner.

"Well, Jamey, I can see that you've been teaching him some of your charm lines in addition to the English language," teased his smiling wife.

"Not guilty on that count, your honor. This kid is a natural. He needs no assistance from this old guy in the charm department," responded JT.

Following his meal, a weary Twan smilingly related the events of his day. It seems that a couple of sixth graders had discovered the home address of Mr. James T. Russell. Aware that Twan listened to them talking at lunch that day, the older boys agreed to sell the "hero-worshipping" Twan the highly desirable information for his lunch, two Hostess Twinkees, and two Hershey Bars. In addition, in exchange for his lunches the next two days and fifty cents in cash, they offered to take him to the location. There was no way that Twan was going to pass up that deal. Therefore, he did not. The three boys left directly after school for their destination that was a considerable walking distance. Upon arriving at the appointed place, the two older boys returned home leaving Twan to his own devices for his return trip. The long walk, the hunger pangs, and the dryness in his throat combined to assault the little boy's stamina. He settled himself against a very large tree and began his vigil until he was overtaken by sleep. As the famous radio reporter, Paul Harvey, would say, "And that's the rest of the story."

"It's time to get you home, buddy," ordered his teacher.

"Good-bye, Twan, it was wonderful meeting you," smiled Tara.

"Bye, Twan," echoed Katie Anne.

Twan delivered big hugs to Tara and Katie, thanked his hostess for the meal, took JT's hand and said, "You drive or me?"

The teacher and his young protégé laughed and joked on the drive home. JT made sure Twan understood the message that his antics of the day were wrong and should not occur again, ever. As they pulled up to the three family home which housed Twan's family on the third floor, Twan turned toward JT, threw his arms around his neck, and whispered, "I love you" into his ear. The teary-eyed teacher squeezed his young admirer and whispered, "Me too."

Twan's grandmother was fast asleep, but his aunt had been awaiting his return home since the moment she first called the Russell home. She could not rest until she saw her absent nephew with her own eyes. The friends walked hand in hand up to the third floor, and Twan opened the door to announce he had at last returned. His aunt Mai Lin said something to him sternly in their language that removed any trace of a smile from his face. He turned to JT, hugged him once again, and headed for his bedroom. Mai Lin Lam began to thank JT, but she was so overcome with emotion that she simply walked into his arms and held tightly. It seemed like minutes until she released her hold on him, but in reality, it was only a few moments. She gently placed her lips against his right cheek and then his left, smiled, thanked him again, and wished him a goodnight. She closed the door behind him and he started down the stairs.

"I told you she digs me, Little JT. They all do."

CHAPTER 50

"Good Morning, Mr. Holloway, how are you?" smiled JT as his boss and friend entered his classroom.

"I'm well, Mr. Russell. How are you? I understand you had some drama in your life recently," grinned the tall, handsome principal.

"Are you talking about the Twan Cheung thing?" asked JT. "How did you learn about that?"

"That's part of the reason I'm up here. I just received a call from a Mai Lin Lam; I understand she is the aunt of your 'happy wander' young friend."

"Yeah, he's a great little kid. You've seen him around," replied JT.

"Well, according to his aunt, Twan won't be at school for a couple of days. It seems that her mother has been taken to the hospital, and she needs to keep Twan at home with her until she knows what's going to happen with mama," related Walter Holloway. "By the way, you made quite an impression on that lady. She speaks of you as if you are a deity."

"And your point is…"

"Does Tara know about this chick?" asked the departing principal.

"Thanks for the info and the update, chief. In addition, no, Tara does not know about Ms. Lam. But what's to know, right?"

"You tell me, Studly," laughed Holloway as the door closed behind him.

She died. The grandmother of that poor little boy succumbed at Lynn Union Hospital on Lynnfield Street following her admittance to the hospital two days earlier. Complications following a stroke caused her premature passing according to the information JT received through the school grapevine. Of course, he felt badly about her death, but his primary concern was the welfare of Twan. The child had experienced so much loss already in his life. Why was he inflicted with yet another? Moreover, his guardianship greatly concerned JT. Would his aunt be able to assume the role that his grandmother had handled so well? Would she want that responsibility? JT did not have enough on his mind already, right?

The Buddhist service for Lai Thi Lam Ho was held in her home. The deceased was displayed on her bed surrounded by flowers, burning incense, and religious artifacts. Mourners were allowed to view Mrs. Lam briefly and exit the apartment. Visiting time was at a premium with far too many people and far too little space in the dwelling. JT and Tara arrived at the home and were greeted warmly by a handsome little guy in a suit who hugged both of them and knew not whether to smile or weep. His aunt, her eyes swollen and red, welcomed JT with a hug and a kiss on each cheek. JT introduced his wife to Mai Lin Lam. Tara offered her hand and condolences to the grieving young woman. Twan then led Mr. and Mrs. Russell into his grandmother's bedroom.

"It looks like she's sleeping, Mr. Russell," whispered Twan. "I remember my mom when she died," he continued. "She looked like she was sleeping too. I don't remember my father. My mom told me he died in war when I was little. Why do people have to die, Mr. Russell? Why can't we live forever?"

"That's God's plan for us, buddy. We have to trust that he knows what he's doing," replied the touched teacher rubbing the boy's shoulder. Mai Lin entered the room and walked directly to JT. She placed her hand in his and squeezed – an action not lost on Tara Anne Carleton Russell! JT gently disengaged his hand, and Mai Lin responded by clinging to his arm. If Tara's look could cause male organs to fall off, JT would have been looking for his! JT turned to escort Tara from the room. He said his good-byes, and Tara walked toward the doorway to the stairs. Before he departed, Mai Lin circled his neck with her arms, placed her head on his shoulder, and whimpered, just as Tara turned to see what was keeping JT. An embarrassed JT joined his wife as they walked downstairs to the car. He knew the look. There was a storm gathering on the horizon. Hurricane Tara struck land as they entered the green Toyota.

'What the fuck was that all about, Jamey?" queried Tara in an elevated voice.

He knew she was pissed. He had never heard her use the F-word in all their years together.

"Why was that 'fucking slut' all over you like a loose suit? What the fuck is going on, Jamey?"

"Tara, please calm down. Nothing is going on. She and her grandmother hold me in high regard as Twan's teacher. Both of them seemed to be very emotional 'touchy-feely' people. Perhaps that's a cultural characteristic."

"I didn't see the bitch groping anyone else in the place! Right in front of me! One woman just doesn't do that to another woman! I trust she knows just how very married you are, Mr. Russell, and that you have a two-year old daughter as well as another child on the way!

"She is well aware… What? You're pregnant, Tara?"

"Yes, but at the moment I'm not quite sure whether it's yours or not!"

"Oh, sweetie, this is super news! How far along are we?"

"What do you mean *we*, buddy?" she asked, now grinning. "I'll tell you later when I decide if you're the baby's father or not."

"I love you, Tara Anne Carleton Russell," whispered her jubilant husband.

"Listen to me carefully, James Thurber Russell. You had better have a heart to heart talk with Little JT. There is and forever will be one and only one home for that little bastard."

"Yes, m'am, did you hear that, Little JT? Oh, ok. He said he couldn't quite hear you. Could you get a lot closer to him?"

"If you decide on having Chinese any time soon, I will never look Little JT in the eye again," cracked his suddenly flippant wife.

CHAPTER 51

"JAMES, IT WAS SO THOUGHTFUL of you to invite us over for dinner this evening. We all know the stresses you've been under lately," announced Charlene Russell.

"Well, Ma, there is an ulterior motive to the family gathering this evening," smiled JT.

"If you're going to hit me up for money, kid, do it after I eat," joked Jim Russell.

"Come on Jamey, what's up?" questioned Bina.

He looked toward his sister and saw a woman. She was all grown up. Her twenty-first birthday was very near as was her college graduation. When did that happen? Had he been so absorbed in his own life that he had let the most important people in his life slide into "taken for granted" status? He vowed to rectify that situation immediately.

"Well, folks, Tara and I have an announcement to make. Tara is expecting. Yes, and she just recently decided that I am the father!"

"Jamey, you are such an asshole," smiled his glowing wife.

Charlie left her chair to hug and kiss Tara along with Jim, toting Katie Anne in his arms, close behind her. Bina hopped over to her brother and leaped into his arms.

"Does this mean I'm going to be a godmother again?" beamed Bina.

"Sorry, kid, rules say only one per customer per family, but you'll still be an auntie again," smiled JT kissing his sister's cheek.

Katie Anne hopped about the kitchen as the adults hugged and kissed each other. Her parents had attempted to explain to Katie what was happening, but her age limited her comprehension of the situation. She did understand that a baby somehow got inside her mother's body and someway was going to come out to join her family. She was going to be an older sister to someone at sometime soon.

"Well, folks, now that we have the small stuff out of the way, what are we going to eat in celebration?" smiled a relaxed JT. "I would suggest Chinese, but I value all of my body parts, right sweetheart? So, who would like Italian food? There is a new place across from the old Coca Cola plant."

So Italian, it was, and it was great. While Charlene and Tara cleaned-up and Jim let Katie give him a new hairdo, Bina and JT had a chance to talk.

"So, B, how's your love life?" asked her inquisitive big brother.

"Obviously not as great as yours, big brother," she teased. "Tell me something, Jamey. Has Tony Delvane ever said anything, you know… in that way, about me?" blushed Bina.

"Gee, B, back in college he used to tell me that he wished you weren't my sister. Being my sister practically made you his sister, you know? Why would you ask me a question like that?" Jamey asked already knowing the answer.

"I have had a mad crush on that boy since I was fourteen years old. Seven years is a long time to carry a torch for someone who may not even know you are alive. Don't you agree, Jamey?"

"Abso-fucking-lutely, B, I tell you what. As soon as we get my partner's head straightened out, if you wish, I could play cupid for the two of you," laughed JT.

"Would you really, Jamey? I think that would be wonderful. You are the best big brother ever," she said with a flash of her beautiful smile.

"I bet you say that to all the boys," cracked JT.

"Only the ones I love, Jamey. Only the ones I love."

As Tara was preparing for bed that evening after finally getting Katie Anne to sleep, a very serious JT came up behind her, sat on their bed, and told her that he had something he needed to share with her.

"If you mention that Chinese thing once more, Little JT is going to get kicked in the nuts!"

"No, this time I am being totally serious. I've held this inside so long now that I feel like its controlling me instead of vice versa," lamented JT dropping his eyes to the floor.

"Jamey, is it about us? Are we all right?" asked a concerned Tara.

"It's about me, hon. It's about war. It's about something I'll live with forever. Only now, it's closer to me than ever," related JT as his voice faded.

"The reason I was sent home from Nam was the wound I received in some pretty brutal hand to hand combat. At the time I was so scared that I couldn't think straight. I knew I needed to fight my way home to you, or it was the end of us. The North Vietnamese soldier that I killed was a family man. He never got home to his wife, Tram, and their son, Twan. I know this because I saved a picture and a letter that fell from inside that soldier's helmet; Phong Ho Cheung, the man I killed, and I know the odds against such a thing happening are unearthly, the man I killed is the father of Twan Cheung, my student, my little buddy. I killed his father. I played a huge part in making him the orphan that he is today."

"Hold on, Jamey. This sounds incredible. Are you certain about your information? Could you be mistaken? God, Jamey, of all the enemy soldiers who died in that war the one you fought and killed had a male child who happened to find his way into a Lynn Public School classroom years later to be taught by the man who was responsible for his father's death? Ripley wouldn't even touch that one, honey."

"I know, Tara, but it's true. I've carried it around inside me for the past five years. I still have the letter, the picture, and the knife removed from my shoulder. I've checked and rechecked the records. Twan has to be my Phong Ho Cheung's kid."

She placed her arms around him as he began to weep. He attempted to hide the tears from her, but she refused to allow him to do so. She encouraged him to cry it out, and so he did.

The following day was a Saturday, but Katie Anne did not intend to allow her father to sleep-in. Their Saturday morning ritual of breakfast in front of the TV, so as not to miss one moment of the continuous cartoon programming that had come to mean so much to them as Katie grew older, awaited. After covering his face with good morning kisses, Katie pulled herself up on the bed and sat on her now wide-awake father's chest.

"It must be time, huh baby? The cartoons await," yawned the smiling JT.

"Jamey, go with her to the living room. I'll fix your cereal and bring it in to you," said Tara as she stretched her previously sleeping muscles.

"Stay in bed, hon. You're sleeping for two now," he cracked.

"Just go," she ordered with a smile.

Off to the living room they went, Katie Anne with legs around her father's neck and his hands holding hers was beginning to have to duck as her father walked through doorways in that fashion. She was growing like a weed. The two plopped down on the sofa, turned-on the TV, adjusted the channel, and got down to some serious cartoon watching.

"Jamey, I think you should see this," called out Tara from the kitchen. She stood holding the Lynn Item that she had just brought inside after searching the immediate area outside the backdoor to find where Timmy Plant's erratic throwing arm left it lying today.

"Be right there. I'll be right back, Katie. Don't let anyone take my seat," requested JT kissing his hypnotized daughter.

"You know you're interrupting some serious cartoon time, lady," he teased.

"Take a look at the headline story, lover," she mugged.

Reading the headline aloud for the pretended benefit of both of them, JT's interest was immediately captured.

"Local Woman Arrested in Call Girl Racket," rolled from his lips. "What? I don't need this when I have my own little hooker, baby," he teased.

"Keep reading, Romeo," she insisted.

"A North Shore prostitution ring was uncovered and halted by local authorities yesterday. An undercover operation had been monitoring the group's activities for months. The well-organized, far-reaching, quite profitable agency, under the direction of Ms. Mai Lin Lam of Lynn and comprised of highly paid Asian sex-for-hire females was terminated as undercover agents arrested Ms. Lam in a raid on the organization's Peabody center of operations. Shit, Tara, this is Twan's aunt!"

"I know that," she said sternly. "I knew that bitch had an angle. That friggin hooker was not after Little JT. She was after big JT's money and contacts."

"Do you have any idea what this means, Tara?" asked JT nervously.

"Yeah, genius, I probably saved someone around here a few bucks and a dose of the clap," she cracked.

"No, hon, I'm serious. Now Twan has no one. Mai Lin maintained temporary custody of the kid after her mother passed. If the chick goes to jail, Twan will become a ward of the Commonwealth. He'll be bounced around foster homes until he's eighteen and fucked up! Tara, I can't let that happen! I won't allow that to happen! I owe that kid, Tara. I owe him… a life."

"Well girls, that's the whole story. I have no idea what to do," agonized Tara to her mother-in-law and sister-in-law. "He insists on taking responsibility for the little boy. His guilt is killing him. Perhaps if I were not pregnant and if we had the room, I could support his wish, but I can't because I am, and we don't. I just feel Jamey is doing it wrong by allowing his emotions to rule his brain."

"Tara, do you know anything about the foster care system?" queried her mother-in-law.

"Nothing, Ma, but I have a feeling I'm going to become quite knowledgeable very soon," frowned the pregnant woman.

"Look, we have the room. James' room is available. If Dad and I qualify for the foster program, we could take the boy in with us. James would then have a good, stable environment for the little boy. He would also be able to see and spend as much time with him as he wished."

"Ma, you'd do that for us?" a teary Tara asked.

"First, Dad has to sign-on with this. Then, my daughter," as she nodded to Bina.

"I'm in. I think it would be wonderful to have a kid around the house," laughed Bina.

"What do you think, Tara?" asked Charlene McDonough Russell.

"I think I really lucked out marrying into this family. That's what I think."

No pressure was needed to convince Jim Russell to bow to the wishes of his wife and daughter. His only concern was his and Charlie's age. Were they too old to get involved in something like that for the first time? Would they remember how to parent a child? Lately, all they had to do was spoil their granddaughter, Katie Anne. Before he committed to anything, he felt a family conference was required. The six of them, including Katie Anne, met at Jim and Charlie's house on Oakville Street, just down the street from the Riverworks, the largest component of the General Electric Company's factory in Lynn. JT was amazed at the generosity of his parents' offer. Yet, he was concerned about the demands of raising a child on folks who had been there, done that, and now deserved their due rest. Jim and Charlie insisted not only did they feel up to it, but the challenge excited them. Bina chimed in that she was ready to finally find out what being a big sister was all about. Everyone seemed to agree; however, JT brought everyone back down to earth when he thought aloud that the family might just be placing the cart before the horse.

"We still don't know what's going to happen to Twan's aunt," stated JT. "Most likely, she'll have to do some time for her business venture.

Secondly, how will Twan react to the life we have already planned for him? All I know at this point is that there is a little confused boy with so much love to give and so much life before him temporarily marking time under the supervision of some child protective agency of the Commonwealth. Thirdly, even if auntie does no time, does she maintain custody of Twan after having her gainful profession revealed?"

All at the conference were in agreement. If the child became available for foster care, if the Russells were acceptable candidates for childcare, and if the child was agreeable to the plan, it was full steam ahead for the Russell family.

CHAPTER 52

"How long have I been here, nurse?" asked the highly medicated, one-legged patient with a patch over his left eye. "When will I be seeing my doctor? How long will I be staying here? When is dinnertime? What day is it? Why aren't you answering me, nurse?"

"Mr. Delvane, I answered those exact questions for you not fifteen minutes ago," responded the exasperated caregiver. "I just don't have the time to talk with you at the moment. I have other patients."

"Hey, Delvane," whispered a voice to Tony's left, "I have plenty of time to talk. How about us being friends?"

Tony looked in the direction of the voice. He saw an unattractive man with a pocked face and hair to his shoulders sitting in a wheelchair. Both of his legs had been removed almost to his groin and one of his arms was missing to the shoulder.

"Hey, I hear your name is Tony Delvane, huh? I'm Lucifer, man. If I don't find someone to talk to in this place that's not totally nuts, I'm gonna flush myself down the john."

The visual struck Tony as being incredibly funny. He went on a laughing jag that lasted much longer than was worthy of the remarks.

"Hey, man, I think I like you. You're not totally nuts are you?" asked Lucifer.

"I'm not fucking nuts a little bit. These bastards are keeping me a prisoner in here, but they cannot break me, dude. The gooks couldn't do it. They can't either," sneered Tony.

"Hey, man, if you want to be friends, I know a way to seal our friendship. I get some great 'shit' from outside, you know, smoke, weed. I will share it with you, man. We'll be brothers," smiled the toothless Lucifer.

"Hold on, buddy. How do you feel about gooks?" quizzed Tony.

"I hate'em, man. They done this to me. I fuckin hate'em," responded the wheelchair bound patient turning red with anger.

"Great answer, man. I think we can try being friends, dude. Call me Lazarus," said Tony extending his hand to the sitting man. Tony's new friend took the back of Tony's right hand in his one and only left hand and shook it.

"Please to have you, Lazarus," responded Lucifer smiling once again.

"Hey, dude, why are you called Lucifer?" questioned Tony.

"Because I'm the fucking devil, of course man," sneered Tony's new best friend.

"Meet me in the john after evening meal. We'll get buzzed, man."

Tony nodded and ambled away seeking new adventures in the "through the looking glass world" he now inhabited.

"Who's next Tweedle Dumb and Dee, that friggin grinning cat, or the white fucking rabbit?" an amused Tony thought to himself. "I have to get my ass out of here."

Lucifer and Lazarus became inseparable in time; however, Tony always refused to partake in Lucifer's pot sessions. He had enough chemicals flowing through his body. He clearly did not need additional non-pharmaceuticals messing up his already clouded mind.

"You know what we need, man. We need a plan," suggested Lucifer. "We need to convince these doctors that we're well enough to leave this place. I'll help you; you help me, and we'll get the fuck outta here.

"OK, what's your plan?" questioned an interested Tony.

"Every time you see me acting crazy, doing something like them nuts, you remind me to correct my behavior as soon as possible. I'll do the same for you," theorized Lucifer. "Yeah, that way we'll look like the normal guys in here, and they'll have to let us go home."

"Great plan, Lucifer, you are the Man," congratulated Tony.

"Of course. Why do you think God kicked me outta heaven? He's a jealous bastard," smiled the devil.

CHAPTER 53

By late April things had fallen into place. Jim and Charlene were perfectly acceptable foster parent candidates according to the Commonwealth of Massachusetts. Twan had met and immediately loved both of JT's parents. Although he did confess to his teacher that he would have preferred living with him, Twan was quite capable of understanding about the lack of living space in his and Tara's home. The little boy had spent two weeks in a group home outside of Boston so hearing that he would have a whole room to himself elevated his spirits. He was further excited to learn that Mr. Russell would visit with him each night in his idol's old bedroom. Twan thought this was a great deal. He saw Mr. Russell all day at school, and he saw him again each night. He did not even have to sell his lunch and snacks, or camp outside of Mr. Russell's house to make that happen. The final obstacle and the greatest was the legal system. Mai Lin Lam, in a plea bargain agreement, would serve eight to fifteen months in the Salem County Jail. Upon release, she would relinquish her custody rights to Twan. The Commonwealth performed in-depth interviews and investigations of not only Jim and Charlene Russell, but also Bina, Tara, and JT Russell before giving the stamp of approval to their petition for the foster parenthood of Twan Ho Cheung. The Russell family was expanding, and it was on the verge of adding another member to the mix. Tara was due on or around the first of August. At her advanced stage of pregnancy, her constant discomfort made her wish to be done with it.

Be careful what one wishes for young lady, for one may be granted one's wish. Tara had been experiencing contractions all morning. She had kept a record of time and duration of each contraction in a notebook. When JT arrived home from his summer school job, he found her in great distress. Off to Lynn Hospital, Boston Street branch, they went. The examination indicated that her cervix had begun dilating and had reached four centimeters of the necessary ten centimeters for delivery. Tara was admitted, and both she and the baby were hooked up to monitors. For the next fifteen hours, there was little to no movement on the cervix front and great to horrendous movement on the pain front. Suddenly progress reinitiated. She was close to full dilation. She had received her epidural, and JT was applying cool packs to her forehead, face, and neck. Her doctor popped in, looked under the covers, and got her into a delivery room. As JT was saying good-bye to his wife, just after he had kissed her, the nurse who was following Tara's bed into the delivery room approached JT.

"Well, Mr. Russell, are you going to join us in the delivery room this time?"

"I wish that were possible, nurse," JT lied. "However, my wife and I did not attend the mandatory child birthing classes, so I'm out of luck."

"Not with me around," boasted the nurse. "Let's get you properly dressed, and we'll be inside the delivery room in a minute."

JT did not know whether to shit or go blind! Either would have been a more desirable choice at the time. He feared that he would make a fool of himself by fainting or vomiting, but he was at the point of no return. The now properly attired father-to-be was led into the room where miracles occur. He would need a miracle of his own to get through this day. When they were eighteen years old, JT had taken Tara to a drive-in theater in Medford for a double feature of "The Birth of Triplets" and "Judy's Little No No". He took Tara to all the classic films. Unbeknownst to young JT, "The Birth of Triplets" was an actual film account of a Caesarian section delivery of triplets complete with all the blood, umbilical cords, placentas, etc. that one could handle.

He was near nausea at the drive-in; he truly feared his reaction to the real life drama. As he entered the room, there was only one person more surprised than he to see him there—Tara.

"Doctor, I can't worry about giving birth and losing my husband to a heart attack at the same time," she smiled.

"I am sure your husband will do just fine, Tara. If anything happens to him during the delivery, we will just push him to the side until we are finished. How is that for a plan?" laughed Dr. Spicer.

"Sounds like a plan to me," replied the new mother-to-be.

"Keep up the giggles you two. This is serious stuff to me," complained JT.

JT stood to the side of the room behind and to the right of Tara's head. His beautiful wife, feet firmly placed in stirrups, had a nurse to each side of her. Most of what happened during the next half-hour to forty-five minutes remained a mystery to JT. Aside from all of the "push" commands, the grunts and groans, and what he thought to be a threat from Tara to cut off Little JT, all Big JT was able to do was focus on the familiar opening between his wife's legs which now had a small bald head emerging from it. A few careful maneuvers by Dr. Spicer and shoulders, arms, and hands came into view. Another twist here, and turn there, resulted in the emergence of the rest of JT's second daughter. He stood mesmerized as the doctor suctioned out her orifices then patted her bottom encouragingly to induce her first cry. He stopped breathing until the little girl cooperated. He watched as the cord was severed, and the nurse took the baby to a side table for cleaning and warming. He remembered sidling over to his wife, looking into her smiling face, and kissing her as they both cried. Within moments, the nurse returned with their new daughter and placed her upon her mother's chest. He was never able to describe his feelings during his tenure in the delivery room. Seeing his child being born was a spiritually energizing experience for JT. From the moment of her birth, his daughter and he shared a lifelong psychic bond. He would have missed that once in a lifetime experience if it had not been for a wise, insistent, head nurse.

CHAPTER 54

JESSICA DELVANE PLACED HER PACKAGES on the kitchen table, closed the back door with the toe of her shoe, and, as was her religiously performed habit, checked her telephone messages. The third message was from Dr. Brown at the VA Hospital inquiring as to whether she and her husband would be available to meet with him the following afternoon. First, she called Mario to confirm his availability. Next, she telephoned JT's home to ask him to accompany them once again. Because his mother and Twan had been pulling double duty at JT's house since Veronica Leigh Russell arrived, combined with the half-day summer school schedule he maintained five days a week, he would be able to meet them at the hospital the following afternoon. After speaking with Tony's mother, JT began to feel guilt pangs for he had not given his hurting best friend a thought in weeks. His conversation with Bina about Tony came to mind, and he made a mental note to follow up on it as soon as Tony was well. At the hospital, Lazarus and Lucifer had become inseparable companions. Known to the staff as the "odd couple" since they seemingly had absolutely nothing in common besides missing limbs, the two attended to each other diligently. They had devised a non-verbal system of communication that served to correct the aberrant behavior of the other when exhibited by either one. They exchanged hand signals to inform each other of poor behavioral choices, as well as the severity of the exhibited poor behavior. The first order of business addressed by the cohorts was to modify any overt offensive actions or verbalizations directed toward those of the Asian culture. To listen to the conspirators discuss the logistics, implementation, goals, and modifications to their plan of action, they sounded more like doctors than they did patients. Actually, the improvement in Tony's condition was the subject of the meeting called by Dr. Brown. The thrust of the meeting with JT and the Delvanes was the good news that effective immediately family and friend visitations were being reinstated during regularly scheduled hospital visiting hours. Additionally, Dr. Brown informed the Delvanes that an overnight home visit was in the offing for Tony should his current rate of progress continue. The visitors were ecstatic over the good news, but they were cautioned by Dr. Brown that Tony was still a troubled young man and would require continued medication and psychotherapy. He then informed them of the one negative aspect of his report. According to the psychiatrist, Tony had developed a close relationship with another patient that could negatively impact his progress. The patient, one Edward L. Conrad, was a triple amputee whose diagnosis and dismal prognosis represented a threat to Tony's well being. Obliged to respect patient confidentially, Dr. Brown was prevented from discussing the condition of that patient. He did offer that the man was extremely delusional and criminally violent. After hearing the good news, bad news routine once again, the visitors left with a shadow of concern. The party of three visited with Tony following their meeting with Dr. Brown. The patient was overjoyed to see and touch the people he most loved. JT was impressed with the lucidity and jocularity of his comrade. Tony shared long, warm embraces with his parents, teased JT about being an old, married man, and cried like a baby when told of Ronnie Russell's birth. He appeared so much to be the Tony that they remembered not the maniacal creature they experienced at Easter. An emotion-filled parting, repeated promises by his visitors to see him the next day, and seemingly heartfelt apologies from Tony for his past behavior preceded the departure of the visitors. On the way to their cars, JT, Jessica, and Mario were in wonderfully high spirits. It had been a great day. They felt the worst was behind them. Tomorrow looked to be a brighter day.

"Dude, it is working. My doctor is pretty much convinced that I am improving. You, my friend, are a genius, Lucifer. We are friends for life, amigo," bubbled a very happy Tony Delvane.

"Longer than life, my friend," smiled the smug Lucifer.

"There is a little problem. The doctor is going to try to split us up. He told my folks that you were a bad influence on me. You could hurt my progress."

"That prick, I'll rip the fucking heart out of his chest and eat it. You don't believe that, man. It's you and me, forever, right? Am I right, Lazarus?"

Tony looked into the eyes of the obviously distressed Lucifer. He had not seen him like that before. The man began to hyperventilate. His countenance took upon a red flush, and his body began to shake all over. The man's unkempt, seldom-washed hair took on a strange appearance. Tony had to look twice at the cowlicks on either side of the man's shaking head about his ears. The arrangement of hair reminded him of horns!

"Hey, calm down. This is not good for you. Relax. Of course, it is you and me forever, dude. Without you, I would be one of the nuts in here. I'll never forget that," spoke Tony softly trying to calm the man.

It seemed to be working. Lucifer's breathing began to return to a more normal level, and he allowed his head to fall back in an attempt to relax and regain control of what was left of his body. Tony continued to speak quietly to the man and rubbed his shoulders until the episode had passed.

"Lazarus, man, you gotta promise me something. Say you promise."

"Anything for you, buddy. Of course, I will promise," whispered Tony ready to say anything to avoid a repeat of the previous demonstration.

"If only one of us gets out of here, that guy will come back for the other. Promise me, man. If they let you out, you had better find a way to get me outta here. You owe me, right? You won't leave me here alone with the nuts, man. You promise, right?"

The man started to exhibit signs of relapsing into the behavior of his just concluded episode. Before he slipped into a full repeat performance, Tony calmingly told him the things he needed to hear which stopped the attack in its tracks.

"Look, Lucifer, if that's what you want, that's what you'll have," whispered Tony.

"I know these guys, outside, man. For a few bucks, they will help you spring me if you get outta here.

"When and if the time comes, you contact them. They'll know what to do," spoke Lucifer haltingly.

"Anything, dude. Anything you say," responded Tony. "I won't leave you here alone, ever."

Edward L. Conrad, a.k.a. Lucifer, knew it was highly unlikely that he would ever be released from that hospital. In fact, he had spent most of the past ten years confined to various VA hospital mental wards in several New England states. Conrad was not the Vietnam veteran that he claimed to be, nor were his injuries remotely war related. Yes, he was a veteran having entered the Navy upon leaving high school on his eighteenth birthday. Yes, his injuries occurred while he was an enlisted man. Yes, the man was crazy as a loon from his early teens on. Only an administrational fuck-up by the Navy, or a miracle, allowed him to pass the physical and mental tests to gain entry. The boy had a long, sordid history of problem behavior at school from kindergarten on up. He was a fixture in special education and chronically disruptive behavioral classes up to his eighteenth birthday. His medical history read like a serial killer in training manual. He was mass murdering neighborhood cats at eleven years of age. He moved up in class to larger mammals in his home state of Maine by the age of fourteen. Death seemed to provide a source of wonder and great curiosity for the boy. He would bring death to various creatures in an attempt to isolate the exact moment when the soul leaves the body – the exact moment when life exits and death enters. Although a court of law never proved him guilty, the young man had graduated to experimenting with human beings. Unfulfilled and dissatisfied because lesser animals were unable to relate their feelings and describe the stages through which they passed during his death experiments, he began to prey upon younger children, always males. His Dr. Mendola-like experiments involved pushing his victims to their maximum level of pain via varied and sundry forms of torture. He would then promise them life and safe release if the specimen continued to cooperate in his grisly practices. How this guy slipped through the cracks of social detection and punishment remained a mystery for the ages. How he could appear as normal as he wanted to be on cue was fascinating. A master chameleon of sorts, he had the ability to be anyone or act anyway to which he put his mind. Following his second acquittal on capital murder charges, the young man and his attorneys thought it best that he seek greener pastures. He bid good-by to Maine and hello to the United States Navy. He was in his glory with all of those young men and himself isolated on a ship for months at a time. Then a strange thing happened to him. Conrad's interest and curiosity in the intricacies of death lessened as his homosexual behavior increased. Perhaps he found more pleasure in live moving bodies than in those used in his near-death experiments. At any rate, he modified his murderous behavior and sublimated it with rough, dominant, sexual behavior. During one such encounter in the middle of the Atlantic Ocean, Seaman Conrad and Seaman Desmond, a handsome young man from California, had stolen away to an infrequently visited custodial closet far below deck. There they experienced each other carnally, relaxed, lit-up a joint, and blew themselves apart when a carelessly tossed match met gallons of highly flammable cleaning products. Desmond died immediately. Conrad, near death for weeks, survived minus two legs and one arm. The fatal explosion and dereliction of duty charges against the survivor ultimately resulted in Conrad's reintroduction to incarceration. While confined to a British hospital in London for lifesaving treatment, Conrad began to exhibit behavior that led his doctors to suggest a complete mental evaluation upon his return to the United States. The triple amputee,

Conrad, failed to convince the stateside doctors of his sanity. He really did not give a shit. What did he care? What did he have to live for? He was a freak. Why should he not be a fucking nut too? Some ten years and several hospitals later, Seaman Edward L. Conrad rediscovered a reason to live – the first time he saw Anthony James Delvane.

CHAPTER 55

THE BABY WAS HEALTHY. TARA was recovering well. Charlene and Twan had control of both their household and JT's. Tony was progressing nicely in the hospital, and a new school year was about to commence. The Russells and the Delvanes were riding a winning streak until Jim Russell dropped dead. One morning following his usual stop at Dunkin Donuts for a regular coffee and a plain donut with jimmies, Jim Russell, at the age of fifty-two, dropped his order, grabbed at his chest, and fell to the donut shop floor. Even the CPR efforts of a fast acting bystander could not resuscitate the man who had suffered a major coronary thrombosis and was dead before he hit the floor. The notification to the family had one redeeming feature. They were all together at JT's house celebrating the homecoming of Veronica Leigh Russell. When the police arrived at Jim's home on Richie Street, no one was at home. Mrs. Burnside, their next-door neighbor of twenty years, met the officers and directed them to JT's home. Following the pronouncement by the officers, Charlene, Bina, and Tara Russell needed medical assistance. JT battled his emotions and worked to comfort his three ladies. Twan, as usual, was taking great care of Katie Anne. JT often saw himself and Rose Marie when he watched Twan and Katie Anne interact. The baby had slept soundly during the crisis period, a blessing of sorts, a miracle considering the wails of agony originating from the smallish four-room apartment on Bernard Street. As the paramedics arrived, JT handed over control of the situation to them walked out the back door, entered his green Toyota, and cried until he was cried out. He knew he had to be the strong one. Playing that role was not anything new to him; however, in the past, if he had failed in that role he always had his father to back him up. His dad was his best friend, closer to him than Tony was if that were possible. He could say anything to his dad. They shared a mutual love of life, family, and fun. JT even began to enjoy the role reversal he and his father began to experience, as both grew older. He became his dad's protector, guardian, and sage. He was able to repay his dad in that way for all the sacrifices he had made for his family over the years. Now, all of that was gone. The man he loved more than anyone on the planet had left him.

JT hated everything about the wake and funeral. He hated the late afternoon meeting at Samuel's Funeral Home on Broadway on the day his father died to make the arrangements. He hated hearing the questions asked for the newspaper release. He hated picking out a casket with his heavily medicated mother and sister. He even hated it when the owner of the funeral home, an old friend of the family, allowed them to make a quick visit with the physical body that was until so recently his father. He stood guard at his mother's side holding her hand throughout the four-hour wake. Tony, who received permission from the hospital to attend, stood with Bina, offering her a comforting shoulder upon which to cry. Tara had to split her time between the funeral home and the baby. Her mother was able to sit with the three children between her social engagements. She even found time to make a visit to the wake with Tara's father. The next day, Jim's family and friends celebrated his life at a funeral high mass at St. Peter's Church. During the burial at St. Joseph's Cemetery, JT steeled his emotions as he continued to attend to his three ladies. The mass was beautiful according to those paying attention. The funeral was well attended, he supposed – he certainly did not care – though his mother did. The gathering of family and friends following the funeral was at his mother's house catered by friends of the family. Almost everyone who attended the funeral stopped back at the house to offer support to the devastated family only to find JT not in attendance. After securing his three ladies in the care of family and friends, JT got into his green Toyota and returned to the cemetery. He walked to the now covered hole piled high with baskets of flowers, knelt before the sign that indicated the name of the deceased, and dropped his eyes to the ground.

"I hope I made you proud today, Dad. I did my best. Don't you worry about Ma and Bina; you know I will take the same kind of care of them as you did. I will miss you so much. I already do." Then he mused to himself: "The world is a little darker today because you no longer grace its doors. On the other hand, Heaven is a little brighter due to the arrival of its newest son. I will do everything in my power to be the kind of man you were so that we will be together once again." Then remembering the words of William Goldman, he whispered aloud, "Until that time, Dad. Until that time."

He stayed there for some unknown length of time crying, smiling, and even laughing aloud at their antics. When he felt it was time to go, he simply stood, turned, walked to his vehicle, and did not look back. Son and father had shared their final good-bye.

CHAPTER 56

Tony's progress was reportedly so good that he received a weekend pass as a reward. The doctor made note to the young man's parents that the amount of time he spent with Edward Conrad had also decreased substantially. The doctor thought that to be a very good sign. The Delvanes arranged to have JT pick-up Tony on Friday afternoon after school and return him to the hospital on Sunday evening before 10 PM. The ride from the hospital was very upbeat considering the degree of grief that JT was still experiencing. He thought the time to be right to address Bina's concern about Tony's feeling about her as a woman.

"Hey, I really appreciated the way you stepped up at the wake and comforted Bina. I did not know where to look first. There were so many of my ladies in distress."

"You're my family, Russ. What else would I do? You know how I feel about Bina," responded Tony seriously.

"No, Tony, I don't."

"Russ, at the wake when I was holding her she looked at me the same way she used to. I mean, she looked at me as if I were the same old Tony, not the freak with one leg and one eye. I have had the biggest crush on that girl for the longest time, but her being your sister and four years younger than me always made me feel like a pervert when I thought about her as a girlfriend. Russ, how would you feel if Bina and I started going out? If you think it's a bad idea, I will forget about it on the spot. Tell me how you really feel, buddy," pleaded Tony to his friend.

"I think it would be great Tony."

"That's a relief, Russ, because I'm taking Bina out Saturday night," smiled his partner.

"You asshole! Have you two already hooked-up?" he asked rhetorically. "I was going through this Dear Abby shit, and you two are already an item?" smiled JT.

"Yeah, man, it just happened at the wake. Weird huh? She was so vulnerable and so beautiful. I just wanted to hold and protect her for always. She does not see me for what I do not have or what I am not. She sees the person inside. Russ, that person wants to come outside and start living again. I couldn't think of another woman that I'd like to have with me more when Lazarus rises from the grave once again."

"As I live and breathe, Mr. Delvane, I do declare that I do not know this man who speaketh of love. You have my blessing. I would love to have this work out for both of you. I know how Bina feels about you. Wouldn't it be great if you became a legal member of the Russell family?" joked JT.

"Hold on boy! We are going on a date, not picking out a china pattern," smiled Tony.

"In due time, brother. In due time," laughed JT.

"I hope you didn't mind picking me up, Bina. I have not received my driving clearance yet. This is not how I wanted our first date to start. The important part is that we are finally together. I guess we have already shocked everyone in the Delvane and Russell families. Who would have thought that you would actually go out with me?" laughed Tony Delvane.

"Excuse me, sir. What is that? I have been harboring one powerful crush on you since I was fourteen. I probably shouldn't have admitted that."

"I love hearing it. As long as we are being up front and honest, I adored you all those years, but you were my best friend's sister. I would have never risked allowing a problem between us to tear Russ and me apart," Tony related seriously.

"Well, what about now, Mr. Delvane?" she queried. "What if we have a problem now?"

"I'd risk pissing off the Almighty to be with you, young lady," he bragged.

"I would say that you tell that to all the girls, but I want to believe it so badly," said a blushing Bina.

"I've never said it to any other girl, Bina, and if my luck continues, I may never have to say it to another," said Tony blushing this time.

"Well, I think this first date is going reasonably wonderfully, Mr. Delvane," asserted Bina. "What say you?"

"I'd say if it were going any better, Miss Russell, I'd have to marry you."

"If you're not careful, you're going to sweep me off my feet, Mr. Delvane."

"God knows, I'm trying, lady. I am just real rusty at this dating stuff. We didn't have many social occasions in the jungle, and the women in the hospital are all kind of stiff," he joked.

"If I were keeping score, sir, I would say you are doing fabulously," she cooed. "Before you sweet talk me out of a meal, pick a restaurant fast."

They mutually decided to dine at Imperial's Italian Restaurant on Route 1 in Danvers. Tony remembered the restaurant as quaintly Italian and very romantic – perfect for a first date. They sat opposite each other and sipped soft drinks as they awaited their food. The conversation was non-stop and riveting from both sides of the table. Bina updated Tony on many of the events of the past five years during his imprisonment. Tony spoke freely and openly about his feelings, his experiences, his fears, and now, for the first time in years, his hopes. Every time he looked into her eyes, he smiled and she blushed. When their veal parmagiana and spaghetti arrived, Tony moved to Bina's side of the table where he convinced her to help him reenact the spaghetti-eating scene from Lady and the Tramp. With a long strand of pasta hanging from his mouth, Bina lifted the other end to her mouth. They ate to the middle where their lips met, and the two old friends shared their first romantic kiss. A great meal, followed by a walk along Good Harbor Beach in Gloucester, several more shared kisses, and he was begging her to see him again on Sunday morning for breakfast. She needed little convincing. She was in love, and she knew it. He was in love, and he knew it. Unfortunately, he did not know whether to trust the judgment of a mental patient.

CHAPTER 57

AT THE END OF THE last school year, JT had to make decisions for the following school year's placements on all of his then current students. The vast majority of his kids went on to the sixth grade in their neighborhood schools. At that time, the protocol for students at JT's ESL Level III was a mandatory year in a sixth grade class regardless of the student's chronological age. Therefore, if JT had a fifteen year old student who spent three months to a year learning the language, that student, at his or her advanced age, was still mandated to spend a year in a self-contained sixth grade classroom before being allowed to go on to junior high school. JT knew the system was doing it wrong because many of his very bright kids left school at sixteen years of age rather than spend a year with a class of twelve-year-old sixth graders. He submitted proposal after proposal that outlined a junior/senior high school tracking system, which would place ESL students in chronologically correct, or near correct grade levels. These students would receive specialized help, tutoring, and attention by a specialist assigned to the ESL program. He got nowhere. The result of those jousts with the administrative windmill was JT's request for transfer from an ESL class to a self-contained fifth grade class. He could no longer justify to his ESL students the necessity of having them follow an obviously flawed protocol that was costing them a year of their lives. Worse, it appeared that he was the only one concerned about it. JT began the new school year in a new and strange role as a fifth grade teacher. He assigned Twan to the sixth grade at TLC Community School, which really worked out well for both of them. He was able to take him to and from school, as well as monitor his progress. One Saturday following his dad's death, he sat Twan down and told him how much he was counting on him to be his mother's man around their house. Twan needed no additional encouragement from his idol. He worked very hard in school, and he performed his role at home better than an eleven-year-old boy ought to be able. Once again, this time without the family patriarch, things started to settle down around the two Russell homes, but the ever-apprehensive JT, so scarred by past events, constantly waited for the other shoe to drop.

CHAPTER 58

BINA AND TONY SPOKE EVERY single day usually more than once. The romance of the long-time friends was in full bloom at the time of Dr. Brown's decision to allow Tony to re-enter society. The doctor released Tony to his parents' custody with the understanding that he would attend outpatient sessions weekly and his parents would maintain a strict regimen of monitoring his medications at home. Tony would have agreed to do that standing on his head nude in the middle of Central Square if it meant his freedom to be with Bina everyday. For him the news could not have been better or come at a better time. The young soon-to-be ex-marine, for the first time since basic training, felt energized, alive, and happy. All the hospital staff in the mental health ward applauded his good fortune. Patients, who were sufficiently cognitive, congratulated him and wished him luck. However, one patient in the ward saw the alleged good luck of Anthony J. Delvane as a threat to his own future well being – Edward "Lucifer" Conrad.

"It seems someone around here has forgotten about an old friend lately," complained a voice from outside Tony's room. "Yeah, someone just doesn't have the time to spare for a friend who saved his fucking ass! Now you just use'em, abuse'em, and toss'em…Is that your game now, Lazarus? You promised me, man! You owe me, big time! Have you forgotten?" raged the irate visitor in the wheelchair.

Tony was swiftly communicating the hand signals that had become so successful for the pair in an effort to snap the angry Lucifer back to reality and allow him to modify his potentially damaging behavior. His now raging comrade paid no attention to the warnings and continued his rant.

"Without me you're shit. You need me, Lazarus. I am all-powerful. I give life, and I can take life," he screamed.

The out of control, Lucifer, kept spinning his wheelchair to block Tony's every attempt to leave the scene of the commotion. At one point, the triple amputee lost control of his chair and barreled into the surprised Tony Delvane. The standing man lost his balance and fell upon the man confined to the wheelchair. Their bodies struck each other and twisted awkwardly as both men hit the floor. The now empty chair skidded across the room as the still crazed Lucifer tore at the clothing of his former friend and confidant. Blow after blow from Lucifer's only good arm made contact with Tony's head and shoulders. The ranting and raging continued until Tony had had enough. He broke free from his attacker and landed one solid right hand to the left side of the crippled man's chin! Lucifer went out for the count. The attendants separated the twisted combatants and called for medical assistance for the unconscious man. Upon arriving at the scene, the head nurse administered to the fallen Lucifer as a second nurse attended to Tony. Tony's immediate thought was whether the incident would have any impact on his discharge from the hospital. He began to weep for fear that life had done it to him again – dangled the carrot just out of his reach before pulling it away entirely. Fortunately, for him, his fears were for naught. The entire bizarre incident , witnessed by a number of patients conscious enough to lay the entire blame at the"wheels" of Lucifer, would not affect Tony's discharge. Once back on his foot, Tony attempted to approach the now conscious Lucifer, but the still offended party would have none of that. His anger continued to the point where restraint was required.

"I'll get you for this, you prick! You are dead to me, fucker! I will pluck out that good eye and fucking eat it. I am going to fuck that little girl of yours! I'm going to kill you both!"

At last, the sedative began to quiet the raging patient and the ranting came to a welcomed conclusion. Tony watched as they wheeled his former friend away on a gurney. After the events of that day, he hoped he had seen him for the last time.

CHAPTER 59

THE BERNARD STREET APARTMENT NO longer met their needs as a family. It was time for the Russell family to lay down some permanent roots. Tara and JT had discussed the move continually over the past couple of years, but Katie Anne would be entering kindergarten before too much longer, and a decision was no longer avoidable. Tara knew well that JT wanted his mother to move in with them, and she had no problem with such an arrangement. That move would require the sale of the Richie Street house and the presence of an in-law apartment for Charlene and Twan in any perspective new house they were to purchase. The lady of the house was also keenly aware of a burning desire in her husband to make Twan a permanent member of their household. That action would require the cost of legal representation in the petition for Twan's adoption. On his side, JT was well aware of Tara's preference for a parochial school environment for their girls as opposed to a public school education. He also knew well that Tara desired to return to the working world when Ronnie was ready for nursery school. They arranged to handle the decision-making process in their usual fashion. As in every other important decision made in their lives together, they went on a date. Yes, Tara and her husband would dress-up, leave the children at grandmother's house, and go to their favorite restaurant, The International, on Route 1 in Saugus. During the evening, they would thrash-out the options available to them, negotiate the details, reach a mutually agreeable resolution, seal the deal with an outrageously priced dessert, and return to an empty apartment to have some loud sex.

They sat opposite from one another at the restaurant laughing and smiling as the waitress took their order. Once she departed, the only interruptions to their discussion were visits from the "popovers girl", the "mushrooms girl", the "fritters girl", and the "meatballs girl". Based on their experience, JT knew his wife to be a clear thinker, a crafty negotiator, overall a very formidable opponent. On the other side of the table, Tara recognized the stubbornness of her husband; his dire need for clarity, order, and organization; and his disarming charm, which had directly resulted in a second child instead of stopping at one as they had originally planned. However, Tara knew she held the trump card in dealing with her Jamey. Tears… if all fair dealings failed, she would cry – end of discussion, case closed, chalk one up for her team. JT just could not handle his wife's tears. She hoped she would not have to resort to such tactics; however…

The evening was going fabulously. The food was great. The appetizer girls were very generous. The negotiations were cordial, timely, and fruitful. JT got his in-law apartment request. Tara got her parochial school request. JT accepted Tara's proposal to have the lawyer selected for their house purchase to serve as their legal representation in Twan's adoption proceedings. The "deal breaker" seemed to arise when Tara insisted that the issue of her return to work not be "tabled" for the time being as proposed by her husband. JT had grown up with a "stay at home" Mom. It was all he knew. He was resistant to having his children grow up differently. Tara, on the other hand, practically raised herself. Though her mother did not work outside of the home, her social calendar more than comprised a forty-hour workweek. JT listened closely to Tara's need to be more than a homemaker. The importance she placed on this issue became more evident as the night wore on. JT's need to have his daughters attended to by their "stay at home" mother during what he considered to be critically important developmental years became just as evident. The swing toward Tara's position eventuated when Tara argued successfully that Charlene, the girls' paternal grandmother, would be available to the girls 24/7, if necessary, as she would be residing in the same dwelling. JT was unable to contradict the logic; therefore, the work issue went to Tara with the condition that Ronnie be old enough to attend a full-time nursery school before Tara sought her return to the business world. They sealed their deal with a kiss as they stood leaning towards each other across the table. Then, they went home and had a wonderful night of loud sex.

The Russells moved into a four bedroom, old, Victorian home on Lynnfield Street. The lower level made for a perfect in-law apartment complete with its own kitchen and bath. Each girl and Twan had her/his own bedroom, JT had a small utility room, which he used for an office, and Tara was happier than a pig in shit with the new housing arrangement. The adoption of Twan Ho Cheung took place in a very timely fashion. Twan, when given the choice, chose to use the surname Cheung-Russell, a decision absolutely supported by his new mother and father. It became almost comical for the first few weeks after the finalization of the adoption, as Twan would call JT "Mr. Dad" or "Dad Russell", or "Mr. Russell Dad". At times, he called Tara "Mrs. Mom" or "Mrs. Russell Mom". However, in a short time, Twan displayed a facility and normalcy in addressing his new parents properly – as if he had been doing it forever.

Charlene's house sold without difficulty. She now had a nest egg for her future. The sale of the house was difficult for her due to the emotional ties to which she clung associated with her home. Before long, she settled into her comfortable new apartment, which allowed her to be with five of her babies everyday and every night of the week forever.

Bina had moved into her own apartment in Peabody shortly after graduating from Merrimack College in North Andover, having transferred from Boston University after her first year. She and her roommate, Cindy Cole, both worked for Norton Investments located in Boston since their senior year internships turned into well-paying first jobs. Things were also going well for Bina and Tony since his return home. Their relationship continued to grow and developed into something serious. The issue became when they would marry rather then if they would marry. The Russells had survived yet another life-altering event, and although their path through life would be harder and sadder without Jim Russell, they circled the family wagons and prepared themselves for the future.

Bettina Charlene Russell became the bride of Anthony James Delvane during the same September that Twan entered the ninth grade at Lynn Classical High School, Katie Anne entered Grade one at St. Peter's School, and Ronnie Russell began Busy Buddies Nursery School. The newlyweds moved into a first floor apartment on Melissa Avenue in East Lynn. Bina continued to earn a decent salary working at Norton Investments and Tony received a one hundred percent disability status from the government. The money to which he was entitled each month was decent, but Anthony Delvane allowed his staunch Italian pride to interfere with his ability to accept the stipend graciously. He found it more difficult each day watching his new wife prepare for work and leave him at home each morning. What was his role to be? What was he to do? Would that be what the rest of his life would be like? As time passed, the longer he accepted the money from what he termed "the pity fund", the more bitter he became. The more bitter he became, the more he drank. The more he drank, the less effective his medication became. The less effective his medicine became, the more bizarre his behavior became. The more bizarre his behavior became, the more distant he and Bina became. The more distant he and Bina became, the more he drank – a classic case of the dog chasing its own tail. The storybook romance was crumbling around Bina and Tony, and they did not know how to reverse the process. Within a matter of six months of married life, they hardly spoke to one another. Their love life was non-existent. The normally sweet, mild-mannered, soft-spoken Bina developed an extremely negative and belligerent attitude toward Tony as his drinking and behavior got worse. She constantly confronted him and challenged his manhood and courage. Bina criticized and berated the man mercilessly out of her frustration over his self-destructive behavior. The situation reached its pinnacle on the evening she arrived home to find her inebriated husband smoking marijuana with two scruffy-looking strangers. Bina began screaming at the three vagrants. She demanded that her husband's new friends leave her home immediately, which they did ignoring her husband's protests.

"I hate you! I never should have married your crazy ass, Delvane. I should have known better than to marry such a loser, such a freak!" she screamed.

That last comment struck the wrong hurtful nerve. The formerly calm, mellow, "feeling no pain" man who had been lounging on the couch when she had arrived home pulled himself to a sitting position, got unsteadily to his feet, and glared at his wife. She was now the sole source of his present pain and that hatred registered on his face. As he approached her, she stood her ground and sneered. Upon reaching her, he slapped her across the face sending her against the wall. Astonished by his actions, she attempted to get to her feet. He grabbed her hair and threw her back against the wall.

"I'll kill your ass if you ever talk to me like that again, bitch!" he screamed at the unconscious woman. "Now get up and make my dinner. Get up, you Italian-American princess."

He grabbed her by the hair and lifted her lifeless head. When he observed no movement from his wife and very shallow breathing, he released her head. A rambling telephone call to the police made by the suddenly terrified husband resulted in a squad car and rescue unit at his door in minutes.

"My wife is hurt bad. Two guys just beat her and ran. I was out. They were looking for money. They pushed past me and knocked off my artificial leg, or I would have caught the bastards. I can identify them both. Please hurry. She is hurt bad, I think. The two guys… maybe she's dead….hurry…please!"

Bina was moaning loudly as she struggled to regain consciousness. Her concerned husband grabbed her by the hair again and looked directly into her face.

"Two guys did this. The two guys you kicked outta the house. I came in, and they ran. You stick to that story, or I'll kill you and your whole fucking family."

He gently lowered her head to the floor aware that he could not afford inflicting additional bruises to his already battered wife. The paramedics tended to Bina's injuries then loaded her into their vehicle for a trip to the emergency ward. The police did not buy her husband's story a little bit. The obviously inebriated man related several versions of the same story upon questioning. The police speculated that the case was a classic example of domestic violence – a drunk, out of control husband, abusing his weaker, defenseless wife. However, there was no evidence, other than the empty beer bottles and an odor of marijuana, to support their theory. The investigating officers assisted the now greatly distressed husband in locating and reattaching his prosthesis. They helped Tony into the cruiser, and the officers sped off to the hospital. The good news came quickly. An emergency room doctor diagnosed Bina with a mild concussion and superficial bruises. She would be as good as new in a few days. The only exceptions were the colorful bruises on the side of her face and several ugly bruises on her forehead, arms, and shoulders, which would fade in time. The bad news came later as the investigating policemen, now entertaining the distraught husband at the Lynn Police Station to secure his written statement, received information that a lucid Mrs. Delvane had told a story confirming some of the elements of at least one version of the story reported by her husband. The officers transported Tony back to the hospital several hours later. Each officer took a turn monitoring the husband as they separately questioned his now in-patient wife in her hospital bed.

The first officer took a direct approach in his questioning. "Why did your husband do this to you, Mrs. Delvane? Tell me, and we'll put the bastard away so he can never hurt you again."

"No," she protested though not strongly, "it was the others. Those men…they were looking for money. Tony didn't hurt me, really."

The second officer took a kinder, gentler approach seeking to establish a comforting relationship with the woman.

"We know that couples have disagreements. Both the other officer and I are married men, Mrs. Delvane. We know how tempers can get of out control when people do or say things to each other that are very hurtful. It's my job, Mrs. Delvane, to make sure that this does not happen to you again."

"Then catch those guys!" she interrupted.

"Please, Mrs. Delvane, I've seen a lot of these cases. Believe me when I tell you that things never get better and most often get much worse."

"Look, Tony didn't do this. He would never hurt me. He loves me. I refuse to answer any more questions about it!" Bina stated sternly.

"Then there's no chance of your filing a criminal complaint against your husband, m'am?"

"No, of course not! Find the guys who did this to me," wept Bina Delvane.

"Yes, m'am, we'll try. I truly hope you know what you are doing," whispered the officer touching her shoulder as he left her side to depart the room.

The two officers escorted Tony into an empty family room.

"Look, you piece of shit, you know and we know what you did. That woman in there for some ungodly reason is confirming your Swiss cheese story."

"You mean the truth, officers?" Tony interjected.

"Look, asshole, don't get me any angrier than I already am at this moment. We are going to be watching out for your wife. If she's back in here for so much as a broken finger nail, we're coming for you. The next time we just might forget that our job is to uphold the law."

"Well, that certainly sounds like a threat," mocked Tony. "What a nice story for the Item – Lynn Officers Batter Double Amputee War Hero for Revenge! Doesn't it have a nice ring to it, boys?"

The first of the two officers to leave Bina's room restrained his partner from doing harm to Tony Delvane on the spot. The restraining officer suggested to Tony that it would be preferable and perhaps healthier for all involved if he arranged for his own transportation home.

"Certainly, officers, I thank you for your concern and quick action. Please contact me when Policemen's Ball tickets become available. My wife and I love to dance..."

Tony turned to leave the family room on his way to Bina's room.

"You miserable fucking coward, you had better pray we don't cross paths again," seethed the still restrained officer.

"Temper, temper, boys, you're talking to a war-fucking-hero here!"

She was less than pleased to see his face. At the first sight of the love of her life, she began to cry uncontrollably.

"You did well, kid. You saved all of us a lot of trouble and your family a lot of pain. Just remember, Bina, I have nothing more to lose, so a wise person would deal with me exercising extreme care and caution. Capice, you fucking Italian princess?"

Bina continued to cry but nodded her head in agreement.

"When you get home, we'll make nice, forget about this unfortunate little stumbling block in our happy marriage, and maybe make a baby. How about that my sweet?" smiled Tony.

Her crying had ceased. She looked upon his mean, evil, smiling face knowing in her heart that she could never again love that man.

"Hey, I'd better notify the family that you're in the hospital, honey. The Russells and their gook stepson will beat down the hospital doors to visit their little girl, Bina. Just make sure, little girl, that you remember our story. Don't forget, thanks to you, I'm privy to an incredibly strange but true Ripley's Fucking Believe It Or Not type story that would cause trouble in Russell Land if it were to see the light of Twan's day."

He bent over her and kissed her brightly discolored cheek, whispered good-bye, and left the room.

"You miserable excuse for a human being, if you hurt my family, I'll kill you myself," she whispered.

Fortunately for her, there was no one to hear her threat.

CHAPTER 60

"OH MY GOD, JAMES, IS she going to be alright? How could this happen? When may we see her?" questioned Bina's mother upon hearing the news from her son.

"Ma, slow down. One question at a time, please," begged JT. "We'll go right now, so calm down, and get yourself ready."

As she left to prepare for the ride to the hospital, JT looked at his wife questioningly. Tara had received Tony's telephone call, now some six hours after the fact.

"What the fuck took him so long to contact us, Tara? This is ridiculous. We should have been with her hours ago," lamented JT.

"I don't know, hon, but he didn't sound too concerned. Actually, he sounded matter-of-factly, no emotion, not like the Tony Delvane I know," responded his concerned wife.

"Well, I'll find out what the fuck is going on. My sister had better be all right," threatened her angry sibling.

Charlene and JT arrived at the hospital at midnight following the ten-minute ride to Boston Street. Neither could comprehend the fact that Bina lay sleeping in her room alone except for the infrequent visits by a nurse or nurse's aide.

"Where the fuck is her husband, Ma? He should be here. Why isn't he?"

"Calm down, James; you'll upset your sister," warned Charlene.

Their conversation caused the patient to stir. JT and Charlene were able to speak with the now awake Bina. She was hesitant to discuss the incident, but JT wanted answers and he wanted them immediately. He excused himself and walked directly to the lobby and a bank of payphones. Searching his pockets nervously for change, he felt like he was about to jump out of his skin. Not having taken his evening dose of blood pressure medication had not helped his condition. Finally, he managed to master the art of using the payphone. The telephone at Tony and Bina's house rang nine times before a drowsy-sounding voice answered.

"Tony! What is going on? Why aren't you here with my sister? I've gotta get some information, buddy, and Bina doesn't want to talk," rambled the excited brother into the handset.

"Whoa! Hold on there, big brother. What is the big fucking deal? She is going to be fine. I am tired, so I am catching some winks. What time is it anyway?"

"Midnight," responded JT.

"What the fuck would I be doing at the hospital at midnight, holding the little princess's hand?" commented Tony, inappropriately at best in JT's opinion.

"I want to see you first thing in the morning. I will be there before school so set your alarm. I'm telling you right now, Tony, I don't like what I've seen so far," confessed JT. "I hope you can satisfactorily fill in the information gaps..."

"Or what, Russ? What will you do, big brother?" mocked Tony at the other end of the line.

Before he said more than he wanted to say, JT hung-up the phone on a Tony he did not recognize. He experienced fleeting flashbacks of that long ago Easter, and the Jekyll/Hyde character that came dressed as Anthony James Delvane. He could not help but be suspicious. The confusion he felt from the actions of his other half made him extremely uncomfortable.

Meanwhile, back in Bina's hospital room, Charlene comforted her daughter as best she could. Having thought she had cried out all available tears, Bina shocked herself when she began to cry uncontrollably and blurted out to her shocked mother:

"He hit me, Ma. He threw me against the wall, pulled my hair, and threatened to kill me...us! Tony's crazy, Ma. I don't know who he is any longer. We don't talk; we don't have sex; all he does is drink, and now he smokes dope. I am so afraid of him. I can never be alone with him again, but, Ma, you can't tell Jamey!"

"Bina, how can we keep this from your brother?" begged Charlene.

"Ma, he'll go after Tony. I know he will. Ma, telling JT would be a giant mistake that could destroy our family. Please, hold your tongue until I can get a handle on this, please," pleaded Bina. "Promise me, Ma, please."

"I won't promise, but I will be watching that son of a bitch like a hawk. One false move, one hair on your head damaged, and I'll come down on that asshole myself!"

Charlene held her daughter and gently rocked with Bina in her arms. JT found them sound asleep in each other's arms. JT got zero sleep on the uncomfortable chair in Bina's hospital room that night so he did the prudent thing by calling into the school administration building for a substitute teacher. He knew that his mother would want to be with Bina until her younger child left the hospital, and both of them wanted to speak with her physician. His mind then drifted to his conversation with Tony. He was still smarting from the tone of voice and attitude, which he encountered in talking with his relatively new brother-in-law earlier that morning. He vowed to find the underlying cause of the suspiciously smelling situation. He went into the bathroom, threw some water on his face, combed his hair, and prepared to leave for Bina's apartment. His mother awoke to his movements. As he exited the bathroom, she called quietly to him to help her off the bed, which he did. He informed her of his plans, which for some strange reason upset her. She did not want him to go to Tony's apartment and made some feeble excuse about his awaiting Bina's doctor with her. He promised her that he would be returning directly after talking to

Tony. JT was adamant about his going. Nothing she could say was going to delay the visit he pondered throughout the night. He kissed his mother's cheek and walked quietly from the room. The ride to the newlywed's apartment was but five or six minutes from the hospital. As he pulled in front of the light green two family house, he looked at his watch. He figured that 7:45 AM was a more than reasonable time to visit family. After only two knocks on the front door, an already dressed and wide-awake Tony Delvane opened the door.

"Russ," he greeted his visitor somberly.

"Good morning," the old friend replied curtly.

JT walked in and looked around the disheveled living room. Food leftovers lay on the floor. The sofa and matching chair were decidedly out of place, and he noted bloodstains on the wall. Waiting for his host to begin the conversation, JT slipped his hands into his pockets and nervously played with the coins he found there.

"Well, Russ, what can I do for you?" asked a serious Tony Delvane.

"The first fucking thing you can do is explain your behavior on the phone last night," quickly responded JT trying to maintain his composure.

"Look, I was way out of line. I awoke badly from a deep sleep. I behaved poorly. Russ, it was a bitch of a day," complained Tony.

"I suppose it was, but I don't exactly know. I'm sure you can fill-in the details for me," responded JT.

"When Bina came home, I was out walking around the neighborhood. She surprised a couple of druggies who were in the house looking for dough. As I was walking toward the front door, I heard her screaming so I moved as fast as this fucking peg leg would let me. At the door, I ran into the two pricks, or I should say they ran into me. I fell down the stairs, and this damn plastic leg of mine fell off. I found Bina unconscious, and I called the cops," sighed the less than upset husband upon finishing his story.

"Do you know where I was all last night, Tony? I was where your ass should have been…sitting with Bina! How could you not have been there?"

"Maybe we all don't believe in the same strong family ties shit as you! Maybe some of us do not need to be handholding, sentiment whispering, overly protective assholes. Maybe," he started to get angrier and he continued, "some of us should mind our own fucking business before someone's fist removes some teeth."

The agitated Delvane now began to turn red in anger and insulting in his rants.

"Who are you to question me, Russell? I am a fucking war hero! I do what I want, when I want, to whom I want! Little sister is learning. She has a hard head, but she is learning. She thinks I'm a freak! We'll see who the friggin freak is…"

JT watched in awe. His host had gone from calm to delirious in a matter of moments. He had begun to storm around the apartment ranting about not being told what to do by an Italian whore, not having his friends thrown out of his own house, not being questioned like a criminal, not being sorry for teaching the little princess a lesson in manners.

"It's time for you to fucking leave, Russell. I am done with you. I am done with your whole "gook loving" fucking family. If you know what is good for you, you will shut your mouth and get the hell out of my life. It is your choice, friend. Your sister made the wrong choice; I hope you're smarter than that bitch!"

"I think I've heard just about enough from you Tony. I just want to hear you tell me. I want to hear it from your lips. Did you hurt my sister?"

"Your sister? You mean my fucking slut. Freak, I will show her a freak! Fucking bitch, next time I will kill her!"

"You just answered my question you miserable son of a bitch!" screamed JT as he lunged at the out of control man.

JT wrapped his arm around the neck of his ranting brother-in-law and engaged him in a headlock. Tony, somewhat unstable on his feet, struck at JT's groin with alternating hands. James Thurber Russell had had it with the stranger in his midst. Protecting the "family jewels", while releasing his thrashing opponent, JT sent a punch that landed squarely on his former friend's jaw. Out popped the glass eye, which JT followed and smashed with the heel of his shoe! Once again, he directed his attack toward the focus of his anger, who was on the floor twisted in an almost comical pose. He grabbed his opponent's prosthesis and yanked with all his might. Off came the leg in his hands. He proceeded to beat the man about the head and shoulders repeatedly with the plastic limb.

"War hero? Is that what you are, you fuck? I'll show you a war hero, you son of a bitch!" he screamed crashing the limb on his head once again. "If you ever come near my sister or my family again, I will kill your miserable ass."

With one last swing for good measure, JT sent the battered coward rolling against the previously bloodied wall. JT dropped the leg, stood looking at the man he once knew so well, felt a tear roll down his cheek, and turned away breathing rapidly. He went to the phone and dialed the police. He gave the officer on desk duty his name and address in addition to the emergency information concerning the injured party. He particularly made note to the officer, that should the police want to talk with him, he would be getting some needed fresh air just down the street at Lynn Beach. Upon hanging up the phone, JT dragged his exhausted body into his car and made the very short drive to his sanctuary. As he walked to a bench looking out toward Egg Rock, a moment returned to his consciousness that had evaded him earlier.

"Did that son of a bitch actually call my son a gook?"

CHAPTER 61

The perception of isolation he received whenever he viewed Egg Rock lay deeply imbedded in JT's memory. He would sit for long periods imagining what it must have been like back in 1856 when the first lighthouse appeared on the island. The very fact that the eighty foot high, three acres in area, soil depleted rock qualified as an island was a compliment to rocks everywhere. Located a mile to the northeast of Nahant, Massachusetts, Egg Rock never belonged to Nahant, Swampscott, nor Lynn, its three closest communities. For some unknown reason, it belonged to the City of Salem, just north of Lynn. In 1856, the City of Salem ceded Egg Rock to the Federal Government for purposes of erecting a lighthouse. By 1919, the government determined that the island no longer needed a lighthouse with a keeper. After employing a number of unique and colorful keepers in the previous sixty plus years, the government created an automated lighthouse in 1919. By 1922, the automated lighthouse also fell into disfavor, and its light was extinguished. The government offered the lighthouse to anyone willing to pay five dollars for the right to move the entire structure from the island at the buyer's expense. A buyer came forward who hired a crew to move the lighthouse onto a barge. As they navigated the lighthouse toward the barge, a rope snapped at an inopportune time causing the structure to crash into the ocean. The remains of the historically rich edifice washed up on local beaches for some time. From the sightings of sea serpents by local

Indians in the 1600's, to Milo, the lifesaving, lighthouse dog belonging to George B. Taylor, the first keeper, to the colorful gallery of eccentric personalities who followed him as keeper, Egg Rock held a special place in the annals of North Shore lore and Lynn legend.

JT sat alone at the deserted beach breathing in deeply the fresh, chilly, salty, air. Before long he was joined by two officers from the LPD. Strange but true, the officers answering that call were the same officers who answered the original call to Bina's house the day of her hospitalization. It seems the officers had made a point of requesting immediate notification from the desk sergeant should an incident involving the Delvanes' Melissa Avenue address or the names of Bettina and/or Anthony Delvane appear on the "calls" list. The officers had no difficulty locating JT since he was the only human being at the beach for miles in each direction.

"You are the James T. Russell who reported the incident at 31 Melissa Avenue?" asked the patrolman.

Following JT's affirmation, the officers requested his version of the incident, which sent the gentleman at the Melissa Avenue address to the hospital. JT informed the officers that the man was his brother-in-law, and they had a disagreement that morning.

"So, Mr. Russell, Bettina Delvane is your sister."

"Yes, sir," JT responded to the more direct of the two officers.

"And she is presently in the hospital, is that correct?"

"Yes, she is," responded a solemn JT.

"Are you aware that my partner and I responded to that call also? Of course you aren't how could you? Let me take a wild guess as what really happened," offered the more empathetic of the two officers.

"That piece of shit brother-in-law of yours is responsible for your sister's condition. You found out in some fashion. You confronted the fucker, and you put a few dents in his head and psyche. Is that about right, sir?"

"Well, yeah, what made you…?"

"We pretty much had that piece of shit pegged yesterday, but we had no proof. We told him that we'd be on him like white on rice if anything else happened to his wife. This is off the record of course, and I'd have to deny it in a court of law, but I'm jealous that you got the bastard before I did. Now, that is not to say you were correct in taking matters into your own hands. In fact, as big a fan of yours as I am at the moment, I'm still going to have to cuff you and take you to the station."

"It was self-defense, officer. He went absolutely nuts," whispered JT.

"It will all come out in the wash, sir. Please place your hands behind your back."

At the station, JT used his one phone call to contact Tara. After explaining his plight, he requested that she contact his mother at the hospital. He directed her to transport his mother and sister to the Russell's Lynnfield Street home were Bina to be released that day. Next, he asked her to check on the condition of their brother-in-law who should now be resting uncomfortably after his admission to the hospital. Following her husband's wishes although desperately wanting to be with him, Tara made contact with Charlene. The conversation was short and borderline hysterical from Charlene's end of the line. Bina was being released as they spoke. Tara arranged to pick-up the pair as JT had requested, and she did her best to calm Charlene. Her efforts were for naught partly because her mother-in-law could hear the concern in Tara's voice. Cutting the conversation off, Tara told the distressed woman that she would be at the hospital within the hour. From across the room, Bina had obviously observed her mother's reaction to the phone call. When the discharge nurse left the room, she immediately questioned her mother seeking details.

"Your brother is in jail, Bina. He and your husband had a fight."

"Oh my God, Ma, did you tell Jamey? I told you not to. I knew this would happen!" yelled Bina.

"I didn't tell him a thing, Bina. But it certainly sounds like he found out," responded Charlene in a rising voice. "Tara will be here soon, honey. Then we'll know more."

"When Tara arrives, she's taking us directly to the police station. I'll straighten-out this mess the way I should have from the start," lamented Bina Delvane.

One flight below Bina's hospital room laid a thoroughly beaten Anthony Delvane. The opening between the upper and lower lid of his left eye socket revealed the absence of his glass eye. The man was covered with bruises, scrapes, cuts, and scratches about his head, neck, and shoulders. His prosthetic leg was being held as evidence; therefore, he was minus a second body part as he lay in his hospital bed. A policeman was stationed outside his room as a precaution. The officer nodded to the doctor on call as he entered the room to examine the patient. Within moments of the doctor's arrival and onset of his examination, the patient began thrashing violently in his bed. He was screaming obscenities, which left the physician in harm's way. The officer on duty entered to subdue the man but found him to be a worthy adversary. The physician called for additional assistance, and within minutes, Tony Delvane was once again in restraints.

During that period of excitement in her husband's room, an unknowing Bina left the hospital with Charlene and Tara having no idea of the condition of her husband nor caring to find out. Bina insisted that Tara take her to the police station to see her brother and straighten-out the mess in which her family now found itself. Arriving at the station, Bina directed Charlene to telephone Jessica and Mario Delvane to discover their level of knowledge regarding the morning's events. Tara walked with Bina to the front desk and explained her situation to the sergeant on duty.

"Delvane? Melissa Avenue? Malloy and Ford asked to be notified if either identifying name was called in to us. Please wait over there for one moment. They might still be in the station," suggested the desk officer.

Within moments, Charlene returned to the group, and two familiar figures in blue uniforms walked toward the women. Bina recognized the first officer as the more direct and blunt of the two who had questioned her at the hospital. Now she was able to give the man a name – Officer John Malloy – which she read from the identification badge on his pocket. The second officer, the one she found easier to talk with, was Officer Gerald Ford. Bina greeted them warmly, yet she felt embarrassed to be meeting with them to reveal her lies. While Charlene and Tara sat at the visitors' area, the officers walked Bina into an interrogation room. Apologizing repeatedly for her deception, Bina's story – the true story – came forth like a bursting dam. The officers received a full and detailed account of Tony's medical history, his behavioral problems, and the events that led to her hospitalization. The officers recorded every word she said. When they finished with her, there was no question as to whether criminal charges were to be filed against her husband. The problem at hand was now JT's status. After five hours of incarceration, the young educator knew that cell-life would be worse than death for him. For his entire time behind bars, he refused to use the communal toilet although the "calls of nature" on both fronts were bordering on emergency status. He made sure that he did not look directly at the other criminals in his cell for fear of having some lonely sole developing romantic intentions toward him. Yes, it had been one hell of a day for JT Russell, and it was not even 1:30 in the afternoon.

The interrogating officers suggested that JT's family contact a lawyer immediately. They suggested that with extenuating circumstances present from the first day's events, a most probable successful self-defense plea, and his first time offender classification, at worst JT could be charged with misdemeanor disturbing the peace. Upon hearing the encouraging news, Tara headed home to pick-up Katie and Twan from their respective schools and Ronnie from Tara's girlfriend Francine's house. Charlene and Bina contacted a lawyer, a friend of a friend, who immediately arranged for JT's release. While meeting with the lawyer, Bina questioned as to whether he handled divorce cases. She also asked him to differentiate between a divorce and an annulment. The very good-looking, young lawyer arranged a meeting with Bina for the following day to discuss her future actions. When finished with the paperwork, Officers Ford and Malloy escorted the stranded threesome into their cruiser and transported them home.

Back at the hospital, Tony Delvane, shot full of all too familiar tranquilizing drugs, took residence in the more secure mental health ward. Things were not looking-up for Anthony James Delvane at that point in time. Perhaps Lazarus had run out of resurrections!

CHAPTER 62

JT FELT WONDERFUL RETURNING TO school following his weekend of healing and relaxation. So fine did he feel that he was in a "no refusal mode" to anything or anybody. When Walter Holloway asked to see him in his office, JT breezed in smiling.

"We have had a real strange case dumped in our collective laps, JT. It involves the soon-to-be thirteen-year-old niece of the Italian ambassador to the United Nations. This young lady will be residing in our city for as long as several months before she returns to her home in Naples or to her uncle's home in New York. The problem is that her English is too advanced for our ESL class and not proficient enough for a junior high school placement. The powers that be have been urged to do whatever they can to accommodate the young lady, and as shit rolls down-hill, we are being urged to do everything we can to accommodate the young lady, capice?" smiled the perplexed principal.

"Walter, this is why I'm out of ESL. You know that. The potato heads running this system have no clue as to how to deal with these non and limited-English speakers properly. Now some high mucky-muck's kid is involved and they're scurrying around trying to protect their asses!" complained the exasperated teacher.

"You're right in this case, JT, but that does not help us out of the situation at hand. I need positive input," complained Walter to JT.

"OK, we could put her in Douglas's sixth grade..."

"Hold it! I said positive in-put. Francis Douglas was perhaps a fine teacher at some point, but we both know that he is marking time to his retirement. I'm in his class at least three times a day to make sure he and his class are awake and covering the sixth grade curriculum. Last week he had them watching the Price is Right on a classroom television, and when I questioned him on it, he became defensive and argued that his aim was a creative mathematics lesson," laughed the weary principal.

"Well then, what about the other sixth grade, Miss Evans class?" asked JT.

"She's a first year teacher, JT, who wanted a kindergarten or first grade class. She took the sixth grade class just to get into the system. The girl works very hard, but I find her crying in her room each day after school. Those older kids are making her life miserable. Next suggestion?" quizzed the principal.

"I know what you're doing, Walter," smiled JT.

"It's about time, kid. I was beginning to think that stint in solitary confinement caused some permanent damage," he smiled. "Look, you have the expertise in ESL to keep her interested and progressing. She'll be a little old for your fifth graders, but we'll tell her that she is to be your student assistant. How's that for thinking on the fly?" asked his boss and friend.

"Whatever you want me to do, Walter, I'll do. I know her fit in my class is nowhere near being appropriate. This fifth grade is made-up of a pretty immature group of characters, and your young lady is almost a teenager," complained JT.

"You're my best bet. Let's give it a shot, and see what happens," suggested Walter.

"Fine, boss, just how much time do I have to prepare for her arrival?" asked JT.

"She should be waiting in your classroom when you get there," chuckled his friend turning around abruptly.

Speechlessly, JT stood and waited for his boss to turn around toward him. JT once again reached out for the principal's hand on which he wore his college ring, kissed the stone, bowed, and retreated from the office without ever turning his back on the hysterical Walter Holloway.

Not all the news was bad. When he arrived at his classroom door, he saw a very old friend, Maria D'Oreo, awaiting him. Ms. D'Oreo had known JT since he was five years old. She had babysat him often "back in the day". In fact, she would take him to her house, a first generation Italian family, instead of sitting with him at his house. Maria's parents, two older brothers, and one younger sister treated him as visiting royalty upon each visit. They introduced him to such delicacies as pigeon, guinea pig, and pig's feet in homemade tomato gravy. They took a little half- Italian, half-Irish child and turned him into a one hundred percent Italian.

"Jamey!" she spoke in her usual loud voice. "It's been so long. Look how handsome you are. I told Antonella all about you," she stated proudly.

"Maria, you know the niece of the Italian ambassador to the United Nations?" asked JT incredulously.

"Know her? She's practically family. She's from our village in Italy. I told her parents that I would get her settled here in Lynn, make sure she's comfortable, and have her placed with the best teacher possible – you," smiled the adoring Maria.

"It seems everybody knew about this before I did," laughed JT.

"Come, let me introduce you to Antonella Lira," bubbled Maria.

JT took one look at the kid and knew he was going to have problems. Antonella stood over five feet in height and possessed an incredibly developed figure for her age. When she smiled at her new teacher a set of immaculately white teeth appeared. She then tossed her long, straight, light brown hair back a la Cher of Sonny and …Her perfectly applied make-up and her habit of alternating licking and biting her full lipstick covered lips made her "your not average fifth grader". Next to the little girls in his classroom, Antonella looked like a major league ball player on a little league team.

"Welcome to TLC Community School, Antonella. I hope you will enjoy your time with us," offered JT extending his hand.

"I am sure I will," she smiled ignoring his hand in favor of the European form of greeting – the embrace.

As she kissed him on each cheek, he knew he was blushing, but what could he do?

"Maria has told me all about you. I feel like I already know you," gushed the young girl.

"Well, you're one up on me," laughed JT nervously.

CHAPTER 63

EVENTS OF THE DAY TURNED quickly. Decisions regarding Tony Delvane's hospitalization, the charges against JT Russell, and Bina's divorce proceedings fell like dominoes in a row. All of the adult Russells attended a competency hearing at Lynn District Court in regard to Anthony James Delvane's fitness to stand trial for spousal abuse. The guest of honor could not attend. At his fitting for his new straightjacket, he injured two nurses and a male attendant. Needless to say, the judge was unforgiving when he recommitted the absent defendant to the custody of Dr. Sheldon Brown and the Veteran's Administration Hospital. Tony was going to his home away from home once again.

The good news was that the same judge, one week later, ruled "no finding" in JT's disturbing the peace case. JT was informed that should he be a good citizen for the next year, all evidence that the incident ever occurred would be eradicated.

Bina had already filed for divorce. There was absolutely no way she would ever again wish to talk to that man so living with him was definitely out of the question. The lawyer who was instrumental in "springing" JT from jail had turned over Bina's divorce case to a colleague because he believed there was a conflict of interest developing as he was now dating his client. Bina had kept her initial meeting with Attorney Mark Morrow the day following JT's jail release. Not only did she receive expert legal advice, but she experienced a chemical reaction to her new barrister that resulted in coffee appointments, lunch appointments, even a dinner appointment or two. The fledgling romance became a source of concern for Attorney Morrow; therefore, he divested himself of her legal affairs and inserted himself into their love affair.

"Welcome home, Tony," smiled Dr. Brown reaching out to touch the restrained man's shoulder. "We will have you better in no time. You just wait and see."

What else could the trapped rat do but wait and see? He was not going anywhere for the immediate future.

"Hey Lazarus," a vaguely familiar voice called out. "Lazarus, over here man. Remember me, Lazarus, man? It's me Ed L. Conrad. Bet you didn't even know my real name, right man? Remember, Lucifer, Lazarus? Yeah, man, I'm a lot better now than before. I don't let anyone call me by that L name anymore. It was bad for my self-esteem, you know."

The wheelchair-confined visitor rolled closer to his returning former friend.

"Yup, now I'm just good old Ed L. Conrad, Lazarus. Do you know what the L stands for, man? Guess. No guess? Left-to-rot, you fuck." The visitor whispered to the new patient, "I haven't forgotten shit, you prick! Your ass is mine, mental boy. See you around campus."

Having completed his mission, the visitor disappeared as quickly and quietly as he had appeared. Had Tony been more coherent, he would have had good cause for alarm. However, the triple scooped tranquilizer sundae given him for his journey from hospital to hospital left him feeling no pain. As time wore on and his meds wore off, Tony experienced some realizations about his current situation. He knew he had been there before; he recognized some of the nuts walking around; he remembered the incessant questioning of that guy in the long white coat. Before long, Tony had regained his firm grasp on semi-reality. He still knew he was a war hero. He remembered his best friend, Russ, whom he had not seen in years. He asked to see his girlfriend Bina, whom he was going to ask to marry him. He knew he had to make a telephone call to someone named Twan, but he could not remember why. One afternoon while watching the Phil Donohue Show on the television in the Recreation Room, the light bulb above his head lit-up! The show was about reunions, long lost friends, siblings, parents and children reuniting on television for the entertainment of millions at home watching. It was as close to a Eureka experience as Tony's "fried" brain was capable of perceiving.

"Uncle Tony wants to speak with nephew Twan about his dad, the dead one, and the live one," he thought to himself. "Russ, you hurt me. I don't know why. I am back in this place because of you. Russell, when you fuck with the bull sometimes you get the horns. Let's just see how bad I can hurt you, fucker!"

Having been on his best behavior, which was no easy accomplishment, the head nurse allowed Tony to make a telephone call. He was to use this privilege to call his parents. Standing in the three-sided telephone carrel he leaned as close to the telephone as possible to guard his secrecy. The perfect scenario he thought would be to have the little "gook" home alone. Tony would plant a seed of doubt in his nephew's mind. Twan would have time to allow it to fester throughout the day. The boy would then need an answer to the festering query and would confront the source of the truth. He was so excited; he could barely dial the Russell's telephone number.

"Russell residence, this is Twan, may I help you?"

Encouraged by his good fortune, Tony responded, "Twan, this is your Uncle Tony. I'm calling from the hospital to see how everyone is doing," lied the patient.

"We're all good, Uncle Tony. How are you doing? I hope you're feeling better. Dad told me you were sick. Funny thing, I just signed a get-well soon card for you not two minutes ago."

"Hey, maybe we have a psychic connection or something, Twan," laughed Tony. "Look, kid, I like you, and I don't like lies or liars. I can't stand to see you deceived the way the Russells are deceiving you," lied Tony.

"What are you talking about, Uncle Tony?"

"Twan, did you know that James T. Russell knew your real father? Did you know he knows exactly what happened to your real father? Do you know he's been keeping it from you all these years? Twan, James T. Russell…."

Twan slammed down the telephone in anger borne of fear. He stood shaking as the phone rang repeatedly. He would not answer it this time.

CHAPTER 64

"OK, GUYS, TODAY WE ARE going to write a full-page composition, that is the minimum length, involving a discussion between two or more people of your choice who are discussing anything you choose. The people may be people from history, television, movies, real life, or cartoons. Your job will be to determine who will be in your composition, what the characters will be discussing, and the correct usage of quotation marks and other internal and external punctuation marks, which we have been studying for weeks. Are there any questions? Yes, Antonella?"

"You are offering us complete freedom in what we write?" asked the smiling, definitely out of place student.

"You have complete freedom within the guidelines of classroom and school appropriateness. In other words, proper language, limited use of slang, nothing from R-rated cable television movies," he smiled.

She raised her hand once more, "Is a love story appropriate?"

"Yes, I believe that would be fine," he replied hastily.

"Are there any other questions? OK, Tina, pass out the large yellow composition paper, please. Put your proper heading on the paper, draw your one-half inch margins, and begin," he directed.

Walter Holloway entered the room as the children were deeply engulfed in their assignment. He walked over to JT's desk, put an arm around his shoulder, and whispered into his ear:

"Is that your new student or Miss February?"

"You mean," JT whispered in return, "you hadn't met the young lady before you tricked me into this ungodly situation?"

"No, I had no idea. For the love of Christ, JT, be very careful in dealing with her. Make sure the two of you are not alone for any reason. I would never forgive myself if I helped get you into a pickle."

"What are you suggesting there, boss man? I'm not a schoolyard pervert," he whispered in mock protest.

"You wouldn't be the first guy to fall victim to a school girl crush. From the looks of that young lady and the way she looks at you, she may be ripe for one."

JT looked him in the eyes and said, "Great, I don't have enough to worry about."

Walter smiled and said, "I owe you a big one."

JT smiled at the principal and responded, "Will you stop talking like that. You're in a public school."

As the principal walked out, JT informed the class that any composition not completed in class would become homework due the following morning. With the dismissal time approaching almost everyone had to take the assignment home.

"OK, guys, do your jobs. Dismissal will be in five minutes," announced JT.

Each student attended to his/her assigned task which when completed would help result in a neatly cleaned, orderly, organized, classroom, just the way JT liked it.

"Mr. Russell, may I see you after school?"

JT turned his head toward the speaker. It was Antonella batting her eyes and licking her lips.

"Certainly, but may I help you now?" he asked.

"No thank you, I will wait until the others go," she smiled.

"Oh shit," he murmured to himself. "Hey, Bruno, did I tell you this morning that you owe me ten minutes for being late last week? " he called out.

"No, Mr. Russell, why?" questioned the shocked student.

"Well, I should have. Tonight – after school – ten minutes," he mumbled.

"Geez thanks," complained Bruno.

"Hey, don't do the crime if you can't do the time, buddy," he cracked.

A quick look toward Antonella by the teacher saw a look of dejection register on her face.

"If I have to live like this for months, I'll go nuts," he said to no one in particular.

"Tara, I'm home," announced JT.

"Oh, honey, could you go back out and come in again? The marching band hasn't warmed up yet," responded his multi-tasking wife.

"Whoa…is someone here having a really bad day? Perhaps someone has that PMS thing, you know… Pretty Mean Shit," he teased.

"Now, I really want you to go out again, and don't come back in, you shit. I have two little female Russells who have been arguing, pinching, teasing, and hair pulling since they both arrived home. I have an out of sorts mother-in-law downstairs who has been vomiting every fifteen minutes for an hour. To top things off, the other male member of this family has locked himself in his bedroom and won't accept callers. Yes, Jamey, I am having a really bad day, but this time it has absolutely nothing to do with my period."

"It sure is lucky you're married to me, Mrs. Russell. I'll just solve all these problems of yours so you can begin to prepare me a wonderful home cooked meal," smiled JT obligingly.

"Jamey, its take-out or bread and water," announced his wife.

He set upon his peace mission first quelling the warring factions in Katieland and Ronnieland. A few prudent suggestions about love and sisterhood, a ringing endorsement on non-violent protest, and a promise to visit the Salem Willows Amusement Park remedied the first near nuclear confrontation. He quickly departed the scene of the now amiable sisters whom he left to discuss the great things they were to do at Salem Willows. He popped downstairs to visit his ill mom.

She was no longer vomiting; however, the nausea had not gone. He placed cold pads on her forehead, and when she felt able, he forced a couple of non-aspirin tablets down her throat. He hand held; he cold-packed; he commiserated; he even got her to fall asleep. With two down and one to go, he confidently walked toward Twan's room. He applied their secret door knock (two long, three short, two long), but received no reply. He called to Twan trying to respect his privacy before entering the boy's room without permission. Still, he received no response. A turn of the handle found the lock engaged. He then became concerned. Privacy or not, JT knew he had to enter the room for his own peace of mind. The doorknob on Twan's door was one of those, which possessed the tiny emergency lock disengagement hole. A pin or needle inserted in the hole allowed the lock to be opened. The fact that he could not find a pin or needle immediately added to his nervous energy. The kid could be sick and unable to respond. He could have overdosed on some heinous drug slipped to him at audio/visual club. Worse yet, he could be looking at JT's old Playboys, which he found hidden in the basement near the furnace and was having his way with himself. Katie came to the rescue having taken a needle from her grandmothers sewing box. Commenting on her ingenuity, JT announced that she had just won the Russell children a second trip to Salem Willows. The announcement brought the house down! JT pushed in the needle and listened for the pop. Once he heard the sound, he announced to Twan that he was coming in. He found his son face down on his bed motionless except for the breathing, which he checked for immediately. He gently shook the boy who reluctantly rolled over. His eyes were swollen and red apparently from extensive crying.

"Twan, what's the problem?" he asked in his best fatherly voice. There was no response from the boy.

"Did something happen to upset you at school today?" he asked trying a second query.

There was still no response from the child.

"Twan, I can't help if you won't talk with me, buddy," he pleaded.

"Mr. Russell," Twan shocked his father by this formality, "do you ever lie? Have you lied in your whole life? Is there ever an OK time to lie?"

Taken aback, JT looked into the eyes of the obviously distressed child. Yes, Twan, I suppose I have lied in my life. Scientists tell us that most humans lie out of fear. The greater the fear, the more we are subject to lie. Is that OK? I don't really know how to answer that question. I guess if a lie prevents someone from being hurt, the reason has some justifiability…, but it is still not the truth. You know, like if you were looking at some new mother's baby who obviously resembles a monkey, most people would not tell her that her kid is a chimp. It's a lie, but it's protecting someone's feelings."

"So there is a time when lying is OK?" asked Twan.

"When a lie keeps someone from feeling bad, a lie is less bad I assume. All things being considered, buddy, as Shakespeare said, 'to thine own self be true', is probably the best test for each individual to use. Hey, kid, why are you doing all this deep thinking? Why did you lock your bedroom door? Why are your eyes big and red? Why did I get the 'Mr. Russell' greeting?"

Looking directly into JT's eyes, Twan asked, "Dad, did you know my real father?"

Shock registered on JT's face, which was easily recognized by his son. He had always known the time would come when the truth would have to be told. He just had not expected it so soon. He had two choices according to his self-preservation mechanism: deny, deny, deny and possibly avoid the pain of the revelation, or answer as honestly and straightforwardly as he knew how. The former offered safety in the status quo with the downside being the possibility of sinking deeper into a maze of lies. The latter, the frightening choice, offered to turn his world upside down. The ramifications could be life altering. He knew in his heart and mind that when this subject was finally to be addressed, he would choose the latter regardless of the consequences to his tight-knit little family.

JT reached for his son's hand, "Yes, Twan, I have some knowledge of your biological father. I have been waiting until I believed you to be capable of comprehending the entire story. Now, you have forced a change in those plans, and I must tell you whether you are ready or not. Before I begin, buddy, just of out curiously, why....how...did this arise now?"

"Uncle Tony called today. He said he hated lies and liars and that the Russells have been lying to me for years about my real father," wept Twan.

JT nodded forlornly, reached out a handkerchief to the weeping child, and placed an arm around his shoulders.

"Wait here, Twan, I have to get something for you. JT walked to his bedroom, knelt on the floor of the walk-in closet, and scavenged through a locked box from his military days. He collected the items he sought, placed them in a tote, and walked back to Twan's bedroom.

"Jamey, what do you want me to do for dinner?" yelled Tara.

"Put it on hold, hon, Twan and I have something to do," replied JT.

JT reentered Twan's bedroom, sat so that an open space lay between them, and carefully emptied the contents of the tote onto his bed. Twan looked at JT questioningly. In front of him on his bedspread lay a knife, a photo, and an unfinished letter.

"You're old enough to understand the concept of war, Twan. War is a condition that usually arises when one country's political ideals conflict with another country's political ideals. Each country's politicians get together on each side and vote to declare war on the other country. Since politicians are exempt from the life and death conditions of war, they need people to fight this war for them regardless as to whether their substitutes wish to fight or not. Now this is where your biological dad and I enter the story. We were two guys from two completely different cultures who hold absolutely nothing personally against each other. We do not even know each other. However, each of our countries tells us that we must hate each other. We must hate each other so much that we must try to take each other's life. Your dad and

I faced such a life or death situation in your native Vietnam. Both sides fought long and bitterly throughout the night. Ammunition ran out a few hours before dawn. My squad prepared for hand to hand combat. Your Uncle Tony and I basically said good-bye to each other before the hand to hand fighting began. We were out-numbered, out-flanked, and apparently out of luck. We prepared our bayonets for the attack. Tony and I stood back to back during the initial charge," JT paused for a moment to wipe his eyes. "Twan, I was never so scared in my entire life. Directly before me was an enemy soldier who I suppose was as frightened as I was. We held our bayonets in each other's direction. Neither of us appeared to want this to happen, but it was war, and it was kill or be killed. I was fortunate enough to disable my opponent first. As he lay dying, he stabbed me in my shoulder with his knife all the way to the hilt," JT said as he removed his shirt to show Twan the nasty remnants of his wound. "Before I lost consciousness, I grabbed a picture and piece of paper that had fallen out of the soldier's helmet. Why? I'll never know. Nevertheless, I held on to those items all the way to the hospital where a nurse had to pry the papers from my hand. Twan, I was the only one from my squad to leave that firefight to safety. My friends and fellow soldiers were either killed or taken prisoner. At the hospital, a Vietnamese nurse translated the letter and the back of the photo for me," he said lifting up the knife taken from his shoulder. The name on this knife is the name of the man I killed in that battle, Phong Ho Cheung, your father."

The boy threw himself into his father's arms and sobbed.

"Was this too much for you, son?" JT asked quietly.

"No, Dad, I needed to hear the truth. After that phone call from Uncle Tony, I began doubting you, Dad. I should have known better."

"Are we OK, then?" asked JT tearfully.

"Dad, there's one more thing I must know. Did you and Mom adopt me out of pity?" wept the child.

"As God is my judge, Twan, we adopted you for one reason and one reason only – we loved you. We wanted you as part of our family," wept JT.

"I needed to know that Dad, because I have never loved anyone the way I love you and Mom."

"I swear to you son, I will spend everyday of the rest of my life proving my love to you."

The two squeezed each other tightly as they cried into each other's shoulder. In the distance, they heard Tara Russell yelling that the girls and she were starving. JT and Twan looked at each other, smiled, and walked out of the bedroom.

CHAPTER 65

"GOOD MORNING, JT, YOU'RE LOOKING your usual handsome-self this morning, "said Marsha Peters one of his favorite women on the faculty.

Marsha Peters was a walking, talking, "wet dream". At fortyish, the five foot five inch, one hundred twenty-five-pound divorcee with "cover girl" looks, a great body, oozing sexuality, and a love for flirting utilized her gifts to their fullest. JT Russell was one of her favorite targets. The two had known each other so long and well that all the lines of propriety had been crossed and re-crossed repeatedly.

"Say, JT, who the hell is that Playmate of the Year you're housing in that bordello of a classroom you run? Jesus, JT, if elementary chicks are going to start looking like that, old chicks like me will never get laid," laughed Marsha.

"Marsha, we would never allow that to happen to you. I am almost sure we could find some derelict to couple with you. If not, I'll do it myself if I can get permission from Tara," teased JT.

"I look forward to it with or without the permission, stud," she said smiling as she spun and walked away.

"Don't pay attention to her, Little JT. She can only get us into trouble," thought JT to himself.

"Geez, JT, you're on a real streak. Nine to ninety, if they can't walk, you carry them," laughed Susan Wright, perhaps JT's closest female friend in the world. Sue and JT had a long history that solidified their friendship over the years. When she became his next-door neighbor at TLC Community School, their casual friendship evolved into something special. He loved her sense of humor, which at first intimidated him. As time passed, he felt more and more comfortable with her and allowed the real JT to come out and play. Susan was a complete package in JT's mind. She was smart, funny, very attractive, and wise beyond her years. He and she would hold nothing back from each other. She was a sympathetic ear, a source of sage advice, and just about the only person on the planet that could cause JT to laugh hysterically. As for her part, she felt comfortable telling him anything and everything often times things she did not share with her husband, Jeremy. There were no limits to their easiness with each other. JT could look into her eyes and know that she was menstruating. When she was troubled, he could recognize it immediately, and he then made it his business to bring her out of her malaise. They were two peas from the same pod, kindred spirits, and inseparable wits. JT often thought fondly of the day Susan explained her sister's theory of defending one's life at Judgment Day. According to Sue's sister, Janey, each of us will be required to view a video of our entire life on earth in the presence of God. The decision to go up to heaven or down to hell depended upon the evaluation of each individual's video by the Deity. JT got a kick out of Sue's suggestion that her life's video would have him billed as her co-star.

"Susan, you know, bedsides that woman who has legal rights to my life, you are the only woman in the world for me," JT smiled.

"Imagine if I had bigger boobs. Tara's position would be in jeopardy," laughed Sue.

"How shallow you must think me, madam. All Tetons need not be Grand Tetons, my dear Susan," JT checkmated her at her own game.

The two walked up to their classroom together teasing and joking in their usual manner. Susan stopped for a moment.

"JT, in all seriousness, be careful with that little hard body. A world of hurt awaits if you are not on your toes."

"Have you been talking to Walter?" asked JT.

"Why did he warn you too?" she asked.

"You wouldn't believe how hyper I get when the little chick gets too close or wants to get me alone," JT lamented. "I even kept a kid after school the other day for something he did last week so I wouldn't be alone with her."

"We both know about Little JT and his ability to run the James Thurber Russell Show, so watch it, moron!" she emphasized as she walked into her room.

The day was uneventful. The kids were on their best behavior. Since Antonella Lira's entry into the classroom, she had done a remarkable job of assisting JT with one on one tutoring, correction of assignments, and classroom management. So intimidated by her physical appearance, all the girls in class wanted to "be" her and all the boys wanted to "do" her. One of her classroom jobs was the checking-in of homework assignments. On that day, there was only one assignment to collect, the incomplete composition from the previous day. Once all the compositions were checked-in, she took hers and placed it on the top. JT was in for some interesting reading that evening! The classroom emptied quickly and quietly. JT grabbed the pile of compositions and put them into his briefcase. He walked through the swinging door to see Susan, but she was involved in deep discussion with her fourth grade colleagues, Angela Noto and Fran Blinska. He smiled at his three friends, waved good-bye, and headed back to his room to gather his briefcase. Off he went down the backstairs to the spot where he parked his car. Waving good-bye to Phil and George his custodian friends, he pulled out of the schoolyard and headed home.

With only the compositions to correct that evening, JT thought he would get an early start on them so he would have a duty-free evening. He retired to his small study and settled-in to correct a couple dozen compositions. His eyes focused upon the first composition on the pile. Antonella Lira was on top. Of course, he thought to himself. What followed set JT back on his heels. The composition read as follows:

Nella waited for the telephone to ring. She knew Jimmy was going to call, but she did not know when. They had met several weeks ago at the school where he taught. She knew right away that she was in love. Nella did not receive the same feeling from Jimmy at that time. As a new substitute teacher at his school, Nella asked him many questions about school rules. By the third time she substituted at his school, she noticed more interest from him. He tried to touch her hands and arms as they moved past each other. Finally, on her sixth day of work at his school, she walked into his room to say good-bye before leaving for the day. He asked her to sit down.

"Nella, do you have a boyfriend?" Jimmy asked her.

"No, I am a single lady. Why do you ask?" she blushed.

"I think you are the most beautiful woman I have ever known, Nella," said Jimmy.

He reached for her hair and ran his fingers through the long straight strands. He dropped her hair and began to trace a line around her face and lips.

"Do you want to kiss me, Jimmy?" Nella asked.

"You know I do, my love," said Jimmy.

"Why are you waiting?" she asked.

He placed his lips against hers and ran his tongue along her lips.

"Jesus Christ," whispered JT to himself. Wondering as he returned to the composition, "What the fuck does this kid have in her mind?"

Nella said, "Put your tongue in my mouth, Jimmy. You know you want to!"

He asked, "Can you read my mind, Nella?"

"Then don't!" she said angrily. "But you'll never know what you are missing!"

They kissed again. She opened her mouth wide and took his tongue deep into her mouth and sucked!

"I know you want to touch me, Jimmy!" said Nella.

"I want you to touch me too," said Jimmy.

"That was the beginning of our love affair," thought Nella.

The phone rang. She picked it up on the first ring.

"Nella, I have great news, my love," said Jimmy.

"Tell me my Jimmy love," said Nella.

"My wife died today. We can be together for now and forever!" said Jimmy.

Nella hung up the phone and dreamed of her and Jimmy together forever.

The End

"I am in deep shit. Walter better help get my ass out of this situation," whispered JT. He dialed the school telephone number. Walter Holloway answered himself.

"Walter? This is JT. I want you to listen to this. Then I want you to tell me what the fuck to do!" rambled JT excitedly.

Following the oral reading to Walter, JT felt worse than after having read it silently the first time.

"Who wrote that, JT?" asked the panicking principal.

"Guess, Walter," JT almost yelled. "Do the names Nella and Jimmy ring any bells, boss? Antonella and James sitting in a tree K-I-S-S-I-N-G…Remember the old verse, boss. Look, I am not laying blame at your feet, but you must get me out of this deal, buddy. Get in touch with her parents, the authorities, and the whole fucking U.N. if necessary. I want out, Walter, before it's too late."

CHAPTER 66

"May I speak with Anthony Delvane, please?" asked the voice at the end of the line.

"Mr. Delvane is not allowed to receive telephone calls at this time," responded the nurse.

"Well, m'am, he made a telephone call recently to my home. I think it only fair that I contact him in return."

"Hospital rules prohibit unauthorized telephone calls, sir," replied the nurse automatically.

"Well, get me authorization!" responded the angry man at the other end of the line.

"I could contact the patient's doctor, sir," offered the nurse.

"Do so, please," encouraged the caller.

"Please hold, sir," ordered the nurse.

The minutes ticked away, and the caller became angrier. After about ten minutes, the nurse clicked-in with permission from Dr. Sheldon Brown to allow Anthony Delvane to receive the telephone call. Another several minutes passed before a voice at the other end spoke.

"This is Tony Delvane. Who is this?"

"This is your former best friend, your former brother-in-law, and someone who used to give a shit about you!" railed JT Russell. "It didn't work, you putrid piece of rancid humanity. You tried to hurt my family, you prick, but it didn't work, freak! Yeah, you heard it;

you're a one eyed, one legged, no hearted freak! That is what you are – a living piece of shit! How does it feel to be in loony land again, Delvane? I pray your sorry ass never sees the light of another day in the sane world. Have a nice, medicated, straight jacketed life, you fucking freak! Good-bye!" screamed JT.

No one knows exactly how much of that diatribe Delvane actually heard. The "freak" terminology had sent him into a rage, which resulted in a destroyed telephone carrel, a double dose of tranquilizing juice, and a refit of his custom-made straightjacket. One interested observer watched the entire episode from his wheelchair in the company of his two new best friends. The three comrades reportedly thoroughly enjoyed the extreme distress exhibited by the man known to them as Lazarus.

CHAPTER 67

TARA TURNED TOWARD HER HUSBAND as they lay in bed. JT's gaze was fixated on the ceiling directly above his head. She weighed her decision as to whether or not to initiate a discussion of the perplexing situations that seemed to have deluged her shell-shocked partner. JT had been detached from the family over the past several days forgetting even the first of two promised Salem Willows trips with the kids. Her choices were simple: try to open him up and help him come to terms with his concerns, or roll over and go to sleep in hope that he would rebound all by himself. Though the choices were simple, the consequences were not. Would she be exacerbating the situation if she brought it to the surface? Would he feel his privacy invaded by her intervention? Would she be causing an emotional rift in their relationship with her unsolicited involvement? It never used to be that hard for her. Their relationship, with the exception of their dating years and Jamey's psycho behavior about the regularity of her menstrual cycle, had always been an open book. She never hesitated in casting her opinions into the mix whenever he got hot and bothered, but things had been different lately. Jamey appeared to be distancing himself from her. Certainly, the recent rash of emotionally charged events could explain that type of behavior. Her gut feeling told her it was more. Their full, rich, sex life, which they had enjoyed forever, had dissipated to a shell of its old self. She found herself having to concentrate lately in order to recall the latest episodes of their lovemaking. Stranger yet, not a week ago, she had offered to "clean Jamey's pipes", their euphemism for oral sex, before he had to leave for his evening school assignment. Jamey had turned her down, not rudely or unkindly, but Jamey never ever would have refused her offer in the past. "Pipe cleaning" was Little JT's favorite. Big JT liked it a lot too. His refusal not only took her aback, but it also hurt her. Perhaps he was losing interest in her as a woman. Was she letting herself go? Had she begun to take her husband for granted? Then it came to her. They needed a date. She decided to put the troubling thoughts out of her mind for the moment and try to sleep. In the morning, she would discuss the plans for a date with her husband. She would outline the topics with him, which she felt necessitated the action, and would encourage him to agree rapidly. The sooner she could get rid of that cloud hanging over her marriage, the sooner the normalcy would return to their life. That night she dreamed of two Jameys. One came home to her each evening, played with the children, and was attentive and loving. At the same time, a second Jamey could not remember her name when attempting to introduce her to friends. The second Jamey could not keep his eyes from other women. When Tara and he were together, he would make crude, sexual comments about what he would like to do to each passing female. During the course of the dream, the first Jamey kept shrinking in size while the second one became larger, more handsome, and extremely aloof. She witnessed herself aging quickly, approaching maximum density, and retreating to a windowless room. Waking up that morning was a blessing for Tara. Unfortunately, she had little difficulty remembering the smallest of details from that evening's nightmare. She needed no additional motivation to initiate her proposal to Jamey. However, had she needed a push, that evening's dream clearly offered the incentive. JT listened to his wife's concerns dutifully and agreed to her wishes without hesitation. Although he failed to view their current relationship at the same critical stage outlined by Tara, he respected her point of view.

That afternoon Tara arranged for reservations at the International Restaurant for the following evening, a Saturday. She asked Charlene if she would mind sitting with the children, which she did not. Tara then went shopping for just the right outfit for the date. On Saturday evening, the couple returned to their favorite restaurant and immediately involved themselves in their task. JT learned from Tara's conversation that his once so confident wife now had self-confidence problems. He felt that she was taking upon herself all of his problems as well as those of her own. JT believed that some of that behavior might be arising from having too much time to ponder family problems both major and minor. From Jamey, Tara surmised that he was at an extremely low point in both physical and mental energy. She listened to a man who sought answers to answerless questions. Still, Tara's innermost thoughts revolved around her Jamey's attraction to her. She finally found the courage to bring the words to the surface.

"Jamey, are we all right?"

"In what respect, hon?" he asked her.

"Are we still the same couple who couldn't keep their hands off each other? Are we the crazy people who made love standing-up covered by a blanket that night on Good Harbor Beach? Will we grow old together, Jamey, or have you grown away from me?"

He took both of her hands in his and looked directly into her eyes.

"First, young lady, I think the time is ripe for you to return to the workforce. I think we should make that our first priority. Second, when I need help with anything in my life, you are the first and only one to whom I come. Third, finally yet most importantly, although I am in a low cycle of psychic energy right now, I have not and will not ever change my feelings about you, our family, our life, and our marriage. Please believe that. It is a truth that will not alter in time."

"Well, Mr. Russell, you seem to have found the key to my trove of problems. I will be there whenever and if ever you need me. Our marriage is the most important aspect of my life. I will protect it with my life. All I ask of you, love, is should we grow apart please talk with me first before acting. I could not live being a "last one to know" wife. I will love us forever, Jamey."

They sealed the deal in their classic style by standing and bending toward each other over the table to share a kiss. After paying the bill, they went directly home and had some "not so loud" sex.

CHAPTER 68

"ARE YOU SURE YOU WANT this done, Lucifer? We could get our asses in a sling for something this crazy," bemoaned Curtis Waltham, a tall, muscular black who had become an intimate of Ed Conrad.

"That's just it, Curtis. We have the perfect defense, man. We're nuts. We're not responsible for our actions. I want this to happen more than anything else in my fucking life, man, and you will help make it happen," smiled the devil.

Buddy Lee Hooks, a monster of a man in height and weight, joined them as the discussion continued.

"I was just telling old Curtis here our plans for our old friend, Buddy Boy," said Lucifer in welcoming the giant to the group.

"I've planned this sucker forever, men, and I'll not be denied. That freak's ass is mine, and I do mean his ass," laughed a maniacal Ed Conrad. "Here's how it goes down. When Lazarus walks into the shower this evening, you two clear the place out, but do it gently, quietly so the nuts don't make a fuss. Once the pigeon is under the showerhead, Buddy Lee, you go into action. Put the sucker on the floor of the shower with his ass up. Make sure he doesn't move a muscle. Curtis, you take me from my chair while I rip off my drawers. When the little solider is saluting, you're gonna set me down on the bastard. I'm gonna give him the ride of his fucking life. When I'm done, you guys can have fun taking turns if you want. Buddy Lee, don't forget the gag. That pig will be squealing loud enough to wake up all the nuts in this place. Any questions, my friends? Good. Until this evening, my brothers."

For so many months, which turned into years, Ed Conrad had monitored every movement of every individual in the mental health ward at the hospital, both patient and staff. He found the best time and place to put into effect his plan for vengeance. The choice of Hooks and Waltham as his new comrades was part of the preparation. He needed big strong men who were not too particularly bright. The men must be susceptible to Lucifer's style of subliminal suggestion or "brainwashing" in its more common context. Conrad had invested months of recruiting time, befriending, and then molding his new puppets to his own specifications. All of this planning by Conrad depended upon his hope that Tony "Lazarus" Delvane would return to the hospital. In Conrad's mind, it was not a question of if he would return. It was simply a question of time. Lucifer had imparted almost everything he knew to his then best friend Delvane. He schooled him well in the art of being a chameleon – to be what they expected him to be; however, he did not share all his knowledge with the released patient. Conrad knew that Delvane would be back because Lazarus had no real control of his anger. He could hide it temporarily. He could moderate it on occasion, but eventually it would be his downfall – his Achilles heel – and Lucifer knew it. In addition, Conrad did not fully inform his cohorts of his plans for that evening. The jilted demon made special arrangements for his former partner that he shared with nobody. Neither man knew that Anthony James Delvane would never leave that shower room alive.

CHAPTER 69

IT WAS TIME FOR A breather. All of his students had left the building after one of those difficult type days. It seemed that on particular days, some unknown being in some unknown way was capable of adding a couple of extra hours to the school day. That was the case this day. JT rocked back on his desk chair, ignored the papers he had intended to correct, folded his hands behind his head, and breathed deeply. He closed his eyes and practiced the relaxation breathing techniques that Paulette "Polly" Edwards, his Reiki master and first grade teacher friend had taught him. JT held a hypnotic fascination for Polly. A short, attractive, highly intelligent woman of forty who appeared younger than her years, the possessor of a truly remarkable spirit and will, and a loyal, dependable confidant with whom JT had the most interesting conversations. Polly was always willing to share her empathetic philosophy of life and healing abilities with those lost or in distress. She and JT would discuss topics of spirituality, faith, and supernatural based subjects. No one else in his world offered access to that particular area of interest and instigated his quest for further knowledge. Polly had gone beyond friendship in sharing her gifts with JT especially during certain life altering events as the death of his dad. He decided he needed to make a point of seeing Polly soon for a much-needed "heart to heart" talk and perhaps even a Reiki session. The first time she worked her "magic" upon him was in her classroom one day after school. She had brought in her folding table and proceeded to try to relax the cowardly JT before a doctor's physical he was to undergo. Few knew, except for those few unlucky physicians and nurses and of course, his immediate family, that JT possessed a terrible case of "White Coat Syndrome". When placed in the same room with a physician, JT's blood pressure would attempt to escape from his body. Strangely enough, that was not the case following a session with Polly. Her ministrations left him very relaxed and usually asleep. His outstanding memory of her was the relaxing effect she had upon him. He marveled at the incredible heat generated from her hands and arms during a Reiki session. A need to reach-out and feel that radiance still lingered in his mind whenever he talked with her. He made a mental note to see her in the morning. As he was about to open his eyes and prepare for his trek home, a familiar voice startled him.

"Are you sleepy, Mr. Jamey Russell?"

It was Antonella Lira. A sense of panic and then impending disaster raced like an electric charge through his body.

"Well, you certainly frightened me, Antonella. Why are you here?" he managed to ask.

She approached his chair as he was attempting to rise. She reached for his hand to help him to his feet. Lifting himself awkwardly from his chair with the help of his surprise visitor and standing before the grinning young woman, he felt extremely self-conscious. She, on the other, appeared composed and relaxed. Still holding his hands in hers, she released his left hand and took his right hand in both of hers as she placed it upon her left breast and sighed.

"Stop that immediately, young lady!" rang out a voice from the rear of the room. You should be ashamed of yourself! Do you have any idea of the seriousness of your actions? Do you realize that you could ruin your teacher's career and marriage?" yelled a brilliantly red-faced Susan Wright. "I watched everything you did, young lady, so let there be no mistake about what just happened here! Were you my daughter, I would lock you in your room and throw away the key. In all my years of dealing with children, I have never seen a more disgusting example of behavior by a student toward a teacher!"

The girl was in tears at this point holding her arms across her chest.

"Mr. Russell, this must be reported immediately to the principal. I trust you agree?" added the seething Sue Wright.

"Absolutely, Mrs. Wright," responded JT.

The girl was hysterical now as the two teachers walked her to the principal's office. Several times, she looked to be on the verge of fainting, but the only assistance she received was an arm on her shoulder by Susan Wright. Walter Holloway was sitting at his desk taking a welcomed respite from the trials and tribulations of the day when his two favorite teachers walked into his office quite flustered. He could not believe his ears. He would have never imagined that a child so young could be driven to an action so blatantly sexually harassing.

"Where is she now?" he asked after hearing the entire story. "Young lady, in here, now!" he commanded. "Do we not have a meeting arranged tomorrow with your guardians concerning your composition writing?"

The utterly embarrassed child nodded her head, stared at the floor, and continued sobbing.

"How could you disrespect this man, a man who has been extremely kind and considerate of you, in such a disgusting fashion?" asked the irate principal.

The girl looked up at the principal in obvious confusion. Her glance then met that of her teacher. "Disrespect? Disgusting? I love him!" yelled the child.

"I've heard enough. Mrs. Wright, please telephone her guardian immediately. I must see her at once. I will not accept 'No' for an answer from her!" continued the flustered educator.

"You, young lady, will sit out in the waiting area until your guardian arrives. Then together we will decide the best course of action regarding your behavior and the continuance of your education at this school. Mr. Russell, Mrs. Wright, I offer my apologies to both of you from the staff, the parents, and students of T. Lewis Carroll Community School. Such behavior is inexcusable. To experience such behavior anywhere, let alone in a public school, is unforgivable. Please accept my apology. We will speak tomorrow after my meeting with Antonella's guardians. Please go home and try to forget the terrible events of this day."

Sue looked toward JT who in turn looked back at her, "Thank you, Mr. Holloway. We will see you in the morning," announced Mrs. Wright as both teachers turned and exited the office.

On their journey back upstairs to their classrooms, the intimate friends shared a hug. JT held her very tightly as he thanked her for being in the right place at the right time.

"Well, dickhead, did I not warn your feeble ass about this very thing?" she teased. "Look there's no accounting for taste, and she is very young so don't get your already overly inflated ego pumped up by Lolita's actions!" laughed Sue Wright.

"You know, if you had been just a few minutes later, I'd have had a date for this weekend," teased JT.

"Sue, tell me, are yours as firm as the kid's?" taunted JT.

"You've copped enough feels over the years you pig bastard. I should have turned around and walked away from you and the little chick. By this time you'd be back in jail with Big Bubba, your old roommate," she smiled. "Besides, stud, all you'd have to do is ask and my boobs are yours," she teased.

"You mean I've been doing it wrong all these years, Sue?" bemoaned JT.

They joined up again after clearing out their respective rooms and began their usual after school walk from the building. He stopped her before he opened the exit door for her, took her hand, and looked into her blue eyes.

"Thank you so much for being you and for being there today. You are the best," he whispered getting overly sentimental.

"We've known that for a long time, buddy. Let's just listen to mama when mama tells Little JT to stay away from the jail bait."

She pecked his lips, turned around, and glided through the now open door.

"See you," she called out as she climbed behind the wheel of her car.

He waved and smiled as her car passed by. Off she went in her direction home, and he drove in the opposite direction. By the time he arrived home, he had just about two hours before his evening school class began. He walked through the front hall announcing his return from the wars. Tara popped-out from the kitchen walked up to him and gave him a monster hug and kiss.

"Well, what was that for?" questioned her pleased husband.

"Oh, I just got off the phone with Sue Wright. She told me you'd probably be horny tonight," laughed Tara.

"Women, I'm surrounded by the creatures...Thank God," smiled JT.

CHAPTER 70

"ARE WE GOING TO SHOWER tonight, Tony?" Tony Delvane asked himself. "Why don't we check?"

He sniffed under one arm and then under the other. Satisfied that he passed the sniff inspection sufficiently, he voted thumbs down on the shower issue. He left his room to go to the Recreation Room using a crutch instead of refitting his prosthesis. The one-eyed, one-legged patient adjusted his black eye patch as he plodded along the hallway to his destination. Moments earlier, the loud, tough-talking attendant that Tony did not particularly care for had hurried into a patient's bathroom for an emergency intestinal evacuation of the three plates of spicy Tex-Mex food he ingested at the cafeteria during lunchtime. The bloated, gaseous, cramping attendant exploded multiple times into the hopper. The fragrance so upset his now delicate stomach that he began vomiting into the now "filled to capacity" bowl. The longer he leaned toward the disgusting refuse in the bowl, the more he vomited. The more he vomited the more the bowl deposited its contents onto the floor. At some point, the poor bastard could take it no longer, so he gathered the strength to flush the bowl hoping for the contents to disappear. Just the opposite occurred. The disgusting combination of bodily fluids had badly clogged the works. The smelly, colorful mess of human excretion poured out of the bowl over the floor and under the door onto the hallway floor. An unsuspecting Tony Delvane was just fortunate enough to be passing the disaster area as the "levee" broke.

His crutch slid through the obscene mixture causing him to lose his balance and land full-bodied onto the gross puddle. As Tony cursed and ranted about his misfortune, a brave soul, who obviously cared more about helping his fellow man than wallowing in a shit storm, assisted Tony from his distress. Tony no longer passed his self-styled sniff test. In fact, he so disgusted himself that he walked directly to the shower room after asking his rescuer to gather a set of clean clothing from his room. They met at the entry to the shower room where Tony continually thanked the man for his assistance.

"I don't even know your name, friend. I thank you from the bottom of my heart, man," said Tony earnestly.

"No problem, brother. You just get yourself straightened out. When you get some time, you come see me. My name is Curtis Waltham, man."

CHAPTER 71

THE NEWS OF THE PREVIOUS day did not take long to navigate through the TLC Community School grapevine. JT was welcomed to school the next morning with a plethora of humorous and near humorous comments from the females of the teaching staff.

"Good morning, Studly," cooed Marsha Peters, edging closer to JT as he walked toward the Teachers Room. "Tell me, lover, I hear that the young chicks go for the 'not so hung'."

"Morning, Marsha, can't you remember that far back?" he smiled and continued walking.

"Good morning, Mr. Russell, could you show me the way to the little girls' room?" Millie Waldron his former ESL teaching partner sing-songed in her best Shirley Temple impersonation.

"It's been a long time since that curvaceous butt of yours could fit a little girls room commode, my dear Millie," he sing-songed back to her.

"JT! Oh, JT! My niece needs an escort to her Campfire Girls Jamboree. She's eight. Is she too old for you?" teased Paulette Edwards sending herself into hysterics.

"Et tu, Polly?" he drolly retorted to the hysterical woman.

As he entered the Teachers Room, he witnessed the absolute prize-winning contribution. Amidst a standing room only crowd, he viewed at the center of the long cloth-covered table, which extended almost to the end of the ten foot by twenty-foot room, three dolls: Ken, Barbie, and Skipper. The Ken doll was in the middle; Barbie was to his left, and Skipper, Barbie's niece or best friend or something, was to his right. An oaktag sign lay at the feet of the three dolls outlining Ken's dilemma:

"Barbie, you've let yourself go as you've aged. I can no longer continue this fraud of a relationship. Skipper offers me youth, and youth, and youth, and natural boobs."

"Ken, she's just a baby! What is she a thirty-two C? What will you two have to talk about? What do you have in common?"

"I can think of three things real fast, lady."

"First, Barbie, we both are deeply in love with me! Second, age is nothing but a number. Third, Skipper has yet to experience mature love. Skipper, get your lunchbox and backpack. It's L-O-V-E time!"

"Very friggin funny, my friends, remind me to invite you to my next tragedy," laughed JT.

All his teaching ladies gave him hugs and kisses as they passed him on the way to their classrooms. He smiled to himself in the now empty Teachers Room at this excellent fortune of having such friends. As he turned to leave, Walter Holloway was walking in.

"I had NOTHING to do with this. My lips have been sealed since the incident, but if I were you, I would look to our friend Sue Wright," laughed the beaming principal. "By the way, kid, she's gone. Your little Lolita's guardians were so humiliated that they could not wait to get the girl out of here. We have seen the last of that little bombshell. In addition, JT, would you please try not to be so irresistible! This shit takes a lot out of me," joked the principal as he pursed his lips in a mock kiss and blew it toward the embarrassed teacher.

"Hey, Walter, I draw the line at pedophilia."

CHAPTER 72

Mildred Waldron, twelve years JT's senior, had been his teaching partner before he moved from ESL to his current fifth grade position. The five foot four inch tall, one hundred twenty pound, brown-haired, Mrs. Waldron was perhaps the sweetest person in JT's world. Because they shared a common ancestry, the former Millie Giadona, immediately discovered the way to JT's heart by making him a variety of cream filled pastries and Italian food leftovers for lunch. The two hit if off instantly. There probably was not a soul on earth who could not get along with and love the woman. The single obstacle in their relationship was philosophical in nature. Millie, in JT's eyes, was perhaps the world's most permissive educator and parent. Millie was just too good for her own welfare. She treated hostility, rudeness, disrespect, and anger with kindness. Each person with whom she dealt was more important to her than she was to herself. Millie had made a career of turning the other cheek with almost everyone in her life. This character trait drove JT to distraction. In his eyes, the reward for goodness should never be abuse, but she continually made herself the target of such abuse by allowing her students, her work friends, and, he supposed, even her family to take advantage of her gentle demeanor. There lay the single area of conflict in the personal and working relationship of Mildred Waldron and JT Russell. The saddest aspect of the situation was that JT spent years trying to change his friend to no avail.

"People don't change, JT. We are what we are," Mildred would recite time after time to her friend.

He would always counter with the fact that human beings are in a constant state of change. Those individuals who adapt successfully to this state of flux are usually the most sane, most happy, most successful on the planet he would argue. The argument always broke down at that point with her issuance of her trademark interjection "horse puckies" which signified that the end of the discussion had been reached; she chose to hear no more; he did not convince her that she and not he was wrong. Millie had the most remarkable ability to "will" herself to be, do, or perform that which was alien to her own wants and needs and to do so without feeling put upon. Should an acquaintance make some out-landish request such as asking Millie to house her three hideous cats for the duration of the friend's six month vacation, Millie would do it without so much as an "ouch". When she was first married, her husband became upset with her because she did not keep house up to his mother's standards. Rather than make the situation a monumental obstruction to their married life, she set about to become a clone of his mother in every facet of her wifely duties whether she agreed with the practices or not. She was just too good for her own sake, and JT believed she needed protecting. Therefore, he named himself her protector with or without her permission. JT became the one who complained to the inquirer when unrealistic requests were made of her. He remained the disciplinarian for her ESL students after he left that program. He listened and gave her sage advice in personal matters. As an illustration to the strength of his feelings concerning matters of her wellbeing, many times in the heat of anger he threatened to terminate all connections to her should she make a decision that obviously favored another's welfare at the expense of her own. JT would often times reach a point of distraction in dealing with Millie. He would debase himself about his fruitless attempts to help the woman. The confused friend had no idea why he should care so much about her welfare until in the midst of a particularly robust argument, JT in a loud voice said, "Rose Marie, you're driving me crazy!"

Millie looked at him strangely and asked, "Who's Rose Marie, JT? You just called me Rose Marie," she responded.

"What? Perhaps you misheard me. I don't know a Rose Marie, Millie," lied JT.

CHAPTER 73

THE CONSPIRATORS GATHERED OUTSIDE THE occupied shower room. They had spent the past several minutes discouraging any patients who sought an evening cleansing and sent each off in the direction from whence he came. Ed Conrad suggested to his accomplices that they give their victim a chance to get himself clean and presentable before implementing the plan. On Lucifer's mark, Buddy Lee stripped down to his shorts and tee shirt and moved into action. Within moments, a frightfully surprised Tony Delvane found himself upended by a huge pair of arms attached to a hairy giant of a man. Once introduced rudely to the shower room floor, Tony Delvane felt the monstrous Buddy Lee sitting upon his back. The attacker applied the cloth gag between his victim's jaws. The giant pulled the gag tightly and double knotted it behind Tony's head. Leaving his wheelchair outside of the shower room, Ed Conrad entered the showering area in the arms of Curtis Waltham. Delvane was kicking his leg and thrashing his arms until the mountain resting on his back grabbed his arms and maneuvered them behind the victim's back in a very precarious position – an errant movement could easily snap an arm, elbow, or shoulder. Curtis had set his friend, Lucifer, on the floor and the legless man quickly removed all his clothing. All the while, Lucifer was describing to his former best friend exactly what he was going to do to him.

"Yo, Lazarus man, I told you so, man. You fucked with devil. Now, the devil is gonna fuck with you. "

"Move me, Curtis," ordered Conrad.

Curtis Waltham hesitated a moment in recognition of fact that he was about to place his arms around a fully aroused, naked man.

"Let's go, man. We ain't got all night!" raged Lucifer.

The muscular black man took a deep breath and lifted the naked, thoroughly excited, legless man. As he held the man airborne, he noticed a glint of something catching the light of an overhead bulb. Lucifer had placed something under the armpit of his missing limb, and he held it there securely under his stump. Waltham laid the crazed triple amputee on the back of Tony Delvane. Buddy Lee had to reposition himself to give Lucifer access to his destination. Now with Buddy Lee kneeling before him holding his arms at another incredibly awkward angle, Tony Delvane felt the presence of a second invader.

"Get ready, you prick. The time for Lucifer's revenge has come," yelled the excited little man.

It was at that point that Curtis recognized what Lucifer had under his armpit. It was a box cutter!

"Hey Buddy Lee, the dude's got a cutter!" yelled Curtis.

"Lucifer, we want no part of this shit!" yelled the huge Hooks.

"Shut the fuck up you two chicken-shits. Lazarus ain't ever gonna rise again!" screamed the out of control patient.

Out of the shower, ran two of the three conspirators, leaving the legless, one armed, naked Lucifer on the back of a man whose throat he had just slit from ear to ear! As the final breath was leaving Tony's lifeless body, he called out, "Russ, forgive me…As his eyes closed, he watched as Rose Marie Lloyd floated toward him with welcoming, open arms.

"Come back here! I command you! By my powers of darkness, I command you to return!" screamed the blood-covered murderer.

The little man could do no more than make a vain attempt to crawl out of the killing room and back toward his chair. Even had he been successful in navigating such a path, he would have found his chair resting on its side, wheels still spinning, against a far wall. Two panicking orderlies, investigating the screams and recent revelations of Lucifer's two former friends, found the crawling, blood-covered, unclothed Lucifer pulling himself from the shower room exit. They subdued the suddenly superhumanly strong, little man and held him at bay until the authorities arrived and escorted the howling maniac to the police wagon along with Buddy Lee Hooks and Curtis Waltham. The three conspirators who took the life of Anthony James Delvane were loaded into the police wagon just as the city coroner pronounced the victim dead at the scene of the crime.

CHAPTER 74

JT SAT IN HIS RECLINER, pulled the handle on the right side toward him, and pushed himself back. Tara, the dear girl, had taken all three kids to the Topsfield Fair. Initially she met resistance from Twan who would have preferred to go to the fair in the evening with his friends. Tara had absolutely no problem with that request; however, she did add a stipulation of her own to his plan. The academically brilliant high school senior had to attend the fair first with his sisters and overly burdened mother who desperately needed assistance in closely monitoring the movements of her two precocious little girls. Twan could appreciate the logic in the request and readily agreed to the arrangement. Therefore, JT sat relaxing in his favorite chair collecting his thoughts while attempting to formulate a financial plan for the kids' further education as the remainder of his family made merry at the fair. At eight years of age, Katie Anne was now in the fourth grade at St. Peter's School. Ronnie, two years her junior, had just entered the second grade at the same school. The education of both his little girls required monthly tuition payments. He lamented silently that such an expense would not have existed had they gone to public school, as he had wanted. Then there was Twan. Since the seventh grade, his son had gotten no final grade lower than an A-. Now with the young man beginning his senior year, the college search was well underway. As a junior, he scored over fifteen hundred on his SAT's in May. At the conclusion of his junior year, he had applied to Harvard

University, MIT, Yale, and Stanford for early acceptance. JT felt sure that his son's credentials merited serious consideration for "full-boat" scholarships at any of the four schools. Well, he prayed that he was sure. Even with Tara's return to J. Hollingsworth Furniture Company as their customer relations specialist, and his four part-time jobs at the CALL Adult Learning Center, the Massachusetts English As A Second Language Education Program, Monitor Counseling, Inc.,and Operation It's Your Time, the family expenses just could not take a hit like the cost of any Ivy League education. JT physically could not spread himself any thinner. The schedule he maintained kept him away from Tara and the kids a great deal more than he wished. He was already beginning to feel the effects of his frequent absences on his body in the form of stress brought about by his personal guilt feelings, and he had become aware of a distancing of the children from their father. What was he to do? He could seek a principalship at another school. The additional money resulting from that promotion could possibly allow him to abandon one or more of the part-time positions. The downside to that scenario would be that he would have to leave the classroom. However, why should he? He was a teacher. The man believed that he held the job for which he was destined. Was he willing to sacrifice his direct involvement in the classroom to make a few more dollars as an administrator? In addition, his part-time jobs, especially the adult education positions, were a source of great satisfaction and fulfillment for him. Which of the positions would he leave were he to take on the additional duties of a principal? Was it to be money or career satisfaction? Was it to be selling oneself out to move up or sacrificing forever financially? He then thought of Laertes standing before his boring father, Polonius, listening to his fatherly advice, as he shared his wisdom in Shakespeare's play Hamlet:

"And this above all, to thine own self be true."

"To thine own self be true," he repeated out loud. "I am what I am. I teach. That is my calling. I would be doing myself a grave disservice by making a decision based solely on monetary gain. I must be true to myself. I will make this money thing work. I must be where

I am needed most – in the classroom," he concluded. Closing his eyes, he dozed off exhausted from the mental combat of the past few moments.

CHAPTER 75

Diana Brian-Wisdom tossed back her long dark brown hair as she sat before the mirror of her make-up table.

"If being beautiful were only not so much work…" she teased herself. "Well, Diana, let's get to it. We wouldn't want to be late on our first day now would we?"

Ms. Brian-Wisdom was the new director of the Calling All Level Learners Adult Learning Center, the Call Adult Learning Center. Chosen over two dozen highly qualified candidates, she was to supervise a staff of three full-time daytime instructors and one part-time evening instructor, none of whom had she met to date. The twenty-nine year old, personable, remarkably attractive woman had recently returned to the North Shore following her divorce from David Wisdom, her husband of three years. She had taken-up residence in a one-bedroom condominium in Marblehead not far from Mr. and Mrs. Theodore Brian, her very well to do parents. She knew she should have listened to them when they quite openly spoke about their objection to her marriage to the politically active David Wisdom, a lobbyist for the oil industry. They just did not approve of the amount of time the couple would be separated by his business demands; neither of her parents approved of his less than nurturing behavior toward Diana; and the amount of alcohol he consumed simply added an exclamation point to their objection to her becoming Mrs. Wisdom. Nevertheless, she married the man, and she lived to tell about it – just barely.

"Spilt milk, Diana. Split milk," she mumbled to herself.

The brief marriage had left her wounded, emotionally scarred, and leery of the male gender as a whole. The physical and emotional abuse occurring during the final nine months of that union had essentially caused her to be suspicious of all men and, at worst, made her a great candidate for heterosexual celibacy. Still, the woman maintained a magnetic, "bubbly" personality and life's energy that drew people towards her. She hoped that this would be true of her new staff, but if that did not turn out to be the case, the lady could also play "hardball" with the best on the block.

"Face on, check. Hair beautiful, check. Perfect outfit, check. Bouncy boobs, check. Pearly white teeth, check. Smell like a million bucks, check. I think we are ready, Diana. How about you?"

She checked her planner for the one thousandth time that morning. Of course, nothing had changed. She was to meet the supervisor of Adult Education for the City of Peabody, Seymour Freed, for breakfast just down the street from the storefront-formatted Call Center. Following breakfast, he would introduce her to the staff as the new director of the center. Fortunately, for her overachieving, stressed self, she did not have to work one of her two long days until the following day since the Call Center operated only two evenings per week, Tuesdays and Thursdays until 9:00 PM.

"So, I'll be meeting Tamara Grus, Annabelle Cerdut, and Candace Arching today. Tomorrow, I will meet with James T. Russell," mused the obsessive Ms. Brian-Wisdom. "It's show time," she whispered.

She popped out of her condominium into her black Ford Mustang. Checking her face in the mirror, probably not for the last time that morning, she smiled and started the car. Off she went on the first day of what she hoped would be a new and improved life.

JT was standing in the second floor bathroom at school making last second adjustments to his outfit prior to entering his classroom. He ran his schedule through his mind.

"I'll be at Operation It's Your Turn tonight and Wednesday night. As per usual, there is MESLEP on Saturday. I'll be counseling my

Monitor clients on Friday evening, and I get to meet my new "boss lady" on Tuesday at the Call Center. Not to worry, right Little JT? If she's a female, she'll love me."

There was so much more fact to that lighthearted statement than fiction. JT always had many more close female friends than male. He never really thought intellectually to dissect that situation. Females nine to ninety years of age just seemed to like him immediately although he had always considered himself an "acquired taste". The reason for this stroke of remarkable good fortune could not be credited to his physical appearance since he possessed neither movie star good looks nor physique. Nor could it be attributed to a purely intellectual basis because there were many brighter bulbs on the tree than he. His personality was most probably part of the answer. JT's total and absolute appreciation for the female gender also entered into the equation. His unbridled nature and uncensored sense of humor helped more than hurt. No matter, wherever the answer lay, JT was greatly appreciative of the results.

CHAPTER 76

THE SAME DAY ANTHONY JAMES Delvane entered his final resting place at St. Joseph's Cemetery was the same day that James Thurber Russell met a fellow educator who would be an important part of his life for the next twenty years. As JT looked back at that day over the years, he always felt strangely because he came to visualize that day as a sort of odd departure/arrival scenario. Out went someone who had played an important role in the "making" of JT Russell, in-came another person who would play an important role in the future of JT Russell. He saw it as a weird example of an even exchange. Following his good-byes at the early morning private family service for Tony, JT left immediately for work. He had promised Walter that he would be at school on that day to welcome the new remedial reading teacher, Jerry Sherman. Walter was thrilled to be getting a teacher of that man's caliber at the Carroll Community School; additionally, he was welcoming a male faculty member into a school that was composed of female educators who held a four or five to one ratio majority. With staff departures and arrivals, Mr. Sherman would be only the fifth male in the building including the two building custodians. Walter Holloway was a strong believer in the male influence in elementary school buildings, not only at the administrational level, but also throughout the classrooms even at the first grade if possible. Although a hollow victory of sorts for Holloway, he saw the addition of a single, highly recommended male to his faculty as a sign of things to come.

Walter combined JT's class that morning with Millie Waldron's small class until the funeral concluded. One could only imagine the scene he would find upon his return. JT knew the rest of the day would be pretty well lost. To pull his students back into a learning environment mentality after having spent a couple of hours in the Disneyland of classrooms would be extremely difficult. He was correct. The kids were a mess. Once he cut his class from the combined herd, he started their attitude readjustment therapy. By lunchtime, after combining his carefully crafted behavior policy with every known punishment threat known to the civilized world, his kids were back to their normal level of functioning. Walter had informed JT upon his return to the building that he and Jerry Sherman would be coming upstairs to JT's classroom for a "get-to-know-you" lunch. As the lunch-aide begged his students to line-up for lunch with little success, JT simply introduced "Rock Hudson" the one-pound bolder he kept on his desk, a souvenir from Donald Trowl, a former student, who threw the projectile through his classroom window yelling to Mr. Russell to stick it up his ass! Once the pounding started, the poor behavior stopped. This was a display of behavior modification at its finest. The children lined-up and off they went on their merry way to lunchland.

Both Walter Holloway and Jerry Sherman had been observing the performance.

"Nice rock, JT," teased Walter.

"Whatever works, boss," replied JT.

"Please explain to Jerry that you don't use that on the kids, JT," smiled Walter.

"Hi Jerry, I'm JT. It's a pleasure," sticking out his right hand. "I don't use the rock on all the kids. Just those really deserving ones," teased JT.

Jerry Sherman was a former Lynn resident who left the city to seek his fortune. After several years away from home, he had decided that a career change was necessary. Upon leaving his former occupation, the six-foot tall, thin, obviously nervous man had spent two years in a Western suburb of the Commonwealth learning the teaching trade. He still harbored doubts about having given-up his previous well paying career as a mortician. However, he was returning home to work in the school system, which graduated him. Strangely, he was returning to the very elementary school he attended as a child. The offer from the Lynn School System was just what he had been waiting for. He packed up his wife, Gwen, and their two children, Samantha and Sherman, and headed back home. Unfortunately, they were unable to find suitable housing in Lynn; therefore, he and his family took up residence in the neighboring community of Saugus. JT liked the man immediately. He was void of pretense and hubris. He laughed at the proper times, added cogent comments to the discussion, and presented himself as a unique character in a building full of unique characters. Jerry Sherman reaffirmed his uniqueness when he removed a whole fish head from his lunch bag and began to devour it immediately. Walter absolutely avoided eye contact with JT for if either had looked toward the other, the resultant hysterical laughter would have been too difficult and embarrassing to explain. Walter managed to explain without laughing that he was placing Jerry in the vacant half-room down the hall from JT's classroom. His and JT's classrooms would be in close proximity of each other. The placement made perfect sense to JT since Jerry would be working with fourth, fifth, and sixth grade students identified with reading difficulties. With all three grades grouped together on the second floor, Jerry's ready access to his students saved important instructional time. Almost immediately, JT had a good feeling about the new teacher – fish head and all.

CHAPTER 77

"Please call me Diana," smiled Ms. Brian-Wisdom as she extended her hand to JT.

"Thank you, I shall," countered JT taking her small, soft hand in his. "And please call me, Mr. Russell."

There was no expected laugh from the lady, just a puzzled look.

"I'm only kidding, Diana. You may call me whatever your heart desires," JT quickly backpedaled.

Now she smiled and then laughed more at the ease with the fashion which her new colleague handled their introduction than at the intended humor.

JT thought to himself, "This is going to be a tough room to play with Ms. Brian-Wisdom in attendance. Hey folks, come-on back. I'll be appearing here all week…maybe."

"I have heard so much about our 'Night Knight' that I was looking forward to meeting you in person, Sir JT," smiled Diana.

"Now that the disappointment has set in, you'll probably not believe another word you hear around here," smiled JT. "By the way, Diana, who came up with the 'Night Knight' thing?"

"I understand a rather large group of your students identify you in that manner, if not to you, to each other," answered Diana.

"This is the first time I've heard it in that context. I just hear people saying night, night to me as they wave and leave. Of course it's appropriate, Diana," he mugged. "It is just a bit surprising to hear about it for the first time from one's new boss."

"Well, JT, I understand that you are tremendously popular with students and staff alike. I hope that we will become good friends, not just employer/employee," responded Diana.

"I know we will Diana," smiled JT.

"Would I be keeping you from anything important were I to ask you to spend a few minutes with me after closing time this evening?" queried his new boss.

"Only an evening meal. If you haven't eaten, we can go over to D'Auria's and share a pizza, if you like," offered JT eagerly.

"How about I take a rain check on the pizza offer, and we run-over a few things right here?" countered Ms. Brian-Wisdom unsmilingly.

"Certainly," answered JT thinking he may have made a faux pas. "But the pizza offer is only good through this century, m'am," he babbled.

"I'll keep that in mind, JT," she said as she turned and returned to her office area.

"Little JT, I think we might be losing it. Nah! She's probably just one of those strange chicks who doesn't dig me," he said to himself.

JT locked the front door from the inside and quickly made his way to the back of the learning center to the open office area of the director. The meeting was relatively brief with Diana explaining her philosophy and the system she planned to implement at the Call Center. JT, impressed by her knowledge and thoroughness, concluded that she apparently knew her stuff. It left little doubt in his mind as to why she won the job over so many other qualified candidates. JT listened intently to the presentation without once bothering to interrupt or question her. When she had completed her talk, JT felt obliged to try to soften any "bad" impression he might have inadvertently made earlier that evening.

"Diana, if I said or did anything that offended you this evening, I truly apologize. I am, and you will find this out, a team player. You will have no difficulty having your agenda carried out during my shifts."

"What are you talking about JT? I thought we got on wonderfully," the boss laughed.

"Well, I kind of think of my sense of humor as an acquired taste that might not appeal to everyone. Just know, please, that I have enjoyed meeting you, look forward to working for and with you, and hope that we can become good friends," continued JT.

"JT, I haven't had a lot to laugh about over the past year or so. I am just probably out of practice. I love to laugh, and I would like to learn how to once again. I think you will be good medicine for me. I love the way you spoke so frankly and sincerely to me. You make me feel as if we've known each other forever or perhaps in another life."

"I feel likewise, Diana. Well, now that that is off my chest I will sleep better. Are you leaving now?"

"No, I am going to finish up my diary entry for today and then head home."

"I'd be happy to wait for you.

"Thanks, JT, that won't be necessary. I'll be fine."

"Then I shall see you on Thursday evening. Good night, boss."

"Good night, JT. Thanks for understanding," said Diana. "Maybe not all men are fucking assholes, Diana," she thought to herself. "We'll have to keep an eye on that one. He just may be a keeper."

CHAPTER 78

AS JT WALKED INTO THE house, he was greeted by Tara who had just kissed the girls goodnight. Charlene had long been asleep, and Twan was in his room studying as usual.

"How did your evening go, Jamey? Did you meet the new director? What was she like? Is she married? How about kids?" she rattled off one question after another.

"Whoa, there girl! How about my welcome home hugs and kisses?"

"Come on, let's get if over with," she teased. "All right, it was not as bad as usual. Now let's have the low-down," she urged.

"She's very old, probably your age, and she is U-G-L-Y! I'm sure that she doesn't wash, and she has hairy armpits."

"Cut the shit, funny boy. I'm serious. I always have to stay abreast of my competition, lover," she laughed.

"Diana is a very attractive, highly intelligent woman without a sense of humor in her fabulous body. She has no rings on the finger, so I am guessing unattached. I sense that she is not as comfortable around men as a beautiful woman should be. She is probably a victim of one or more unsuccessful relationships. She has an outgoing personality. I am not sure of her sign, but I would guess Virgo. Her periods usually last five days with the third day being just dreadful! She prefers pads to tampons; shaves her beaver clean; and adores the reverse cowgirl position for coitus."

"You know, Jamey, sometimes you...."

"I know, honey. I know."

"I'm going to bed. There is sandwich stuff in the fridge if you are hungry. Maybe in the morning you will be in a more cooperative, communicative mood. Good night, dreamer," she smiled as she blew him a kiss.

"Dreamer. Right. The chick obviously digs us, right Little JT?" he whispered and off he went to have his evening meal.

CHAPTER 79

"So it's not a problem, JT? I won't have a car for about a month," complained Millie Waldron. "Hamilton's friend who usually drives him to work is having some serious surgery. Hamilton needs to take our family car to work."

"No problem, Millie. I will pick you up and get you home. You are right on my way home. If I'm ever in a hurry, I'll just slow down, and you can jump out if it makes you feet better. When do we start?"

"Is tomorrow morning too soon, JT?"

"Do you need a ride tomorrow morning, Millie?"

"Yes."

"Then tomorrow morning is not too soon. Do you need a ride home after school today?"

"No, I can walk."

"Why can't this woman hear me? Millie, I am not carrying you home on my shoulders. Wait for me, and I'll even let you sit in the car with me."

"You're sure?"

"Oh my good lord, one of us will not live through this next month."

"Thank you, JT."

"You are most welcome, Mrs. Waldron."

As ordered, Millie Waldron was ready to leave when JT walked through the door between their rooms. Following JT were Sue Wright and Jerry Sherman as had become their ritual since Jerry's arrival. The four friends walked down the back stairs to the parking area making small talk until reaching their vehicles. One of the activities in which most staff members participated at TLC was the "Jerry Watch". Watching the man maneuver a car invoked memories of Mr. Magoo. Staff members would stop in their tracks, partly for safety, to watch the man enter and park in a near empty lot! The maneuvering of the vehicle mesmerized the observers. They particularly enjoyed watching the repeated journeys from reverse gear to drive gear to not only straighten the vehicle, but also to insure the proper depth in the parking place. Once "the Eagle had finally landed", he began another ritual that consisted of stepping from the vehicle to eyeball the results of his ministrations. Finally, when the deed was given his seal of approval, observers would watch in wonder as they would catch glimpses of the open vehicle which appeared to be void of a single non-refuse covered inch of floor space, with some areas two and three layers high. Driving and car care just were not a priorities for Jerry Sherman. JT had learned that the first week of their friendship. For some ungodly reason, JT agreed to look when Jerry had opened his trunk to show JT his spare tire. There in the clutter of the trunk lay an opened bag of lawn seed. Around the perimeter of the inner trunk, grass had taken hold and had begun to grow! Jerry never heard the end of that one from JT. By the way, neither of them could locate the spare tire.

The four friends entered their vehicles and began their treks home. JT and Millie waved as Sue and finally Jerry passed. Millie asked JT if he had a moment before they departed. She was acting stranger than her normal strange.

"JT, how long have we been teaching together?" she asked rhetorically. "Eight years, my dear friend. Moreover, do you have any idea how I truly feel about our relationship? Well, let me tell you while I have the courage. JT, I have been in love with you since the first month of our friendship. I am totally obsessed with the idea of being with you, of having you for myself, of us being together in every way."

JT was speechless, not a common occurrence in his life. All he was able to do was concentrate on the face of his friend.

"You are shocked. I can see that. I am not blind. I realize the differences in our ages, our marriages, our children; I have been over those things a million times in the past eight years. I just cannot help myself. Do you know that I usually come home from school and cry for an hour or two? No, how could you? This has been going on for lo these many years. You did nothing to encourage me except make yourself the perfect man. I realize that I may well be doing it wrong at this moment, but I have an urgent ulterior motive. JT, I'm dying…"

The listener's ears perked up, and he shot back into the real world looking at his friend intently as she spoke.

"I have ovarian cancer, my friend, and my doctors have been kind enough to give me as few as six months or as long as a year to live."

JT felt the tears slide down his cheeks. He reached for his longtime friend and held her tightly as they both crumbled into despair. He rocked with her in his arms. She planted little kisses along his cheek and neck. Following several moments of quiet, Millie composed herself enough to explain her actions.

"When I was told the news, my first thought was my kids and their futures without me. My second thought was you. I had to tell you everything before it was too late. I cannot even understand why it became so important to me. Hamilton, he needs a house cleaner and nanny. He will get along fine with the proper help from his family. I have already sat with the kids and explained the situation as gently and as best, I could. It was the hardest thing I have ever had to do. Today with you was the second hardest. So my friend you are now privy to the inner most thoughts of one Mildred Rosa Waldron. Please do not feel the need for reciprocity of feelings. Please do not pity me. Please continue to be my closest friend if you are still able. In addition, please, share this information with no one. It is not often that you are speechless, JT. I think I may have found the secret, huh? Look, I have taken up enough of your time. Why don't you take me home? If you want to talk, we can do that in the morning. You are still picking me up, right?"

"Right," repeated JT automatically as he backed the car out of its space.

CHAPTER 80

"IT SOUNDS LIKE SHE'S ASKING for a pity fuck, Jamey! I'm sorry, hon, this is too strange to be true," cried Tara Russell.

He could blame no one but himself for immediately breaking a sworn confidence. However, what could his out-of-work for the day wife do but interrogate a husband who had walked into the house in tears? After several minutes of badgering, imagining only the worst of possible scenarios, did Tara extract the cause of JT's so out-of-character behavior.

"Just like that she tells you that you are the love of her life? After all these years of teaching together, and being in the same building, suddenly you are the only one she wants to scratch her itch! I am at a loss, Jamey. Then she tries to seal the deal with a terminal illness. How fucking obvious is that? What happens next, a miracle cure after you screw her brains out? Call me anything you want, Jamey, unsympathetic, cruel, jealous, whatever, I think the whole story sucks."

"Won't we know for sure in six months to a year, Tara? Why would anyone put themselves in such a no win situation?"

"No win? She obviously struck gold with you judging from your reaction. If she affects Little JT in the same way, she will have struck the jackpot," reasoned Tara rather loudly.

"That could never happen, Tara. It would never happen. Millie sees our relationship completely differently than I do."

"Jamey, did you learn nothing from the Rose Marie thing? You can't go spreading your special something over the women in your life ignorant of the fact that one, some, or all of them will mistake your well-intentioned friendship for much more."

He looked at her unable to respond. The mention of Rose Marie's name compounded his current pain. Was she correct? Could the entire Millie episode be a terribly misguided attempt by a desperate woman to raise a relationship, existent only in her mind, to the next level? If so, he was probably as much to blame as she. Unconsciously, had he been leading her on? Was the situation a revisiting of his and Rose Marie's story?

"Look, Jamey, until this thing plays itself out, do me a favor. Do not allow yourself to be alone with Millie at all if possible. For safety sake, always have someone else there with you. If all of her story is true, then I will probably burn in hell for my reaction. If it is not, as I suspect, one need only imagine the lengths to which such a person might resort. Please, for your sake, for our sake, be on your guard. You should have learned your lesson from the Antonella Lira incident. Always expect the unexpected."

"Hey, it's late. I've got to get ready for Operation IYT," he interrupted.

"Jamey, could you work with only guys tonight?" smiled Tara.

She watched her husband disappear into their bedroom and then dropped exhausted into her favorite chair. Everything had happened so rapidly since JT arrived home. He did not ask why she was home at that time of the day. Nor did he ask where the kids were. Clearly, he had yet to see Charlene since his arrival. Everything was on hold due to the latest Russell revelation.

"Jamey? Don't you think it strange that I am home this early in the day?"

"What? Yeah, Tara, why are you home so early?"

"I had a doctor's appointment."

"Doctor? What's wrong, Tara?"

"Friggin Little JT did it again, buddy, we're pregnant!"

"Holy shit! You just went back to work, hon."

"Thank you for the update."

He hurried out of the bedroom and drew his wife to her feet. They kissed, hugged, and cried.

"Can we afford this, Jamey? There are options, you know."

"Together we can do anything, Tara."

"Right answer, buddy! So, now I will give you the other great news. Twan received his Harvard University early acceptance today, a full academic scholarship! Charlene took the girls and him out for a celebration dinner at Fuddruckers."

"What a freakin day!" he yelled, as his feet landed back on the floor. "I wish I could stay at home tonight. But, we're gonna have another mouth to feed so Daddy has to go to work."

"Jamey, please tell Little JT that his reproductive services will no longer be required. We're going the tube tying route after this one, right?"

"Anything you say, sweetie, as long as it's not a vasectomy. Little JT absolutely would not abide by that."

"Naturally, my two, big, strong pricks," she murmured.

CHAPTER 81

THE FOLLOWING MORNING HE ARRIVED at the Waldron home at the agreed upon time. Millie Waldron came hopping down her side stairs with a large smile on her face. JT wondered if he would ever be able to smile again were he told he had a terminal disease that would take his life in a year or less. He shrugged it off thinking that it takes all kinds to fill-up the planet. Millie, still smiling from ear to ear, entered the car through the door opened by her driver. Once in the car she leaned over toward JT and kissed his cheek. That was shock number one of the day for JT. He was sure he was doing a poor job of hiding his embarrassment so he chose not to look at the grinning woman to his right. Small talk did ensue on the trip to school initiated in most part by Millie. She spoke about how wonderful it was to have released such pent-up emotions. She spoke of feelings that had tortured her over the years. JT noted that little bit of information. What was the torturing element about which she spoke? Clearly, she had not known about this alleged life threatening disease for years. So that would be a misrepresentation of fact should she be alluding to the terminal cancer. The only other interpretation of her statement would be the relief she felt in allowing herself to confess her feelings about him. The highly analytical man could not envision those two events existing together in equal degrees of importance in any sane person's mind. On the one hand, one will be dead in a year, a fact confirmed by medical evidence. On the other hand, one admits to being emotionally, romantically, or sexually attracted to an already married, thirty-five year old father of three who to that point in time had in no way reciprocated those feelings. There were just no scales in existence, which could perfectly balance those two options! However, the doomed woman appeared to be on a self-induced high on the way to school. They arrived at school much earlier than to which JT was accustomed. In fact, aside from the boiler man, who opened the school, they were alone. After a brief stop in the Teacher's Room to check their mailboxes, the two teachers made their way to their own classrooms. JT felt some relief as Millie entered her room and did not continue to his room with him. He began perusing his lesson plans for the day when he heard the door between his and Millie's room swing open. Slightly startled he looked over at her and smiled.

"Is there anything at all I can do for you, JT?" she blushed as she walked toward him.

"What do you mean, Millie?" JT queried.

"I'm not very good at this kind of thing," she said as she reached the area where he stood.

"Now that you know how I feel, I want to show you how I feel in every way," she purred as she reached out and touched the front of his pants tentatively.

JT froze as she gave Little JT a pat and began to pull down the tab of his zipper! Unless he was grossly misreading her intentions, she was intent on meeting Little JT up-close and personal.

"Millie, I'll give you three hours to get your hand off my zipper," he teased trying to make light of the situation.

"Do you like what I'm doing, JT?" she asked as her hand pulled on his zipper.

"Yes, but no, Millie, I can't do this," he stuttered attempting to act contrary to Little JT's will.

"You feel like you are enjoying it, JT," she whispered as she patted his crotch once again.

"That's it! Just stop! I can't do this!" he insisted as he pushed her hands away brusquely.

"I just wanted to show you the depth of my desire for you. I've never even attempted this before this moment. I wanted to give you something I've given to no other man. Are you rejecting me, JT? Do you have any idea how fucking important, how difficult this was for me?" she asked her voice rising in anger.

"It can't happen between us ever, Millie. If I've given you the wrong signals, I apologize, but I couldn't live with myself if I allowed such a selfish act on my part to take place especially now that Tara is pregnant again."

She looked at him in shock. "What did you say? Tara is pregnant! How could you, JT? I want your baby! How could you do this to us? I offer you what I've given to no man, and this is my reward!" Oh my God, I think I'm going to pass out."

JT reached for her, but she pushed him away.

Holding him off at arm's length she yelled, "Keep your hands off me. Don't ever touch me again!" She was getting louder at the time when more people would be entering the building.

"Relax, breathe deeply, Millie."

"You shut your pig mouth, you bastard!"

Obviously close to a collapse, the woman turned carefully and stumbled toward her classroom.

"Now you've fucking done it, Little JT. What do we do now? I have a new psycho with whom to deal. My life is almost like an open audition for a new game show 'Next Nut, Please'!"

As he walked to the bathroom, Sue Wright came through the upstairs doors.

"JT, you look like you've just seen a ghost. Are you sick?"

"Morning, Susan. Yeah, I feel just a bit under the weather today. I need to throw some water on my face."

"JT, let me know if there's anything at all I can do for you."

"Oh, shit no," he thought to himself.

Upon hearing those words again, he half ran to the bathroom.

Awkward would have been too tame a description of his dealings with Millie that day. Adversarial would come to mind. Vindictive would have been an appropriate choice. However, hostile best described the atmosphere originating in the Waldron classroom and permeating into the Russell classroom. JT made several peace-making attempts throughout the day to appease the distressed woman to no avail. As dismissal time approached, he received a communication from the injured party via one of her students. The note was short and to the point:

> *You Prick,*
> *I will not be needing a ride home today, a ride to school tomorrow, or a ride anywhere with you in the future.*
> *Your Plaything*

"What have I gotten myself into this time?" he mumbled as he folded the note and tore it into small pieces. "Why didn't I listen to Tara? Do not be alone with the woman she warned me. However, my fucking independently thinking penis and I just would not listen, or perhaps we're just incapable of listening when it comes to S-E-X!"

CHAPTER 82

JT HAD YET TO SEE Twan since he received his excellent scholarship news. Fortunately, the young man was arriving home just as JT pulled into the driveway.

"Hey you! Come here!" he shouted to his startled son.

Twan smiled, blushed, and walked toward his father who was now out of his car.

"Hi, Dad. I didn't get to see you last night. Was it a long night?"

"They're all long, buddy," he said as he hugged his son as tightly as he could.

"I could not be any prouder of you than I am right now. No, no, let me correct that. Never a day in our lives together have you ever given me cause not to be as proud of you as I am this day. I love you, son. You are everything a parent could wish for."

"Thanks, Dad, I owe you my life. Now I have some bad news for you. You remember Janice Corcoran, don't you?"

"Of course I do. Isn't she that gorgeous little blond that you have been squiring around town for months now?"

"Yes, sir, that's Jan. She and I are pregnant, Dad, and I was expelled from school this morning for striking her guidance counselor."

"Twan!" he screamed.

"Just pulling your chain, Dad! See, the Vietnamese apple doesn't fall far from the tree."

"If you ever do that to me again in any form in the future, you will be the first goddamn surgeon having to operate with no friggin hands, you little bastard."

They hugged each other and walked into the house smiling – something that JT had done little of that day. He was due at the CALL Center that evening so the family, as usual, did not eat the evening meal together. JT had just enough time to clean up, prepare his paperwork, play with the girls for a bit, and welcome Tara home before he had to leave. Understandably, he had a difficult time looking into her eyes, a fact that did not go unnoticed by the lady of the house. After kissing everyone good-bye, he was off to work again. There were days when he marveled to himself as to how he ever got to his destination. Automatic pilot was about as accurate an explanation as he could conjure. How he was able to pull into the CALL Center parking lot without a single conscious memory of the drive there was scary. What had he been doing during the drive? Was he experiencing periods of selective amnesia? Without a doubt, he knew of one event having taken place that day that was deserving of selective permanent amnesia. He said his "hellos" and "good-byes" to the three teachers who staffed the center during the daytime hours and spoke to each student who chose to remain at her/his study carrel or table to continue studying into the evening session. Once he had completed his initial check of the center, he stopped by Diana's desk to say hello. She was her usual bubbly, personable self, but there seemed to be more. She seemed to be more receptive, less guarded in her behavior, as if a wall she had been scaling had been successfully negotiated.

"Well, Mr. Russell, how nice to see you," she teased. "Oh, that's right, I believe I do have permission to be more familiar with you as I recall."

"Touché, Ma ami. I believe you will soon become a formidable opponent, mademoiselle."

"It isn't easy keeping up with you especially when one's laugh and smile have been in mothballs for a while," she quipped.

"We'll have you back on track before you know it. In fact, I would venture to say that you will soon be seeking sanctuary from all the smiling and laughing you're going to be doing. You'll probably be applying Ben Gay to your facial muscles."

"You are something else, JT. How you disarm people amazes me. Where did you learn to do that? Was it just developed as part of your pick-up patter?"

"Please, madam, you see before you a one hundred percent natural, gifted by God and Mother Nature, All American, Italian boy just trying to get by in this old world."

"Well, Mr. All-American Italian boy, I have, in a very short time of having your acquaintance, realized a charm which must have cost many ladies their undergarments."

"Diana, you make me blush. Not to mention the undeserving flattery from your lips that reaches both God's ears and mine."

"I'm out of my league matching wits with you. Please take mercy on me," she laughed.

"Now, I am truly embarrassed," he lied.

"All kidding aside, what are the chances of cashing in on that pizza offer tonight?" she smiled. "I have a proposal which I would like to discuss with you."

"That sounds great, boss, as long as it doesn't involve a ring of any kind."

"It's a little bit different type of proposal, my friend, I can guarantee that," she laughed.

Following the departure of the last student, JT and Diana locked-up the center, and he walked her to her car.

"A gentleman as well...My, my, my, Mr. Russell, you certainly know how to treat a lady."

"That, Ms. Brian-Wisdom, would depend upon the lady," he flirted.

She followed him in her car to D'Auria's Restaurant in Salem not more than a ten-minute ride from the CALL Center. JT was a frequent visitor to the restaurant; therefore, most of the wait staff knew him by name. Whenever he visited, his server would always attempt to seat him at the same table; hence, when he arrived and a familiar girl was on duty, he always impressed his guests by asking if his table were ready. He got such a charge out of that! It just made his night. Diana excused herself to visit the women's room, and JT found the opportunity perfect for a visit to the men's lounge. On cue, the two diners walked out of the doors facing each other at precisely the same time. JT offered his arm to his beautiful, smiling boss who hooked her arm into his without hesitation. Drinks and a pizza with everything on it was Diana's choice. JT knew that indigestion would be his companion that night. They made small talk for a while until the alcohol in Diana's first drink loosened her lips. He then learned of her abusive marriage, her relocation to Massachusetts, her European travel, her present aversion to the male gender, and her plans for JT Russell.

"JT, I am quite familiar with your busy schedule; however, I would like you to consider the following proposal. I would like to name you the evening supervisor of the center, the 'Night Knight', or whatever title you would like. I want the center opened five nights a week under your guidance."

"I am flattered, Diana. For me to make this move I would have to resign from Operation IYT on Mondays and Wednesdays and Monitor Counseling on Fridays. Financially, I'm not in a position to take a cut in pay now that there is another child on the way."

"Oh really! Congratulations, JT. Please do not worry about the compensation. I have already adjusted our budget for the extra hours and have increased your hourly rate by a dollar an hour. How would that impact you finances?"

"Really? That would be fabulous. I'd actually be getting a raise," marveled JT.

"So, what do you think, Mr. Russell?"

"Give me a time frame that will allow me to offer a two week notice to both Monitor and IYT, and I am yours."

"You have a deal. Let's drink to it, JT."

They touched glasses and nodded toward each other. Then, JT went and did it. He winked at her, and she winked back. If he had just stopped at the clink of the glasses, Diana might not have insisted on a second, third, and fourth drink. JT found himself telling her his life story. He complained about Millie's case of unrequited love and the dreadful situation in which he found himself without getting into the sexy details. She listened intently with her hands folded beneath her chin, commenting appropriately, just listening to the painful anecdotes coming from the man.

"Well, JT, I know one thing for sure. I would never do anything like that to you. I would never put you in so hurtful a position where you would have to choose between maintaining my friendship and encouraging my fantasies."

"JT, is there anything at all I can do for you....anything?" queried Diana.

The shell-shocked man could not believe what he was hearing. The coincidence was too mind-altering. That was the third time today he heard that same offer! What was this some new addition to the "woman speak" sexual vocabulary? He swallowed hard, thanked his boss, and suggested that they call it an evening. As he walked with her to her car, she reached out and took his arm. After opening the door for her, she threw her arms around him in an overly friendly happy embrace. Diana then kissed the pleasantly surprised man on the cheek before sliding into her Mustang.

"Thank you, JT, for everything. I have a feeling that I have already known you forever. You make me feel so comfortable and safe that I have no need to erect walls with you."

"That's me, Diana, the neighborhood eunuch, a danger to no one but myself."

"Stop it! You know what I mean," she laughed.

"Drive safely, boss. I will see you on Tuesday. Have a great weekend."

She smiled once more, touched his hand, and off she went. JT got into his car, took a deep breath, and mused to himself, "Little JT, what the fuck are you doing to me lately?"

CHAPTER 83

"I WANT TO APOLOGIZE FOR my behavior, JT. I acted in an unforgivable fashion, and I would completely understand were you to terminate our relationship."

The words from the mouth of Millie Waldron surprised JT who was about to turn the doorknob to his classroom when the woman, like a free-floating spectra, appeared unannounced behind him. She had said all the right things in the correct way leaving JT with little choice but to accept her apology. He once again apologized to her for his ungentlemanly-like behavior. At that, the two agreed to forget the painful confrontation and try to move their friendship forward. As far as JT was concerned, that was the best and easiest course of action. He would be dealing with the woman for the rest of the school year. Looking forward to a lengthy period of animosity and open hostility did not particularly appeal to JT. As Millie turned to return to her classroom, she looked at JT with an expression of embarrassment then quickly looked to the floor.

"JT if there is anything I can do for you, anything, anyplace, any time, all you need do is ask."

With that, she turned and headed to her classroom.

Conferencing with Little JT, Big JT thought aloud, "Holy shit, Little JT, she isn't finished with us yet! Do you know what we need? Reinforcements!"

He immediately set about recruiting his reinforcements to help protect him from the lovesick woman. Taking both Sue Wright and Jerry Sherman into his confidence in separate but identical discussions, he explained his plight. Both friends offered suggestions for future action and agreed to safeguard JT from finding himself alone with Millie – oh, you were so right, Tara. The primary suggestion from both cohorts was the total elimination of private rides with Millie to and from school. Should she be in dire need of transportation, Jerry volunteered to either offer his services to her or travel with both JT and Millie to and from school. Not only had his friends' agreement served to protect him from the emotionally impaired woman, but also it served to protect JT and Little JT from themselves. From that point forward, JT was never to be alone in the company of Millie Waldon.

The plan was a good plan, not a great plan, for it did not include a provision for JT's protection away from the school setting. Thinking he had become paranoid, JT began to see flashes of someone watching him or following him on foot and in his car. As the days passed, he experienced a dramatic increase involving the episodes of these stalking incidents. Tara had even commented to JT about reports from Katie and Ronnie of a strange woman in a car watching them as they played. Tara, herself, sensed similar out of the ordinary instances of covert observations, as well as telephone calls with no response and quick termination. Nevertheless, what was there to do? No crimes were being committed until that December evening.

Tara, now just over two and half months pregnant, had left the girls with Charlene while she and Twan went to do some Christmas shopping at the North Shore Shopping Center. Tara asked Twan to drive in order that she could save her energy for the actual shopping. The mother and son chatted and laughed with each other as Twan entered Route 128 at the Route 1 and 128 Junction. The evening was quite cold and at that time of year darkness arrived very early. The highway was surprisingly scarcely traveled; a factor in the avoidance of what could have been an even greater tragedy to take place that evening. While driving in the middle lane of the three-lane highway, bright headlights in his rearview mirror momentarily blinded Twan. Snapping the adjustment on the mirror from daylight vision to nighttime vision, Twan was able to adjust his vision sufficiently in time to see a large white commercial van tailgating his vehicle. He tried to remain calm in order not to panic his pregnant mother. However, the van was clearly invading his driving space. He made a quick check of his mother's seatbelt and then his moments before he felt an impact that sent his vehicle swerving into the adjoining lane striking the rear end of a third vehicle. Twan did everything he could think of to keep his vehicle stable, but the second impact on the rear of his car caused the vehicle to spin out of control, hit the safety railing, leave the ground, turning over twice before coming to rest on its roof in a sea of frozen turf along the highway. Fast acting motorists approached the vehicle fearful that it might explode into flames at any moment. Both passenger and driver were hanging upside down suspended by their seatbelts. Observers reported that both appeared to be breathing; however, a copious amount of red liquid covered the interior of the vehicle and the front windows. The good Samaritans attempted to communicate with the trapped occupants, but they were unsuccessful. Shortly, the screaming sirens of emergency vehicles approached from the south as police and fire department vehicles raced their way to the scene. Extrication of the injured parties from the vehicle required the use of a mechanical device shaped like huge pliers. Within a matter of moments, the firefighters were slowly lowering the unconscious female victim from her safety belt swing onto a waiting stretcher. The alert male victim, in obvious physical distress, assumed his position on a second stretcher. Paramedics worked on both victims simultaneously. Upon learning from the young male victim that his female companion was pregnant, the rescuers immediately loaded her onto a vehicle and transported her to the hospital. Twan pleaded to go along with his mother to no avail. Several minutes passed before a second ambulance arrived to transport the young man with the arm and leg injuries to the same hospital.

JT was about to leave for the CALL Center. He was running later that day than usual due to several scheduled parent conferences. When Charlene received the telephone notification of the accident, she received no information about the condition of the victims. Very simply, according to the caller, the closest relatives to the victims were to meet with the staff in the emergency room immediately upon arrival. JT gave Charlene directions to call the Call Center, keep the girls as calm as possible, and pray for their family. JT virtually "flew" out of his house and into his car. The "not knowing" was a hideous experience for JT. What would he discover when he arrived at the hospital?

"You are Mr. Russell, father of Twan Cheung-Russell and husband of Tara Russell?" asked the on-duty ER doctor as he led JT to a chair.

"Tell me please, what's going on?" begged a teary JT.

"Your son and wife were victims of a hit and run accident which left them suspended by their seatbelts in an overturned vehicle, Mr. Russell. Mrs. Russell is still unconscious."

"And the baby, she's pregnant..." questioned JT.

"She's lost the child, Mr. Russell. I am truly sorry. We are trying to determine the severity of her injuries presently. Her unconscious state is of extreme concern to us at the moment."

"Will I lose my wife, doctor?"

"We are doing everything we are able to do to prevent that, Mr. Russell."

"And my son, doctor?"

"Twan Cheung-Russell received a compound fracture of the tibia of the right leg and a broken humerus of the left arm. The leg will require surgery; however, he seems to be checking out well on his other tests. Our major concern, Mr. Russell, is your wife's condition. She is presently undergoing a CAT scan. We should have some information for you shortly."

"JT, what's going on?" Jerry Sherman nervously inquired. "I just talked to your mother. Have you found out anything?"

"Twan is pretty broken-up, but his broken bones will heal. Tara… has lost the baby…she is still unconscious. We should know more shortly. Jerry, you'll never know what it means to have you here."

"Where else would I be at a time like this, JT?" asked his friend as he encircled him with his arms.

Tara's CAT scan revealed a large hematoma or blood pooling on her brain. JT immediately reacted with extreme panic for not twenty-four hours earlier had he watched a lightweight boxer on a televised bout receive such a beating about his head that he required emergency surgery to relieve pressure on his brain. That unfortunate gladiator died on the operating table. The more he thought, the more he panicked. He began to imagine life without Tara. How could he explain to his girls that they would never see their mother again? He knew he was incapable of such a task, but what would he do? The doctor to whom he had spoken earlier approached JT and Jerry followed by a second white coat.

"Mr. Russell this is Dr. Arnstein. Dr. Arnstein, a brain surgeon here at the hospital, is a specialist in traumas to the head. I think it would be prudent of you to listen carefully to his report," urged the ER doctor as if reading from some soap opera script.

"We have completed your wife's battery of tests, Mr. Russell, and to be frank, the results are very disconcerting. She has suffered a major trauma to the right hemisphere of her brain, which has caused a considerable amount of bleeding in her cranial cavity. This build-up of blood is causing extensive pressure on her brain, a situation we must address immediately. Once we have this condition of immediate concern controlled, we will be able to evaluate the overall damage to your wife's brain. We need your permission to continue her treatment."

JT was barely able to comprehend the severity and frightening consequences of the situation. Jerry held him tightly about his shoulders and encouraged him to allow the medics to help Tara. Upon being reminded by the surgeon that time was not an ally, JT signed the necessary documents before he slumped onto an unsightly stained chair in the emergency room. Two loves of his life were to be in two separate operating rooms at approximately the same time. Was that to be his punishment for his weakness? Was he responsible for the pain, suffering, and possible...He could not even think it! Goddamn you Little JT! You weak little prick! Later, he might look back on that statement in amusement. Not now. There was not the slightest reason nor sufficient time for him to enjoy the health enhancing benefits of a hardy laugh. Perhaps there may never be again.

Twan's surgery went well. He was out of surgery and taken to the Recovery Room. JT was assured by Twan's surgeon that save for a possible lingering limp, his son would be good as new with no threat to his future medical aspirations. JT reminded himself that he was halfway through the nightmare. He prayed to a God to whom he spoke when he was in need of divine assistance. He was not a stupid man. He knew how hypocritical his actions were, as were his ludicrous requests for divine intervention. Nevertheless, if not God, who? If not now, when? The surgery lasted forever or at least that long in the JT time zone. He made every promise that a human is capable of making to a deity in repayment for his favorable intervention. It did not work. Tara Anne Carleton Russell, thirty-five year old wife of Lynn educator, James Thurber Russell of Lynn, Massachusetts, mother of Twan Cheung-Russell, Kathryn Anne Russell, and Veronica Leigh Russell all of Lynn, daughter of Franklin and Maryanne Carleton of Nahant, and daughter-in-law of Charlene Russell of Lynn died from injuries sustained in a motor vehicle accident on December 10th.

CHAPTER 84

THE FOLLOWING DAYS WERE A blur. Without Charlene's incredible strength and leadership, JT would have been lost. She exhibited a courage and fortitude few knew she possessed. Fortunately, someone in the immediate family was capable of assuming control, for the main cast of characters was devastated by the life altering events of the days following Tara's passing. As usual, JT internalized his grief though not as completely and privately as was his want. His girls with the constant support, reassurance, and love from Charlene and Bina were able to comprehend the situation though not totally; however, JT feared for the longer-lasting impact to each of his girls over time. Twan was unable to attend either the wake or funeral according to doctor's orders. His path was perhaps the hardest to follow of all in his family due to his inability to say a proper good-bye to his mother. The outpouring of kindness and attention toward the family by relatives, friends, acquaintances, and friends of friends was heartwarming to all the Russells. Tara Anne Carleton received her final rest following a high mass a Sacred Virgin Church and internment at St. Joseph's Cemetery. Her legacy to the world was her children and the values she strove to impart to them. JT prayed that all of their children, in particular their girls, had inherited and would exercise the virtues, attributes, drive, determination, and love possessed by their mother. It was paramount to him that their girls never forget just how wonderful and special a woman their mother had been. He made a vow at her graveside to make that happen.

Christmas was unbearable for JT in particular. His children were unable to celebrate the most important of all childhood holidays; he wept for a son so severely beset with guilt that a course of antidepressants was required; he, himself, harbored a gnawing guilt regarding his unforgiven, unfortunate indiscretion with Millie; and he could not get past the unbearable anger toward a murderer not yet brought to justice. Altogether, these factors represented a recipe for total and absolute mental exhaustion for the man. JT was able to take the time up to the Christmas vacation away from the classroom, followed by almost two full weeks of vacation. Together this period served as a reasonable block of time to reestablish some semblance of a routine for his children. He and Charlene had daily discussions about their sharing of duties and responsibilities, which would lead to the implementation of a structured life style and environment for the girls. By day, his energies focused upon accomplishing that immediate goal. By night, he experienced an existence composed of crying himself to sleep, sleeping on Tara's side of the bed, beating himself up psychologically for his shortcomings, and berating the authorities through which he sought to attain his revenge. In the three plus weeks since the accident, he had heard nary a word about solving the crime. Yes, the abandoned white van turned-up shortly after the accident. Yes, a stolen car report listed it missing from a mall parking lot on the day of the accident. Yes, all the witnesses to the accident, including Twan, submitted signed statements. No, the authorities were no closer to solving the case than they were immediately after it happened.

The time was at hand for the family members to continue their lives. Twan still bound in leg and arm casts had the most physical difficulty of all in the family; however, the regiment of antidepressant drugs and the beginning of weekly sessions with a psychiatrist had indeed improved his perspective on the death of his mother. JT still feared what the long-term effects of losing their mother at such young ages would have upon Katie and Ronnie, but Charlene more than stepped-up and loved her girls to pieces. It became a daily debate in JT's tormented mind as to whether his daughters should attend some form of grief therapy sessions. For the time being, he decided to leave the decision in the hands of the girls' teachers who would be among the first to identify aberrant behavior in the classroom setting. Were this to eventuate, he would then take the next logical step of engaging a therapist. Charlene with constant support from Bina became the rock upon which the newly reorganized Russell family depended. JT's constant fear revolved around the mental and physical energy required of his mother. The woman who had already raised her own family and was now supposed to be looking toward her kinder and gentler years took on the responsibility of two young children at her advanced age. He gave little thought to himself. He continued to grieve privately, to bottle up his emotions, and to isolate himself more each day from all except his immediate family. JT missed Tara terribly. Somewhat more than her physical absence, the man missed her mental strength, her emotional support, and her soothing, nurturing way. Having been with her since they were seventeen, he was highly out of practice in making important, family-based final decisions on his own. There were just too many adjustments for the man to absorb at one time. The most obvious truth that JT had to face and accept was that he was simply just not as tough as he imagined himself to be. The realization that Tara had been more than a partner in their lives became more apparent each day that he lived without her. It became so clear to him that she and she alone was the heart and soul of their relationship. Tara had the family care and concerns firmly on her shoulders. She had been the money magician who turned the rewards of her husband's extensive labors into a sound financial foundation for the family. She was everyone's band-aid for both physical and emotional wounds, and she considered herself least in a family of high-maintenance individuals. Tara Anne Carleton Russell was irreplaceable, and he never had the chance to tell her he was sorry.

CHAPTER 85

THE COLD CRISP DAYS OF the New England winter slowly but thankfully turned to the burgeoning days of spring. Twan was quickly approaching his graduation from high school and soon after that his move from the family residence to his dormitory residence at Harvard University. JT and Twan talked long and often about that next stage in Twan's life. The young man needed his father's encouragement to leave the motherless nest. The thought of separating himself from his wounded family both scared and concerned him. How could he go now when each needed the other so desperately? When he proposed commuting to the university in order to remain in the home, a hastily called family meeting, several weeks before his graduation, convened. Each family member, starting with Ronnie, expressed her/his opinion about the importance of Twan following not only his dream but also Tara's dream. Katie Anne spoke eloquently, for a fourth grader, emphasizing the fact that Twan should do this for their mom who would not allow him to choose otherwise were she there. Charlene told him that although they will miss him terribly, he will be living-out his family's dream for him, and he had the responsibility to the family to abide by their wishes. JT very simply said to his son, "Twan, this above all, to thine own self be true." He hugged the boy who had lived both a nightmarish and fairytale life. The family met in the center of the room for a group hug and cry. The decision was unanimous. In mid-summer of that year, seven and a half months following the passing of his mother, Twan Cheung-Russell would test out his wings as a new member of the freshman class of 1985. And so, it was.

In his wallet, JT kept an excerpt from the inspiring speech given by the Valedictorian of the 1981 graduating class of Lynn Classical High School, Twan Cheung-Russell. Whenever he missed Twan too much, whenever he needed a reason to smile, whenever he needed to rejustify his existence, he would remove the neatly folded typed parchment upon which he found the following:

"As a child I was an abandoned soul tossed from whitecap to whitecap on the sea of life. To my great and good fortune, He who watches over all of us chose to have that helpless child, the man you see before you today, grasp and cling to a 'life preserver' that kept me afloat. This salvation brought both love and stability to my troubled waters. He who knows all first sent this 'life preserver' to me to be my teacher, my mentor, a model of strength, knowledge, compassion, understanding, and love. Everyone he touched very easily loved this man. I was certainly no exception. Later, during the darkest hour of my young life, He who protects the innocent allowed that same man to rescue me from my sea of despair and make me a member of his family. Only the two of us, he and I, will ever truly know the depth of love we hold for each other as well as the heartbreaking truth that may well have destroyed that bond. Today, as the Valedictorian of the graduating class of 1981, I, Twan Russell, wish to share this moment with my one and only family, the Russells. I know my mother, Tara, is looking down upon us at this moment smiling at her husband, Jamey, daughters Katie and Ronnie, mother-in-law Charlene and sister-in-law, Bina. Please join me in honoring the family that saved my life."

Reading the passage never failed to bring tears to JT's eyes and chills throughout his body. If he and Tara had done nothing else correct in their entire life together, they certainly were not doing it wrong with the young man who became a most loved son.

CHAPTER 86

"WHAT ARE YOUR PLANS FOR the summer, JT? Rest and relaxation or work?" inquired Walter Holloway.

"You know me, Walter; I'll be in Gloucester for eight weeks running the site there for the Massachusetts English as a Second Language Education Program. Hey, I even recruited Jerry Sherman for this summer."

"Will you still be doing the CALL Center?"

"Yes sir, five nights a week whether I need it or not. You know, Walter, about idle hands, right?"

"Yes, JT, and I also know about working yourself to death! You have to slow down. I cannot imagine what it is like being you these days, but you still have two little girls who need their daddy around. Stop and smell the fucking roses, JT, before they're six feet above your dirt-napping, worm-eaten, poor excuse for a body!"

"Nice talk coming from an educator, babe."

"Seriously, kid, you can't stop the memories by working 24/7. Take it from one older and almost as wise."

"I know what you're saying, Walter, and please never think I am not appreciative. I just have to get through this thing the best way that works for me."

"JT, is there anything I can do for you, anything at all?"

JT looked at his friend and smiled, "Walter, you've been around all these women too long buddy." JT laughed at his inside joke and soon became downright giddy.

"Is there something I missed here, JT?"

"It's a long story, my friend. Perhaps one day I'll have the courage to share it."

JT began his duties as site supervisor for the MESLEP summer program shortly after school let out for the summer. When he designed the plans for his site each summer, he always tried to arrange for a minimum of ten days preferably two weeks of vacation time before having to return to school in September. He was able to arrange a full two-week break at that program's end. He thought a trip to Florida and Disney World would be great medicine for the girls, a nice reward for his mother, and a means of missing Twan less. Therefore, he went about making all the necessary arrangements for a road trip to Florida. The family was terribly excited. Ronnie and Katie marked-off each day of the MESLEP schedule on their calendar as their father arrived home. Five days before the end of the summer program, the Gloucester site and the Lynn site held a joint field day in Lynn. The children of migratory workers for whom the program existed experienced a day of games, fun, food, and prizes as a reward for their diligence throughout the program. JT also had the additional opportunity to visit with friends from the Lynn site that he had not seen recently. To his surprise, Millie Waldron was on that summer's Lynn site staff. The relationship between he and Millie had taken a strange turn to say the least. She rarely spoke to him unless the topic was school or education related. Millie and Hamilton Waldron never appeared at Tara's wake or funeral nor did they send a sympathy card. Although strange, JT thought it was all for the best. Then it hit him. Had it not been almost ten months since Millie's admission of her undying love for him and of her terminal disease? Not being a doctor of course, JT thought Millie looked pretty health participating in the three-legged race, staff tug-o-war, potato sack race, and one mile run.

"Maybe impending death agrees with her," he mused to himself. "Tara had the woman pegged from the get go. Millie, the pity fuck, how pathetic was that?"

Shaking his head in disdain, the seed of a thought entered his mind. He quickly allowed it to slip through the cracks of his memory. However, unconsciously the seed had taken root.

CHAPTER 87

"SO WHAT DO YOU SAY, boss, are you going to miss me when I'm away?" smiled JT at Diana Wisdom.

"Oh, didn't I tell you that the center would be in need of your services for those two weeks, JT?"

"Not a problem, boss. If you take Ronnie and Katie to Florida, I will be happy to stay and work.

"Mr. Russell, you just don't know how tempting an offer that is to me."

"JT, there's a telephone call for you. It's your mother," yelled Stella, the center receptionist.

"Oh shit! What now?" He quickly walked to the nearest phone, which happened to be on Diana's desk.

"Ma? What's up?" he nervously inquired.

"How many times have I told you to watch your step on the staircases? What did the x-ray show? There is a crack in the bone? Are you sure? Let me talk to Bina. Bina, what happened? How many stairs? Is there any other damage? You are at the emergency room now. What is the course of treatment? Off her feet for two weeks! How does one do that at Disney World? Obviously, she will not be able to go. What do I do now? What do I tell the girls? No, how can you go? You will have Ma if I figure out a way to do this thing. Look, give her a kiss for me. Do not let her say anything to the girls until I get home.

Drive home carefully. They're getting to know us on a first name basis at the ER."

He placed the telephone into its cradle, slipped into Diana's chair, and placed his head in his hands.

"JT, I couldn't help but hear. Will your mom be all right?" quizzed Diana.

"Yeah, she'll be just fine two weeks too late. Diana, have you ever had the feeling that you're walking around with a dark cloud hanging over your head?"

"For the past three years, JT. Until recently of course," replied his boss. "Can't you handle the girls by yourself?"

"Let me tell you a short story of a recent adventure of mine. I took the girls to the movies. Ronnie had to go the bathroom badly. I walked Katie and Ronnie to the women's room and asked Katie to keep her eye on Ronnie. Then I waited and waited and waited. By now, I am beginning to get worried. Finally, Katie emerges from the women's room with the news that Ronnie did not quite make it to the toilet and her underwear was soiled. Embarrassed, Ronnie threw her panties away into the bowl! Now, she refused to leave the bathroom because she had no underwear. I sent Katie back in to get Ronnie, but she would not budge. What does a male do when entry into a women's room is involved? To make a long story short, I finally coaxed Ronnie to the door of the bathroom where I wrapped my sweater around her waist several times. Fathers alone with young daughters make for an accident waiting to happen."

"I see," said Diana trying not to smile.

"Diana, what would you do if you were me?" asked JT.

"Well, JT, most of the obvious choices involve disappointing your daughters. Exactly when are you supposed to leave? Saturday? Here is what I would do if I were you. I would ask me if I would go with you. I would then tell you that if you could move your trip to later on Saturday afternoon, I would love to go!"

"Are you jerking my chain? You would do that?" asked JT in a surprised tone.

"In a heart beat, buddy! All I'd need to do is get coverage for myself at the center by calling in a favor or two," she bubbled.

"Do you think your girls will be all right with this?" she asked.

"If the choice were Disney World with you or no Disney World without you, I'd bet my life you're in."

"This will be great, JT. I have never been to Disney World, and I know I can trust you to be a gentleman. You should get used to sleeping in the car by the third night or so," she laughed.

"Ok, Ms. Wisdom, if your offer is for real, I most heartily accept it. We will discuss our ground rules on the trip down South, m'am! Should we shake on it?"

Diana Wisdom gave JT a hug and kissed his cheek.

"Deal!" she said.

CHAPTER 88

To LISTEN TO HIS MOTHER'S reaction to the new plan for the Florida trip, one would have thought that her son had hired a hooker to satisfy his carnal urges day and night and monitor her granddaughters in between fucks! However, he had expected about that very reaction from her. She implored him to alter his current thinking by using a very unconvincing argument that she could use a motorized chair to get around the amusement parks. He thought that to be a nice attempt at a compromise until he questioned her need for daily bathing, dressing, bathroom trips, etc.

"Ma, I love you, but bathing you or carrying you in and out of the shower is a little too kinky even for me."

She then used her Bina scenario.

"Take Bina. She can take the time off, and the girls would be so much more comfortable with her."

"Ok, Ma, and who do I leave here keeping an eye on Peg Leg Bates? Yeah, Ma, it will be a great trip for all of us wondering each moment of the day while on the amusement park rides whether you are alive or not. Honestly, Ma, you have no idea how fortunate I feel having Diana step-up to help us. Ma, she is a quality person and a first class woman. Believe me; I have no ulterior motives in bringing Diana on this trip. I am still and will always be in love with Tara. I grieve for her now as much as I grieved for her last winter. Please do not do this to me. I'm just not strong enough right now to handle your disapproval or unhappiness."

"James, I need to meet this young woman. My granddaughters are just too precious to me to…"

"And you think they aren't to me? Do you think I would in some self-serving way place my daughters in harm's way? Do you really believe such a thing?"

"It's not that James. They have been through so much. I can't have them hurt again." She was crying continuously now which meant that JT would do whatever he had to do to make her stop.

"Ok, Ma, I think it would be a great idea to invite Diana to dinner so that she can meet you and the girls. In fact, I'll do it right this minute if tomorrow evening is all right with you?"

On her affirmative nod, JT dialed Diana's home telephone and got the answering machine. He left a brief message for her to call him as soon as she received the message. Within a minute of his hanging up the phone, it rang.

"JT, it's Diana."

"That was fast, boss."

"I was screening calls. You know how it is with all the suitors and pervs ringing-me up at all hours."

"Yeah right, Diana, poor beautiful you."

"What's up, JT?"

"If you are free tomorrow evening, the Russells request the pleasure of your company at dinner. I think it will be a great opportunity for you to meet and get to know the girls. What do you think?"

"You're mother wants to check me out, right?"

"Yeah."

"I'm on, buddy. What may I bring?"

"Yourself."

"Helpful, JT, very helpful. What time?"

"Sixish or whatever is convenient for you, Di."

"Di, that's new. I kind of like that. Six is fine. I'll find your place, don't worry."

"Deal?" he asked.

"Deal," she replied.

Right on time, the doorbell signaled the arrival of Ms. Diana Brian-Wisdom. Two very beautifully dressed young ladies answered the door and were complemented warmly on their looks and dress.

"You must be Ronnie, and you have to be Katie Anne. These flowers are for you, Ronnie, and these are for you Katie. Oh my goodness, they match both of your dresses. Your dad didn't tell me that he had two beautiful princesses for daughters."

"Well, he should have," responded Ronnie as Katie blushed at her sister's lack of the social graces.

"Thank you, Diana, the flowers are beautiful and so are you. Dad didn't tell us you were gorgeous. He just told us you were his boss."

"Really? You are such a love, Katie, thank you."

"Maybe you should fire him, Diana!" yelled Ronnie.

"Hey, don't give her any ideas," laughed JT entering the room dressed to kill.

"Thank you for coming, Diana."

"Thank you for inviting me, Mr. Russell."

"She calls you Mr. Russell, Dad? Just like your kids at school," said Ronnie seriously.

"It's a long story kid. Let's get Diana inside and comfortable."

"I'll take this hand," said Katie.

"This one is mine," yelled Ronnie.

"Doesn't leave me with much," joked JT.

"Really, Mr. Russell?"

It had taken her all of two minutes to captivate the girls. Diana's obvious beauty, wonderful smile, and bubbly personality had made the Russell girls her fans immediately. Now came the harder part, the inspection and interview of Mrs. Charlene Russell.

"Diana, this is my mother, Charlene Russell."

"Ma, this is my boss, Diana Wisdom."

"Please call me Diana, Mrs. Russell," offering her hand.

"Then please call me Charlene, Diana," taking her hand in hers.

"I was listening to my granddaughters welcoming you to our home. They are so correct. You are lovely, dear."

"Thank you so much, Charlene. Now I can see where JT has gotten his good looks."

"You are too kind dear. Would you like a drink before dinner?"

"Ma," JT interrupted, "remember I told you about her drinking problem? She is a fish, for heaven's sake. Hide the good china."

"JT Russell, Ronnie's correct; I should fire you!"

"Only kidding, boss. Ma, she has no drinking problem. The chick has a hollow leg. I've seen her drink sailors under the...."

"JT! Please don't make me more nervous than I already am, OK?"

"Well, then, why don't we dine?" suggested JT.

As he walked by Diana to the kitchen, she kicked him on the ankle hard enough to elicit an "ouch" from the deserving jokester. The dinner went marvelously. JT had followed all of his mother's directions to perfection. He offered an antipasto and minestrone soup, followed by lasagna, sausages, and meatballs. He had left the Gloucester site early that day complaining of a stomach illness and called-in sick to the center. Conversation was light and constant. Laughter and smiles were copious. After eating their fill, Katie and Ronnie adjourned to their bedrooms for some much-needed playtime. Even with the three adults alone, the atmosphere was relaxed and pleasant. Before Charlene had an opportunity to bring-up the Florida excursion, Diana addressed the subject proactively once JT had left the table.

"If I were going to send my grandchildren or children on a 2600-mile round trip for ten days with a stranger, I would insist upon meeting that person who will share the guardianship of the most important people in my world. I have known JT for a relatively short time, but it did not take me long to realize the quality person that he is. Now, we grownups know that this does not happen by accident. I am a firm believer in the "apple doesn't fall far from the tree" adage. Having met the woman who raised this wonderful man, there are no questions left in my mind as to one major source of his strength, warmth, and compassion. Please believe this, Charlene; I will protect your granddaughters as if they were my own. I have only the deepest respect and admiration for your son and the fashion in which JT has dealt with the loss of Tara. I would love to call you a friend as I do now with JT. Please feel secure that the girls are in good hands with both of us."

Upon saying that, Diana rose from her seat, walked over to Charlene, and hugged the woman tightly. Both women were teary-eyed as JT reentered the room.

"Oh shit, did I miss something? Everyone was laughing when I left. Now it looks like you two were cutting onions."

"We are just learning about each other, son."

"Yeah, JT, it's a female thing."

"Good. Is it almost over?"

"What do you think, Charlene?" asked Diana.

"I think that you and I are going to be good friends, my dear," whispered JT's mother.

"Deal?" asked Diana as she proffered her hand to Charlene.

"Deal," acknowledged Charlene taking Diana's hand into both of hers.

"Congratulations. I hope the two of you will be very happy together," laughed JT.

As JT walked Diana to her car that evening, he thanked her profusely for her kindness. Winning his mother over as quickly as Diana had bordered upon a miracle.

"I loved meeting your family, JT. Your girls are fabulous. It is obvious that you and Tara did such a wonderful job raising them. Your mom is a sweetheart wrapped in barbed wire. Nevertheless, I think we understand each other. Moreover, you, my friend, are a very lucky man to be surrounded by so many that love you so much. By the way, Mr. Russell, how many people address you as Jamey?"

"Bina is the last of the line, I believe."

"May I call you Jamey? I just think it fits you so much better than JT."

He thought for a moment and replied, "You get Jamey if I get Di. Deal?"

"Deal," she whispered as she hugged him goodnight.

CHAPTER 89

THURSDAY WAS THE FINAL DAY of the Massachusetts English as a Second Language Education Program summer project for the students. The day was full of award presentations and public acclaim for kids who voluntarily attended an eight-week summer project in hope of diminishing the gaps between where their learning level was and where their learning level should be. JT felt proud after each project because he knew in his heart that he gave as much of himself as he possibly could have given in making the programming an enjoyable learning experience for the kids. JT would address each new summer staff prior to each new project to emphasize the importance of their mission. If one entered his staff thinking it a "throw away" summer job, the shock was real and immediate. Knowing how highly accountable MESLEP was to both Commonwealth supervision and internal supervision, JT insisted on implementing a project that was "by the book". His concluding message to staff each summer at orientation was quite simple:

"If you are doing what you're supposed to be doing when you're supposed to be doing it to the best of your ability, you will have no problem with me, the program administrators, or the Commonwealth of Massachusetts. Please remember, I will never ask you to work harder than I work."

His style was effective. He always had a model site. The final Friday of the program, while his staff was celebrating the end to one more summer project, found JT at MESLEP headquarters "closing out" his site. The director of the program and the site supervisor sat together evaluating a checklist of thirty or so areas of programming along with the site supervisor's written response to each area before the site was officially closed and the summer officially over. On the way home from "closing-out" his site, he picked up Bina who drove him in his car to pick-up the luxury van he had rented for the trip south. He knew from experience that car travel with young children was difficult at best and could tend toward horrible at the opposite end of the spectrum. The van he rented had all the amenities he could muster. The fold-down back seats made great beds. The "backy-back" as his kids called it gave them stretching and distancing space. The van had a radio and a tape player, a small television that plugged into the lighter, activity books up the ying-yang…he was ready!

That evening none of them could sleep. The girls were incredibly excited. He was just plain nervous. Being 1300 miles away from home with two babies and his beautiful boss now did not seem like the formula for a relaxing vacation. He spent some time requesting celestial assistance from Tara and his father before finally surrendering to the sleep fairy. Boy oh boy, did the sleep fairy have a treat for JT that night! Somehow, he found himself in an African village hut curled into the fetal position on a bed of woven palm tree fronds. He heard a noise at the entrance of the hut; he sprung to a sitting position to find a totally unclothed Diana Wisdom facing him. Her long brown hair fell over her shoulders and along side of her beautiful full breasts; her body was alabaster from head to toe with the exception of the beautiful dark triangular thatch below her naval. He rose to his feet now fully aroused in response to her nakedness. He took her gently into his arms as she dropped his loincloth to the jungle floor. He led her by the hand to the palm mat and lay her down. As she assumed a comfortable position, and readied for him, the wall of the hut fell down revealing a safari boat full of Disney World visitors standing and applauding!

Thankfully, morning finally arrived. From her perch on the couch, Charlene directed the Russell girls in their preparation for departure.

The evening before, Charlene had given JT a list of items for each girl. In turn, each girl assisted her dad in obtaining the required articles. Once each girl's suitcase was filled, JT could relax and concentrate on preparing himself for the trip, which he did. The pre-packing was a twist of genius. That morning the girls were ready to go in no time at all. What was initially to be a late afternoon departure, at Diana's request, was altered by the lady herself when she cancelled a hairdressing appointment. JT mercilessly teased her that it would just be overkill anyway if she looked any better. Following a round of kisses good-bye and a good-bye telephone call to Twan, JT packed his girls into the van, waved good-bye to Charlene and Bina, checked his itinerary and finances, and drove off to pick-up the fourth member of their happy troop.

CHAPTER 90

HARVARD UNIVERSITY COVERED A MASSIVE portion of the City of Cambridge, Massachusetts. The size of the spiraling school all by itself was intimidating to new students. When one considered the history and tradition of the school, the quality of the graduates it sent forth into the world, and the burden of living up to a full academic scholarship, Twan Russell definitely needed an infusion of confidence and a period of adjustment to his new surroundings. The young man knew how to be a student. He had proven that his entire academic life. Now he had to learn how to be a Harvard University student who must maintain an average of B in all subjects to keep his scholarship. Pressure? Just a bit. But what a way to go! Food and boarding, a part-time job for spending money, and an excellent education free, and all he had to do was make straight B's! Hell, he had not seen a B on any final grade in his whole life. Now was not the time for that to change. However, in the recesses of the young man's mind was hidden the anger, guilt, and pain of his mother's unsolved death. He vowed to make time in his schedule to do anything and everything he could to resolve that open, festering wound on his heart and soul. At least once per week he would contact the Peabody Police Department to speak with the detective assigned to his motor vehicle accident. In that the accident and subsequent death occurred in the City of Peabody, the police department of that sister city to Lynn maintained jurisdiction over the case. Twan's contact at the police station was Detective Harry

Manos, a two-eyed Peter Falk clone of Greek heritage who would have given twenty years of his life to help Twan find the perpetrator of his mother's demise.

During his most recent conversation with the detective, after almost eight months of dead ends and false leads, Manos related an interesting piece of new information to Twan. It seemed the stolen van was property of one Dawn Woodruff, a thirty-five year old female from the City of Peabody. Upon interviewing the woman initially, she made it known to the investigating officers that since her ownership of the van no male had been inside to the best of her knowledge. The young woman volunteered that she was a member of a pro-female empowerment group whose philosophy discouraged socialization between the sexes. According to her, the only possible male fingerprints in her van would belong to employees or clients of the dealership because she bought the van brand new. When the investigating officers checked the van for fingerprints following the accident, they found no male prints at all, but they found multiple instances of female prints. After identifying the owner's fingerprints, the investigating officers ignored police procedure. Their oversight at that point was that they mistakenly assumed that all the female fingerprints inside the vehicle were those of the female owner. They neglectfully failed to follow the evidence stream for some unknown reason. Two weeks ago, on a lark, mostly out of desperation, Manos requested permission from Dawn Woodruff to have the van's interior checked once again. The second check turned up five different sets of perfectly clear fingerprints, those of the owner and those of four other females. Ms. Woodruff was able to send to Manos a list of twenty to twenty-five females who were in the van since the accident. Manos invited all of the women on the list to the police station to have their prints matched with the prints found in the van. His labor resulted in the identification of three sets of prints. The owners of the now identified prints were interviewed and eliminated from suspicion following a thorough check of their whereabouts on the night of the incident. One set of prints remained unidentified. The fingerprints did not appear on any of the current fingerprint databases available to the Peabody Police Department. Manos theorized to Twan that the driver of the van on the night of the accident might well have been that unknown woman.

CHAPTER 91

SAFE, The Society for the Advancement of Female Empowerment, founded in the late seventies as a socio-political group, sought not only to raise the societal status of females equal to that of males but also to demonstrate the decaying role of the male of the species to the continuation of our society. The founders and supporters of that group advocated causes as socially conscious as equal pay for equal work, non-hostile working environments, extended paid pregnancy leaves, and a variety of quota systems to enhance the number and status of women in the work place. However, the organization also received mockery and disdain for its advocacy of sexual reproductive alternatives, same sex marriages, non-socialization of the sexes, and masturbation as the primary form of human sexuality. The extreme nature of the group's platform was not widely accepted immediately, which was a much-appreciated fact from the male perspective. The Commonwealth of Massachusetts's branch of the budding nation-wide movement had at its leadership several dynamic role models for woman of the Bay State. Dawn Woodruff of Peabody, Massachusetts, was one such person. At the age of thirty-five, Ms. Woodruff held several degrees from area colleges including her Doctor of Philosophy in political science from Radcliff. Following a disaster of a nine-month marriage, at the age of twenty-three, the tall, slim, blond, Daryl Hannah look alike, had reached and surpassed her threshold for abuse from the opposite sex. She sought solace in the company of creatures like herself who had experienced the intolerable cruelty of their male counterparts. In such a protective, nurturing environment, she was able to heal and grow. The experience was a resurrection of sorts, a life-altering period of time that gave her life direction and meaning. She chose to dedicate her life to those who were as injured as she was. SAFE offered her a forum from which to spread her beliefs. The stronger she grew intellectually the higher she rose in the Massachusetts SAFE hierarchy. As a woman's advocate specialist, she sought to bring new members onto the SAFE rolls. She fought for the rights of her sisters across the Commonwealth. Her voice became a powerful force in the arena of women's rights.

At an informational session at the Temple Shalom in Marblehead, Dawn met one of those damaged creatures – Diana Brian-Wisdom. Having just returned to Massachusetts, Diana arrived emotionally limping to that Monday evening discussion session sponsored by SAFE. Diana's disastrous three-year marriage was behind her, but the scars of the abuse, treachery, and deceit left in their wake an esteemless woman searching for direction, comfort, and protection. Dawn could not help but notice the gorgeous brown-haired woman sitting at the back of the room hanging intently upon her every word. At the session's end, Dawn quickly sought out that young woman, leaving several poised questioners in her wake with a simple "excuse me for a moment". Diana had already risen to leave the hall when Dawn approached and immediately introduced herself. Diana, taken with the self-assuredness of the woman, her control of her audience, and her passion for her subject, felt both flattered and embarrassed by the woman's directness. Apologizing for being too forward, Dawn inquired as to whether anyone had told her she looked like a brunette, straight-haired Farrah Fawcett. She then asked Diana if she would be interested in having coffee with her following the question and answer session. There was something magnetic about the speaker's presence. Diana said "yes" before thinking, something she was never prone to do. That evening the two women shared confidences over several "stronger than coffee" beverages at a nearby pub. Dawn allowed Diana an opportunity to discuss issues that she had kept bottled up inside her for years. Not only a wonderful speaker, Dawn proved to be an empathic, supportive listener. There came a point in the latter part of the evening when both women realized that their consumption of liquor had exceeded their maximum capacity. After experiencing difficulty navigating their way to the parking lot, both highly intelligent women reasoned that driving should not be an option that evening. Being that Diana's condominium was just several blocks away from the pub, she suggested that they walk there and really consume some coffee this time in an effort to improve their present lack of sobriety. Much later that evening, there in Diana's home, Dawn Woodruff introduced her inebriated host to the world of female-to-female sexual activity.

Everything felt so natural and right. Diana's sense of security and comfort had not been so strong in years. Dawn was very adept at the art of female-to-female love. She guided the novice, as a sighted person would lead the blind. Dawn had been with many women in her "new" life, but Diana was different. An intense desire to caress and possess the entire being of her newly found partner occurred within Dawn. She had yet to experience such passion! With Diana, everything was so natural, so new, so fulfilling. The two women slept in each other's arms until the light through the skylight awoke Dawn. She gently separated her naked body from Diana's and adjourned to the bathroom. The movement on her bed roused Diana from her deep sobering rest. As the sleep left her eyes and sensibilities, it occurred to her that she was unclothed. Where were her pajamas? Then from the bath, she heard a female voice singing, and flashes of the evening's happenings began to return to her consciousness. Dawn slipped out of the bathroom in all her naked splendor and greeted her newly made friend. Diana was speechless! She pulled the bed coverings around her nakedness and looked questioningly at Dawn.

"Diana, are you alright? You look so strange."

"I always look like this when a strange naked woman walks into my bedroom; in particular if I am naked as well!"

"You don't remember last night, Diana?"

"I remember that we tried to out drink the town drunk. The rest is a blur. Dare I ask you to fill-in the blanks?"

"We shared the most beautiful night together, love. You were simply angelic."

"No, Dawn! That could not be! I'm not like that!"

"Like what, Diana?"

"I've never been with a woman like that. Never! I could not. I would not. Dawn, please!"

"Diana, are you telling me that I was your very first woman?"

"So, I did do it!"

"Yes, love, and you were wonderful."

Not knowing proper lesbian etiquette with which to respond to Dawn's complimentary play by play of last evening's exchanging of body fluids, Diana resorted to her immediate initial reaction. She vomited all over her bed. The distraught woman wretched and wretched until she whimpered in exhaustion. Throughout the cleansing, Dawn held Diana's forehead and kept her hair out of harm's way. The patient, older woman coaxed her protégé to rid her system of the previous night's alcohol overload. Apparently, both women were not reading from the same page, for the source of Diana's projectile vomiting was a reaction to the visualization of her participating in a disgusting form of sexual behavior and not the gastronomic reaction to her liquor intake. Dawn lovingly held Diana until the young woman regained her composure.

"Dawn, we have to talk. There has been a terrible misunderstanding here. I am not a lesbian. I have never been one nor can I see myself ever being one. I am so sorry if that was an impression you received from me. I find you a remarkable woman; your accomplishments are to be admired; I just don't do that!"

"Calm down, love. I totally understand. I should be apologizing to you. I absolutely misread the signals emanating from you. Believe me; I would never dream of attempting to sleep with a "straight" woman with no interest in me whatsoever. In my world, such an action is contrary to all I believe and advocate."

"I believe you, Dawn. I am so terribly embarrassed. I hope that you will forgive my uncouth physical reaction. Please don't take my vomiting personally."

"Personally? Of course, I will not, love. You would have vomited over any woman who had just introduced you to your conception of perversion 101."

"Dawn, I still wish us to be friends. Is that possible in your world?"

"Diana, I have many straight girlfriends. It would be an honor for me to include you as one of them. But I must know in my heart that you forgive me for taking advantage of last night's circumstances."

"Let's not talk of blame again. Last night happened, and I will deal with that. I have never been a "spilt milk" kind of person. Please tell me that with your comforting words, you are not just trying to make me feel better."

"No love, you are a very special lady. I would love to get to know you better and to have you in my life. Now, I'd better dress because I'm starting to feel self-conscious."

"Self-conscious? You have a fabulous body, Dawn. I can say that, right?"

"Yes, you can, love, and I thank you."

When Dawn departed that morning, Diana in her heart of hearts never expected to see her again. She surprised herself in the way she had come to accept her actions of the previous evening. This factor alone was enough to instigate her questioning of her true sexuality. Her thoughts about the incident vacillated. First, it was "girl, was I drunk last night!" Could she have unconsciously wanted Dawn sexually? Had her terrible experience with marriage altered her sexual preferences? How would she know? She had not had heterosexual relations for almost two full years. Do people turn homosexual? Would she be able to recognize it if it were happening to her? Each new query she proposed gave rise to several more. Diana was obviously out of her element. What she needed was expert advice and information. On the spot, she made-up her mind to contact Dawn Woodruff whether or not Dawn wanted to contact her.

Several days passed with no communication between the two. On Friday morning, Diana telephoned SAFE headquarters and left a message for Dawn to call her. Within fifteen minutes of leaving this message, Diana's telephone rang as she was stepping out of the shower.

"Hello?" answered the still wet Diana.

"Hi! It's Dawn Woodruff. How are you? I was so happy to receive your call."

Unconsciously, Diana moved her arm to cover her naked breasts and squeezed her thighs together tightly.

"It's great to hear your voice. Thanks for getting back to me so soon."

"The truth be told, I've been waiting for you to make the first move. I guess in my convoluted way of thinking if you called me, we were all right about the other night."

"We were fine when you left my house, Dawn. That is the reason I am calling. If you are free this weekend, I thought we could get together for dinner."

"Both tonight and Saturday I have SAFE commitments. However, on Sunday, I am having a few close friends over to my house for a homemade meal. I would love you to come. I am sure you would fit in just fine. And I know they'll love you."

Once again, without so much as a thought, Diana accepted the invitation. What was it about that woman that caused Diana to ignore lifelong habits?

"I'd love to come. Just tell me where and when, and I'll be there."

CHAPTER 92

"RONNIE, KATIE! CAN YOU SEE that sign?" asked Diana.

"Welcome to Florida! We're here, Ronnie!"

"Where's Mickey?" asked Ronnie in all seriousness.

"What's going on?" asked the newly awakened JT.

"Daddy! We are here! We're here!" yelled Katie.

"But where's Mickey?" reiterated Ronnie.

"Welcome back to the conscious world, Mr. Russell. Man, do you snore or what?" teased Diana.

"Isn't it better that you found out now, dear?" teased JT. "Weren't you supposed to wake me up when we left South Carolina?"

"You looked so adorable sleeping. I just didn't have the heart to wake you," cooed Diana.

"So you drove straight through South Carolina and Georgia all by yourself? You are strong Wo-man. Have many babies. Make Chief much happy," he teased.

"That, my dear, would most certainly depend upon who the chief is," she retorted.

"Well, now we have about two and a half hours to the condo which is only, get this Ronnie, four minutes away from where Mickey lives!" screamed her father. "You must be tired, Di, let me take over."

"Really, Jamey, I'm fine, unless of course you would prefer to drive."

"No m'am, I'll passage with you anywhere," he cracked.

"Yeah, you say that to all the girls," she teased.

"Only the Farrah Fawcett look-alikes, my dear."

"Don't think those compliments will get you anywhere, buddy! They will probably get you everywhere," she smiled as she glanced from the road to the smiling passenger.

"I didn't realize we had a condo, Jamey. Now you won't have to sleep in the car. I'm sure the condo will have a sofa," mugged the driver.

"Wake me up again when you see an Orlando sign, wise guy. Our check-in time is 4 PM. If we're going to be a lot later than that, I want to call to confirm that we are still on the road."

"Yes, sir. Is there anything else, sir?"

"Yeah, try to miss at least one bump in the damn road will you?"

"Yes sir! Not a problem."

She diligently searched for every bump, crack, pothole, and road kill she could find from there to Orlando, and hot damn she missed nary a one! Shortly after 6 PM, the weary travelers pulled into Blue Sands Resort in Kissimmee not four minutes from the Magic Kingdom. JT checked in and received the directions, keys, and informational package.

"Di, take a right here. Now it is your second left. Good, girl. Pull right in here."

"Katie, Ronnie, the Russells have arrived!" announced their dad.

Diana looked into JT's eyes, flashed her gorgeous smile, and blushed.

The condominium was great. There were two large bedrooms downstairs and a huge master bedroom in the loft. It offered them every comfort of home. It even had a microwave oven in the kitchen and VCR's attached to both the upstairs and downstairs televisions.

"Why don't we put Katie and Ronnie in the bedroom next to me," suggested Diana to JT. "You take the master bedroom, appropriately titled I might add."

"Are you sure?" he asked.

"Yeah, I think it gives the girls and me more of an opportunity to bond, don't you?" she smiled then looked down.

"Yeah, and if you came upstairs, we'd have an opportunity to bond. Only kidding, boss," he lied.

"About what, Jamey?" she smiled slyly.

Ronnie who wanted to know when they were leaving for Mickey's house interrupted their pitter-patter. Accepting the suggestion that Mickey was probably asleep at that time, Ronnie was overjoyed that they were to wake up early the next morning to be first in line at the Magic Kingdom. However, for that evening, JT had convinced the girls that an expedition exploring the wonders of Kissimmee was the next best thing in the world to do. He was right. Kissimmee was a magical place for children and adults. Water parks, dinner shows, helicopter rides, amusement rides, more food places than a county fair, and more souvenir stores than should be allowed under the "be fair to parents' wallets" ordinance. The girls were mesmerized, all three of them. Diana and the girls were giddy with excitement. JT watched how the three females meshed, and then he thought about how much they must miss their mother.

"What do you say, guys, want to take a break from all of this fun and get some food?" he joked.

"Well girls, are we hungry?" asked Diana.

They walked into a STEAK AND SHAKE Restaurant and had the best burger Ronnie had ever tasted, the best fries that ever passed Katie's lips, and the best dinner company Diana had ever had. As the girls walked ahead of Diana and JT toward the next amusement center, Diana slipped her hand into JT's, turned to him, and thanked him for bringing her with them.

CHAPTER 93

"Twan Russell, please. This is Detective Harry Manos, Peabody Police Department."

"Hello, detective, this is Twan Russell."

"Well, kid, I have some news. It may be nothing, or it may be a lead. You impressed upon me that you wanted to be informed about anything to do with your mother's case that crosses my desk, correct?"

"Yes, sir, what's up?"

"The unidentified fingerprints in the van have been identified. Some seemingly insignificant database requiring fingerprints of all registered Washington, DC lobbyists and their spouses for security reasons "kicked-out" a match to our missing prints. Our prints from the van match those fingerprints of one Diana Brian-Wisdom, the wife of a big shot oil lobbyist."

"Did you say Diana Brian-Wisdom?"

"Yeah, Diana Cassandra Brian-Wisdom is the full name. According to our research, she is originally from this area. She left the Commonwealth after marrying David Wisdom, a major political lobbyist. That's all I have at the moment, but we're still working on it."

"I think I can help you out, detective. Ms. Brian-Wisdom has moved back to this area, Marblehead to be exact. She is the director of the CALL Center for Adult Education in your city."

"And how do we know this, son?"

"At this moment, sir, she is at Disney World with my father and sisters."

"You wouldn't be pulling an old detective's Johnson now, would you kid?"

"No, sir, Diana Brian-Wisdom is my father's superior at his part-time position at the CALL Center.

"And excuse me for asking a personal question, but it's an old detective's bad habit. What the fuck is she doing with him at Disney World, research?"

"She's substituting for my ailing grandmother so that my two little sisters wouldn't be terribly disappointed by having their trip down South cancelled."

"So it was her idea?"

"Yes, sir, she suggested it to my father who was more than appreciative of the gesture."

"Uh huh, I am just thinking aloud here, kid. Why do you think her name did not show up on the list of van passengers we received from Dawn Woodruff? Would you have any insight into that relationship too?"

"No, sir, I didn't even think of it until you mentioned it this very moment."

"Well, kid, we may not have taken a giant step, but I kinda feel we're at least on our way out of the dead end we've been locked into for eight months. I will be in touch. Oh, by the way, when is the happy family due home?"

"I suspect they should be here ten days from this past Saturday."

"You're the damn Harvard student, kid, do the math!"

"They should be home by Sunday night or Monday morning at the latest."

"All right, kid, I'll be talking to you."

"Thanks, Detective Manos."

The cagey old detective leaned back in his chair with a pen between his teeth.

"A guy who has been a widower for just eight months takes his tootsie boss to Florida for a vacation. The tootsie is connected in someway to the owner of the stolen van that caused the death of the guy's wife and near death of his kid. If I were not such a trusting son of a bitch, I'd say that's just a tad fucking suspicious. Manos, you should have your own friggin television show."

CHAPTER 94

ON THE RETURN TRIP FROM Kissimmee to the condominium, the girls could not keep their eyes open. No sooner had they gotten into their pj's and argued over sides of the bed, they were well on their way to the only free "land" in Florida – dreamland. JT and Diana sat in the living room/dining room area and relived the highlights of their day and night.

"Jamey, your girls are wonderful. I love them to death already."

"I know they're nuts about you. When I was tucking in Katie just now, she whispered in my ear that she and Ronnie had talked, and they want to keep you when the trip is over! Can you believe that, Di? Di, what's wrong?"

The face with the beautiful smile had transformed into a tear-stained countenance. He walked over to her, but he did not know what do to.

"Did I say something, Di? If I offended you, please forgive me."

"Oh, Jamey, you have been nothing but the most fabulous man since the first moment I met you."

"Please, madam, you'll turn my head."

"I am so serious now, Jamey. Today was the best day of my entire life!"

"Then why the tears, boss?"

"I am now actually aware of what my life is missing, Jamey. I watch the way the girls idolize you. I love the way they respond to me. You and I have such a relaxed relationship. I know now that this is all I ever wanted my whole life. I just made some very poor choices in my life in seeking that goal.

He placed his arm around her, and she rested her head on his shoulder. They remained that way for quite a while. Silently staring at each other and smiling. He felt so much more comfortable now that she was no longer crying.

"Jamey, I'm falling into something so alien to me far faster than my intellect should allow me. Do you think me terrible to covet another woman's family, Jamey? Have I the right to seek happiness so soon after a tragedy? Is that pure selfishness on my part? I am helpless, my friend. I am slipping deeper and deeper into that helplessness by the moment."

She took his face into her hands as she turned toward him.

"I truly understand what a terrible time you've had and the difficult future you face with the kids. Please stop me now if I am moving too fast. Your discouragement would be easier to accept now than later. Jamey, I would love to share so much with you. I have feelings for you that I have had for no other man, ever. If this is the wrong time, or if I am the wrong woman, would I be too forward to ask for a warning from you? Oh shit, I hope I haven't fucked this up! I never thought it out. I've been free associating like a woman ready for a straight jacket."

He pulled her face gently towards his and kissed her lips. Her return kiss caused her to feel dizzy. She clung to him until her heartbeat subsided and the disorientation passed. JT returned his lips to hers repeatedly. The tears from both of them made the couple laugh at the soggy kisses that they were exchanging.

"So what do you think, Russell? Am I the kind of girl you could get used to having around?"

"Before I answer that, I have a question of my own. Will my answer have any impact upon my current position at the CALL Center?"

She smacked him on the shoulder demanding that he be serious.

"I have never felt so vulnerable to anyone in my life, Jamey, as I do to you at this moment. I know I am absolutely one hundred percent in love with you – did I just make another mistake, Russell? Never mind, I'm up to my ass in shit so deep now, what does it matter?"

"You are everything any man could ever need or want, Di. The fact that you could love me scares me. I haven't been very good luck most of my life for those who have loved me. The last thing I would wish for you is a dose of JT's curse. I cannot say that I am over Tara. I do not know if I ever will truly be. My grief seems to have no limits at this point; however, if you possess the patience and determination to be more deeply involved in the life of this humble educator, there's not a woman on the planet that I would rather be with than you."

"So, are we like going steady, Russell, or are we a monogamous couple?

"We're anything you want us to be, love."

"Deal? she asked.

"Deal!" he responded.

They kissed several more times unable to leave each other's side. For the first time in what seemed like hours, Diana began to relax and absorb the magnitude of their commitment. JT walked Diana to her bedroom door and told her to sleep on all that had transpired. He wanted to give her a "cooling off" period to allow her to think unemotionally about their discussion.

"If you don't change your mind by morning, boss, we may have to alter the sleeping arrangements around here."

"You can bet your ass that nothing is going to change at this end, buddy! Nevertheless, the same goes for you. If you change your mind, Jamey, I'll spend the rest of the vacation walking around bare ass until you return to your senses!"

"Deal?" he asked wide-eyed.

"Deal!" she smiled back.

CHAPTER 95

WHEN DIANA AWOKE THE FOLLOWING morning, the remnants of her dream that night amazed her. One would have surely thought that the baring of a heart and soul to another, confessing an all-consuming love for a man, and wetting through two pair of panties would have led to dreams of her and Jamey, but that was not the case. She dreamed about the early days of her relationship with Dawn Woodruff. The small dinner party at her house after the "incident" remained in her consciousness as she awoke. She lay back in her bed and listened for movement from the girls' room. Hearing none, she allowed her mind to wander to her dream source.

The evening of the dinner party arrived quickly. Diana purchased a very nice bottle of wine at Slappy's Liquors on the way to Dawn's home, which was located in a gated community just off Route 128 in Peabody. Her condominium was located on the eighth floor, which presented her with the most stunning view of the surrounding communities. Diana had been the first of the guests to arrive. Dawn answered the door looking elegant in a very stylish long skirt and beautiful blouse. They hugged genuinely feeling happy to see each other.

"Am I the first to arrive, Dawn?"

"No, I'm here."

"Right. You're even funnier sober than you are drunk," she teased.

"Come in. Sit down. Relax."

"This is for you. I hope you like it," handing her the bottle of wine.

"Many thanks, love. Excuse me for one moment; I must check the oven."

"I love your home, Dawn."

"I'll give you the grand tour in a moment."

The gracious hostess seemed to glide from the kitchen into the living room taking her guest by the hand to begin the home tour.

"Before I do another thing, I have a small confession to make, "admitted Ms. Woodruff. "We will be here alone tonight. After your call, I uninvited the others. I pray this does not upset you. I felt I needed time alone with you because of the other night."

"You needn't have done that, Dawn. I trust you didn't hurt the feelings of your friends."

"Not to worry. The girls know my 'subject to change on a moment's notice' life style and me. But please, believe this, I had no ulterior motive whatsoever in changing our plans."

"If you tell me it's true, than I accept you at your word. Isn't that what friendship is all about, Dawn?"

"You are a love."

They continued the tour of the beautifully decorated, perfectly tidy condominium, and then sat down to a deliciously prepared meal of French cuisine. Dawn Woodruff was the complete package: brains, looks, class, taste, wealth, unfortunately for Diana she was not a man! That evening was memorable for Diana. Dawn answered her every query about her chosen lifestyle and gave sound counsel to Diana about her search for a happier existence. She was a woman at whose knee Diana could learn and grow. It was that "sex thing" that haunted the younger woman.

"I want you to know one thing before you leave me tonight. You struck a heartstring earlier this evening when you told me that you would accept my word at face value because that is what friendship is all about, Diana. Now I have to confess something in the name of friendship that may cause you to rethink your desire for a friendship with me."

"You're scaring me, Dawn. Good Lord, what could be so ominous?

"In my life, I have never had such an emotional connection to any other human being as I have had with you. I think of nothing else. You totally occupy my waking moments. I absolutely understand and respect your personal preferences and would do nothing to coerce you to 'change teams' so to speak. I don't know if I am strong enough to be your friend when I ache to be so much more. I have never truly fallen in love before, Diana. Even my marriage was more of a fulfillment of a societal obligation. I am in love with you, Diana, and I know not whether I am able to just be your friend."

Diana allowed her eyes to drop from her friend's face for the first time since her declaration of love.

"Dawn, all I know at this moment is that I will be the poorer for not having you in my life. I regret that I am not able to be what you need and want, but you will not find another who will hold you in higher esteem than I will. If it must be a black or white decision in your mind, so be it. However, please know that I am willing to take the chance of possible future pain in order to have you in my life."

They embraced and separated smiling.

"I think you have a best friend, Ms. Wisdom, at least until I can't bear it any longer."

"I'm honored and so happy that you are willing to make such a sacrifice for the sake of our friendship, Dawn. Don't ever hold anything back from me either. Talk to me when things get bad for you. Christ, Dawn, there can't be anything more personal left to be embarrassed about sharing than we've already shared!"

On parting that evening, the tentative best friendship began. Dawn was the person responsible for directing Diana to the job opening at the CALL Center. Diana helped introduce Dawn to a stress reducing activity with early morning and late evening runs at the beach. In fact, now that she had been thinking about it, Diana used Dawn as her only shoulder to cry upon in her burgeoning case of mad love for a married man. The two shared, as would sisters, as intimates. Suddenly, though not totally unexpected, it was all gone.

CHAPTER 96

"Diana, Diana, are you awake?" whispered Katie Anne Russell. "Ronnie and I are."

The girls cracked open the door to see a smiling Diana with her arms spread wide. Both little girls rushed to her bed and hopped on top of her. She hugged each one separately and then together. Each happy little girl planted a big kiss on Diana's cheek.

"Should we get ready now, Diana?" asked Ronnie.

"How about just the three of us get cozy under the covers here for a little bit, then we'll all go upstairs to wake up the big guy?"

She did not need to convince the girls. Both scurried under her bed covering, and the three ladies snuggled together as if they were one. At the same time, with not so much as a creaking stair, JT crept down the stairs from his loft bedroom with the ever-present video camera on his shoulder. As he approached the girls' bedroom, he was narrating the audio to his videotaping. Thinking he was going to find the girls sleeping and the target of a great cinema verite recording, he pushed opened the door of an empty bedroom. Disappointed, he moved to the next bedroom with his camera still recording and his narration of unscripted material continuing as he navigated the hallway. Once he turned the corner and peeked into the room, he noticed a remarkably large lump in the center of the double bed completely covered by bed covering. He crept in slowly, stopping his narration in hope of capturing the occupants of the room unaware. Just as he reached to pull the bedcovers up and off, the three females scared the life out of JT by beating him to the punch! Up jumped Katie and Ronnie screaming "surprise" under the direction of the Lady Diana who had anticipated the voyeur's plan. Along with some great video of the three ladies in action, JT got some fabulous video of the ceiling and walls as he fell backwards from the bed. He also captured some interesting audio of him uttering several words for which Ronnie later chastised him.

"Girls, go help your father get up," teased Diana. "A man his age should not fall like that because he could break a hip. Next thing you know, you're pushing the old geyser around in a wheelchair."

"Daddy, is your hip all right?" yelled Ronnie. "Are you OK to go to Mickey's house? We can get a wheelchair, right Diana?"

"I'm fine. No help needed, thank you very much," he replied indignantly. "You'll rue this day, Missy Diana!"

"Rue? I'll rue it? Rue hoo hoo. Rue hoo hoo. I'm already rueing it, buddy," she laughed.

They were not the first in line at the Magic Kingdom, but they were darn close to it. The entire process of parking thousands of cars, transporting dozens of people in dozens of trams, loading hundreds of folks on paddleboats and monorails just to get them to the main entrance was fascinating to JT and Diana, but it was not fast enough for the girls. JT's faithful video camera rolled continuously keeping a video-tapped record of every move made by Diana and the girls. The first six hours just flew by. By the ninth hour, JT was ready for an ambulance. By the twelfth hour, the girls finally agreed to go home and return the next day. By the time they got back to the condominium, it was close to 11PM. JT carried Katie, and Diana carried Ronnie into their bedroom and put the "dead to the world" little girls to bed still in their clothes.

The adults adjourned to the living room/dining room area with assistance from each other.

"Oh my God, this was only the first day, Jamey," cried Diana. "How will we ever get through the week?"

"Now, who's the old fart, Diana?"

"Kiss me, you fool, before I forget what you taste like."

Jamey held her closely and kissed her for a very long time.

"Well, have you changed your mind, boss? I forgot to ask you this morning. You females had me running around in circles."

"Yes, Jamey, I believe I have," she said with a sad serious face.

He looked at her with a bit of a start. He uneasily waited for the next words from her mouth.

"I love you more than I did last night, and if I'm any judge of character at all, I believe I will love you more each day that we're together."

"Will you not scare me like that, Di? I may not be around much longer if you're going to be the cause of my having a stroke!"

"I want to be with you tonight, Jamey."

"I must be with you, Di."

"Please be patient with me, Jamey. It's been a very long time for me."

"We have the rest of our lives, sweetie; there's absolutely no rush."

He ran his hands through her long brown hair and kissed her lightly on the lips before taking her by the hand and leading her upstairs. She thought her heart was going to leave her chest it raced so. At the top of the stairs, they embraced again. Now, she was unsure whether it was his, hers, or their hearts thumping loud enough to be heard outside the condominium. They began to undress each other tentatively. With each new article of clothing deposited on the floor, each of the lovers exhibited more confidence. To pull off JT's jeans shorts, Diana pushed him on to the bed without warning.

"There you go again! Are you trying to kill me or what?"

"Shut up, you wuss, and help me get these briefs off."

"Yes, m'am, anything you say."

As he made himself naked for her, she slowly did the same for him. She was breathtakingly lovely in her nakedness.

"Diana, I have an introduction to make. Little JT, this is Diana. Yes, you are correct. We have been dreaming about this one. Isn't that cute, Diana? He stood right up as soon as he saw you?"

"Are you ever serious, Jamey?"

"Let's show her how serious we can be, Little JT."

Not only had it been a long time for her, but he also had been without release for many months. He had to harness the pent-up needs of Little JT to insure that their first experience as lovers would be a memorable one. A thought ran through his head about a piece of advice his father had given him when he abortively tried to tell JT the facts of life. Both of them knew that he would never get through the "birds and bees" talk without cracking-up, so he simply said, "Kid, never stop being her lover first and foremost." JT had taken that piece of advice to heart and tried to practice it his entire sexual life. He took a great deal of time stroking, massaging, bussing, and kissing her entire body. Her whimpers of pleasure were like aphrodisiacs to his brain, yet he restrained himself. Although he was not sure if it really happened or not, but he swore she grabbed him by the ears following her second release and whispered, "Is anyone going to get fucked around here?"

"Little JT, you're on," he murmured.

He tried to impress her with his coital skills. Within the first fifteen minutes of their coupling, he had had her in four different positions. By the time Little JT gave it up and was in need of a rest, Diana had ridden on at least six different rides at JT Land!

"Whoa there, buddy, you are something! You went from a comedy show to a magic show. Are you for real? Where did you come from? No, don't tell me, if I find out you might disappear like Rumplestiltskin!"

"Rumple-fucking-stiltskin? Here I think I'm loving you like Warren Beatty, and you come out with Rumplestiltskin."

"Just a figure of speech, stud." Then she paused, "Jamey that was remarkable. I have never even been in five of those six positions. You are like Clark Kent. When your drawers come off, you become Superman, and you don't even need a phone booth."

"Now, that's better. Rumple-fucking-stiltskin, my ass."

"I am so in love with you. If you had been a lousy lover, I would still love you to pieces…

"Little JT, close your ears! The woman is talking heresy."

"But you are absolutely perfect for me."

"As Woody Allen said, my dear, 'I practice a lot when I'm alone.' Really, honey, I'm not that good. I just try hard."

"Seriously, Jamey, I'll get better. I want to do everything I can to please you."

"You already have, boss, and now if I am any judge of character, it'll only get better and better."

"Deal?" she smiled.

"Deal," he grinned back.

"Oh by the way, Di, what did you use for birth control?"

"Birth control? I completely forgot about that part! Did you use anything, Jamey?"

"I haven't had much reason to carry anything around with me lately."

"Even knowing that you'd be on a ten day trip with a hottie like me, you purchased no protection?"

"How'd I know you'd be so easy?"

After punching him in the arm, she looked at her partner in crime and whispered, "This vacation may be one for the ages, Daddy."

"Que sera, sera, sweetie."

"Really, Jamey?"

"Really, Di."

"Deal, Russell?"

"Deal, Diana."

CHAPTER 97

EIGHTEEN MONTHS EARLIER AT THAT familiar pub in Marblehead, Diana and Dawn were trying to drink each other "under the table" again. The differences that night were that Diana was on her guard about doing anything contrary to her sexual nature, and she was drinking this time for a reason. The woman was in the throes of depression over her on-going obsession to possess the impossible…her married man. Not only was the object of her compulsive desire still unavailable to her, his wife, she had recently been informed, was pregnant with their fourth child. The bartender, in all his wisdom, finally stopped serving the two inebriated imbibers. He went so far as to send the waitress over to their table with several cups of black coffee over the next half-hour.

"You realize, Diana, that you have never told me the identity of this object of your obsession," complained Dawn.

"What good would that do, Dawn?"

"Why don't you try, and we might just find out, Diana."

"It's JT Russell, the guy who works nights at the center. He appears to be a 'very married' guy with happy kids and a story book life, I guess. I just cannot stop fantasizing about the man. I really don't understand why. I just love everything he does and says. I love the way he smells, and the way he looks at me. I love his polite ways and his magnetic persona. He draws me closer and closer to him each day. I fight it. I try to get mad at him. I look for his faults. Yes, he has faults. I am just losing the battle. I feel like that crazy chick in 'Play Misty for Me'.

Soon, I will be stalking the poor bastard and stabbing his housekeeper. I need help, and I don't mean another drink."

"Well, you have sufficiently depressed me, my friend. It kills me to see you like this. No man, not a single, living, breathing one of them, is worth the pain that you are experiencing. I wish I could shake you to your senses. Do you not agree that we, humans, should choose that which is in our best interests and not necessarily that which we desire most? Your object of desire, as is mine, appears to be unobtainable. My advice to you and myself is to cut your losses and run. Any other choice perpetuates an illusion and is not a viable option."

"So what you're saying, Dawn, is that I should forget about JT, and you should forget about me."

"Yes, love, the time has come. You told me to talk to you when the pain grew to be too bad. Well, the pain was too bad the moment after I found out that you were a straight woman. Since then, I have dealt with an unbearable situation, like you, hoping upon hope that some incredible set of circumstances might arise that would magically change our lots in this life. I have now accepted the fact that it 'ain't gonna happen' for me, love. You and I are on self-destructive paths, similar yet different, but correctable with a dose of willpower and a bucket or two of common sense. I shall miss us together. I will probably not ever recover from your spell, but I cannot handle the pain of being so close to you without any hope of possessing you. I cannot bear to hear your acrimonious bullshit about some asshole that cannot see the best possible thing he could ever ask for in his life. Therefore, I must go. When I say good-bye to you tonight, it will be for the final time. I will not look back. For if I do, I face the reality of falling headlong into the abyss."

"Dawn, please."

"Good-bye, Diana, please remember I am doing this not to hurt you, but because I love you. However, I must start loving myself once again."

She dropped several bills on the table, smiled at her companion, turned, and walked out of Diana Wisdom's life.

CHAPTER 98

OVER THE FOLLOWING FIVE FLORIDIAN days and nights, the happy band of vacationers had so much fun that had they died on the spot, it would have taken a mortician days to remove the smiles from their faces! The girls were in heaven. From the brand-new Epcot Center and the Magic Kingdom, to Gatorland, back to Kissimmee, to Sea World and everything in between, if ever there were a heaven on earth for children of all ages; JT had found it for all three of his girls. At night with the children soundly asleep, the newly connected lovers utilized whatever energy remaining from their daily park visits to bond together, to experiment in all aspects of physical love, and explore each other in every possible way. By their Saturday departure time, the girls were ready to be home with their grandmother, and the lovers were ready to begin the next chapter of their lives.

"Girls, double check everything. If we leave anything behind, it will be lost for good," reminded Diana.

"Ronnie's under the bed now, Diana," yelled Katie. "I think she's stuck."

"I'm not stuck, Diana. I just don't want to leave. I'm staying!" yelled Ronnie.

"How about if you come out, you, Katie, and I will talk about our next trip?" coerced Diana.

"Diana! Is Daddy gonna let us keep you?" screamed Katie. "Ronnie did you hear that?"

In record setting time for seven-year-old girls, Ronnie slid from beneath the bed into the arms of Diana where her sister was awaiting her. Still laughing, Diana held the girls tightly and knew she was where she should be.

"I guess we'll have to ask the big guy about that, girls. Why don't you go talk with him?"

"Diana, do you want to stay with Ronnie and me?" asked Katie very seriously.

"Girls, more than you will ever know. I want to spend as much time as I can with you guys."

JT entered the condominium to view the lovefest going on.

"When I left, you were getting ready to leave. I come back, and it looks like you're planning to stay."

"Daddy, Ronnie and I have an important question to ask you, and we can't leave until we get your answer," calmly stated Katie Anne.

"This sounds important. You had better let me in on it," said JT seriously.

"Daddy, we love Diana, and she loves us. We want to keep her," pleaded Katie.

"Katie Anne, Diana is a grown woman not a homeless puppy!" replied JT.

"But Daddy, she wants us to keep her!" responded Ronnie. "Tell him, Diana!"

JT and Diana looked at each other and smiled.

"I tell you what. Diana and I will have a long talk about this important decision, and after we have come to an agreement, you two will be the first to know."

"You mean no decision now?" asked Katie.

"Boo!" responded Ronnie.

"Your dad is right, girls. This is a very big decision for him. We certainly don't want to push him."

"Not just for him, Missy Diana. What about the rest of your life?" proposed JT.

"Jamey, I already know my answer," she winked.

The trip home, as did the trip to Florida, required an overnight motel stay. JT figured that they would probably stay the night in Virginia or Maryland depending upon traffic. However, he had one more surprise left for his ladies – a stop at Pedro's South of the Border. Located at the border of North and South Carolina, that sprawling assembly of amusements, oddities, motels, eateries, souvenir shops, tourist information, and auto care was advertised from one hundred miles away in both directions via billboards. Going to Florida, the girls started reading the "Pedro" billboards until finally they saw the huge sombrero and tall tower of South of the Border. They begged to stop, but the time was not right for a pit stop of any duration due to their condominium check-in time. On the way home, with time much less of an issue, JT thought he would surprise the girls with a Pedro tour. As they passed through Georgia and South Carolina, the girls eagerly awaited the first Pedro billboard. Sure enough, about one hundred miles from South of the Border, the billboards began. Each girl took turns reading a billboard with Katie Ann assisting Ronnie over the harder vocabulary and explaining most of their humorous meanings. The applause from the backy-back of the van erupted when JT signaled his turn to enter Pedro's South of the Border! Mentally, he set a time limit for their visit, which he barely met due to his own miscalculations. As they were strolling through one of the several large souvenir shops at Pedro's trying to walk off a very nice mid-day meal, JT noticed a room at the rear of the building with the following sign on the door: Dirty Old Men's Shop. He just could not resist the temptation, so he excused himself from Diana and the girls, slipped on his dark glasses, and stole into the adult's only section of Pedro's. He was like a kid in a candy store. There were rubber and plastic mechanical sex toys of every possible description – those for the gentleman and those for the lady. Unable to control Little JT's appetite for the unusual, Big JT ended up purchasing a shopping bag full of devices with which he and Diana could play. Putting off the girls' questions about what was in his bag, JT kept the bag behind his knees partially under the driver's seat while he was driving. When it was Diana's shift to drive, the bag transferred to the passenger seat with JT. Diana became as curious as the girls had been.

"Hey, Russell, what are you hiding in that bag? Are you wearing women's clothing again?" she laughed.

"Very funny; it just so happens that I bought you some presents."

"For me?"

"Yes, and just look at the way you treat me," he complained in mock despair.

"I'm sorry, sweetie. What did you buy me?" she sing-songed.

"Diana," he whispered, "you won't believe this shit. I got vibrators, body paints, massage oils…"

"And these are presents for 'moi'? I am already having enough of a time keeping up with Little JT. I need more stimulation like I need another breast on my back."

"Interesting concept," he murmured.

"Remind me to keep Little JT on a short leash when you are shopping in dangerous territory," she whispered.

"Oh my, we are getting kinky aren't we?" he mugged.

"Incorrigible, thy name is Russell," she sighed as she looked to a higher consciousness.

CHAPTER 99

"WELL MS. WISDOM, YOU ARE home at last. Girls, this is where Diana lives, remember? Time to say good-bye for now," announced JT.

The three females shared hugs and kisses as well as a few tears that almost immediately ceased when the only gentleman in the van told his daughters that Diana would be coming to their house the next day, Labor Day, for an end of summer cookout. At that moment, he was the most popular male on the planet. He left Katie Anne in charge of Ronnie, locked the van doors, and proceeded to carry Diana's luggage into her condominium. Following several fleeting kisses and declarations of love, the couple separated with promises of a later telephone conversation. Back in the van, JT returned to two sleeping children. He then drove in dark quietness for the only time in the past ten days. Bina and Charlene had been eagerly awaiting their arrival. JT hated to wake the girls; however, to carry them, their bags, his bags, and himself into the house required more energy then he had left in his reserve. The homecoming was jubilant. Charlene had desperately missed her girls. Her injury had made positive strides in their absence so she was able to stand and walk with crutches to greet them. As both Bina and Charlene were opening the souvenirs that the girls had picked out for them, the telephone rang. Not wanting to interrupt the festivities, JT volunteered to answer it.

"Twan! Yeah, we just this moment got in. It was wonderful. Yeah, she was terrific with the girls. You will be here tomorrow, won't you? Great! I want you to meet her. She is a terrific lady, Twan. Yeah, what is it? He wants to talk with me. With you and me? Do you have any idea what's going on with Detective Manos, Twan? Really? New evidence after all these months. Great news, buddy. I am free all afternoon Tuesday. Yeah, I am going to be at school for a few hours in the morning to get my classroom set up for Wednesday. Tell him any time after twelve on Tuesday is fine with me. I love you too, son. See you tomorrow."

The chat with Twan left JT with a positive feeling about perhaps finally making progress on the mystery of Tara's death. For the first time since it happened, he could think of the incident and not shudder. He had more or less unconsciously given up hope that the perpetrator of the crime would ever be found. That new information may be a reason to hope for a solution. Knowing himself so well, he could predict his not being able to relax until he spoke with Manos. Nevertheless, that was for another day. He returned to the living room to rejoin the festivities.

The girls had dispensed their presents and snuggled on the sofa with Bina and Charlene. Neither of the girls could stop talking about Diana and Disney World, in that order. Charlene recognized immediately the remarkable impact that the young woman had had on her granddaughters. A feeling of sadness borne of jealousy surrounded the previously smiling grandmother. It was time to put the girls to bed, but before they left, JT coaxed them into telling their Gram and Aunt Bina about the cookout the next day. They asked Bina to bring soon-to-be Uncle Mark with her so he could meet Diana too. After he had sat with the girls and talked about their incredible adventure, he kissed each goodnight, wished them pleasant dreams, and tucked them in for the evening.

"They are so excited, James. I haven't seen them like that since...," Charlene stopped before verbalizing something that would only be painful to all in attendance.

"...And that Diana made quite an impression on them didn't she?"

"She's an amazing woman, Ma. Bina, I cannot wait for you to meet her. The girls actually asked me if they could keep her."

Two of the three people in the room laughed at the notion. Charlene allowed it to pass without note.

"It seems she's had an impact on someone other than the girls, brother dearest. What's up?"

"It's hard to explain, but when she's around I can't feel sad. I don't hurt. It's almost like she's a pain medicine."

"Sounds serious, Jamey. How does the lady feel about the situation?"

"What situation, Bina? My goodness! She and James are friends and working acquaintances," interrupted Charlene agitatedly.

"Well, Ma, to be completely honest, I'm going to be seeing a lot more of Diana from now on. I thought you and Bina should be the first to know."

"James, you have two young daughters to consider above all else," protested Charlene.

"You think I don't think about what their lives are going to be like every friggin waking moment of my life! I think about them growing up without a mother, with a memory so horrible that I hesitate to mention Tara's name! Yeah, Ma, I consider my children every moment I breathe. Remember who my teacher was. Look, I do not want to anger anyone or get angry. My personal life is just that. Whom I choose to share it with and for what reason are my personal decisions. Moreover, I assure you that I make absolutely no decision involving any of my children without the most profound contemplation."

"James, I didn't mean..."

"I know, Ma. Let's just let it lie here for now. I am tired from all the driving and need to hit the sack. Goodnight, Bina, Ma."

He kissed each of them on the cheek and walked slowly to his empty bedroom breathing deeply as he moved in order to maintain his composure.

On Monday morning the girls were awake early watching Jerry Lewis raise all that money for sick kids, as Katie put it. The sound of the television woke JT who had to get up anyway to shop for the cookout. He lay in bed and waited a respectable amount of time before dialing up his sweetheart.

"Hi, Jamey, I was just dreaming about you. How could you cheat on me you, bastard?" she emoted. "Just kidding, sweetie."

"You keep pushing that stroke button, Diana. One day it will be the big one. Then will you say, 'Sorry, I killed you Jamey. I was just kidding'?"

"Relax, lover, you're as strong as a horse. I certainly found that out first hand."

"If you're gonna start talkin like that I have to get in a more comfortable position, lady."

"You, Mr. Russell, will keep your hands off of Little JT. He's all mine now."

"I love when you talk like that, honey, but don't let Little JT hear it. He's much more sensitive than I."

"Hey buddy, I know exactly how sensitive Little JT is, remember? Moreover, as for you, I know how to sooth my man. Why don't you come over? We haven't christened my place yet, big boy."

"I'll pick you up, and we'll shop for the cook-out. Before or after the errands, your choice, you may have your way with me. Deal?"

"Deal," responded Diana.

"Oh by the way, Jamey, I have a doctor's appointment late in the day tomorrow so I won't be at the center."

"What's wrong, Di?"

"Nothing at all, sweetie. I called my ob-gyn from Florida following our first night birth control debacle. I needed a check-up anyway, and I need information on the current birth control options. I just cannot stand those condoms. I can't feel your real warmth, you know?"

"Are you trying to wake Little JT, or what? Too late, he's up and searching the area for you."

"I'd best say goodbye then before the little guy injures himself by slamming his head against your tighty, whitey briefs."

"I'll pick you up in about an hour and a half. Love you."

"I love you so, Jamey. Bye."

Simultaneously though more than twelve miles apart, each hung up the telephone, lay flat on his/her back, looked up at the ceiling, and smiled and smiled and smiled.

The shopping was the hard part. JT could not keep his hands off the woman. By her choice, the "christening" was to take place after the errands. This more than explained the poor man's neediness. Once the last item was in the bag and the shoppers packed the car, JT broke more than several laws in returning to Diana's home.

"Thank goodness we made it here alive, Russell. Was that your foot on the gas or was it Little JT?"

"Silence, woman! Chief want make much good love to lady chief. Will do only if she shuts mouth."

Off she ran out of the car and into the condo followed closely by Chief WANSOMENOOKIE.

They met at the bathroom, made a pit stop, and walked hand and hand to her bed.

"One request, Jamey. Please no condom, sweetie. We will be all right. After tomorrow, we won't have to worry at all. Please, it is a christening."

Against his better judgment, he agreed. What he did not take into account was her definition of a christening. For the next almost two hours, they had christened four rooms!

"We are going to need a lot of good fortune to get away with this one, my dear."

"Why, Mr. Russell, would it be so terrible for you and me to bring a child into the world? God forbid, you might even be forced to marry me."

"Do you want to be a wife again, Di?

"No, I want to be your wife. I want your children. And I want our children."

"How do you feel about it, Jamey?" she asked not really knowing if she wanted to hear his response.

"I love you. I would love to bring you into my family. And I would love to make a baby with you."

She threw her arms around his neck and almost cut off the flow of blood through his jugular veins.

"Was that a proposal, Mr. Russell?"

"Do you want it to be, Ms. Wisdom?"

"Do you want to see a naked woman do cartwheels through Old Town Marblehead?"

"Is that a trick question?"

"Are we engaged, Jamey?"

The naked man knelt on the floor.

"Ms. Wisdom, will you do me the great honor of becoming my wife?"

"Deal," she smiled.

They decided to keep their official status to themselves for the time being to allow significant others in their lives, such as Charlene Russell, the opportunity to know and accept them as a couple. At that point, Diana would have agreed to anything Jamey suggested. Her real-life dream was coming true. The hard part was going to be their behavior at the cookout or, to be more specific, the control of their behavior at the cookout. Diana picked up exactly where she left off with the girls. After several moments of frosty conversation, Diana had disarmed Charlene and had her enrolling in her fan club. Bina agreed with her brother's description of the "complete package" of a woman represented by Diana. She thought how fortunate of her brother to have been loved by two such remarkable women in the same lifetime. They eagerly awaited the arrival of Twan to the cookout, as he had not been home since the middle of August. Upon his arrival, his reaction to meeting Diana was quite unexpected. The normally warm, effervescent, personable, young man acted cool, almost aloof, to his father's friend. Both JT and Diana sensed a wall the boy had started to construct the moment he met Diana. JT passed it off to nerves, and the awkwardness of meeting such a special person in his father's life. He placated Diana's concern with that theory and hoped for an improved reaction as the day continued. It never happened. Twan was obviously avoiding the newcomer and did little to hide the fact. JT at last felt he had to make his feelings known to his uncharacteristically ill-mannered son. He cornered the young man and gave him a big fatherly hug, which Twan returned. As they hugged, he whispered in his son's ear.

"Look, buddy, I don't know what crawled up your ass in Cambridge, but your behavior toward someone very special to me is becoming embarrassing! I think I deserve an explanation, Twan."

"Yes, sir, you do. May we speak privately later this evening, Dad? I have a head full of questions that require answers that you might have."

"Fine. Until then, please exercise those gentlemanly manners instilled in you by you mother and me."

"I apologize, Dad. Please don't forget our talk."

Driving Diana home to Marblehead that evening was uncomfortable. Twan's behavior towards her upset the young woman. The other family members fell in love with her, but Twan seemed to want nothing to do with her. JT sensed her sadness in the quiet as they drove. At the same time, she knew that she would hurt Jamey's feelings by accusing his son of being rude to her. Feeling compelled to keep their burgeoning romance as open and honest as it began, Diana turned to Jamey to approach the problem. Almost simultaneously, he broached the subject explaining to her about his meeting with Twan later that evening. He also filled her in about the possible new leads in Tara's death, as well as the meeting with Detective Manos the next day. All of those factors had perhaps taken a toll on the young man sensibilities thus explaining his unusual behavior. He assured her that he would have an answer one way or another before he slept that night. Strangely enough, as a result of that very conversation, he slept not at all that night.

CHAPTER 100

SHORTLY AFTER 11PM, JT PULLED into his driveway. Charlene and the girls had been long asleep. Twan, who was to sleep at home that evening to be available to Detective Manos the next day, had been passing time by watching television. The young man had rehearsed various ways to approach his father concerning the sensitive subject matter, which was at the core of his request for their meeting. He finally gave up the idea of preparing for the session in favor of practicing his father's lingering advice, "This above all, to thine own self be true". There could be no protecting feelings, no smoothing over potentially revealing issues, no holds barred. After all, they would be talking about the events that removed his mother from her family.

JT poured himself a cold drink, reminded himself of the importance of his maintaining his emotions, and began his walk to Twan's room. The door was slightly ajar as he approached. He knocked in their old secret code (2 long, 3 short, 2 long) which brought a grinning Twan to the door. They hugged and retired to Twan's bed.

"Well, buddy, you called the meeting so why don't you begin?"

"Dad, you know that I've been communicating with the Peabody Police Department on a regular basis since the accident. I realize that I have become obsessed with finding the person responsible for my mother's death. At times, I feel consumed by my need for answers. I am like Captain Ahab seeking his revenge on the great white whale. Over time, I have come to understand the grief and guilt motivations driving my behavior. Thus, I have been better prepared to deal with the situation as it invaded my consciousness. Well, Dad, after eight months of no progress, due to the dogged determination of Harry Manos, we may have a viable lead. My problem tonight is the unveiling of this information that may well have a serious emotional impact on you in more ways than one."

"Twan, you're speaking very carefully and now cryptically. Say what you have to say."

"Detective Manos had Dawn Woodruff's white van, which you'll recall was stolen from the North Shore Shopping Center and used in the collision with our vehicle, re-examined recently. He had proposed the possibility of error by the investigating officers on the night of the accident. Ms. Woodruff was very helpful in allowing his new search. Manos discovered that the investigating officers assumed that all of the female fingerprints in the van belonged to the owner. Bad assumption, bad police work. The re-examination uncovered five different sets of female fingerprints. Ms. Woodruff, who has little to nothing to do with the male of our species, gave Detective Manos the names of twenty-four women whose prints might be in her van. Manos had all twenty-four of the women printed and matched to the van prints. He was able to eliminate four of the five sets of prints based upon the suspects' alibis. One set was unidentifiable. Manos theorized to me that our perpetrator may well be a woman."

"The man seems to be a candidate for his own TV show, Twan."

"I'm not finished yet, Dad. Several days ago, he identified the final set of prints from a Washington, DC database. They belonged to Diana Brian-Wisdom."

"My Diana Brian-Wisdom?"

"Yes, sir."

"There must be some mistake or some logical explanation…"

"I was able to fill-in some missing information about Ms. Brian-Wisdom for Detective Manos who seemed astonished that she was at the time vacationing with you in Florida."

"Ms. Woodruff never included Ms.Brian-Wisdom on her list of passengers or drivers of her van. Therefore, if I read Harry Manos correctly, and I have gotten to know the man pretty well, he has developed a scenario of a straying, lovesick husband who wants to get rid of his wife so he and his girlfriend can be together. The girlfriend borrows a friend's van and performs the fatal deed. Eight months later the mourning husband and his new girlfriend are vacationing in sunny Florida."

"Ridiculous! Twan do you believe any part of this?"

"Dad, you have been moved to the top of the suspect list if I'm any judge of Harry Manos.

Personally, I want answers to how Diana and Dawn are connected. Why didn't Dawn include Diana on her list of passengers? How and when did Diana's prints get into the white van? Why was Diana so eager to give up ten days of her vacation time to help an employee of hers? Dad, we have the makings of a major shit storm on our hands. I had to give you a 'heads up' before you meet with Detective Manos this afternoon. And now I believe you will also be better able to understand my mixed emotions about being here today and dealing with Ms. Wisdom."

JT placed his fingertips on his temples, closed his eyes, and tried to process Twan's information. Twan moved over to his father and put is arm around his shoulder.

"I'm sorry it had to be me, Dad, to give you this hurtful news. I have been struggling with the proper way to tell you. Then I remembered a quote from a wise old mentor of mine, and I saw clearly what needed to be done…"

"Jesus, Twan, I used to consider myself a moderately intelligent guy. How have I gotten myself to this point? I have loved only two women in my life, and now I am told that one might be responsible for the death of the other."

The two men sat quietly together each pondering what they now knew and wondering what they were to discover next.

CHAPTER 101

COINCIDENCE, PROBABILITY, HAPPENSTANCE. COINCIDENCE, PROBABILITY, happenstance. Coincidence, probability, happenstance. Repeatedly he pondered the terms as each related to his current predicament. He tossed and turned unable to find the sanctuary of sleep. Morning could not come fast enough for James Thurber Russell for it became apparent to him that there would be no sleeping for him that night. The three terms kept moving through his cluttered, confused, assaulted mind. Surrendering to the inevitable, he reached for his bedside lamp and illuminated the nightstand that housed his evening reading materials. JT opened the top drawer of the double-drawer, pine nightstand and withdrew the pocket dictionary, which was nestled next to his current reading selection, "To Sir, With Love".

"Probability is the quality or condition of being probable; the likelihood that a given event will occur, " he read aloud from his bedside dictionary. "Probability, all right JT, what would be the probability of your new love having a connection to the woman whose van caused your wife's death? Of all the females on the North Shore or in the Lynn/Peabody area alone, what would be the probability that Diana's fingerprints were in the murder vehicle?"

He leafed through the well-used research text to his next destination.

"Coincidence is the state or fact of occupying the same relative position in area or space; a sequence of events that although accidental seems to have been planned or arranged," he read as he perused the term. "Had it been a coincidence that Dawn Woodruff omitted the name of Diana Wisdom from all the possible passengers to have frequented her van? Was it a coincidence that Tara's death resulted in Diana's good fortune?"

Seeking to find the final term of this futile exercise, he stopped, placed the text upon his chest, and breathed deeply several times in order to calm his trembling hands.

"Happenstance is an event that might have been arranged although it was really accidental," he read aloud. "Had it been coincidental or planned that Diana increased my CALL Center hours to five nights a week? Why was she so readily available to drop all commitments in her life to rescue our Florida trip from cancellation? Was she working on her own agenda under the guise of selfless generosity?"

The pieces of the puzzle had begun to fit together so neatly yet so horribly wrong. He knew he had absolutely no desire to rid his life of Tara. On the contrary, she was the center of his universe. However, from a completely objective viewpoint, the coincidence, probability, and happenstance factors appeared to be damning even without actual physical proof. He was ripe for conviction in the court of public opinion. With far more questions than answers in his possession, he closed the dictionary, looked to the ceiling, and lamented to himself,

"Were I the police," he admitted to himself, "I would suspect me as well."

The clock showed 5:30 AM. He decided to dress and drive to Marblehead. Waking Diana from her night's rest was the least of his current concerns. He needed answers immediately. In the span of the past six or seven hours, his life took upon an aura of sadness and despair. The passionate happiness of the past two weeks seemed light years away. He feared that the "curse" following his family had struck once again. He wrote a note to his mother informing her that he would be back by noon in order to meet with Twan and Detective Manos. On his journey to Marblehead, he rehearsed possible scenarios, practiced various approaches to his questioning, and attempted to remain in at least a moderately calm demeanor. He continued in that vein until the moment he pulled up to Diana's condominium. Letting himself into the condominium with the key she had entrusted to him as a gift upon their engagement, he made one last run through his mental checklist before pushing open her bedroom door. She lay there before him like an angel, a beautiful creature even clothed as she was in her pajamas. Not wanting to startle the sleeping beauty, he gently bent down and breathed upon her cheek before kissing it lightly. She stirred for a moment, then her eyes opened, and she smiled.

"My God, I thought it was a dream. Are you really here, Jamey?"

He kissed her lips and sat down on the edge of her bed.

"I'm here, Diana."

"Now that's what I call service. I dream of making wild, passionate love with you and presto. There you are. Hop in, love, there's plenty of room for two."

"Sweetie, we have to talk."

"Oh shit, Jamey, that sounds like an introduction to a breakup. What? What did I do? Talk to me, please."

"Nothing, Di. You did nothing. Take some time to wake-up while I go to the bathroom. I need to fill you in about my conversation with Twan," he said as he walked to the bath.

"And he has to do this at 6:15 AM?" she mumbled.

She left the bed and shuffled into the kitchen where she snapped on her coffee maker. Within a few moments, the pot supplied her with a single cup of caffeine with which to combat any reappearance by the Sandman. When she heard the toilet flush and the sink water run, she headed back to her bedroom. JT walked over to the same side of the bed he had left moments earlier.

"Can I get you anything, Jamey?"

"No, thank you. I'm good."

"Well, love, what's so important that you don't have time to allow Little JT to wake me properly?"

"Di, why have you never mentioned knowing Dawn Woodruff?"

She immediately went on the defensive thinking that somehow, someway, Jamey found out about the night of their tryst.

"Why would I make a point of discussing Dawn Woodruff with you, Jamey?"

"You realize, of course, that hers was the van involved in Tara's death?"

She was relieved for the moment to hear the connection was not that which she feared.

"I honestly did not make that connection, Jamey. Dawn befriended me when I first returned to the North Shore. She is involved with a women's empowerment group called SAFE and was a good friend to me when I needed one desperately. We saw each other socially several times; however, we had a parting of the ways almost a year ago, well before Tara's accident."

"Were you ever in that van, Diana?"

"Dawn's van? Not that I remember, Jamey. Why do you ask? Jesus, honey, I feel like you're interrogating me."

"Diana, your fingerprints were found in Dawn's van by the Peabody Police."

"So, I must have been in her van at some point that I don't recall. I told you we socialized. What are you insinuating?"

"This afternoon I have a meeting with Detective Harry Manos of the Peabody Police Department. According to Twan who has been in weekly contact with this detective since Tara's death, this cop is theorizing that yours truly is the number one suspect in the death of his wife."

"What?" she gasped in shock. "That's not possible, Jamey. How could he think…?"

"Listen to this scenario. Twan laid it out for me last night. A love-struck married man begins an affair with his beautiful boss. His wife is obviously a roadblock to the lovers being together. The lovers devise a plan to rid themselves of the man's wife. Knowing the exact location of where a friend's van is to be, the man's lover takes the van with or without the permission of the owner. The owner reports the van as stolen. While the man is at home awaiting the completion of the deadly deed, his lover uses the van to run the man's son and wife off the highway. Wife dead, man free! Eight months later, the man and his girlfriend are vacationing together in Florida."

"Oh my goodness, Jamey, who could possibly believe that we could do such a thing?"

Diana broke-down at that point and wept uncontrollably. He did what he could to comfort her but neither his heart nor head really cared if she stopped or not.

"Of course it's all circumstantial evidence, less than that, it's only a theory at this point," related JT. "However, after this afternoon, don't be surprised if you receive a visit from Detective Harry Manos. He is going to want some answers to the probability, coincidence, and happenstance factors that have kept me awake all night. Your relationship with Dawn Woodruff, your relationship with me and my family, and your whereabouts at the time of the accident will all be fair game to the detective. If we tell the truth, we should have nothing to fear from the police; however, Di, I can only swear to the truth as it relates to me. I can't vouch for anyone else's version of the truth."

"JAMEY! she screamed in disbelief. You do not think that I would… Do you believe that I could have hurt your family? Talk to me right now, Russell! I love you, but I could never..."

"I don't think anything right now, Diana. I question everything."

"Then you do think I could have been involved in Tara's death!" she ranted. "How could you even imagine that? I think you should leave now! Get out! Get out of my home!"

JT tried to calm her down but in her state of irrationality, he simply thought it best to abide by her wishes. As he walked toward the door, he turned to her and said:

"I'll let you know what happens with the detective this afternoon."

"Don't do me any favors! Just get out!"

CHAPTER 102

"MR. RUSSELL, TWAN, THANK YOU for meeting with me. As you probably know by now, Mr. Russell, we have turned up a new lead in your wife's death. I am sure Twan has kept you informed. By the way, Mr. Russell, you have one hell of a kid here. You've done a wonderful job raising the young man."

"Thank you, detective. Both his mother and I are very proud of Twan."

"Twan, if you wouldn't mind, I'd like to speak with your father alone."

"No problem, Detective Manos, I'll be upstairs in my room catching-up on some reading. Just call when you need me."

"Great kid! Now, Mr. Russell, can you refresh my memory as to your whereabouts on the evening of your wife's death?"

"Don't you mean won't I tell you my alibi, detective? Look, Detective Manos, Twan and I had a long talk about this new lead and where it seems to be 'leading' you. Let us get one thing clear between us. I loved my wife. We were together from the age of seventeen on. There is no one on God's green earth who would want her back or do anything more than I to have her back."

"Right, Mr. Russell. Now, your whereabouts?"

The detective's aloofness angered JT. He wanted to lash out at him for his callous treatment of his just completed declaration of love for his deceased wife. The widower had to remind himself to stay composed. He had no reason to become defensive in answering the man's questions other than the unabashed anger and humiliation he harbored. Through his mind fleetingly swept the notion that the gentleman "doth protest too much". Realizing the significance of that fleeting thought, JT took a deep breath and attempted to suppress the anger slowly simmering within.

"After meeting with several parents in conference sessions after the school day, I arrived home later than usual. I knew I was going to be late getting to the CALL Center, my part-time job, so I called the secretary. Twan and his mother had already left for their Christmas shopping. Shortly before I was to leave my house, I received the notification of the accident."

"And we can get confirmations of those parent conferences?"

"I can give you a copy of my date book as well as names and telephone numbers of the parents involved."

"Please do. Whom did you speak with at the CALL Center? The secretary?"

"Yeah, Stella Demos. I can supply her address and phone number should you need it."

"I will," he replied curtly.

"How long and in what capacity have you known Diana Brian-Wisdom, Mr. Russell?"

"Here comes the curveball," JT thought to himself.

"Ms Wisdom became the director of the CALL Center about a year and a half ago. She is my immediate supervisor. On a personal level, Ms. Wisdom and I are engaged to be married."

"Really?"

"Yes, really, detective!"

"Look, Mr. Russell, I'm not your priest or your conscience, but there are just the two of us here at the moment. Why not unburden yourself…"

"You can stop right there, Manos! The only relationship between Ms. Wisdom and me prior to my wife's death was a working relationship that developed into a close friendship."

"How close, Mr. Russell?"

"You're trying to engage me in an angry debate, but I refuse to allow that to happen. Diana Wisdom and I were not lovers until recently."

"On your trip to Florida would be my guess, Mr. Russell."

"And what does that suggest, officer?"

"Just thinking out loud, sir. So, you're telling me that following a couple of weeks of 24/7 contact with this woman, you fell so madly in love with her that you proposed marriage?"

"It's not that cut and dried. There were a lot of factors involved including her relationship with my daughters and my mother, our comfortable caring relationship, a deep mutual respect and admiration…"

"A killer body?" smirked Manos.

"You're out of line, detective. One more insult, and you'll be talking to me with my lawyer."

"No offense intended, Mr. Russell. What can you tell me about Ms. Wisdom's relationship with Dawn Woodruff?"

"Very little, actually. They became acquainted through some women's group and socialized some. About a year ago, the acquaintanceship died out."

"The reason?"

"I don't know. Ask them."

"I will. Were you aware of their acquaintanceship prior to your wife's death?"

"No. I found out very recently."

"Don't you think it odd that your fiancé would withhold from you such pertinent information since Ms. Woodruff was indirectly involved in the event causing your wife's death?"

"I don't know. What do you think?"

"I think coincidence can explain things only to a point, Mr. Russell. What I am hearing, Mr. Russell, is that your future wife and her friend had direct access to a vehicle used to cause the death of your deceased wife. I am hearing that both ladies neglected to volunteer information to the police that has been shown to be revealing. I'm hearing that a lonely widower, after only two weeks of intimacy with his employer and friend, proposes marriage. I'm hearing what sounds like a classic case of extreme extraction from a marriage!"

"You know, detective, your smugness offends me more than your misguided assumptions. Months ago, I reported incidents to you involving the stalking of my children and me! I reported an increasing frequency of telephone pranks. What came of that, detective? And while you are thinking about that, why not do some checking on a Mildred Waldron, a woman who at the time of Tara's death was not real happy with me for not accepting her advances! If you are going to start tossing stones at me, detective, have the decency to delay judgment until all the information is available. You are full of theories but empty of evidence. I tried not to get angry, but now I am. Should you wish to deal further with me, I want my lawyer in attendance."

"I think I have all the answers I need, Mr. Russell; I'll just speak with Twan and be on my way."

"Fine."

"By the way, sir, would you repeat the name of that woman you just mentioned? Do you have an address and phone number also?"

Upon receiving the information from the now very flustered interviewee, JT directed Detective Manos to Twan's room. As he turned to leave, he looked back over his shoulder at JT.

"Nothing personal, Mr. Russell, it's my job."

"Then you'll forgive me for not feeling likewise, detective, after all it's just my fucking life!"

CHAPTER 103

"HINDMAN, PEARLY, AND DAVIS...THIS IS Elanie speaking. May I help you? I am sorry; all three partners are in court this morning. Would you like to leave a message? Yes, Mr. Flagg, I will make sure Mr. Pearly receives your message the moment he returns. You are welcome. Good-bye."

Elanie Patsos loved those days when she was totally in control of the business as she had been that morning. In her late thirties with a fashion model's face and figure, Mrs. Patsos enjoyed the role of being the only female in the offices of Hindman, Pearly, and Davis, Attorneys at Law. It was true that the workload at times bordered upon unbearable; however, her compensation for her duties greatly pleased her considering the fact that she had not even finished high school. She had fallen one semester short of graduation upon the death of her father. Financial demands upon her family and the custodial care of her chronically ill mother created a situation that never allowed her the opportunity to return to graduate. She considered herself very fortunate to have secured a position with a fledgling Beverly, Massachusetts, law firm. The partners hired her as a seventeen-year-old receptionist/secretary-in-training, and twenty years later, she was an indispensable presence in the proper functioning of the premier law offices on the North Shore. Elanie also thoroughly enjoyed the massive amount of attention she received from her three employers. Having been an only child and a certified Daddy's girl, the loss of her father was devastating to her. Much of her life following her father's death seemed to mark an unconscious search for his replacement. The amount and quality of the attention she received from the males in her life reinforced her self-esteem. At the age of twenty-five, immediately following an aborted extended relationship, both her self-esteem and her life were in disarray. She vacationed in Greece, the home country of her parents, and found herself a husband. Stavros Patsos, four years younger than she, was more than ready to cross the big pond to explore the streets of gold in America. Elanie became the perfect vessel for that opportunity. After almost twelve years of marriage, the couple had fallen into an acceptable yet unsatisfying marital relationship. As long as Elanie followed the mandates of her "old-country values" husband, the marriage was tolerable. That would necessarily include the requirement that she ignore his extramarital affairs. She would serve her man without question or complaint. Her home would be kept clean and orderly. Her money was his money, and his money was his money. Even the thought of her unfaithfulness was absurd. The marriage was able to continue as long as he lavished the appropriate amount of attention on her, and she kept out of his personal life. The trade-off had worked so far.

While dictating a job opportunity at the firm to a local newspaper recently, Elanie noted the inclusion of the provision requiring a high school diploma, two years of college preferred. She was sure Ben Pearly wrote the copy for the job opening because he could be such an educational snob. Her insecurities immediately rose to the surface. Were they seeking her replacement? Was she capable of supervising a more highly educated person than herself? The imagined threat to her position in the law firm motivated her to take "step one" in her newly formulated career path. At her home in Beverly, her next-door neighbor mentioned the CALL Center to Elanie in a passing conversation. The neighbor, Hilda Markos, was incredibly excited about her recent return to school at the center to study for her GED, a high school equivalency certificate. Hilda went on and on about her teacher, JT, who was just about the smartest man on earth and cute too. Their conversation lit a fire beneath Elanie's perfect ass, and she decided to visit the CALL Center, Stavros permitting, to discuss her educational plans. Getting her husband's blessing was not as difficult as she had anticipated. The number of evenings and amount of time required of her were his chief concerns. Elanie pacified him with a promise that he would miss zero home cooked meals and her work about the house would not suffer. After hearing her proposal, he made some lame comment in Greek about whatever she wanted to do was fine with him. Elanie thought to herself that her husband must truly think her a blind fool. With her out of the house three nights a week, he was free to pursue his other interests. Playing the grateful wife, she thanked him for his understanding and love. When he left the table to get ready to go to his social club, she lamented about the shit she had to put up with in that loveless union just to maintain her standard of living.

First thing on her agenda the following morning was to telephone the CALL Center to indicate her interest in their programming. During a quiet moment at work, she called information for the telephone number and dialed with a sense of urgency. She spoke with a kindred spirit at the Center, Stella Demos, the center receptionist/secretary. Identifying Stella as a compatriot, Elanie carried on her conversation switching from English to Greek and back again. Stella had made the potential new student feel comfortable and curious. Elanie asked about the teachers, the learning center's philosophy, Stella's personal opinion, and so on. Stella encouraged her to come in to speak with Mr. JT Russell who was the evening supervisor of the center. He would be able to answer all of her questions, evaluate her current ability levels, and prescribe a course of study that would lead her to her personal goals. Sold on the entire concept, Elanie wished she were able to start immediately; however, previous commitments would prevent her from visiting the center until the beginning of the next week. Stella indicated to her that Monday would be a fine time to visit, and she tentatively scheduled an appointment for her at 6:00 PM to meet with JT Russell. Hanging-up the phone, Elanie felt an excitement she had not known for a very long time.

CHAPTER 104

WEDNESDAY MORNING MARKED THE OPENING of school for yet another year. JT was already behind in his preparations having been unable to get to school the day before due to the Diana and Detective Manos incidents. Feeling unprepared, he arrived at school very early to begin to catch-up on his plans for the day. After arranging the furniture in his classroom and securing the materials that he would need for the day, JT wrote on his front blackboard:

Welcome to Grade 5.
Select a desk.
Get Comfortable.
Do not make the teacher crazy!

He then applied his WTL 3 trademark to the blackboard that would serve as the basis for his introductory remarks to that new class of inquisitive minds. By now, he was perspiring profusely so he retired to the men's bathroom to prepare himself for his charges for the second time that morning. Following the bathroom session, he felt at least presentable although his normally finely ironed clothes had wrinkled from all his physical activity of the morning. As he reentered his classroom, he was happy to see Walter Holloway sitting at his desk.

"Long time, no see, JT," smiled Walter. "I figured to see you here before the first day, kid."

"Unavoidable conflicts in scheduling," he smiled in return. "How the hell are you?"

"I'm fine. The question is how are you and why are the Peabody Police calling me about my star teacher?"

"Was it a detective Manos?"

"Yeah, does that guy think he's Columbo or what, JT? He asked a bunch of questions about you, and then started asking questions about Millie Waldron."

"Really?"

"JT, you're not banging old Millie are you, son?" Walter laughed long and hard not knowing how close to true his question had been. "Of course you're not at the moment because she's been hospitalized for the past week and a half. I was told that she was taken from her home by ambulance to the hospital the day after she completed working her summer job."

"Do you know when she'll be back?" asked JT curiously.

"Look, I was sworn to silence, but she is your close friend, and I know that anything we say goes no further. JT, she will not be coming back. Millie is dying…"

JT swallowed hard trying to look surprised at the revelation. He knew Walter was still speaking, but all he could think of was one less suspect in the case. Millie had been telling him the truth all along. A "pity fuck" may have been her goal, but at least she was not lying about dying.

"What are your plans, Walter? A long-term substitute teacher?"

"I found someone with ESL experience to take her class until a resolution to her situation is reached."

"Well put, boss. That was very diplomatic and sensitive."

"And you can begin by thanking me now for the present that I picked-out for you. Yes sir, I brought on board a lovely young thing to work with you who is going to need to be 'hand fed' so to speak, JT. She is fresh out of college with several weeks of substituting experience to go along with her teacher practicum experience. I looked for a veteran teacher to replace your old partner from the current list. The substitute roll was threadbare. You'll make do, you always do, kid."

"Right, Walter. What's her name?"

"Melissa something...Mamry, yeah like the tit."

"Great, now I won't even be able to look her in the eyes."

"Believe me, boy, it may take you a few moments to get that high on her body. This lass has been faithful to her pectoral muscle exercises."

"Any other bad news? Now, I'm going to have to warn Little JT about his behavior whenever I'm with the young lady."

"Of all the problems you could have had this morning, Mr. Russell, this is perhaps the best you could hope for. You'll be thanking me before too much times passes."

"Yeah, and you'll be waving good-bye to me when they lead me away in a straightjacket."

"Oh to be young and virile again," lamented the senior educator.

"It ain't what it's all cracked up to be, my friend."

"What say you to meeting the young lady, JT? I believe I just saw her enter next door. I think you're going to appreciate the physical upgrade that this model offers as opposed to the older model you've worked with in years passed."

"Just stop! I will be absolutely unable to deal with this woman if you don't stop now!"

"Follow me, young man." He pushed open the swinging door between the classrooms. "Ms Mamry, as advertised, perhaps a little later than expected, this is JT Russell. JT this is Melissa Mamry."

"Welcome to T. Lewis Carroll School, Ms. Mamry (he almost swallowed hard between syllables). I look forward to working with you."

"Mr. Russell, I have heard so much about you from so many different people."

"Believe about ten percent of what you heard, and I had nothing to do with the Kennedy assassination."

"I see I wasn't being lied to, Mr. Russell."

"Please call me, JT," he suggested.

"Thank you, I shall if you will call me Missy."

Old Walter was not lying to either Big JT or Little JT. Melissa Mamry was a tall, slender (too slender for the set of mammary glands she possessed) raven haired, green-eyed goddess. In her heels she was taller then JT, probably well over six feet in height. Her olive skin, which he surmised stretched from her forehead to her toes and everywhere in between, and the long, black curly hair that framed her face gave the young woman an exotic look. JT thought immediately that before the cameras, not the students, was where that gorgeous example of young womanhood belonged.

"I'm really nervous, JT. I need all the help I can get."

"Missy, I'm here for you. I will keep an ear open. If I hear you struggling, I will come in if you wish. Or better yet, something I would do with my former partners, we could bring both classes into my room, and we will give the introduction to the fifth grade together."

"You'd do that for me, JT?"

"Is that what you need and desire?"

"I would be forever grateful."

"Fine, let's do it." After the words came from his lips, he knew he was blushing. He could hardly bear to look at her in the eyes. When he did, she had the biggest brightest smile on her face.

"When do you want to do it, JT?" Now it was her turn to consider her words, but she was not blushing. She was still grinning from ear to ear.

"I'll come in to get you and your class, Missy. I'll see you in a bit."

"Thank you JT, really."

Walter led the pathetic example of studliness through the swinging door back into his classroom.

"Smooth, Russell, very smooth. You know the poor girl for three minutes, and you're asking her to do it with you!"

"It – is – all – your – fault -, Walter! You filled Little JT's head with all that dirty talk!"

CHAPTER 105

THE PAST TWENTY-FOUR HOURS HAD been unbearable for Diana. Within a matter of minutes only one day ago, she fell from the top of the world into her own personal hell. The feelings eating away at her were not unlike those that she experienced during her miserable three years of marriage to David Wisdom. Somehow, the situation with JT hurt her worse, much worse than that doomed coupling. If she had not been positive about the truth of her love for JT before yesterday, she knew now. Torn between the potential loss of the love of her life and the incredible wounds she experienced by the very idea that JT could believe her capable of such hideous acts, she cried her way through most of Tuesday. Only her doctor's appointment offered her a period of respite from her tears. Diana chastised herself for her behavior and urged herself to deal with the situation. She had not spoken to nor seen JT for over twenty-four hours. The need to communicate with him, to apologize for her anger, for treating him so rudely weighed on her mind. On the other hand, the desire to rip his heart from his chest for even imagining that she had anything to do with Tara's death balanced her emotional mindset. Her schedule called for her to be at the CALL Center from 12 to 9 PM that day. JT was due to work that evening. Whether he wanted to see her or not, it would be unavoidable. All she knew now was that she had to get their relationship fixed. No matter what else was to be gained or lost, she had to make them right once again. The phone rang as she had been debating with herself over a plan of action.

"Hello," she was disappointed that it was not Jamey. "Yes, this is Diana Wisdom. Whom did you say? From the Peabody Police Department? Yes, I will be available today until around 11AM. The Russell accident case? Would you be coming over immediately then, Detective Manos? Fine. That is the correct address. Good-bye."

Diana quickly entered the bathroom to prepare for her visitor. Within fifteen minutes of the telephone call, her doorbell rang. Composing herself, she walked to her front door to greet her visitor. The disheveled detective held up his badge and identified himself as Detective Harry Manos of the Peabody Police Department. Convinced of his identity, Diana led him into the living room. Always the gracious hostess, she offered the officer a choice of beverage. He thanked her but politely refused the offer.

"Ms. Wisdom, I'm here to discuss your knowledge of the events which led to the death of Tara Anne Russell, wife of James T. Russell."

"I'm not sure how much assistance I can be to you officer."

"I just need some informational holes filled-in that perhaps you can help with."

"I will do whatever I can to help, detective."

"Ms. Wisdom, would you discuss your relationship with Dawn Woodruff?"

"Dawn and I became very good friends when I returned to this area after my divorce. As a women's right activist, Dawn Woodruff, in my opinion, has no equal. The moment I heard her speak on that subject, I was captivated by her knowledge, empathy, and passion."

"So, you met at a meeting?"

"Actually, I attended a lecture sponsored by her organization."

"And you met how?"

"Dawn approached me after the speaking engagement and asked if I would join her for coffee following the question and answer session."

"She approached you."

"Yes, that's correct."

"Did you know at that time of her sexual preference, Ms. Wisdom?"

"That's not a question I usually ask a new acquaintance, detective. And had I known, it would have meant nothing to me."

"So you do know now that Ms. Woodruff is very openly and proudly lesbian?"

"Yes, I do. What does this have to do with...?"

"Please allow me to ask the questions, m'am."

"Did you go for coffee with her that evening?"

"No, in fact, we went to a pub not far from here."

"For coffee?"

"Well, we ordered beverages of a stronger nature."

"And then you both went home?"

"What do you mean?"

"You went to your home, and she went to her home."

"Oh yes. We made plans to see each other again for dinner. From there our friendship evolved."

"Ms. Wisdom, did Ms. Woodruff ever approach you in a sexual manner?"

"What has this to do with...?"

"My questions, your answers, remember?"

"No, never."

"You mean to tell me that a beautiful woman such as yourself never interested Dawn Woodruff in that way?"

"That's correct. Dawn knew my sexual preference and honored it, as I did hers."

"And the two of you still socialize, Ms. Wisdom?"

"Unfortunately, we no longer do."

"Why is that?"

"People change; interests change; responsibilities change. People drift in and out of each other's lives all the time, detective. Haven't you ever lost touch with an acquaintance?"

"That's a question, Ms. Wisdom. While you were seeing Ms. Woodruff, did you have the opportunity to ride in her van?"

"I suppose. In the many times we socialized, I suspect I might have driven with her in her vehicle."

"How about driving her van?"

"I'm less likely to say yes to that; however, I suppose I could have driven it or sat behind the steering wheel."

"Are you aware that your fingerprints were found in Ms. Woodruff's van?"

"Yes, I was told."

"Of course you were. Are you aware that your fingerprints were found on the ignition and driver's side seat belt buckle?"

"No, I didn't know that."

"Of course not, I neglected to tell that to Twan or Mr. Russell. Do you have any idea whatsoever why Ms. Woodruff neglected to include your name amongst the more than twenty other names listed as drivers or passengers in her van?"

"Perhaps, she had a memory slip. Other than that, I cannot."

"Would you now discuss your relationship with James T. Russell? How and when did you meet?"

"Mr. Russell was the final member of the CALL Center staff to whom I was introduced. That would have occurred on the second day of my term as director of the center."

"What exactly was and is your relationship to Mr. Russell? For the past year and a half, JT Russell and I have been employer/employee, colleagues, close friends, and at this point in time we are engaged to be married."

"You knew he was a married man, correct?"

"Of course. And I respected that."

"Were you attracted to Mr. Russell early on in your relationship?"

"I was taken with Mr. Russell's wit and charm immediately. As our friendship grew, my admiration and affection for the man grew. But I did not act upon my feelings."

"So, you're working three or five nights a week with a guy who makes you weak in the knees, and you do absolutely nothing about it?"

"That is correct. However, to say I did nothing about it would not be accurate. I fought against my emerging feelings while still trying to maintain our close friendship."

"Did you ever discuss Mr. Russell with Ms. Woodruff?"

"Not by name. We discussed our personal lives, and she knew I was unhappy over a relationship that could never be."

"And she never knew the object of your affection and pain was JT Russell?"

"Perhaps at the end of our seeing each other regularly, I might have mentioned him by name. That would have been at least a year ago."

"Mrs. Russell was still alive a year ago, Ms. Wisdom."

"And what should that mean to me, detective?"

"Another question, Ms. Wisdom. Following the death of Tara Russell, what role did you take in JT Russell's life?"

"The same role I had from the beginning of our relationship. Only then, I served as more of a shoulder to lean and cry on."

"The two of you became closer as the months following his wife's death passed?"

"I believe we became the best of friends."

"He had no idea about the feelings you harbored toward him?"

"You'd have to ask him that question."

"I did. Now I'm asking you."

"After Tara died, perhaps I allowed myself to be more demonstrative toward JT."

"Tell me about the Florida trip."

"JT's mom injured herself several days before the departure date. He and I were talking at the CALL Center when he received the telephone call about her accident. The trip seemed to be in jeopardy because JT felt uncomfortable traveling with two little girls and no adult female support. I suppose I allowed my fantasies to drive my offer to take his mother's place on the trip."

"So, Ms. Wisdom, you're telling me that from the time you met JT Russell to the moment you volunteered your services to save his children's Florida trip, you and he had never had a physical relationship."

"That is absolutely true."

"Then, something happened within the next two weeks or so. He fell madly in love with you and asked for your hand?"

"I wouldn't use those exact terms, but the gist is pretty correct. It sounds strange, but it is essentially true."

"So your physical relationship began only very recently on that trip?"

"That is correct."

"Can you tell me, Ms. Wisdom, why you never mentioned to Mr. Russell your relationship with Ms. Woodruff who coincidentally owned the van responsible for his wife's death? Don't you think he deserved to know that piece of information?"

Diana felt herself flushing. She was sure Manos would notice that tell tale sign and presume her to be lying. She paused and thought for a moment. She realized she had made a serious mistake in misanswering some of the detective's previous questions.

"I have a confession to make, Detective Manos."

"I thought we might get to this point. Please continue."

"First, if I tell you something in confidence, something personally embarrassing, that really isn't pertinent to the death of Tara Russell, do I have your assurance that it goes no further than your ears?"

"I can't make you any promises, Ms. Wisdom, but my only interest is bringing the person responsible for Tara Anne Russell's death to justice."

"I understand. Earlier I lied to you about my relationship with Dawn Woodruff. On that first evening we met, we drank so much that neither of us were in any condition to drive. We left both of our vehicles at the pub. We wrote notes as best we could and I placed them in both vehicles to explain the reason for their abandonment. We walked to my condominium several blocks away. I made a strong pot of coffee, but we never drank it. When I awoke the next morning, I found I had slept naked, which I never do, and Dawn Woodruff walked naked out of my bathroom. You see, Dawn thought I was of her persuasion, and she initiated a sexual relationship between the two of us. She did not realize the truth until I vomited all over her and my bed for the next hour! She apologized repeatedly as did I. As hideous an experience as it was to me, I could understand the miscommunication."

"Why on earth did you continue to see the woman? Weren't you playing with fire?"

"Dawn represented many of the things I wanted to be in life and some that I could never be. After several dinner engagements, we came to an understanding concerning our friendship. When either one of us found the demands of the relationship too difficult with which to deal, we would go our separate ways. That is what happened about a year ago. She wanted more from our relationship than I desired or was able to provide. We parted for that reason. I trust you can see why I had no desire to talk to JT about Dawn Woodruff. I was terrified by what his reaction toward me would be if he viewed me as a lesbian or bisexual."

"All right, Ms. Wisdom, I appreciate your honesty. Is there anything else that you fabricated during this interview?"

"No sir, nothing else."

"Both you and Mr. Russell are very interesting people. I hope the case turns out favorably for both of you. Thank you for your time. Good day, Ms. Wisdom."

CHAPTER 106

"Twan, this is Harry Manos. I am sorry to bother you at school, son, but I want to bounce some ideas off you. Great. I left your father's house with a head full of questions that needed answering, motives that needed affirming, and a lingering feeling that he is an honest guy. Yeah, I know you are prejudiced. Then I spoke with the lovely Ms. Wisdom. I cannot see her as a murderer, kid. She is forthright, opinionated, and intuitive. Yeah, of course they are only impressions, Twan. What am I a mind reader? No need to apologize kid. This case is getting to me too. Here is the real reason for my call. I have developed a second theory. Yeah, I know. Nevertheless, having a second theory does not mean I throw out the first, kid. Now I cannot tell you certain details, but I have reason to believe my assumptions may well have substance. Ready? Suspect #1 meets suspect #2 at a women's rights meeting. Suspect #2, an openly gay woman, makes a play for an emotionally crippled young woman newly returned to her hometown. Suspect #1 interprets suspect #2's interest as friendship. She develops a strong attachment for the woman's strong personality and character. Suspect #1 puts off the advances of suspect #2 because she is a 'straight woman'. However, Suspect #1 is so desperate for a friend that she encourages the relationship with suspect #2. Yeah, that is what I thought…playing with fire, bright kid. They socialize a number of times, develop a close friendship, and agree in advance to terminate the relationship if the emotional strain on either party gets to be too great. Do you have any questions so far? Suspect #1 uses suspect #2 as a shoulder to cry upon in a case of unrequited love going-on in her life. What suspect #1 does not fully understand is that talking about her desire for her 'non-responsive' man is like waving a red cape in front of a bull to suspect #2! Suspect #2 develops intense anger feelings toward the source of suspect #1's affection and pain. Suspect #2, approaching an emotional overload herself, disengages herself from the relationship. No, I am not finished yet, kid, hold-on. Suspect #2 is still deeply enamored with suspect #1 although the feeling is not reciprocated. Suspect #2 develops a plan to get rid of the competition, not Tara Russell or Twan Russell, but JT Russell. I think that our suspect #2 might have thought she was getting rid of her chief competition the night of your accident, Twan. You and your mother may have become the innocent victims of a woman's bizarre method of obtaining the object of her affection. So what do you think so far, kid? Yeah, the finger prints in suspect #2's van. According to suspect #1, on the first evening the two met, each was too drunk to drive so they left their vehicles in a pub parking lot. They wrote an explanation for each vehicle on a separate napkin fearing that the police would tow the cars. Suspect #1 placed the notes in each vehicle. Thus, we have the possibility of suspect #1's fingerprints appearing in suspect #2's vehicle. Yeah, I know Twan. In addition, the reason that suspect #1's identity did not appear on suspect #2's list of potential vehicle passengers was the self-serving protection of #2's love object. What about your father? Well, if we stay with theory number one, he is definitely the prime suspect along with his mistress. If we develop theory number two, not only are suspect #1 and the prime suspect cleared, the poor bastards were actually the victims. Yeah, Twan, I know. Your mother was the real victim. No one, other than you and your family wants to see this case end with the perpetrator behind bars more than I do. What's next? Well, I am going to pay a visit to Suspect #2, Ms. Dawn Woodruff, to see if I can shake her out of the tree. Yeah, of course. As soon as I hear something. Study hard, kid. I have a feeling we are in the home stretch, Twan. Keep your fingers crossed. You know where I am if you need me. See you soon. Yeah, you too, buddy. Bye."

CHAPTER 107

"CALL CENTER FOR ADULTS, THIS is Stella. May I help you?"

"I hope so, Stella. This is JT. Is the boss in?" He looked at his watch. It was just past 3:30 about an hour and a half before he was due at the Center.

"Hi, JT, I'll transfer your call."

"Thanks, Stella."

"Diana Brian-Wisdom, may I help you?"

"Yes, could you tell me if James Thurber Russell still works there?"

A smile creased her beautiful face immediately recognizing the voice.

"He does if he gets his ass here on time today."

"In that case, you still have the business of me and my many friends. There was a rumor in the community that poor JT was no longer employed at the center because he made an ass of himself in dealing with his boss."

"Yes, sir, all of that is true. However, Mr. Russell has a loving, forgiving superior who maintains the enormous capacity to overlook the shortcomings of her staff, friends, and lovers."

"Really? Could you now tell me if Mr. Russell still qualifies in the final two categories, what were they again--friends and lovers?"

"Although Mr. Russell has been skating on incredibly thin ice of late, his standing in the center in all categories has not changed. However, that does not mean said standing is not subject to change if Mr. Russell doesn't come to his senses the moment he sees his director."

"Well, I thank you, m'am, for your time and insight. Should I personally see Mr. Russell, I will pass-on your good news. Good-bye."

"Good-bye and thank you for calling the CALL Center for Adults."

She hung up the telephone, had a good laugh for herself, and then cried in relief. She hurried into the bathroom to fix her tear-lined face. For the first time in a while, the face looking back at her from the mirror actually looked glad to see her.

At precisely 5:00 PM, a smiling JT Russell walked into the center, waved, and blew a kiss to Stella. He then walked directly to the rear of the center to the director's cubicle. He knocked on the wall and waited until he heard "yes". He proffered a bouquet of roses around the end of the cubicle's wall. The recipient of the peace offering ordered the gifter to enter her area. Holding the flowers to her face, and then dropping her arm to her side, Diana in the privacy of her three-sided office leaped toward JT and showered him with the affection he needed from her. When she finally pulled away from him or rather when he allowed her to pull away, she straightened herself out, then straightened him out, as well as removed the lipstick from his mouth and cheeks.

"Not ever being here during the day time hours, boss, is this the greeting given to each staff member?"

"Only the ones I love and cannot live without."

"So what's that 2, 3, 4, of us?"

"You suck. Go to work before I change my mind about you."

"Does this mean I'm forgiven? How about joining me for a pizza at D'Auria's after work?"

"Sounds all right, but I was thinking more of a bite at my place."

"I'll check with Little JT and get back to you."

"No need, Big JT, Little JT has already made his intentions known to me as we were hugging." JT quickly looked down to see if he were in a presentable condition to visit his students. Little JT was now on his best behavior presumably resting up for this evening.

"I'm off, boss, but I shall return."

"You did, Jamey, and I love you for it."

At six o'clock, Stella visited the study carrel where Jamey was working on an algebra problem with a new student.

"JT, a young woman who made an appointment to see you on Monday just told me she could not wait to get started so she cancelled all of her previous appointments."

"Yeah, Stella, that's what all the girls say, right Tony?" smiled JT winking at his current student.

"I shall be there directly. Tony and I have just about solved this killer problem."

After a few brief directions to Tony about his next area of study, JT walked over to the front desk and Stella introduced him to Mrs. Elanie Patsos.

"I understand you are in a hurry to start our program, Mrs. Patsos."

"I feel like a kid, again."

"Come on, that certainly couldn't have been very long ago."

"Watch out for him, Elanie, he's dangerous," smiled Stella.

"Are you dangerous, Mr. Russell?"

"Yes, m'am, I am. But I have had all my shots."

"Apparently, what I have been told about you is true."

"Only the good stuff."

"I've only heard good stuff."

"Then, it's true. We are very informal here. I would love you to call me JT."

"I shall if you call me Elanie."

"I think you have a deal, madam."

JT's first order of business with each new student was establishing an individual comfort level. He utilized his counseling skills and his contagious, outrageous personality to disarm new students, put them at ease, and slowly immerse them into his programming lecture. Years of experience in the field of adult education had taught him that walking through the door of such a program, taking that first step, was the most important act an adult learner would make. To have reached that point, the adult learner probably had to debate him or herself over and over about his or her ability to succeed in the undertaking, come to terms with the ghosts of the past which led to the initial discontinuation of his or her education, and fortify his or her self-esteem in order to successfully deal with the challenges ahead. There were two main classifications of students at the center, ABE students and GED students. ABE students (adult basic education) were not sufficiently skilled to be successful on the high school equivalency exams. ABE students could be students who left school with a third grade education or learning level. Generally, the center's goal was to raise their ABE students to at least a ninth grade learning level before allowing them to enter the GED (general educational development) portion of the programming. The CALL Center fostered the concept that an adult learner will learn better working at his or her own pace under the guidance of an instructor in a one on one setting than would a person in a classroom full of students struggling to stay up to the speed of the instructor. People coming to the center with a sixth grade education expecting to have their GED certificate in a month were sadly mistaken. The process moved as fast or slow as the individual required. However, the center would not set-up students to fail; therefore, only those individuals deemed ready to be tested, were encouraged to apply to take the battery of tests. The Commonwealth was not giving away these equivalency certificates. Were they, the Commonwealth would have opened itself up to a world of hurt. Students would leave school in droves to take the easier way to a high school education causing chaos in school systems across Massachusetts. By maintaining rigid standards of achievement for GED students, the high school equivalency certificate had value. The Commonwealth's junior college and four year college systems accepted the GED as a means of satisfying their high school graduation requirement. All employers in the Commonwealth accepted the GED certificate in lieu of a high school graduation diploma. One of the very interesting and very strict rules employed by the Commonwealth was the prevention of any student from receiving a GED certificate prior to the graduation date of his or her projected high school class. JT felt strongly about that factor as it prevented the unfair rewarding of a premature high school dropout. People have their educational lives interrupted for any number of reasons. According to JT, for the Commonwealth to offer what amounted to an educational "discount" would be a disservice to the students and to the society.

In JT's system, he worked on each new student's confidence and self-esteem. The reasons for their past education difficulties or failures were just that—past. He would tell each of them that the most difficult thing that he or she would ever have to do at the center is walk through the front door, which has been now completed. He was good at what he did. People learned to like and trust him very quickly. Such was the case with Elanie Patsos. She and JT were speaking as if they had been old friends after their initial meeting. He was so easy to talk with that many revealed so much more than they had ever dreamed capable of sharing. Elanie was such a student. Before he had begun her placement testing, he knew her life story. He listened to what sounded like an intelligent woman involved in an unhappy marriage. Her educational goals seemed well thought-out, sound, and reasonable. Mrs. Patsos appeared to be a woman with whom he would enjoy working. While talking about their younger days, she mentioned having such a great year in 1969. That year stuck out in her mind for a variety of personal and professional reasons. JT coincidentally had an excellent year in1969 as well. He recalled incidents with Tony Delvane that he had not thought of in years.

"Gee, Elanie, it looks like you and I both love 69," blurted out the usually more careful instructor. Realizing his Freudian slip, he peeked up at her as she bit her bottom lip in an effort to keep from smiling. It is funny how long lasting relationships evolve from the most innocent double entendres.

Leaving Elanie to her placement testing, JT circulated about the center seeking students in need of his assistance. As he approached the director's cubicle, the director requested his presence within.

"Yes, m'am, you called."

"A new student, JT?"

"Yeah, Diana. She is a great lady. You'd love her."

"Uh huh. And very attractive isn't she?"

"I suppose, but I've lost my eye for that sort of thing. I'm spoken for again, you know."

"Uh huh. Does Little JT know he's spoken for again?"

"Diana, give me a break, please. I cannot do my job on a short lease, sweetie."

"Just remember, my love, you and Little JT are mine, and I don't share my toys."

"You really should work on that 'getting along and playing well together' thing, boss. Remember, I only have eyes for you, dear. And if you wish, I'll sing it for you."

"Thanks for the visit, love. Please remember that we want to keep Little JT in good health, and that he is in my hands much more often than he is in your hands."

"Just barely."

"What?"

"Lust fairy! I called you my little Lust Fairy."

CHAPTER 108

BY THE END OF THE first, short, three-day week of school, Missy Mamry and JT Russell were fast friends. The gorgeous creature followed her mentor around as if he were giving away diamonds. Her end of day routine now included an end of day meeting with JT to help her plan for the following school day, an almost embarrassing display of gratitude and compliments, and a kiss on the cheek goodnight.

"I'll come back when you two are finished," volunteered Sue Wright as she walked in mid-kiss.

"Hi, Mrs. Wright."

"Hello, how are things going in fifth grade?"

"Thanks to this wonderful man, I'm more than just surviving. Isn't he just adorable?"

"I've always thought so," mugged Sue Wright, "and I'm sure he has as well."

"You are so funny, Mrs. Wright. I have to run. Good night, Jamey."

"Bye."

"Jamey? Jamey? You are Jamey after three fucking days. You know, I should have let you introduce me to Little JT thirteen years ago when you first harassed me. There has to be something more about you than is visible to the naked eye!"

"Give me a break, Sue. She is a grateful kid who is in way over her head. I'm just keeping her above water at the moment."

"Sweetie, with tits like those the last thing that chick needs is help floating! There's no way in hell she could ever drown."

"That's what I love about you, Sue, you're abundance of empathy, your sympathetic ear, your support for the underdog."

"And here's what I've always loved about you, Jamey, your absolute worship of the female body, your selective memory regarding past near-disasters with the female of the species, and your abject support of Little JT's never-ending need to find a nice warm patch to hammer."

"You are a lady to the end, Susan. Have you already completed your studies at Longshoreman's Finishing School?"

"How many times do you think I have left in me to pull your ass out of the fire? If you're still letting Little JT run the show, it's time to put the adult in charge, JT."

"I hate it when you scold me so. I feel so unloved. Come here and make me feel better."

Susan walked over to him shaking her head in mock disgust. She wrapped her arms around her longtime friend.

"Whatever will I do with you, James T. Russell? You're a child in a man's body."

"Just keep being a person who loves me, Sue. I need that from you. Sue...

"Yes, JT."

"Are you wearing underwear?"

"Jesus, JT, just when I think you're serious."

"White, right?"

"For Christ sakes, JT here look!" She pulled her pants away from her waist to reveal her Hanes Her Way white panties. Happy now?" she asked her voice rising.

"No, but if you pulled the whitey's out a bit I'd be ever so grateful."

"At our age JT, there's not all that much left to see, honey."

He threw his arms around a woman he knew he would love to the grave. There was no one like her in his life, and there never had been.

The woman was a living, breathing, original model whose mold had been broken at birth certifying her uniqueness.

"Well, if I'm not going to see any bush, I'll be on my way, thank you very much."

"One day, JT, I am going to shock the shit out of your perverted self!"

"Promises, promises. Get your stuff. It's time to go."

As he looked down to gather his homebound materials, Sue walked to her room, and Walter walked through his door.

"Walter! Did you drop by to tell me about some big-titted new lunch aide or a two-pussied reading teacher? Here he is, Little JT, the guy who always gets you riled up!"

"JT, Millie Waldon just died."

JT attended the wake that Monday evening having taken the time off from work. Walter also named him to represent the faculty at the funeral the following day. In his harried and troubled mind, he pleaded with fate to slow down the pace of his quickly turning world. For a few days, his plea appeared answered by the proper celestial authorities. The wildest incident with which he had to deal with was an invitation to Missy Mamry's weekend long birthday party at her parents' summer home in New Hampshire. He had been hearing stories at school, which bordered upon legend, involving Melissa Mamry's collegiate antics. According to one source that must remain nameless, Missy Mamry had a propensity for exhibitionism as an undergraduate, a fact that must have put smiles on the faces of legions of Salem State College males! A second source repeated a story of a marathon sex contest during her senior year during spring break in Florida. A third report allegedly quoted the young woman verbatim involving her talent for oral sex. Now his only problem was getting away alone for the weekend.

"Dare I? No way! That is just Little JT thinking aloud. I have to let the adult take charge here. Besides, Diana would rip Little JT from my body if I did something stupid like that."

However, in his heart he knew that the big head was tempted as much as the little head in that instance.

CHAPTER 109

"Hello, Mr. Russell? This is Harry Manos. Wait a moment, please. I know we did not exactly hit it off the last time we talked. I apologize for offending you. Well, I have two quick questions for which I need answers. I understand, and I promise you will not need your lawyer. Yes, sir. How many cars did you own at the time of the accident, and whose car was involved in the accident? Yes, sir. Both are critically important in finding the perpetrator. You and Mrs. Russell left your car at BTW in Danvers the night before the accident to have four new tires put on. How did you get to work the following day? If you had her car, how did she get to work? Your mother drove her in. Please be patient with me, sir. How and when was your vehicle returned to you? On his way in from Harvard. So, what you are telling me, Mr. Russell, is the car involved in the accident was your primary vehicle and not your wife's? Thank you very much, sir. You have been very helpful."

Manos still had some loose ends to tie up before he interviewed Dawn Woodruff. He arranged to meet with the officers responding to the stolen car report allegedly made by Dawn Woodruff on the day of the fatal accident. The officers were not pleased to have to meet with Manos again after taking a not so private beating over the fingerprint mess deposited at their doorstep. Nonetheless, it was part of their job, and it was unavoidable. Carrying an 8 1/2" by 11" color photo of

Dawn Woodruff, which he purchased from the SAFE web site, Manos met with the officers at Arnold's Restaurant during their dinner break.

"I realize all of this happened almost three quarters of a year ago, but I need both of you to strain your memories. I think I am closing in on the answer to Mrs. Russell's death. Correct me, if I am wrong. You proceeded to the North Shore Shopping Center at approximately 1:00 PM on the day of the Russell accident. You engaged a woman who identified herself as Dawn Woodruff. She reported her white van stolen. Did you check a picture identification of the person reporting the theft?"

"She only had a social security card in her possession, detective."

"No picture id's at all?"

"None that she volunteered."

"Did you request one from her?"

"We must have, right Bruce?"

"Yeah, we must have."

Manos placed a large manila envelope on the table in front of the officers.

"Bruce, would you stand at the other side of the restaurant for a minute?"

As one officer left the table, Manos withdrew the color photo of Dawn Woodruff from the envelope.

"Tom, I want you to examine this picture very carefully before you tell me if this is the woman that you assisted at the scene of the stolen car report."

"Yes, sir."

"That's not her, detective."

"You're sure?"

"Yeah, the woman in the picture looks like Daryl Hannah; the woman we spoke with looked more like Darryl Strawberry."

"She was a black woman?"

"Yes, sir."

"And you never mentioned that fact to anyone until this fucking moment?"

"No one asked, sir."

"Send Bruce over and you wait there. Don't say anything to him."

Manos followed the same procedure with the second officer. He received a very similar reaction. He thanked the two officers as he left them and cursed affirmative action under his breath. He must now make arrangements to meet with Dawn Woodruff. Things were starting to get very interesting.

CHAPTER 110

"Is SHE ALWAYS UNFRIENDLY, OR is it just me, JT? When I am at the center, she hardly leaves her office. I can count on one hand the number of words she has spoken to me besides 'hello'."

"Elanie, believe me, she is really a very fine person. Perhaps Diana is allowing her personal problems to affect her work life. I am sure it is not you personally. Let us get back to you. Your placement testing was great. I am going to place you directly into the pre-GED testing materials. Now, I want you to rate your ability in these three areas: math, English language arts, and reading."

"That should be easy. I hate math, and I love to read."

"Great. Therefore, here is the plan. You are going to spend the majority of your time here studying from the math preparation materials; you'll follow math with English language arts; at the moment, reading will be our last concentration."

"What about science and social studies, JT?"

"The science and social studies tests are reading comprehension tests in content areas. This means you need not learn four years of science and social studies in order to be successful on those two tests. What you must be able to do is comprehend what you read, identify main ideas, identify supporting details, and draw conclusions from your reading. Your test scores indicate that this area is a strength of yours. Too often, people will come in and work on those areas that they feel comfortable with, their strengths. This is a big mistake. Those areas of weakness indicate where the bulk of your studying should lie. If you are going to be here for three hours, I would like you to do one and one half-hours of math, one hour of language arts, and a half-hour of reading in that order. If you stay less time, divide your time so the majority of your study covers your areas of weaknesses, not strengths. What do you think?"

"You're the boss, JT. I put myself in your hands. Do you think you can handle me, JT?"

"I've had tougher cases, Elanie, and I've had no complaints so far."

"I'm sure you haven't, Mr. JT Russell."

"Start whenever the spirit moves you, lady."

"I'm off, professor."

"JT, telephone call," yelled Stella.

"I'll take it in Diana's office, Stella."

"JT, this is Sheila Holloway."

"Sheila, it's so nice to hear from you. What's up?"

"Bad news, JT. Walter is in Union Hospital with what doctors believe to be a stroke. He ordered me to contact you so that you would know to serve as acting principal in his absence."

"Don't worry about anything, Sheila. You stay with Walter, and I'll be there after work."

"Thank you, JT."

"I couldn't help but hear, sweetie," remarked Diana. "Why don't you go now? I'll cover the remaining students."

"Are you sure, Di?"

"I wouldn't have suggested it were I not sure, Jamey. Get going. I'll speak with you later."

JT got his things together and drove straight to Union Hospital, which was only down the street from his house. He found Sheila in the waiting area of the Emergency Room. She had heard nothing since her arrival, but the triage nurse promised to find out whatever she could as soon as she could. After an hour, the emergency room resident came to speak with Sheila. She pulled JT by the arm to insure his inclusion in any discussion. The resident confirmed the suspicion that Walter

Holloway had indeed suffered a stroke. At that moment, he had lost his movement on his right side, and everything possible was being done for him. The encouraging factor was the speed with which he and his wife identified the symptoms and his speedy arrival at the hospital. Both conditions have shown to be key factors in stroke recovery.

"We have several more tests to perform, and then we will send him to a room in the Intensive Care Unit," continued the physician. "He's in the best of hands, Mrs. Holloway. Please try to relax."

JT stayed with Sheila until Walter went to his room in the Intensive Care Unit. After calling his mother, he decided to stay with Sheila for as long as she needed him. On the very limited bright side of this terrible incident was the fact that now he did not have to lie to Missy about missing her birthday party. Walter had done it again.

"Hi, Di, I'm fine, really. I'm staying with Walter's wife as long as she needs me here. I know you do, sweetie. I want to be with you too. No, I don't think you are selfish. Look, honey, if Walter is going to be out of commission for an extended period, my hours at the center will change. Because, Diana, the principal's hours are about one and one half hours longer each day than the classroom teacher. I am not sure right now, but I may have to take a leave from the center. I know, but we will still see each other every day. Please, Di, don't make this harder for me than it already is. If you wish, I will see if I can get a substitute for my hours at the center. I know you can handle that. I did not call you to upset you nor to get myself upset. I know. I love you too. I will call if I have anything new to share. Right. Sleep tight, love. Bye."

Diana Wisdom hung-up the phone and cursed aloud. Within days, her new fairy tale love life had encountered stormy weather that seemed resistant to change. Would she ever again be as happy as she was during the Disney World trip? Was she simply doomed to tragic relationships with the male of the species? Perhaps, she should have hooked-up with Dawn she thought to herself in jest. Nothing could be more painful than what she had been feeling of late.

Thinking about Dawn brought back conflicting memories. Their time together was not lacking in emotional investment or pleasant memories. She soon felt a feeling of loss unfelt for many months. She drew herself out of her momentary melancholy by thinking of her Jamey. She was so thankful that they seemed to be back on track. However, the experience sowed a seed in the depressed woman's mind as to whether or not to act upon her inclination to have Dawn in her life once again.

Earlier that evening as Diana was circulating through the center monitoring the remaining evening students for Jamey, she approached the dark, attractive, impeccably dressed woman whom for one reason or another she just did not care for. As she passed Elanie's study carrel, the student asked if she had a moment.

"You're Ms. Wisdom, the director of the CALL Center, correct?"

"Yes, and if I recall correctly," she fibbed, "you are Mrs. Elanie Patsos."

"That's correct. Please call me Elanie."

"Surely, and I'm Diana. I love the way you dress. Your outfits are always so stylish and coordinated to the smallest detail."

"Oh my, you make me blush. That is one of my many compulsions, Diana. Everything I wear must match, or I cannot get through the day. Sick huh?"

"Whatever it is, it certainly works for you. You never fail to attract the men folk as well as the women when you arrive at the center."

"Now I'm really embarrassed," she lied loving the attention she was receiving from her imagined foe.

"Coming from a beauty like you, I am truly complimented. Has anyone ever told you that you look like..."

"Farrah Fawcett?"

"Obviously you've been told before."

"Once or twice. Personally, Elanie, I cannot stand the bitch."

The two beauties had a healthy laugh together. Elanie's laugh appeared more forced than real.

"I'm pleased we have had this time to speak, Diana. I have heard such wonderful things about you, and the work you do here. JT sings your praises all the time."

"He'd better, or the wedding is off."

"What? What wedding is that?" she asked taken unaware.

"Oh, I apologize if you didn't know," she lied. "JT and I are engaged to be married."

The smile on her face faded to a grin, and she was sure her face had reddened. She found her voice just in time.

"Best of luck to you and congratulations to the perspective groom, you have a wonderful man there, Diana. You're both very luck people."

"Thank you," she grinned as she thought to herself, "Take that bitch!"

CHAPTER 111

THE NEWS ON THE MEDICAL front was not good for either Walter or JT. The doctors had suggested to Sheila Holloway that Walter would probably not be going back to work for months; however, a full recovery could and should be expected. For JT the news had far-reaching consequences. He must leave his classroom for the administration position he never really wanted. The impact on his students would be less damaging now at the beginning of the school year than later. He must leave Missy Mamry to her own devices although now as her Acting Principal, he would still have close contact with the bombshell. He must convince Diana that his absence from the center would not disrupt their relationship; he must then convince his CALL Center students that they would be as successful without him. Whoever said that the Lord does not give a person more than he or she can handle was full of shit!

Settling into the leadership role was nothing new to JT. He had been a leader of educational programs for years at MESELP. His problem now was that he was the temporary leader of his close friends and admirers. He must learn to walk the narrow line between getting the job done properly for Walter and maintaining the respect of his colleagues to whom he must return with Walter's return. Could he separate his friend persona from his boss persona? If the occasion called for it, could he confront a malingering friend? He would find out as he began his journey as the Acting Principal of TLCCS. His first order of business was to find himself a permanent substitute. The fifth grades at the school were going to be a problem for the duration of his tenure. With two substitute teachers, he would have to work overtime getting both of them on the same academic page so to speak. Both must be in command of their classrooms to salvage that year's 5th grade class. As was Walter with Missy Mamry, JT was limited in his selection of a substitute for himself. He knew he wanted a male teacher preferably one with some classroom presence. He found Seymour De Dupree, a former linebacker on the University of Massachusetts, Amherst, Minuteman football team. Classroom presence he had. At six foot four, two hundred fifty-five pounds, Seymour had presence up the ying yang! Seymour fell just a bit short on the teaching aspect of the position, but JT theorized that with his tutoring, Seymour would be able to do the job for him. In a conversation with Missy Mamry, JT confided his confidence in her now being the senior teacher at her grade level. He spoke to her as Knute Rockne spoke to the Fighting Irish at Notre Dame. When he was finished, she was in tears, but ready to run through a wall for him, if necessary.

"So Missy, we'll still be meeting each day after school to plan-out your week. We will do that for as long as you feel necessary. We can include Seymour in our meetings if he is available, or I can leave his planning up to you, kid. Have you met Seymour yet, Missy?"

"Seymour and I go way back to our freshman year in high school. I will have no problems dealing with him, JT. My problem is that he's no you."

"True you are, Missy, but on the other hand I'm no him, though I wish I had his physique."

"You're not so bad for an older guy, Jamey. I wouldn't kick you out of bed. Should I have said that, JT?"

"Only if you're ready to give this old guy CPR to get his heart going again."

"You are a package, Jamey. You rock! You just make sure that I don't get short-changed on my personal Jamey time, boss man."

"I will do everything in my power to avoid that happenstance, Missy."

"You know you missed a fabulous party last weekend. Most of my girlfriends are just outrageous. It was lucky for them that the October lake water was warmer then usual. There were more bare asses bobbing around our lake than donkeys in Mexico."

"We have to go now, Missy."

"Who is we, Jamey?"

"I mean I have to go, hon. I'll catch you later."

"I hope so, Jamey."

Melissa Mamry sat down at her desk and noticed she had an itch that needed some attention very soon.

"You're no JT, you big black stud, but I guess, Seymour, you'll have to do in an emergency. Yo, Seymour, do you have a minute? Let's talk shop."

Later that evening at the center, JT composed a letter to all the evening students describing his need to take a temporary leave of absence. Diana agreed to have Stella take care of his mass mailing. To those students in attendance, he explained his situation in varying degrees depending upon the length of time he had worked with the student. Universally, the resultant effect was disappointment bordering upon devastation.

"How about private tutoring, JT," asked Elanie Patsos. "Is that a possibility?"

"It's the time factor that's the problem, Elanie. I hate to disappoint so many people. Let me speak with Diana."

"You mean the future Mrs. Russell, don't you?" asked Elanie.

"I was not aware that anyone at the center knew."

"Were you keeping it a secret, JT? Still have some wild oats to sow before settling down again?"

" It's not that, Elanie. I just wasn't aware that anyone at the center knew.

"Diana didn't have a problem passing the good news to me. In fact, she was ecstatic. But who could blame her?"

"Really? Well, look Elanie, I am going to rethink the center situation and see what I can do. I'll talk to you in a bit."

He walked over to Diana's cubicle and knocked, as was his habit.

"Come on in, Jamey. You're the only one who knocks."

"Di, I want you to hold the mailing about my leave. I am going to try, with your permission of course, working three nights a week from six to nine o'clock instead of five nights a week from 5 to 9 PM. What do you think?"

"Great! I just went from having my best teacher (and lover) no nights a week back to three whole nights a week. Don't think I'm going to raise your pay to make-up for your lost income."

"I would have never considered such a thing. Besides, I have a rich chick girlfriend who pays me for sex. I'll just bump-up my prices."

"And it will be worth every freaking penny! Kiss me you fool."

"Speaking of which, weren't we keeping the news about us 'cool' around here?"

"Yeah, why?"

"Elanie Patsos just congratulated me on my future marriage in so many words."

"I just had to, Jamey. I had to ram it up that phony bitch's ass. It felt so good, hon."

"Who is this? Do I know this woman?"

"This, love, is the mother bear protecting what is hers. Mess with her and hers and suffer the consequences."

"You can be scary, Diana."

"And don't you or Little JT forget it," she responded laughing.

At that moment, they decided that it would be a reduced schedule not a leave of absence for JT Russell's career at the CALL Center. Rather than do the smart thing and eliminate some of the demands on his time and life, JT took the selfless way and would add to the existing stress and strain currently in his life. He would surely be the first to learn if he were doing it wrong!

CHAPTER 112

HARRY MANOS HAD BEEN A busy little detective. He had visited SAFE headquarters only to find that Ms. Dawn Woodruff was in California attending a meeting of SAFE branches nationwide. While there, he made a head count of the number of black women working in the office. His final count was five. Interestingly enough, he found that Dawn Woodruff's administrative assistant was a tall, thin, black woman with a close-cropped hairdo. She did not exactly remind him of Darryl Strawberry, but he thought a word with her would be time well spent.

"Excuse me, miss."

"Yes."

"I'm Detective Manos from the Peabody Police Department. I am investigating a possible murder case. May I have a moment of your time?" he asked holding his badge and ID picture at eye level.

"What may I do for you, detective?"

"Am I correct in assuming that you are Dawn Woodruff's personal assistant?"

"I am her administrative assistant, Carline Williams."

"Of course, you are. I am sorry. Could you tell me your whereabouts during the day on December 10th of last year, Miss Williams?"

"That certainly tests one's memory, detective. May I check my date book?"

"Please do that, m'am. This is an open book test."

His attempt at humor was lost on the woman.

"Oh my, she said that I would not get in trouble. It was just a prank. Am I in trouble? I cannot go to jail, detective. I wouldn't survive,"

"Slow down, lady. Let's take this one step at a time."

"I agreed to be part of a prank that Dawn was playing on her girl friend, Diana, for her birthday. I was supposed to meet Diana at the shopping center in the food court to give her a ride home. When we were to return to Dawn's van, it would be gone, stolen, out of there."

"So you're saying, Miss Williams, that Dawn Woodruff initiated this plan? Do you know if her girlfriend, Diana, had knowledge of the plan?"

"I said it was a prank on her, didn't I?"

"And the plan worked as she planned it?"

"No friggin way! Excuse me, detective."

"Please, go on, Miss Williams."

"There was no Diana to meet me at the food court. I waited and waited, but no one came. When I returned to the van, it was gone! Within five minutes, two cops pulled up to assist me with my stolen van problem. I did not know whether to shit or go blind, detective. I had only worked for the woman for a month before she asked me to join-in on her prank. I certainly did not want to piss her off. I liked my job, and I felt I had a future here. Therefore, I proceeded with the plan as if I had met Diana. I identified myself as Dawn Woodruff showing the social security card she left with me. Those two fool cops did not even ask me for a photo id. Are you hiring just anyone off the street these days?"

"Please continue, Miss Williams."

"They asked for the plate number, make, model, and color of the van. Then they offered me a ride home, which I politely refused. I did not want to be nowhere close to cops if they found out I was lying. I told them that my girlfriend would be meeting me at Filene's very shortly. The officers called in the report, thanked me, then one of them said something about lunch. I walked to the nearest telephone and called the office. Dawn was not there. In fact, I did not see her for the next two days. Luckily for me, my sister was at home; she came to pick me up and take me home."

"Are you aware that making a false police report is a crime, m'am?"

"I didn't make the report, detective. I just gave those two fools Dawn Woodruff's social security card."

"Yes, m'am."

"You've been very helpful, Miss Williams; may I have your home address and telephone number should I need you in the future?"

"Detective, am I in trouble? I cannot go to jail, man. I wouldn't last a day in a prison cell!"

"I assure you that your cooperation has more than balanced your poor judgment in cooperating in this alleged prank, Miss Williams."

"Thank you, detective, because I can't go to jail. No way can I go to jail."

"Yeah, I know, lady. Have a nice day."

CHAPTER 113

"YOU'LL BE AWAY THE WHOLE weekend, Di? Even Friday evening? Do you have to go? Yeah, I know. When did this thing come up? Today? Not much notice. Where is the conference? Well, you will still be in the Commonwealth if I need an emergency cuddle session. All right, please be careful. I love you, too."

JT hung up the telephone and sat back in his chair. That Wednesday night at the center was slow probably due to the heavy rain. A few regulars straggled in, but the place was empty the entire evening.

"Well, we're single this weekend, Jamey boy. What should we do?" asked Little JT.

"That's for me to know, Little JT, and for you to find out."

"Don't mess with me, buddy, I might not be there when you really need me."

"I'm sorry, friend. You know it's always you and me forever."

One of the many demented habits JT enjoyed was his conversations with the imaginary Little JT. The jury was still out as to whether they were truly imaginary discussions, or whether Little JT actually had a direct line of communications to JT Russell's "brain-central". Someone tapped him on his shoulder as he was in the midst of apologizing to Little JT.

"Sleepy, professor?"

"Elanie."

"Boy is it wet out there."

"A hurricane couldn't make you look bad."

"My, my, professor, are you flirting with me? What would the future little woman say?"

"She would most probably say that I continue to exercise great taste in women."

"Are you ever at a loss for words, JT?"

"The moment you walked into the center perhaps."

"Let me in on it. What is the deal with all the word play, JT? Are you pranking me?"

"I want you to know that I am the same JT I was before you found out about my engagement. I do not change according to my circumstances. I am a 'what you see is what you get' kind of guy for better or worse."

"So, if I were to suggest for example that we have a friendly drink together this Friday night after school, you wouldn't be offended and the little woman wouldn't mind?"

"I'd be honored, but as I seem to recall, you have a husband. Might he take umbrage at his wife going for drinks with some male other than himself?"

"He won't even notice I'm gone."

"There is absolutely no way you'll ever get me to believe that, Elanie. If you were my wife…"

"What a lovely idea, JT."

After he finished blushing and staring at the floor, he continued.

"If you were my wife, I'd put a homing device on you so I could track your every movement."

"And do you have such a device on Ms. Wisdom, JT?"

"Not yet."

"So, are we on for Friday after school, professor?"

"I would love to, Mrs. Patsos."

"Wonderful! Now, I'd better get to work. My teacher is a real taskmaster. He even paddles me when I'm bad."

"I wish."

"What, JT?"

"Nothing, young lady, get on to your studies while I heat up the paddle."

He refocused to the moment prior to Elanie's arrival.

"Perhaps, JT, you're rushing into this remarriage thing. You have pretty much been agreeable to everything Diana has proposed. Why not step back a bit. Look at the big picture. See what the world has to offer. You know you are not getting any younger, buddy. Your youth and good looks may soon be a memory. Are you so sure of your feelings about Diana that you can turn your back on every other woman in your world? Tell me you would not want a shot at Missy Mamry's mammary glands. Tell me that you would hate getting your socks blown-off by that exquisite young woman. And Elanie, what about that piece of Greek pastry? Is she not the most elegant woman you have ever laid eyes upon? Tell me you would not love to kiss every inch of that beautiful woman. Tell me you would not risk a coronary to introduce her to all the wondrous rides at JT World. What are you doing, Jamey boy? You are holding us back. You are shackling us to the prison walls. It's not too late, but it soon will be, my friend."

"Go to sleep, Little JT, you're starting to make too much sense."

CHAPTER 114

His first full week as Acting Principal of TLC had finally concluded. No worse for wear than usual, JT collected his thoughts about the rest of his day. Then he remembered Elanie. The drink. After work. That night. He cringed. Had he made a tactical error in agreeing to her invitation? After all, he was a "promised" man, and she was a married woman.

"Oh, fuck it!" he thought to himself.

"What's the worst thing that could happen?" As per usual, JT would soon find out.

When he arrived at the CALL Center, Elanie had already begun her studies. She gave him an incredibly sexy wink as he walked past her study carrel to the rear of the center.

"Good evening, Mrs. Patsos, and how are we today?"

"Kali spera, professor, I don't know how we are, but I am fabulous." She looked at JT as if he were the main course at Thanksgiving Dinner.

"Right you are. I'll be back in a moment," he mumbled, and then to himself, "as soon as Little JT sits the fuck down."

He sat down in Diana's empty cubicle and placed his bag on the floor.

"I think you've gotten my ass too close to the alligators again, Little JT," he mused to himself. "If I had as good a feeling about tonight as you, my freakin leg wouldn't be twitching, and I'd be standing upright smiling at the world too. How could I get out of this without hurting her feelings and/or looking like the world's biggest pussy? How about a family emergency? Lame. Sickness? Next. Previous engagement? You have definitely lost a step as you have aged. Face it son, Little JT stuck your hand in the cookie jar, pulled out one mouthwatering snack, so now you're going to have to eat it, so to speak."

"JT, I'm stuck," whispered Elanie from around the wall of the cubicle.

With Little JT finally behaving himself, Big JT was able to respond to her dilemma without embarrassment.

"I'm on my way. Ladies in distress are my specialty."

Would he ever learn to shut his mouth?

"I know. I've been told about the Night Knight, Mr. Russell."

"Right… Well, let's see if we can fix you up?"

"I'm sure you can, JT."

"Right…"

They walked back to her carrel and he pulled a chair next to hers. As usual, she smelled incredible, practically illegal to human males.

"Is it algebra again, Elanie?" he asked as he looked over her shoulder to the book directly in front of her. The low cut white sweater she wore so highlighted her gorgeous olive skin that he could not resist a quick peek.

"No fucking bra, JT! It's the middle of fucking autumn, and there's no bra!" he panicked.

"So, what do you think, JT?"

"Beautiful," he murmured then snapping back to consciousness, "that's one beautiful problem. I have had more trouble with more students on that single problem than any other in the whole book."

"I meant my breasts, JT," she whispered.

Caught like a rat in a trap he was. However, she was good. She set the trap, practically sent out invitations to the goddamn rat, and then led the bloody vermin to the cheese that she left uncovered. The rat did not stand a frickin chance. Nor did JT.

"I apologize, Elanie. I…."

"Don't, I like that in a man."

"Really? Well, I've got plenty more where that came from."

They both had a good laugh. Then she went and did it. She put her hand on his knee.

"Please don't wake up, Little JT," he prayed.

"Are we still on for tonight, professor?"

"You bet, Elanie. Would you mind if I brought a chaperone?"

She chuckled at that and then whispered, "Don't worry, professor, I don't bite...unless it's by request."

It was too late! Little JT had answered the alarm and had begun to engage in calisthenics.

"Elanie, if I don't take my leave from you at this moment, I may not be capable of leaving this chair for the rest of the evening, if you catch my drift."

"Well, professor, that is a very tempting offer. Perhaps I should just keep you to myself all evening, but if you must 'walk-off' that erection, c'est la vie!"

"Are you like this with everyone?"

"Absolutely no one, ever, JT. I guess I am just a late bloomer."

"Soon, I'll have no secrets from you."

"Nor I from you, professor.

"What are we talking about now?"

"What do you think?"

"I have to go find a male student or an ugly female to work with for a bit. Keep a good thought, Elanie."

With that, he walked slightly stooped-over to a group of students opposite from Elanie's study carrel.

"Did you hurt your back, JT? asked one concerned student.

"Just an old age twinge, Jack. It's nothing major."

He walked quickly to one of his favorite and oldest students.

"Mrs. Pellow, how are you tonight? You look different, did you have your hair done?" remarked JT.

"I just came from an electrolysis appointment. I had my moustache removed along with those hairs growing from my moles."

"You look great. Let me sit here and work with you."

The next to the last student replaced her materials in their proper locations, bid JT a good weekend, and walked out of the center. The last student was still in the bathroom so JT took the opportunity to call Charlene informing her of his plan to be out for the evening. As he hung up the telephone, Elanie Patsos exited the bathroom with reworked make-up, impeccable hair, and a dazzlingly smile. She must have been cold because JT noticed the headlights protruding from her sweater front.

"Let me get your jacket, Elanie. You look cold."

"On the contrary, JT, the jacket will just make me hotter. Where shall we go? Remember it is my treat. I invited you, professor."

"There is a place in Salem that we frequent after work on weekends."

"Do you mean you and the little lady?"

"Yes, as well as students and visitors to the center. We're an equal opportunity entertainer."

"So, I'm not you're first, JT? You've had other students invite you for a drink?"

"Not really. You know that group of young kids who usually sit together each night. They've gone to have pizzas with us, and they've gone with me alone, but they just kind of invite themselves."

"I didn't see the little woman tonight, JT."

"She's at a conference in Worcester."

"Is that the only reason you accepted my offer, because the cat's away?"

"Of course not," he lied. "If Diana were here, I'm sure she would be joining us."

"Would I then have been required to call my husband to invite him? she asked curtly.

"I seemed to have upset you, Elanie. If you wish to change your mind, I would understand."

"I've a feeling you wouldn't be upset if I did change my mind. Have I scared you off, JT Russell?"

"Don't be silly."

"So you wouldn't be upset if Diana found out about tonight?"

"No, I believe not, probably not anymore than you would be upset if your husband found out."

"JT, please know one thing. I live with a man who treats me as if I am second best to his whores. I will not ever accept that from another man. I will not be anyone's second choice again. If you are here with me simply because Diana is not available, I would prefer to go home. If you truly wish to be with me, then we should be on our way."

"I think we both need that drink, lady. Let's go."

"I'll follow you in my car, JT."

The animated couple walked into the restaurant and stopped at the hostess station.

"Good evening, JT. Would you like your table?"

"Yes, thank you, Ellie," JT winked and smiled.

Boy did he love it when they did that for him. He pulled out a chair for the elegant creature who would sit opposite him.

"Is this your personal table, JT, or did you pay her to say that?"

"Of course I didn't pay her. I come here a lot, and I tip well if I must say so myself."

"I don't know whether to believe you or not."

"Which way would it be easier for you?"

"Well, so far I've believed everything you've ever told me."

"There you have it. You must then believe me. I am starving. How would you like a pizza? What kind do you like?"

"Anything you want, JT, is fine with me."

"Really?"

"For real."

"Hi Tracie, we'll have a large salami and mushroom pizza."

"Would you like drinks while you wait, JT? asked the waitress.

"Elanie, what would you like?"

"I would love a glass of white wine, please."

"I'll have a Tom Collins, Tracie."

"Be right back, JT."

"Is there anyone who does not know you, professor?"

"My dear, strangers are only friends we have yet to meet."

"That is profound, professor."

"I got that from a fortune cookie. My all time favorite fortune is, "You are what you are in the dark."

"And what does that mean?"

"I think it means if you act the same way when you can be seen as when you can't be seen, that is the real you?"

"Like tonight?"

"When will I ever learn to shut my mouth? How long have you been married, Elanie?"

"Thirteen years give or take a decade."

"It's funny, Elanie, from everything I've heard from you on the subject, you appear not to be a fan of the institution."

"Oh no, JT, you have misread me. The institution is wonderful. When you marry someone who belongs in an institution that is a real problem!

"Where do you hide this funny lady when you're at the center?"

"It takes a lot of time and patience with me to get me to lower my walls. It has been that way probably since my father died. There has been only one exception to that rule in my entire life."

"And..."

"You are that exception, Mr. JT Russell. You may not be the most handsome man I've ever met, or the funniest, or the smartest, or definitely not the richest..."

"Stop your turning my head with these compliments."

"Let me finish. This is not easy for me. Where was I?"

"You were telling me I was an unfunny, ugly, stupid, poor guy."

"I've never met a person who possesses so many qualities that appeal to others. I see people attracted to you like you are magnetic. In the short time I have known you, I have personally witnessed it a number of times. Hilda Markos, my neighbor, talks about you as if you were the savior. I watch the way Diana's eyes follow you around the center."

"Jesus, I'm never going to feel comfortable there again."

"It's just you, professor."

"May we speak about tonight at the center, Elanie?"

"I have nothing left to hide, JT."

"Were you just teasing me to get a reaction from me? I'm not saying it didn't work, mind you."

"I plead guilty on all counts. You penetrated my walls, so to speak. You released the imprisoned Elanie, JT. When she sees something she likes, or wants, or must have, there is no dissuading her from her quest. Tonight you met the Elanie that I want you to know. I am incredibly attracted to you, and tonight I wanted to let you know."

"Given our current circumstances, Elanie, where does that leave us?"

"That depends upon your feelings about me. How do I affect you, JT? What is it about me that you are attracted to, if anything at all? Do you see me as more than an attractive face and body with a welcome sign on its sex organs?"

The final comment made him cough on his sip of water.

"Here are your drinks, folks," announced Tracie.

"Saved by the bell," whispered JT.

"Temporarily, professor, only temporarily."

CHAPTER 115

WITH THE MASSACHUSETTS ENGLISH AS A Second Language Education Program not due to commence another Saturday and vacation weeks program until January, JT was able to sleep-in the following morning…sleep-in until Katie Anne and Ronnie used his bed for a trampoline. Now wide-awake, he gathered his girls in his arms and gave them hugs and kisses.

"Oh Daddy, you have morning breath," complained Ronnie.

"Ronnie," chastised Katie Anne, "that's not polite. When people and dogs get old their breath gets stinky, right, Dad?"

"Whatever you say, honey."

"Hey Dad, did Diana talk to you about next weekend yet?"

Just the mention of the woman's name left him feeling an unfamiliar pang of guilt, and strangely enough, he had not even done anything. All right, she kissed him goodnight and slipped in a little tongue, other than that, nothing. It was a pleasant evening between two friends involved in a burgeoning friendship who want to fuck each other's brains out.

"What about Katie?"

"Diana wants Ronnie and me to sleepover at her house next weekend. We're going to go shopping, and to lunch, you know, girl stuff."

"That sounds fabulous, girls. Are you two up for it?"

"Daddy, is that a trick question?" mocked Ronnie.

"I'll be talking to Diana sometime today. I'll ask her what her plans are for you guys."

Just what he needed a standing ovation by two little girls on his stomach and chest.

"Ladies, do you think I might have a little bit more privacy, before I get up for the day? I'm still tired."

"Of course, Daddy," answered Katie. "They also get tired easy too when they get old, Ronnie."

"Out! Get out of here! All female Russells be gone immediately!"

Alone at last once again, he closed his eyes to evaluate last night's events. After her third white wine, Elanie was free-associating like mad. He learned every despicable thing with which she had had to deal in the past two years. She endured finding colored condoms in hubby's pants pockets that were not theirs. Elanie related tales of having to cover facial bruises with extra make-up when she dared disobey him. She told him of being put on display at the Greek Club for all his friends to obsess about and drool over, but having to watch helplessly as he overtly flirted with any new young female present. He demanded that Elanie work a full-time job and maintain a picture-perfect home with no assistance whatsoever. The picture she painted was that of a woman desperate for change. Therefore, he had asked her why she put up with all of his antics. She replied very simply that it was a financial decision. Her salary alone would not allow her to live in her accustomed fashion. She was willing to sacrifice her dignity in order not to surrender her standing in the tightly knit Greek community. In this loveless marriage of convenience, her only satisfaction involved the accumulation of material possessions and her perceived elevated social status. He commiserated with her without casting judgment. By the end of the evening and her fifth glass of wine, he was uncertain of her sincerity when she declared her lust for him and a burning desire to feel him inside of her. She also lamented about wanting to have his baby, but by that time, he was suffering from sexual stimulation overload and a moderate alcohol buzz so he just sloughed it off. At departure time, he was concerned for her safety after having watched her consume so many glasses of wine. Elanie pooh-poohed him telling him that she did not even get tipsy until after drink number seven. Nonetheless, he followed her all the way to her house, watched her go into the darkened split-level home, and awaited the appearance of a light. Once, she had illuminated her home, he felt comfortable enough to leave her and head home.

The phone rang startling him back to the present. Charlene had answered it from the living room and called to JT that Diana was calling. Talk about your basic coincidences.

"Hello sweetie, how's the conference?"

"Jameyless."

"Besides that, Di, how are things going?"

"I suppose everything is fine. I miss you. Do you miss me?"

"What do you think? Hey, the girls just told me this morning that you invited them over next weekend. What's up with that?"

"I sort of promised before this damn conference came up. That will make it two weekends in a row that we could not be together. Are you upset?"

"Of course I'm not upset. I love you for the way you love the girls, Di."

"I hope that's not the only reason, Mr. Russell."

"Someone on the phone sounds insecure, and it's not me."

"Jamey, I have a confession to make."

"What did you do now?"

"I really feel terrible, Jamey, and I can't keep anything from you."

"Jesus, Di, tell me before I have a stroke."

"I had dinner last night with an old boyfriend. I should have said no, but he started talking about some old friends and old times, and I finally agreed just to get him off my back. I feel so guilty."

"Why? Did you do anything you shouldn't have done?"

"James Thurber Russell, you should know better than to ask such a question!"

"Well then, Diana, what's the problem?"

As she spoke, he had what he considered a brilliant idea! By firing a preemptive strike about his adventure last night at the same time she is apologizing for her imagined indiscretion, she would not have grounds to be angry with him.

"Look honey, I was in a similar situation last night."

"What? What do you mean, Jamey?"

"Last night I went to D'Auria's with Elanie Patsos…"

"You did fucking what?"

"Diana…"

"You piece of shit! As soon as I leave town you go hound dogging the town slut!"

"Will you calm down and let me explain?"

"Go on, asshole. I'm all fucking ears."

"She's having problems at home, and she asked if we could talk privately. Since I had not eaten, I suggested D'Auria's. That's all there was to it."

"You know how I feel about that bitch, Jamey. I cannot believe you would do this to me. My situation is so innocent compared to yours, you dickhead."

"How do you figure?"

"You were talking about emotional, personal issues usually restricted to intimate acquaintances. Are you two intimates, Jamey?"

"Diana, you're reading too much into this."

"Maybe we are moving too fast, Jamey. Perhaps we should take a step back from this relationship and look at us objectively. I just realized that I do not know you as well as I should. You know I cannot be with someone I cannot trust completely. I've been wounded too deeply in the past."

"Di, you're blowing this way out of proportion."

"And did she blow anything last night, Jamey? Of all the women in the world, why did it have to be her, Jamey? I cannot speak anymore. We'll have to talk later."

Without saying good-bye, Diana hung-up the phone, threw herself onto her hotel room bed, and cried hysterically into her pillow. JT ran his hands through his hair shaking his head in disbelief.

"Do I want to spend the rest of my life with someone who has a tendency to lose control so quickly and so irrationally? She is a wonderful woman, but at least twice now, she has shown me this scary, psycho side of herself. Maybe she is correct. Take a break. It has been a whirlwind romance. Maybe we have been doing it wrong. Perhaps slower would have been better. Time apart may be helpful, or it may mark the end of our ride."

CHAPTER 116

DIANA'S FIRST SESSION ON SATURDAY was a ten o'clock to one o'clock workshop entitled Curriculum Development for the Adult Learning Center. Following lunch, she was to lead a group discussion from three o'clock to five o'clock on Counseling the Adult Learner. At the last moment, the conference sponsors were able to reinstate a previously postponed session scheduled for Saturday evening after dinner. Because of a stroke of good fortune, the availability of that speaker changed due to the early arrival of her flight from California. Diana was one of the last informed about the program change. She needed and looked forward to a block of private time following dinner. When she learned of the additional session, she felt somewhat upset though she restrained herself from displaying her displeasure. Discovering that the speaker presenting Women's Roles in Adult Education Administration was to be Dawn Woodruff gave Diana a sense of conflicted emotions. She had not seen Dawn for over a year. Though they had parted on friendly terms, Diana harbored an irrational deep-seated guilt that she was responsible for the demise of their friendship. Were she able to be more like Dawn, their valued friendship would still be alive and well.

As Diana prepared for her day, thoughts of Dawn ran through her troubled mind. She had learned that she could count upon Dawn to be there for her in times of conflict to offer sage advice and emotional support. Clearly, she could use some of that presently.

Putting on her face that day had taken longer than usual due to her need to mask her reddened eyes and flushed face. Nevertheless, Diana appeared on time for the onset of the day's events. She daydreamed through the first three-hour session unable to bring herself to concentrate on anything other than her morning's telephone call to Jamey. Not wanting to become emotional at such a public forum, she forced herself to disengage her personal thoughts in favor of flights of fancy and fantasy. At lunch, she dined with several newly discovered colleagues and did her best to meld into the conversation. Her afternoon session required her to assume a leadership role; therefore, she gave herself a pep talk via the mirror in the ladies room about her responsibility to act professionally. A motivated Diana Wisdom took full control of her group discussion session. As a result, she received praise from those involved for her role as moderator. Although she was required to attend that additional session after dinner, Diana's spirits brightened because of her successful presentation. Instead of dreading the evening session of the conference, Diana had actually looked forward to it. In the recesses of her mind, she speculated about the possibility of seeing and spending time with Dawn.

Making small talk and seeming to be enjoying herself at the sit down dinner, Diana turned to acknowledge a tapping on her right shoulder.

"I thought that was you Ms. Brian-Wisdom," smiled Dawn Woodruff.

"Dawn!" responded Diana as she rose to her feet to embrace her estranged friend.

"I just this morning found out that you were to be here. You look wonderful. Your hair looks fabulous."

"Thank you. You are as gorgeous as ever. I am so happy to see you. I have missed our conversations too much. I was hoping that you would be coming to this thing. Perhaps we might have a chance to talk. Originally, I had sent my regrets thinking that my California itinerary would make an appearance here impossible. As luck would have it, I was able to return home early from the 'left coast', and here I am in living color."

Conveniently omitted from Ms. Woodruff's explanation of the facts was the telephone conversation with the Worcester Conference sponsors that confirmed to her that Diana Brian-Wisdom was indeed in attendance that weekend. She also neglected to inform Diana that her "good luck" in catching an earlier flight from California had been the direct result of her feigning illness thus canceling her attendance at all sessions of her final day in California.

"For old times sake, how about coffee after the presentation?" smiled Dawn.

"Déjà vu, Ms. Woodruff, it seems as if I've done this before."

"What say you, friend?"

"We both know we won't be drinking coffee."

"I'll take that as a yes, Ms. Wisdom. I'll see you directly after the session."

"Absolutely. It is wonderful seeing you, Dawn."

"It's been far too long, Diana."

"And in particular to all you strong women in attendance tonight, please hold these words close to your breast. Together we have strength. Unity enables the Davids of the world to slay the Goliaths. When women stand together in a committed, impassioned, united posture, no one ever again will dictate to our sex who or what we should be! Thank you and good night."

The standing ovation from all the women in the audience and the vast majority of men had convinced Diana that Dawn had not only maintained her hypnotic mastery over an audience, but if possible, she had improved. The standing ovation went on for at least three minutes. Well-wishers, converts, die-hard followers, and academic groupies, all migrated toward the guest speaker. Everyone wanted to be Dawn Woodruff except perhaps the lady herself. The past year had found Dawn jumping from one short-term relationship to another.

Never before had she possessed such a clear image of that which she sought in her personal life. Unfortunately, her search had led her into many unfulfilling personal and sexual relationships. Prior to knowing Diana, Dawn had lived the relaxed life of the commitmentless. Diana's entry into Dawn's life had changed all of that. Dawn truly desired Diana, and as she could not have her, Dawn sought a Diana clone. Foiled in her romantic odyssey time after time only made her desire for the prize that much greater. She would have committed herself whole-heartedly to Diana in a heartbeat had Diana and she been sexually compatible individuals. Therefore, woman after woman, relationship after relationship had fallen by the side of Dawn Woodruff's road because there was just no substitute for Diana.

CHAPTER 117

EARLIER THAT SAME DAY THE phone rang at the Russell residence.

"May I speak with JT Russell, please?"

"May I ask who is calling?" asked Katie politely.

"This is Elanie Patsos. I am a student of Mr. Russell's from the CALL Center."

"One moment please. Daddy! There's a lady on the phone for you."

JT had just walked out of the shower when he heard Katie Anne's announcement. At his current state of undress, he thought it better that he take the call in his bedroom.

"I'll get it here, Katie. Hang it up when you hear my voice."

"Yes, Daddy."

"Hello, this is JT."

"Should I apologize for calling you at home?"

"Elanie?"

"Who was that adorable child who answered the phone?"

"That was Katie, my older daughter, and of course you needn't apologize for calling me here. It's great to speak with you anytime, anywhere."

"Even after last night, professor? Did I embarrass you with my forward behavior? I feared I may have crossed a line or two that I ought not to cross. I value your friendship, JT. I would hate to think my behavior put our relationship in jeopardy."

"Please, Elanie, you have nothing to apologize for. If anyone should apologize, it should be me. I ate almost all of the pizza."

"JT, you are unique. Here I call you praying that I did not screw-up last night, and you brighten my mood in two seconds."

"I totally enjoyed myself last night. In fact, I told Diana this morning that we had a very nice evening."

"You did?"

He could not help but notice the great surprise in her voice.

"Sure. Why not? Did I do anything wrong?"

"Well, JT Russell, you continue to surprise me. May I ask how the lady reacted to the news?"

"To be honest, she could have been happier. Let's face it, Elanie, you would represent a threat to any woman even one as self-assured and attractive as Diana."

"My, my, professor, is that yet another compliment?"

"Elanie, telling you that you are drop dead gorgeous simply indicates that I have a firm grasp of the obvious. Your beauty and our friendship are factors that Ms. Wisdom simply cannot control."

"Am I hearing the undercurrents of trouble in paradise, JT?"

"It's not for you to concern yourself with, Elanie. You did nothing wrong, nor did I. If Diana chooses to create something from nothing that is for her to deal with.

"But I want to JT. I want to do everything wrong with you. Everything I said last night is true. If you find yourself in need of a friendly ear or any other organ, run my way, professor."

Totally forgetting about his current state of undress while being absolutely mesmerized by Elanie's words, the presence of Little JT standing at attention reminded him of his need to cover up.

"Listen, Elanie, I am absolutely naked at the moment…"

"Are we having phone sex now, JT?"

"No, you misunderstand me. With two little girls in the house, closed doors mean little. Please forgive me, but I must go. If I were to contact you, when would be an appropriate time?"

"Wait a moment, JT. I am trying to recover from the visual. All right, my heart has slowed sufficiently."

"Give me a break, will you lady?"

"I'll be alone for the remainder of the day and evening until the early morning hours most probably. I will also be available from noon to midnight on Sunday. Would you like my schedule for the rest of the week, professor?"

"I'll call you."

"I will be waiting."

CHAPTER 118

"MERCY, I THOUGHT I'D NEVER find you."

"You are a very popular woman, Ms. Woodruff."

"It isn't too late for drinks, is it Diana?"

"I don't have a curfew, Dawn. Do you?"

"Great! Let's go drink the local drunk under the table in this town too, Wisdom."

"I've really missed you, Dawn."

"I can't tell you how wonderful that is to hear."

"Shall we find a new pub, Woodruff, or would you prefer to buy a dozen or so six-packs and drink-em on the corner?"

"I feel very feminine this evening. Let's find a nice little pub. When they kick us out, we'll buy the six-packs."

The laughing women walked out of the main-room arm in arm. Not very far from the hotel was a clean-appearing bar and grille which seemed to welcome both sexes in equal numbers. Once the two attractive women sat comfortably in their booth, a number of eager to please males visited with offers of free drinks. An equally eager Dawn Woodruff politely hustled each away until the local lounge lizards appeared to get the point.

"I see you haven't changed teams, Ms. Woodruff."

"No, I'm afraid this dog's too old for new tricks, Ms. Wisdom. And for whose team are you playing these days?"

"Same team, but it appears that I may be on the trading block."

"Is it the same problem with the same guy, Diana?"

"It's the same guy but a different problem."

"Well, let's get some liquor in us and see if we can cheer each other up. What'll you have, Diana?"

"I would love a margarita, senorita."

"Waitress," called Dawn Woodruff, "two margaritas, please."

"So, what have you been up to for the past year, Diana?"

"Before we start sharing our tales of whoopee and woe, have you had any contact with Detective Manos of the Peabody Police Department?"

"Do you mean about my van?"

"Yes."

"Maybe a month or two ago he called me asking for my permission to have the van rechecked for fingerprints. Why do you ask?"

"That 'Columbo wannabe' seems to be working on the theory that Tara Russell's husband, my present fiancé, and I did away with the poor woman."

Dawn could not hide her shock and disappointment upon hearing fiancé roll from her love object's lips; however, the absurdity of the proposed theory allowed her to mask her pain in righteous indignation.

"He actually believes you and what's his name?"

"Jamey."

"You and Jamey killed his wife so you could be together?"

"In a nutshell, I guess."

"Is there any proof?"

"None that I know of, Dawn, but this detective is a driven man. I suspect you'll be seeing him."

"Why would he want to see me?"

"He asked me why you left my name off of your list of women whose finger prints might appear in your van."

"Put me in jail and throw away the fucking key. Does 'I forgot' make any sense?"

"He also asked me about our relationship, and why I hadn't told Jamey that I knew the woman whose van was responsible for his wife's death."

"If this is the best he has, he's barking up the wrong lesbian."

The waitress placed their drinks on the table. Dawn suggested that she "run a tab" for the pair.

"I am just giving you a 'heads up' about the overly eager detective, Dawn."

"I'll deal with him if and when he approaches me. Until then, let's forget about all that sad stuff. What is this fiancé business?"

Dawn knew she would have to give the acting performance of her life to survive this portion of the conversation.

"Yup! Jamey asked me to marry him, and I just came apart, Dawn. It was like the impossible dream coming true, you know?"

"But what's the deal with this 'up for trade' business that you mentioned earlier?"

"When I telephoned him this morning, he told me that he had gone to dinner after work with the CALL Center's resident bombshell. Dawn, you have to see this chick to believe her. She dresses to the nines, has perfectly coifed hair, smells as if she bathes in Shalimar, and has a face and body to die for. The bitch comes to the center that way. What the fuck does she look like when she dresses-up? I hate the bitch, and she hates me although both of us are too classy to show it. I know what she is trying to do, and my shit head fiancé made it easier for her by dining with her last night. I went off on him as if he told me that he 'did' her."

"Do you think he may have?"

"That's my problem, Dawn. I thought I knew him and could trust him implicitly. Now all my past insecurities have been awakened and are working overtime."

"You sound like the wounded woman I first met more than two years ago. I thought you had learned from your past mistakes, Diana. It seems to me that you have jumped right back into a relationship that suppresses your worth and enhances your partner's. You are too smart for that shit, Diana. As a gender, males are limited creatures. The primary drive of their existence following the need for sustenance and the need for shelter is the constant need for pussy. They are so unlike our gender, Diana. We nest and nurture. We seek monogamous lifetime relationships. Our sexual drives do not control us in the same fashion that they control our brother humans. Diana, I believe there is so much substance to the often-stated semi-humorous little head thinking for the big head contention. Males as a whole are incapable of the scope and depth of emotions that we females possess."

"Waitress, would you bring four more of the same please?" requested Diana.

"Wasn't that an excerpt from the first lecture of Lesbianism 101, Dawn? What about us foolish heterosexuals? We envision the more traditional view of male and female relationships. Do we just kiss-off the concept of having a home and family? Do we simply accept the male creature and all his weaknesses? It's not all that easy to just out of the blue decide to change teams, as I recall, Ms. Woodruff."

A dazzling smile came to Dawn's face. Diana had struck the single chord of their relationship that Dawn was incapable of erasing from her memory.

"Perhaps you just need a refresher course, Diana," smiled Dawn. As I recall, you were an apt pupil. Were we to eliminate the whole vomiting thing, the experience may be entirely more pleasurable."

The two laughed hysterically at the notion that brought them back in time. For a moment, Diana allowed a long-censored thought to enter her consciousness.

"What would life be like now if Dawn and I 'connected' that night? Would I be as able with Dawn to experience the absolute joy I feel with Jamey? Would I be capable of sinking to the bowels of depression with Dawn as I have with Jamey?"

"Cat got your tongue, Wisdom?"

"I was just reminiscing, Woodruff. I had a quick case of the 'what ifs'."

Dawn reached across the table and covered Diana's hands with hers.

"If ever you need me, if ever you change your mind, I will be there regardless of my situation at that time. Do you really want to know how I have spent my last year? I have been looking for you. I do not mean your physical being. I am talking about your essence. I look for your qualities and nuances in every woman I meet. I seek your genuineness and spirit. The problem is resolutionless. Even were I to clone you, I would still have a copy of a straight woman! I did not mean to get into this, Diana, honestly. As you can see, I have not changed since last we were together. I so wish you could be privy to the lengths to which I've gone to have you in my life."

"Why not just tell me, Dawn?"

"That's for another time and another place, love."

CHAPTER 119

"Do you think it wise of me to visit you at your home, Elanie? Yes, I know that, but why would your professor be visiting you in the evening? I guess. So, do you think I should carry my bag? No, not the bag full of tricks. All right, I will give it a shot, but if Mr. Patsos comes home one of us better have a convincing story. Yes. In about an hour. Bye."

No sooner had he hung-up the phone than it rang again. Knowing that Katie Anne and Ronnie were downstairs in Charlene's apartment, Jamey answered following the second ring.

"Hello. Hello. Is there anyone there? No one wants to talk with me? Good-bye."

He went back to his preparations for his night out when the phone rang a second time.

"Hello!"

"You needn't sound so hostile, Jamey."

"Diana? Did you just call here?"

"Yes, but I chickened out."

"It sounds like you've been celebrating."

"Celebrating? No, Jamey dear, I've been drowning my sorrow, old friend."

JT already did not like the tone or direction of the conversation.

"I am surprised to hear from you after this morning, Di. I hope you've recovered from that incident."

"I shall never recover from that incident, James Thurber Russell. That is why I called."

"Are you positive you wish to have a discussion in your present condition, Diana?"

"My condition is fine, thank you. I am calling about your condition. After long, thorough, and due diligence, I have concluded that this relationship has moved much too quickly. I believe that if either or both of us wish to salvage anything from our present situation, a separation of sorts is necessary."

"Di, may we please have this conversation when you're feeling better?"

"Feeling better? I am feeling fucking fine…feeling fucking fine… funny huh, Jamey? Alliteration at its best, buddy. Look, I am not angry anymore. I will not say I am not hurt. Why don't we talk in a couple of weeks?"

"Di, this isn't necessary."

"Oh yes, it is, my friend. It is imperative for my peace of mind and future mental health."

"If this is what you want, Diana…"

"What I want? You know what I want! I cannot make it any more clear to you about what I want! Jamey, it is what it is. We are what we are. If we are to go on, then we shall. Be well, my friend."

"Di?"

She had hung-up.

"Where the hell have you been, Diana?"

"I had to make a phone call. I forgot to send my regrets to a friend on the passing of his fiancé."

"Are you ready for another drink, woman?"

"Dawn, I think I'm maxed-out."

"Yeah, I believe I am too. What time is it?"

"It is eight-thirty on the dot."

"I need to get to a phone. I need a taxi to Peabody."

"You're going to take a taxi from Worcester to Peabody at this hour? Besides costing a fortune, you will not get home for a couple of hours.

You'll stay in my room tonight, and we'll drive home together after my final session tomorrow."

"Diana, we've tried this before."

"Yeah, I know, but now I'm ready for you, big girl."

The two inebriates laughed themselves out of the bar arm in arm.

"Don't try any tricky stuff tonight, Woodruff."

"Anything you say, I shall abide by, Wisdom."

Finding the hotel was difficult for the alcoholically challenged young women. Getting the door unlocked had been a comedy of errors until a kind room service waiter negotiated the task for them. The room had a very commonly viewed hotel/motel configuration. There were two double beds on one wall with a large dresser across from the beds. A small round table surrounded by two upholstered chairs awaited company in front of the huge double windows. Diana drew the curtains as Dawn retreated to the bathroom for a much needed bladder evacuation.

"We have to have some signal to stop us from drinking this much, Dawn. Perhaps one of us should learn how to say 'no thank you'!"

"Diana, I am 'night clothing embarrassed' once again. Do you have an extra?"

"Only dirty stuff. Do whatever you have to do."

"Really?"

In a matter of moments, Dawn Woodruff for the second time in her life stood naked before Diana Wisdom. Then, she gracefully dove onto to the closer of the two double beds.

"Well, that takes care of that problem, Ms. Woodruff. You are a gorgeous creature, Dawn. If I were a man, I would be all over you right now."

"Don't let that stop you, for heaven's sake. You must not tease the poor lesbian like that, Diana."

"I'm serious. You have a fabulous body and incredible self-confidence about showing it unclothed."

"Not to everyone, fool!"

"You mean there are times when you're not so self-assured? You're not always the omnipotent, Ms. Woodruff."

"Right at this moment, I feel more vulnerable with you than I have with anyone, man or woman, in my life."

"Do you think it would be terrible of me to ask if we could cuddle, Dawn? I don't want to sleep alone tonight."

Not waiting for the answer to her rhetorical question, Diana stripped to her underwear, snapped off the lights, and lay down next to the rapidly breathing Dawn Woodruff.

"Are you sure this time, Diana?"

"I'm not sure of anything. Why not just let happen what is going to happen?"

CHAPTER 120

"WELCOME TO MY HOME, PROFESSOR. Would you like the grand tour?"

"But of course, Mrs. Patsos."

Elanie had a lovely home, a split-level house with a finished basement. Her choices in furnishings were as impeccable as her choices in fashion.

"And this is the master bedroom which I have come to call 'The Great Wasteland'."

"You have a beautiful home, but I expected nothing less. And where is the master of the house this evening?"

"He and his friends are in Boston. He called a while ago to tell me he would be quite late."

"Why would any man go out for a hamburger when he has filet mignon at home?" asked JT aloud.

"Professor, if you keep complimenting me like that I shall be obliged to show my appreciation."

"Elanie, a woman such as you should be complimented profusely and often."

"Now you've done it, professor."

She moved toward him and stepped into his arms. Her lips reached up to meet his as he lowered his head. Her kisses were intoxicating. Her smell, her skin, her posture, she was a living breathing love doll.

She hesitated to break their embrace seeking to explore their kiss fully. Finally, she had to come up for air.

"You are an excellent kisser, professor. By the way, how do you like my outfit?"

She was wearing a pink teddy with a pink penoire over her shoulders.

"I was trying not to notice it. I didn't want to upset Little JT."

"Who?"

"I'll tell you later."

"Professor, would you like to remove these?"

She pulled her clothing away from her body as she asked.

"Is that a trick question, Elanie?"

He held her close to him in the darkness of the living room. He brought his face to her neck, shoulders, and cheek taking in every bit of essence that she offered. He dropped the penoire to the floor and ran his hands over her back and shoulders. She allowed her hand to settle at the front of his pants.

"Elanie, that is Little JT. Little JT, that is Elanie. She's the one responsible for all the sit-ups you've been doing lately."

Grasping his crotch through his clothing, Elanie whispered, "We finally meet at last, Little JT."

CHAPTER 121

"I HAVE NOT STOPPED THINKING of you for a single day during this past year. Every woman I meet I compare to you, and all have been lacking. I could be so good to you, Diana. We could be so good together. Give me your hand."

Diana tentatively reached out her hand toward Dawn. The woman gently captured her hand and moved it over and above her left breast.

"No one makes my heart beat as you do, love. No one will ever make my heart beat as you do."

Diana's fingertips ran across the woman's chest then under her left breast as she held its weight in her palm. She then moved her index finger to the woman's erect nipple and made slow circles with her fingertips. With each movement made by Diana, there was a reciprocal sigh, moan, or both from Dawn. Encouraged by her effect on the woman, Diana brought both hands to both of Dawn's breasts.

"If I were to die right now, I would have no regrets," moaned Dawn Woodruff.

"So this is what it's like to be the aggressor?" thought Diana.

The power that she held over another was mesmerizing. She became bolder by the moment. Her left hand rubbed its way down to the only hair remaining on Dawn's tanned body below her forehead. The woman lying to her left shuddered at her touch. Diana slipped her finger along the lips that protected the flower of life. Moving the tip of her finger upward, she located the protrusion of Dawn's pleasure.

Dawn began to grind against Diana's hand leading her to a shaking, moaning release. With Diana's hand held firmly between her thighs, Dawn's hands encouraged the novice to enter her. Diana manipulated Dawn's interior until once again a quaking, moaning release took place. Unwilling to discontinue her exploration, Diana moved her imbedded fingers up and forward. Dawn began to move up and down on them. Within moments, Dawn released again. Repeatedly, Dawn found release without respite. Finally, she lay spent on the bed with her arms encircling her object of desire.

CHAPTER 122

"Let's go into my bedroom, JT."

"Are you sure, Elanie?"

"I am surer of this than of anything in my life."

Taking him by the hand, she led him to the bedroom she shared with her husband. She wanted him to finish undressing her as if she were giving herself to him as a present. As he gazed upon her beauty, he could not keep his hands from exploring every inch of her satin smooth skin. He kissed and caressed her from head to toe, but soon learned that she did not wish him to kiss her there. Disappointed yet not perturbed, JT continued to kiss, rub, and caress the object of his attention. Something was not quite right from JT's perspective. The human love doll, which he fondled so eagerly, surprisingly lacked the response he expected. Her responses were awkward, almost emotionless, and his intellect began to take control from his passion. She disengaged herself from their embrace and made it known that she wished to undress him. As he lay on her bed, she removed his clothing article by article until there was not a single stitch of clothing between them. Viewing his quite hairy body next to her flawless skin stimulated him immensely once again. She began kissing him and rubbing her body upon his although her actions appeared mechanical and rehearsed. Where was the spontaneity that befits a woman of such grace and beauty? She moved about his body planting kisses and little bites as she journeyed downward. She made no attempt whatsoever to greet Little JT. Apparently as she did not want to be kissed there, neither did she wish to kiss there. JT, knowing he was being very selfish found that to be another major disappointment of their coupling.

"I want you inside of me, JT. Now! Do you have something to wear? If not, open the draw on the night table to your right."

Another major disappointment. He had to use a condom. Not just any condom, but her husband's fucking condom! He followed her directions although by that point he felt fortunate that Little JT was still interested in performing. JT tried his hardest to involve himself in the moment, but the stiff, motionless woman beneath him left him less than enthusiastic. He felt that he performed satisfactorily or so he thought, but he realized with all of his positioning of her and his practiced ministrations, she did not seem to have a release. A fourth major disappointment! Call him selfish. Call him narrow minded and insensitive. Call him whatever you will. When it came to sex, JT knew exactly what he wanted and needed from a partner. He got neither of those from Elanie.

"All that glitters is not gold," ran through his mind. "How in the name of everything holy could such a physically beautiful woman be so unresponsive sexually? She sure as hell talked a good game. She could tease with the best of them; however, when it came to the decisive moment, it simply appeared that she was a fraud."

The woman resting against him to his left should be a first-class fucking machine, but that did not turnout to be the case. Was he willing to invest the time and energy in a new relationship, predicated on clandestine meetings and deceit, which harbored a trove of potential dangers? In trying to reeducate that gorgeous creature in the art and appreciation of lovemaking, he might still possibly end up accepting less than he required of a sex partner.

"Food for thought" he mused to himself.

CHAPTER 123

IN THE PRE-DAWN HOURS, DAWN Woodruff awakened from her fabulously restful sleep to the sounds of retching.

"Not a-fucking-gain!" she murmured. "This can't be happening again! I won't let it! Nothing is going to ruin this for me! No Diana, no Jamey, no dead wife or crippled kid, no one will do this to me again!" The crazed woman approached the bathroom.

"What the fuck is going on, Diana? Do I still disgust you that much? Well, fuck you, doll! You owe me, and I'm gonna collect!"

"Dawn, please calm down. I have been sick most of the night. It must be alcohol poisoning."

"If it weren't for me, your precious Jamey wouldn't even be available to you, bitch!"

"Dawn, what are you saying?"

"Pretty little doll, always gets what she wants. There is a price to pay for everything, precious! I was willing to give up everything for you. I risked my life and future for you. I killed an innocent woman for you!"

A distraught Diana continued retching into the bowl.

"What are you saying, Dawn?"

"Do you have ears, bitch? How much of your shit do you think I can take after all I have done for you? I do believe Ms. Wisdom that you have just cured me of you! What was I seeing in you anyway? Tell me Diana, have you ever masturbated? You handle a pussy as if you had never seen one before. You're a hopeless piece of shit for whom I wasted far too much of my life."

Dawn moved toward the retching Diana and kicked her high upon her right shoulder. Diana sprawled against the bathtub. The attack continued. Dawn kicked Diana in the chest and then in the stomach. The already ill woman was approaching unconsciousness. One final closed fist punch to the facial area rendered Diana unconscious. The heavily breathing, maniacal woman stood over her conquest screaming at top capacity for her victim to stand and fight. She began to tear down curtains and throw items both breakable and unbreakable around the bathroom. Totally out of control and possibly out of her mind, Dawn picked-up a shard of glass from the broken mirror and for a moment wanted to cut the unconscious woman's throat. Then there was banging at the door.

"This is hotel security. Is everything all right in there? Are you in need of assistance? Open the door, please, or we will enter by force."

"Trapped," she thought. "What now, Dawn?"

CHAPTER 124

ELANIE WAS SNUGGLING UP AGAINST a non-reciprocating JT. Hungry for his undivided attention and failing to receive it, Elanie rose to a sitting position to address her new lover.

"JT, I love you; I need you; I must have you in my life."

"Elanie, how can you say those things and be sincere about it? You do not really know me as I found that I really do not know you. Are you forgetting about that little detail called your marriage? What about Mr.Patsos?"

"I'd leave that prick in a second for you."

"Elanie, please don't make me wish this hadn't happened. I'd hate to regret our time together."

"What don't you want me to make you regret? Is it the fact that I allowed someone like you, a prick beneath my station, to fuck me like I'm some common whore?"

"Hold on there, lady. We'd better slow this down before things that can't be retracted are spoken."

"Fuck you, professor. You think I need you. I'm a gorgeous fucking chick that any man in this city would die to fuck! You, you're a pussy-whipped, spineless, piece of shit lay that wasn't worth my time."

JT had been dressing all the while the lady ranted and raved.

"Well then, Elanie, I assume then with that opinion of me you'll not want to be seeing me again."

"Did I say that?"

"I don't know. Did you? Maybe it was your evil twin who just ripped me a new asshole!"

"Stay, JT!"

"Sorry, Elanie, I think it best that I go."

"Walk out that door, and I'll scream rape!"

"You do that lady, and I'll tell hubby more personal, despicable shit about himself than he probably knows about himself. Now how would a common rapist like me come into possession of such intimate information, including his three inch dick?"

"I'm sorry, JT."

"Sorry is just not good enough, lady."

"What can I do to make you forgive me?"

"You've done quite enough already."

CHAPTER 125

SPRAWLED ON THE BATHROOM FLOOR were two women. The one closest to the door was bleeding quite freely from both arms. The other, curled against the bathtub, had shown signs of returning to consciousness. An emergency call to the local paramedics by hotel security, as well as some fast action on their part in applying and maintaining pressure over two vertical slits, one in each wrist from the hand toward the elbow, most probably saved the life of Dawn Woodruff. After stabilizing both women, the paramedics transported them to Worcester County Hospital in separate ambulances.

At 7:00 AM on Sunday morning, the telephone at JT's home rang. Having been unable to sleep after the night he had had, JT answered the call on its first ring.

"Mr. JT Russell, please."

"This is he."

"This is Dr. Monroe Peters, Emergency Room physician at Worcester County Hospital. I'm calling in regard to a Diana Brian-Wisdom."

JT swallowed hard and steeled himself against the possible bad news the next few seconds could bring. It was Tara's accident all over again. Was he being punished again for another indiscretion?

"Yes doctor, is she all right?"

"Ms. Wisdom has had an accident."

"Is it life threatening, doctor?"

"No sir, she has some bumps and bruises.

"I found nothing serious. In fact, I have her right in front of me. Would you like to speak with her?"

"Please."

He tried to compose himself before she reached the telephone; however, the moment he heard her voice, he went to pieces.

"Jamey, don't. I'm fine. I'm so sorry, love. It's my entire fault. I need you to forgive me. Please tell me you forgive me, hon."

"I'll forgive you only if you live. Deal?"

"Deal."

CHAPTER 126

IN HER HOSPITAL ROOM AT Worcester County Hospital, Dawn Woodruff watched as several members of the Peabody Police Department arrived.

"I've waited a long while to speak with you again, Ms. Woodruff. I wish it were under more favorable circumstances," said Harry Manos.

"I was expecting you, detective."

"Ms Woodruff, I have reason to believe that you initiated and carried out a plan that resulted in the death of Tara Anne Russell on December 10th of last year. Would you like to make a statement at this time, Ms. Woodruff?"

"Yes, I would."

"Would you like your attorney present?"

"No, it's not necessary."

"Anything that you say may be used in evidence against you in a court of law…"

"I know."

"Officer, send in the stenographer please."

The stenographer sat at a small table in the corner of the patient's room and awaited her commencement.

"Are we ready, Mrs. Pulio?"

"Yes, detective, we are."

"Ms. Woodruff, in your own words please relate any information you have concerning the death of Tara Anne Russell."

The utterly depressed woman looked up at Manos.

"It was an accident. She was not supposed to die. Her son was not to be hurt either. I had been monitoring the family habits for several weeks. I wanted to be sure if I were going to take such a drastic step. The night of the accident, I thought I was following JT Russell. I wanted him out of Diana Wisdom's life permanently. He was the source of so much pain for her that I could not stand to see it any longer. You see, I loved Diana Wisdom although she did not reciprocate my feelings. I believed that with him out of the picture, Diana would turn to me, learn to love me, as I loved her. I also wrongly involved Carline Williams in the false reporting of a stolen vehicle. I removed the vehicle from the North Shore Shopping Center. I, later that evening, used the vehicle to follow Mr. Russell's automobile. I assumed he was at the wheel of that vehicle. I struck the Russell vehicle from behind twice causing it to go out of the driver's control and roll over. I later abandoned my vehicle and made my way home on foot. I am so sorry for that poor woman and her unborn child. I never meant them any harm. Please, believe me. Fate has allowed that son of a bitch of a husband of hers to go on living. How do you figure?"

"Is that it, Ms. Woodruff?"

"I guess."

"Mrs. Pulio, thank you."

The stenographer exited the room.

"I'll tell you how I figure, Ms. Woodruff; I don't give a good shit whether you say you're sorry all the way to prison! Regardless of who died, your intention was to end a human life for your own gain. You can be sorry until the cows come home, lady, but were it not for you, three kids would still have a mother, and the happy family would be awaiting a new edition. Live with yourself, lady. I know I can. Finally after so many months, I'll be able to sleep at night."

CHAPTER 127

HARRY MANOS WAS FEELING GOOD about himself. The first person he thought of calling was his partner in crime, so to speak, Twan Russell. He wondered if he would be able to catch him at school.

"Twan Russell, please. Harry Manos here, kid. I have great news, Twan. Your mother's case has been solved."

"Get out of town, detective!"

"Yeah, son, we did it!"

"Ms. Dawn Woodruff confessed to being the driver of the vehicle that caused your accident."

"She confessed?"

"Signed, sealed, and on its way to Peabody, my friend."

"Harry, I'd love to thank you in person, buy my dad just called and wants me to go to Worcester County Hospital with him to pick-up Diana Wisdom and her automobile."

"Great, Twan, coincidentally, that's exactly where I am at this moment."

"Dude, this is getting to be too far-out for me!"

"I'll wait here until you and your dad arrive. I'd like to apologize to him in person."

"Yeah, I have an apology to make also. I treated Ms. Wisdom horribly when we first met."

"I'll take some of the responsibility for that son. It was my theory that got both of us hot on her trail. Twan, I would like to talk to your father before you break the news to him if you don't mind. Will I be able to catch him at home now?"

"He should be leaving to pick me up in fifteen minutes or so, Harry."

"Good, I'll call now. I'll see you when you get here."

"Right, Harry. You are the best!"

"Good enough for my own TV show?"

"Too good."

The detective enjoyed the feeling of finally sharing some good news with Twan Russell. It had been a long, frustrating, heart-breaking case. However, with all the pain and frustrations he endured, his reward was meeting and getting to know a fabulous young man.

"Mr. Russell, please."

"This is he."

"This is Harry Manos, Mr. Russell."

"What is it now, detective?"

"I have some wonderful news for you, sir. We solved your wife's case. I have a signed and sealed confession from one Dawn Woodruff."

"You mean it's over, detective?"

"Yes, sir, it's over. I just talked with your son. He told me about your plans. I will be here at Worcester County Hospital awaiting your arrival. I have a couple of apologies I'd like to get off my chest person to person."

"Thank you, detective. We'll see you there."

After hanging-up the telephone, JT left a note for Charlene and quickly went to his car to pick-up Twan at his dormitory room in Cambridge. He felt one giant weight leave his back.

The trip to Worcester was now going to be a lot more fun for the father and son than it appeared to be at its inception. Twan had been outside of his dorm room on the street below when his father's car pulled-up. JT jumped from the car, ran toward the young man, and hung on to him as if his life depended upon the sureness of his grasp. The two rocked back and forth in relief and cried on each other's shoulder.

"It's finally over, Dad. Mom will rest now."

"You, my son, are the single greatest gift I have ever received. You have been my rock when I should have been yours. You have never disappointed your mother, or me. I feel incredibly thankful that fate found a way to have you enter my life. I love you more than you'll ever know, son."

"Don't we have a pick-up to make?" asked the teary-eyed son. I believe it is some terrific looking lady who for some unaccountable reason is smitten with you."

"Get into the Bat Mobile, Robin!"

"Can't I be Batman just once, Dad?"

"Yes, you can when you are older, son."

The happy father and son hustled into the hospital and received directions to Diana's room. As they were navigating their way to the correct location, Detective Harry Manos was sitting on the edge of Diana Wisdom's bed.

"So please, accept my heartfelt apology. I know you were subjected to great pain and suffering. After our talk, Ms. Wisdom…"

"Diana."

"After our talk, Diana, I knew you were incapable of the crime. Moreover, if you don't mind a little advice from an old married man, let the past stay in the past. Start your life over again today. Anything that happened prior to this day was practice, a learning experience. Do you get my drift, Diana?"

"I believe I do, detective, and it sounds like a very wise path to follow."

"I'll be going now. I want to meet with Twan and Mr. Russell. I wish you the best of luck on your upcoming marriage. Mr. Russell is a lucky man, or he will be when you lose that black eye."

"Right, detective. Thanks a lot."

As Manos left the room, he watched as Twan and JT walked off the elevator.

"Harry!" called Twan. The young man could not contain himself even in a hospital setting. He grabbed the detective around the shoulders and squeezed.

"You are the best, Harry! I owe you so much. You didn't give up on me, and I'll never ever forget that. You have a friend for life."

"Geez, I never had a Harvard friend before. I don't know exactly how to act. Should I invite you out to tea or to the polo matches, Twan?"

"You are an original, Harry. Thank you. Dad, I'm going to slip into Diana's room while you're with the detective."

"I'll be right along, son. Detective Manos, I want to thank you for not giving up on my wife's case. You have a strange method, but one can't argue with the results."

JT thrust forth his hand to shake the unsmiling detective's hand.

"I owe you an apology, Mr. Russell. I know I had you hating my guts, but I was going to solve this case if I had to piss off the Pope! I hope I didn't cause any permanent damage between us."

"At this point, detective, I have nothing but admiration and respect for you and your diligence."

"One more thing sir, if I may. Congratulations on your engagement to a wonderful woman. If you would not mind accepting some advice from an old married man, start your life from day one today. Anything that happened prior to this day was practice, a learning experience. Do you get my drift, Mr. Russell?"

"That is a point well taken, detective. Now, I have a lady to visit who for some insane reason still loves me. Stay well, Harry Manos. You're one hell of a cop."

"Do you think I should have my own TV show, sir? Oh, Mr. Russell, don't say anything about her black eye. She is a little bit sensitive about it. Good-bye."

CHAPTER 128

"Ms. Wisdom, may I come in?"

"Please call me Diana, Twan."

"Diana, my behavior toward you was inexcusable. That was not the real me. That frustrated, frightened, angry young man suspected most anyone of his mother's death. You did not deserve such rude treatment by me. I would wish to die if I were to treat you like that again. I hope you will find it in your heart to forgive me. You make my father very happy. He has always been the most important person in my life. Whatever brings him happiness brings me happiness. From the moment I saw you as I walked through these doors, I vowed that I would do everything in my power to make us good friends. So, Diana, it may be a little premature, but I welcome you into the Russell family."

The two crying people hugged and held tightly to each other.

"You know, Diana, my mother, you, and I all have a couple of things in common. We all have an all consuming love for JT Russell, and the man adopted all three of us."

Twan once again hugged and kissed Diana. At that moment, all was forgiven and forgotten. Day one of her new life had begun.

"Hey, get your hands off my woman, young man!"

"In another minute, I would have had her convinced to run away with me," smiled Twan.

"Yeah, I'm sure she'd love sharing a dorm room with you and Gilbert. Now you get out of here!

I have a lady to romance."

"I'll meet you guys at Diana's house. Where are your car keys, and your car, Diana?"

"I was told that the hotel security brought the car to the hospital with all my belongings. The keys must be here in the room somewhere."

"Could this be them? They have a Jamey and Di tag on them. I'll meet you at home, folks."

"Bye, Twan, and thank you, honey."

"Drive carefully, son."

"Well, young lady, have we had a weird couple of days or what? Oh, by the way, I love what you've done to your eyes."

"You suck, Russell."

"I have either apologized or have been apologized to for the past two days."

"I have too, Jamey."

"I have a suggestion to make, Di. Because I love you more than life itself, I want us to be married as soon as possible; however, I am a bit hesitant because of that crazy thing you do. Jesus, Di, you scare the hell out of me when you go off. Is there a way we can eliminate that from your emotional repertoire?"

"Certainly there is dear, don't piss me off. Seriously, love, were I not so absolutely, crazy, mad in love with you, I could probably control myself."

"Then it's not your fault, poor girl. You're only human."

"You suck again, Russell."

"Look, sweetie, I don't know what happened last night, and it's not important. The important thing is that we are together again. I suppose we will be getting our share of notoriety in the tabloids. Whatever happened is in the past. Today is the beginning of our lives. Everything that happened before today was practice, a learning experience."

"That is so beautiful, Jamey. Did you think of that all by yourself?"

"A wise old cop came up with that, Di. I think it is very valuable.

"I know, Jamey. That same old cop told me the same thing."

"I'll be damned. If we follow his advice, Di, I don't think we'd be doing it wrong this time."

"I agree, my love. Now about the wedding…"

"Are you sure you feel well enough to discuss this now?"

"Are you shitting me? I've been waiting for this from the moment I met your sorry ass!"

"Really? So I didn't have a prayer did I?"

"Of course not, lover. Men are light years behind woman in personal and social development."

Later that day on the drive home, JT approached a subject that just might test their new "the past was practice" agreement. As Diana cuddled against his shoulder, he thought it time to introduce his proposal.

"Di, are you asleep?"

"Of course I'm not. I'm just breathing in your smell."

"Great."

"Yes, it is, sweetie."

"Di, as my immediate superior at the CALL Center for Adults, I am submitting my formal resignation."

"That's fine, honey," she said not even looking up.

"I mean that's effective immediately," he emphasized.

"Of course it is, love."

"You're all right with this?"

"Absolutely, I want whatever makes you happy."

"I must say I am pleasantly surprised by your reaction, Diana."

"I must say I am pleasantly surprised by your resignation, Russell. Now, I won't have to follow through on my plans to fire you!"

"You were going to fire me?"

"Russell, I can't have my teachers socializing with their students. In particular, I can't have my own private teacher socializing with any hot to trot, horny chicks!"

"Excuse me, Ms. Wisdom, what happened to the 'forget the past deal', and we'll start new today?"

"Forgive me, love, it must be the head trauma from my black eyes."

CHAPTER 129

"JAMEY! JAMEY! WAKE-UP! WHAT THE hell have you been doing since you called me almost four hours ago?"

"Apparently this was it, Di. Was that wrong of me?"

"Knock off the wise ass stuff, or I'll give your steak to the dog. Have you even checked-in with your mother?"

"I believe I did just before I called you."

"Have you heard from Katie, Ronnie, Twan, Billy, or Susan?"

"I believe not. What is this Twenty Questions for the Newly Awakened?"

"You're going to do just fine as a retired gentleman. You're already a CPT."

"What?"

"Couch potato in training."

"Come here lover. I just finished dreaming of you."

"Did you really, Jamey? After all these years, you still dream about me?"

"Who said anything about still? It was a first!

She lay down her groceries on the kitchen table, walked toward her now wide-awake husband and plopped down on his lap.

"I don't tell you often enough Di, but I love you more each day that we're together. You saved my life. I do not know where I would be today had you not thrust your possessive claws into me and forced me to marry you. I would probably be deciding which hot babe I'd be rewarding tonight with my attention."

"You are an ass wipe! Someday you'll be able to get through an entire paragraph without fucking-up"

"But you love me."

"Guilty as charged."

"Di, I don't know how good I'll be at this retirement business. Do you know what I mean? Idle hands are the devils workshop."

"Yeah, like you've had trouble finding something to do with your hand."

"That's just what I need now. I bare my soul to you, and you make jerk-off jokes."

"You're right sweetie. I should be more sensitive. I apologize, Jamey. I think you should write a novel. God knows, you have some insane anecdotes to share in your inimitable, perversely humorous, fashion. One or two people may be interested in reading it. One thing, buddy, if you use me in it and mention Farrah Fawcett and me in the same line, it will be a warm day in Antarctica before Little JT and I resume our up-close and personal relationship."

"That's it? Everything else is fair game?"

"Knock yourself out, Hemingway!"

"Amazing how you come up with these things, Mrs. Russell. Let's seal this with a big, old, wet, kiss. Are you ready, Little JT?"

"You so suck, James Thurber Russell. Sometimes you…"

"I know, Diana. Nevertheless, I have this incredible feeling that we are the folks not doing it wrong.

"Whatever, Russell, I'm stuck loving you at least for the rest of this lifetime."

"Deal?" he asked.

"Deal," she answered.

The End?

About the Author

William N. Rappa, Jr. retired from the Lynn, Massachusetts, school department at the conclusion of the 2004-2005 school year following a thirty-six year teaching career. During this thirty-six year career, Mr. Rappa taught students at all levels of public education: elementary, junior high school, middle school, high school, and adult education. In addition, he developed, implemented, and administered supplementary remedial programming from pre-kindergarten level through adult education. He received his Bachelor of Arts Degree in psychology from the University of Massachusetts at Boston in 1969 and his Master's Degree in Education from Salem State College in 1973.

Mr. Rappa, a lifelong resident of Lynn, Massachusetts, the setting of his novel, resides in that historically rich city with his wife, two daughters and their families.

Doing It Wrong? is his first novel.

Breinigsville, PA USA
21 December 2009

229607BV00002B/2/P